Praise for

Cruel Me...

"A lush tribute to female rage, both visceral and epic, with a tender, poignant sapphic romance at its core. This book smolders—in every sense of the word."

—Ava Reid, #1 *New York Times* bestselling
author of *A Study in Drowning*

"A fiery tale of vengeance, magic, and love that will keep readers spellbound. Vita's journey from forgotten princess to a force of reckoning is absolutely thrilling. There's nothing I love more than a cunning and vengeful sapphic main character stepping into her power, and Maren Chase delivers. This novel weaves a mesmerizing tale of alchemy, slow-burn romance, and a heroine's fight for justice. I can't wait to see all of the Vita and Soline fan art that is sure to come from this story."

—A.K. Mulford, bestselling author of
The Five Crowns of Okrith series

"*Crueler Mercies* immerses readers in the depths of female strength, love, and rage. I loved going on Vita's journey, and I know countless other readers will feel the same."

—Ryan Graudin, author of
The Enchanted Lies of Céleste Artois

"A fearsome reimagining of the girl locked in the tower, Chase's tale vibrates like a thousand crows taking flight. At turns violent and tender, tragic and uplifting, it will break your heart and then bring you roaring to your feet with vengeful satisfaction. Naomi Novik fans who want it queerer and angrier will love this new foray into sapphic fantasy."

—Bethany Jacobs, author of *These Burning Stars*

"A slow-burning alchemy of forbidden sapphic romance and heartrending vengeance that pits charm, cleverness, and compassion against man's brutality. Haunting and sharp edged."

—Susan J. Morris, author of *Strange Beasts*

Crueler Mercies

Crueler Mercies

Maren Chase

This book contains depictions of violence, the death of a parent, child neglect, misogyny, animal death, starvation, extended scenes of warfare, cannibalism, murder, a coercive relationship, and sexual assault.

Published by Fantasy & Frens, an imprint of Bindery Books, Inc., San Francisco
www.binderybooks.com

Copyright © Maren Chase 2025
All rights reserved. Thank you for purchasing an authorized copy of this book and for complying with copyright laws. No part of this book may be reproduced, or stored in a retrieval system, or transmitted in any form or by any means, except in the case of brief quotations embodied in articles and reviews, without express written permission of the publisher.

Acquired by Zoranne Host
Edited and designed by Girl Friday Productions
www.girlfridayproductions.com

Cover design: Charlotte Strick
Cover illustration: Camille Murgue
Map: Ilana Blady
Crow silhouettes: Shutterstock/Diwas Designs; Shutterstock/gfx_hamza

ISBN (hardcover): 978-1-964721-04-0
ISBN (paperback): 978-1-964721-03-3
ISBN (ebook): 978-1-964721-05-7

Library of Congress Cataloguing-in-Publication data has been applied for.

First edition
10 9 8 7 6 5 4 3 2 1

This is a work of fiction. Names, characters, places, and incidents are either the product of the author's imagination or are used fictitiously and not to be construed as real. Any resemblance to actual persons, living or dead, organizations, events, or locales is entirely coincidental.

Printed in China

For Poppy, Fe Lea, and Tere,
without you, there would be no story.

And for Zoranne,
without you, there would be no book.

PART I

There Can Be No Comfort

Chapter One

The birds chirped merrily from the boughs in the castle garden on the morning that Vita's mother was killed.

During her lessons, Vita had gone to great pains to be as willful as possible so that Governess would let her run around outside. Usually once she'd been permitted to play, she would tire herself out and behave better for the rest of the afternoon, a fact that Governess knew and Vita always used to her advantage.

Her favorite place was the courtyard in the center of the castle with the hedge maze, and though eyes watched her from windows at every angle as she played, it always seemed like running through the perfect shrubbery hid her away in a world all her own.

Many such eyes followed her that morning, all censorious, but with bare feet and sweat on her brow, she ignored them in favor of dodging the servant tasked with chasing her.

After nine and a half years, she considered herself an expert on the courtyard maze, but sometimes she would spin around at an intersection to lose her place or make turns with her eyes closed to try to keep things fair.

"My lady!" Governess called from outside the maze, her voice carrying on the summer air. "Until ordered otherwise, we are supposed to spend the day studying as usual."

"'The Mother gave the world a sun, the Father took its light,'" she sang, scurrying away when the serving boy nearly cornered her. "'The Father stole the winter chill, the Mother brought the blight.'"

"Studying *language*, Princess! Not silly children's rhymes."

Vita giggled, turning on her heel to sprint down the long passage that would take her to the fountain at the maze's center. The servant was only a step behind, panting as he ran, but he did not scold her.

When Vita finally saw the fountain's relief, the figure of some great-grandparent or other whose name Governess would not be pleased she'd forgotten, she smiled at the servant boy. "I win," she said, giving a teasing curtsy before allowing him to flush her back out of the hedges.

Hands on hips, Governess stood, angrily tapping her fingers against the chain of keys hanging there. "My lady, you must—"

Her rant ended prematurely when a guard walked into the courtyard and stooped to murmur in her ear. Vita was busy trying to convince the servant to chase her around the perimeter by arguing that it would *really help her focus on her lessons, honest.* Still, out of the corner of her eye, she noticed that the guard bore the sigil of her mother on his breast. One of the queen's household guards.

"Oh!" she shouted, spinning on her feet in excitement. "Has my mother sent for me?"

The hem of her skirt was not as tidy as it ought to be, but her mother never cared about that when they met in private. And anyway, it would give her an excuse to beg to have a pretty dress made for her tenth-birthday celebrations.

Lessons always concluded when her mother called for her, so she might escape doing work for the rest of the day.

Governess's lips were pinched as she nodded toward the guard, who melted back into the shadows. "Come." She waved Vita forward impatiently and grabbed her arm when she moved into reach. Vita drew back, eyes wide.

No one ever tugged her arm. Even when she was very bad, they just made her copy lines from her books or do extra sums. No one was permitted to be rough with Vita.

"Did you not hear me? I told you to come," Governess continued. "We don't have much time. This, I imagine, will be more instructive than any lesson I've been permitted to teach you."

Governess did not wait for Vita to agree before hauling her out of the bright courtyard and down one of the endless halls of the castle.

Vita spluttered out a half dozen questions, trying to keep pace with Governess's long legs hidden beneath her somber, severe skirts. When she lagged too far behind, Governess switched her grip to the back of Vita's neck, holding tightly and pushing her forward until nails bit into her skin.

"Ow! Stop, I'm behaving. I—"

"Now, Vittoria. There's no time for delays."

For all the years Vita had known Governess and watched the hair in her bun fade from brown to gray, she'd never once heard the woman call her *Vittoria*.

Everyone had always called her *Your Highness* or *Princess*. Even the earlier use of *my lady* had felt strange to hear given Governess's penchant for using only the most formal manner of address toward her charge. Sometimes, she went so many days without seeing her parents and hearing them speak her name aloud that she was forced to whisper it to herself at night as a reminder.

Vittoria, Vittoria, Vittoria. Little Princess Vita, the daughter of the king.

"Are you taking me to see my mother? Because I would like to see her." She scratched her nails along the sand-colored stones of the castle wall as she ran to keep pace. "And you cannot refuse me."

Governess had done so plenty of times, but there were rules to going about it. Often, Vittoria was the highest-ranked person in a room, and if her orders did not contradict her parents', then there was no official way to stop her unless Governess wanted to interrupt the king's day to see his daughter scolded.

Her parents learned to give strict instructions, but sometimes she could weasel around them just enough to get her wishes.

They passed the hall that led to her mother's apartments but did not turn down it.

"We're going the wrong way."

The older woman grabbed her shoulder, pulling her around until they were face to face. "You will *behave*, Vittoria," she said, slow and overenunciated. "Now is not the time for a tantrum."

Tears welled in Vita's eyes, but she nodded, cowed by Governess's behavior.

They traveled downward together, deeper into the innards of the castle than she'd ever been permitted to go. The light faded as the windows disappeared, and they were forced to make their way by the glow of the wall sconces alone, though it was the middle of the day. Then, she started hearing the moans.

They passed a line of cells, the prisoners inside all so skinny that Vita could probably wrap her arms around their waists without struggle.

"I'm not allowed to be here. Father wouldn't like it," she whispered, trying to dig her heels into the flagstone. Smears of dried brown *something* covered one wall, and the scent of rotting hay and feces forced Vita to press her sleeve against her nose. All around them, manacles rattled as the prisoners shifted, and a shiver crept up Vita's spine as she imagined the metal around her own ankles.

"Quiet, child."

Never one for total obedience even in the face of her fear, she lowered her voice further and asked, "But *why* am I here? I don't—"

Her complaint died on her lips. In the last cell on the left sat a woman Vita would have recognized in blackest night, or by scent alone, or from a single touch. Her long brown hair, usually arranged in an elaborate style, now hung messily around her slumped shoulders. Tears rolled down the scrapes marring her cheeks.

"Mother!" she shouted, wrenching herself from Governess's hold and throwing her face against the bars. Her arms reached through, and her mother grabbed her hands and placed kisses on her fingers. "Mother, what are you doing here?"

There was a bed of half-rotten hay in the cell. Something in the corner squeaked, and Vita jumped back. A rat—dark and massive—scurried across the floor.

"My darling, my darling. You're here. They were gracious to bring you to me."

"I don't understand." She tried to steady her voice, remembering all the rules about never crying in company. That was for babies, not princesses. "Let's go back upstairs."

"Beloved, you must stay in your rooms today. Can you do that? Do not look out the windows. There will be a great crowd in the courtyard making all kinds of noise. But stay inside and do not look. Promise me."

A tear trickled down Vita's cheek, but her mother would not release her hands long enough for Vita to wipe it away. "Why?"

Her mother's fine dress was torn at the shoulder, as though she'd fought back against whoever forced her in here. It was also limp and soiled with sweat. How long had she been down here, wearing the same damaged dress without a maid to attend her? She hadn't seen her mother in nearly a week by her count, and though that was longer than usual, Governess always imparted to her the many duties that kept a queen occupied. Had she been here this whole time?

Vita's gaze darted around, looking for someone to bark orders at in her best imitation of her father's voice.

"You must promise me," her mother whispered. She transferred both of Vita's tiny hands into one of her own before cradling Vita's cheek in her other palm, forcing her attention back. "Stay away from the windows."

"I—" Vita swallowed thickly. "I promise. I will stay here with you instead."

"You cannot. You will have to go back to your rooms. Don't worry, my Vita. All will be well."

Her mother leaned closer, kissing her forehead through a gap in the bars.

"Will I see you tomorrow?" Vita asked, trying to sound cheerful. "We can read together in the library after your duties are done. Or we can take a walk in the gardens. They look so pretty with all the flowers blooming." Her nose tingled. "Or—"

It had been weeks since they had walked together in the hanging gardens or strolled through the maze or read books side by side in the library. Each of their recent meetings had been shorter than the last, but Governess kept Vita so busy with her studies that it hadn't seemed strange.

Her mother frowned, and before she could say anything, Vita cut in, desperate.

"I will even . . . even practice my conjugations! So that you will see more improvements in me."

"I'm afraid we cannot see each other tomorrow."

"But—"

"You will need to be—be brave for me, Vita," her mother said, voice hoarse. She repeated Vita's name like she wanted to press it upon her soul. "I know that you can. You've always been so fearless."

Vita shook her head, wanting to shed the ominous feeling creeping between them, brushing against her until it was close enough to cling to her skin and make her itch.

"No, Mama, I—"

Vita reached into the cell until her arms clutched as much of her mother as possible. They were both squashed against the bars, the wrought iron cold against her cheek.

Vita was helpless and stupid and young. Not brave at all. But while they were still together like this, she could pretend that things were normal for a little longer.

"Tomorrow," she whispered. "We will read together tomorrow."

Her mother ran a hand through her hair, arm awkwardly contorted. "I love you very much, Vita."

She had so many questions, but she could not bring herself to voice them. They sat, lumpy and foul, in her throat.

"I love you," she said instead, wanting it to be enough. It had always been enough before.

Mama placed another kiss on her forehead, and Vita cried in earnest.

Vita tried to pretend that the walk back to her rooms was a game, leaping through passages and pressing herself up to the walls to stay as far from any windows as possible.

If not for her violent sobs or the aggrieved governess at her back, urging her on, it could almost have been a game for real.

She'd sworn to her mother that she wouldn't look, but she couldn't escape the noise.

In her quarters, she buried her head against her knees and pressed shaking hands to her ears, whispering silly rhymes again and again until the words lost their meaning. The rhythm, steady and songlike, calmed her racing heart.

The door opened long enough for two whispered voices to converse before it closed again. Governess returned to Vita's side and prodded her shoulder. "Come. You're being summoned."

It was different from her usual strictness. In the past, Governess's irritation was matched to a pinched respect, like Vita needed discipline to become something good.

Now the warmth in her voice was gone. Vittoria shrank back in fear of the woman she spent most of her life with.

"I don't want to. My mother told me to stay."

"And your father has ordered you to come."

She shook her head back and forth, curling in on herself. "No, no, no, no. Mother *said*—"

Governess dragged her to her feet and out of the room. She did not bother to change Vita's unkempt dress or tidy her hair.

She was forced to scamper beside Governess again until

they reached the grand balcony situated above the square. Her father used it to give public speeches on celebration days, often allowing Vita to join him and her mother now that she was old enough. Governess handed her over to the king with an audible sigh of relief.

Vita's tension bled away at the sight of her father. Though her mother had ordered her to stay in her rooms, she was suddenly glad to have been summoned. She threw her arms around him and buried her face in his torso. "Father! You must help me. Mother told me to stay in my rooms, but she was being so strange. Surely you know how to fix this. They've thrown her in the dungeons!"

The king pushed her back, keeping a warm, firm hand on her shoulder. "Hush, Vittoria. You'll see soon enough. And then tomorrow you will travel, and it may be quite some time before we see each other again."

Vita drew away, strings of hair falling in her eyes. "Travel?"

When her parents went on progress, they never brought her along. For years, she'd stared wide eyed as hundreds of horses left the castle courtyard in uniform lines, and each time she'd cried that she should be with them, but Governess always sent her back to her rooms after they saw them off. "Where am I going?"

Long caravans traveling down dirt paths sprung up in her mind. Men with weapons to guard her and all of her trunks filled with her best dresses. She would be accompanied by carts of gold, and thieves would want to rob her but would find themselves too in awe of the splendor to try. And she would sit atop a horse—that was, after all, what warriors did, and though she was only skilled enough to ride her pony, she was certain she could learn along the way. She could wave to the people working the fields they passed.

He guided her toward the edge of the balcony, and Vita peered over the balustrade. She had to push up on her tiptoes to see, but as soon as she did, she wished she hadn't.

"I am sending you to Novogna."

She tried to smile, but a sudden bout of acrid bile crept up her throat.

It wasn't because of Novogna itself. The son of a nobleman used to boast to her about the city when they were forced to take lessons together. He claimed it was even brighter than their own city of Messilio, and only very important people got to go there. She had wept to Governess about it for weeks after. Back then, Governess had rolled her eyes and rubbed Vita's back, reminding her that she would be going on more than enough journeys in the future, and that little girls were meant to stay at home under their father's protection while they still could.

But she could no longer focus on traveling or horses or shimmering cities; ahead of her, visible just over the balustrade, was a great wooden scaffold. Straw covered the front where a square block lay. Dozens of people waited in anticipation, jeering and shoving each other to get closer.

She swallowed a great nervous gulp. "Why Novogna, Father?"

"Your Majesty," he returned, his grip tightening on her shoulder until his fingers dug in painfully.

She corrected herself quickly, straightening her spine as though Governess were there prodding her. She was never made to call him that except at formal state occasions, and even then, he often did not make her abide by the rule as strictly as he ought to have. "Your Majesty."

"Novogna will be your new home."

This answer did not please her, and ordinarily she would have waited to see Governess and ask *why* as many times as it took to get a satisfactory answer. Instead, she only asked, "For how long?"

"Indefinitely."

"And when will I see you again? I would not like to be apart forever." Then, struck by a sudden good idea, she said, "You could send Mother with me."

"I think not, Vittoria. Now, pay attention."

A group emerged from a door below, and the crowd swarmed forward. Vita could not see who was at the center, and as long as she could not see, then it could be anyone.

The swell of people separated just enough to expose the woman at its heart: her mother, wearing a simple black dress with her hair pinned high on her head.

"I don't understand, Father," Vita said, voice desperate as she tugged at his fine doublet. "Your Majesty. Why—"

"Shh." He steered her in front of him so there was no escape, his body caging her in. "I know you do not understand. Perhaps it is my fault for shielding you from the truth these last months, but no more. Watch."

A man dressed head to toe in black read out a list of crimes, and for all that the words twisted around Vita's heart, she could not have repeated a single one back. The sounds of the crowd were muffled in her ears.

Her mother raised her chin, face calm, to stare up at her husband. The man in black gestured for her to kneel and lay her head upon the block of wood.

Vita screamed, waving her hand over the balustrade. Her mother's attention cut from the block before her to Vita, and if a tear traced down her cheek, Vita could not see it, but she would always imagine it there anyhow.

"Pay attention, Vittoria." When she tried to turn away, he

gripped her chin so that she could not. "Your mother is no longer a queen. No longer my wife. She made the choice that led her here. The final lesson I have to impart to you as your father is to not make her mistakes."

The axe hitting the block was the loudest sound she'd ever heard.

Chapter Two

The weeks of travel between Messilio and Novogna were blank in her mind, an empty wasteland that she could never quite recall. The only thing she knew was that she dreamed of blood and violence and screaming—except, of course, for all the nights when she dreamed of meals with her parents in their finest clothes, dressed up for no one but each other in an otherwise empty room. Servants refilled their cups, and Vita laughed from her seat between her parents, legs kicking each time she was forced to hide her amusement behind her palm.

The beautiful dreams were as terrible to wake up from as the ugly ones. Those joyful days were over now, and she could not return.

When the cart they'd shoved her in finally reached the central square in Novogna, the guards dropped her at the feet of a noble family. The woman wore a beautiful dress, though the fabric was worn at the hem, and the man did not bother to don a coat to meet her. Two boys elbowed each other beside their parents. They stood a head taller than Vita and smiled with too many teeth. No one bowed or called her *Princess*.

She was almost grateful when the lord and lady locked her

away in a room high enough in one of the fortress towers that no one would have cause to think of her again.

Vita worried every night as she lay down that she'd see her parents in her dreams again, bloodied and biting and half-human. Fear choked her, and each morning she woke with crescent indents dug into her palms from the terror.

Eventually, those dreams stopped coming.

Her mother was dead and gone, and her father was far away, sitting on his throne.

Without his blessing, Vita could not return to the sun-warmed stones of her home. She would never again walk the long hall between her rooms and her mother's to practice their needlework together, or visit her father in his study with the dusty bookcases, tugging at his clothes until he looked up from his work to press a quick kiss to her cheek. She would never play in the dirt beneath the gardener's hedges or act out court politics with the dolls in her room.

She could never go home. Even if she did eventually receive an invitation to return, it would be coming from the man who might decide on a whim that he liked having a daughter as much as he liked having a wife. She was not safe anywhere that he held sway.

Vita paced her small room each day, biting at her cuticles until they bled. When the servants delivered her food, she tried to sneak past them into the hall. Once, she made it halfway down the dizzying spiral staircase before they forced her back into her chamber.

Weeks crawled into months, until she was tall enough to peer over the wide window ledge and see down into the street below, where children ran between homes and women tied up laundry lines covered in colorful clothes. Vita called down to them, trying to get their attention, but nobody looked up.

The furniture was solid wood, too heavy to move. Vita stockpiled knives from her meals as little weapons, until one day she woke up and the pile was gone.

The next night at dinner, there was no knife on her tray.

Months dragged on into years. She did not take lessons with the nobleman's sons. She was never sent outside to play or bask in the light.

Instead, Vita drew up escape plans, fingers tracing routes into the soot in the fireless hearth. She ran through each in her mind like her father planning for battle. And yet, no matter what she attempted, she never succeeded.

She tried to make friends with the girl who brought her food, seemingly far older than Vita and yet her exact height, but after a few days, they replaced the girl with someone else.

After long enough, Vita stopped trying to speak with them at all. She was alone.

"Well," she whispered, delighting in hearing any voice, even if it was always her own, "not entirely alone."

The windows were tall and narrow. If she wanted to make a daring escape, she likely wouldn't fit through anymore. Perhaps her willowy nine-and-a-half-year-old figure could have made it, only to tumble out the other side and drop headfirst fifty feet. But now, when seasons had come and gone and she'd stopped bothering to track her age, Vita would never manage to shimmy through to the other side.

She drew in the glass pane with a murmured *hello*. Three crows perched on the sill, and a fourth circled past the window without landing. "I am glad you've all come to see me. Although I must apologize. Only bread again today."

She would save eggs or berries if she was given those, but even after so long in this place, she'd never worked out the meal schedule. They came thrice each day, but there was no consistency. Sometimes meals were nearly a banquet, too much for one girl with no place to go. And sometimes they were prisoner's fare. The work of either a mercurial cook or mercurial orders. There was no one to ask.

When she found bugs crawling around her room, she trapped them for the birds, but the weather had not been fair recently, and wherever the bugs were hiding from the cold, it wasn't with her.

The crows never seemed to mind. Eda gave a little trill, higher pitched than her normal caw, and Vita grinned. Their friendship was far less fickle than her food supply and far kinder than anything else she knew.

Sometimes other birds joined them, singing sweet songs in return for treats, but they were inconstant companions. Vita's crows did not leave her.

"Eda," she said, stroking her plumage before turning to the next. "Zeda, Jeda. Good morning."

Eda had been the first to befriend her, and she kept closest to Vita as a result. It had been in those first days of grief, when disbelief and painful, unending horror consumed her nights until she felt like a husk of a girl. She'd often refused to sleep for fear of nightmares.

When Vita first saw the bird, resting in the window and making a guttural clicking noise that gave Vita no peace, she'd wanted nothing more than to rid herself of the crow and every other reminder of life outside. With no compunction to stop herself, she darted her hand out toward the bird. She'd needed to kill it—to snap its neck between her own two hands. That was how she remembered power. Her father could kill a woman—kill a *wife*—with just a word. If she could kill that *stupid, terrible, no-good bird*, then things might still make sense.

Her hands had wrapped around its little body, needing to pulverize it and let the dust be a warning to others. But when the creature cried out, she found she could not quite bring herself to be the one to end its life. Fear and hatred sat like lumps in her throat, waiting to be wept away or bitterly swallowed.

The bird made no further entreaties, only staring back at her. Waiting.

Finally, Vita had put the bird back on the ledge as though it were a trinket she'd thought to break and not a living thing. She expected it to attack her, to peck at her eyes in retaliation.

Instead, the crow had only looked down at its disheveled appearance with as much disdain as a bird could muster.

"Sorry," she whispered, choking back tears. The bird was probably just tired, wanting nothing more than a place to rest before returning to its nest, and Vita had tried to kill it.

Her hands felt dirty.

Carefully, nervously, Vita reached out to stroke a feather so it was in place again.

To atone, she'd started saving part of each meal, even when it was only bread and a bit of porridge, to set on the windowsill for the bird. And though the crow did not seem to like her much, she always returned. When a second bird followed several weeks later, Vita felt she needed to give them names. She could always tell which bird had been there first. They moved differently—the original hopped from place to place while the other, her partner, stepped with a clear trepidation.

And so the first became Eda—the Alstrin word for *first*—and the second, Jeda. The number-names were meant only as placeholders, counting upward eventually from *first* to *fourth*, until they stuck too firmly to change. On occasion, even Neda, the fifth bird, joined them, but that was not so frequent that Vita ever came to expect his company.

Often during their visits, she recited old Carcan poems taught to her as a girl. Where she forgot a word, she would add a new one in, until the poems were patchworks half-remembered and half-rewoven. She could not recall if they had always rhymed, or if she had added those in to create a more memorable cadence.

Vita recited the poems dutifully, their rhythm matching the strokes of her knuckle against Eda's back. If she stopped saying them, she might find tomorrow that she could not recollect them at all, and then what would be left to her? The knowledge of the six hundred and fourteen stones that made up her walls, some crumbling until they nearly counted for two? The massive tapestries she wove when her fingers were restless and her jailers felt kind enough to give her cotton cord? The birds whose caws sounded sometimes more like language than anything Vita could muster?

Even her age was something that she could only guess at. Though she could mark the passing of days and seasons, whole parts of her life seemed to blur together, entirely unremarkable, until she could not recall how long ago each minute change had occurred. She had spent so many of her earliest days in the tower, either planning escapes or lying listlessly in bed, unable to fathom even pacing the floor for exercise.

Very rarely, the family of the house would send a maid up to dress her and trot her out to a dinner as though to meet a quota of expected care. The nobleman's sons would kick at her under the table each time, causing bruises all along her shins, and their mother would smile into her wineglass.

Eventually, Vita began to sob so fitfully before these dinners that they no longer forced her down.

"That's all right," she said now when the last line of the last poem crossed her lips. She nearly forgot the third stanza, and it rattled her so much that she pasted on a smile to convince herself that nothing was amiss. "We'll be fine here together. Another rainy morning. Maybe the children down in the lane will run inside shouting for their mother again when the downpour starts. Just like last time."

Vita had long ago stopped calling down to them with any expectations of her overtures being returned.

Meda finally swooped in to land, dropping a shiny stone at Vita's fingertip. Vita's false smile shifted into something real as she picked the offering up and turned it over.

"Thank you, Meda. It's your prettiest one yet." Meda preened as though she could understand Vita—which Vita often pretended was possible, to the extent sometimes of forgetting otherwise.

Vita scrambled to her bed, where she'd chipped away at the back of the wooden frame for so many years that there was now a small niche hidden there. She added Meda's stone to the collection of trinkets that lived inside.

Each weathered coin, pearl earring without its match, and lost marble that the crows brought her was a prized possession she could not part with. They were her proof of a world beyond, where women still wore beautiful things and children played with dice while their parents weren't looking.

More importantly, they were gifts. Love made tangible.

All she could give the crows were bits of food and a gentle hand to stroke their feathers. They could fly away and go anywhere. They could find a hundred girls in a hundred towers to feed them and forget Vita entirely. And still, they brought her presents and spent their days with her.

Something in the world loved her. Something saw her face and remembered it fondly.

Chapter Three

Vita knelt by the window, a heavy tome in her hands. It was the thickest book the family allowed her to keep, its cover green leather with faded gold embossing for the title: *The Histories*. She turned its thin pages with careful reverence.

It told the story of the Alstrin Islands, their gods, and their kings, and for some time each day, Vita read it to whichever crows visited.

"Before the world and the island kingdoms and the distant shores of the mainland across the water, there were only the stars and the gods," she recited. This part she did not need to read at all. Ever since she was a child sitting at Governess's knee, all the stories she'd heard had started with the gods and the stars.

"The Mother circled the sky for so long that she created the warmth of the sun, and the Father walked among the comets, stealing her light until he formed the moon. And when they met in the center of it all, the world sprung forth. The Mother molded the clay of the world into mountain peaks, and the Father dug it back into ocean floors. They called into being all the lands, including the Alstrin Islands, and populated them with plants and animals and people.

"The Mother created and created and created, giving to the

people all that they could need. But the Father needed to take, to devour whole parts of existence to sustain himself. The people came to hate and fear him, but his wife loved him more than anyone, and in her anger and despair for him, she created new things. Terrible things. Things that the people would pray to the Father to take away from them. To protect them from.

"Sometimes, when the people forgot themselves, they blamed her for that. But there is no moral weight to giving and taking—both must be done. The Mother blesses; the Father defends. But the Mother also brings plague, and the Father takes lives.

"And so on the islands, the people prayed, knowing that—"

A knock sounded at her door, and Vita stuttered into silence. "Yes?"

Cosima's knock always sounded the same, a pattern and a vibrancy that no other could replicate.

Also, Cosima was the only one who bothered to knock.

"Hello," Cosima said, dragging a basin into the room. Servants brought buckets of tepid water to fill the tub. "It's time to wash your hair."

Vita closed her book and tucked it carefully away, hands trembling. To be the center of someone's attention for any length of time was uncomfortable. It had been too long. Her skin itched at the thought of someone else's touch, warm and unpredictable, but there was nothing to be done. She nodded and stripped out of her clothes, unbothered by her audience. They would forget her again when the door closed.

"Cosima. Hello. I did not expect you today."

"I come every fortnight, Vittoria."

Vita could not be certain, but she didn't believe that this was true. She'd tried on a few occasions to make note of the passing days, and it seemed that Cosima came on no fixed schedule at all.

On one occasion, Vita's hair went so long without being washed that she had to try to collect rain from the gutter and save bits of her dinner water to amass enough to scrub it herself. But every time Vita asked about it, Cosima said the same thing. *I come every fortnight, Vittoria.*

She wondered if maybe she couldn't keep count of the days after all, and if sunrises still meant what they ought to mean. How strange it would be to learn that each gap really was a fortnight. They could be. How would Vita know otherwise? There was no other person to ask.

"Yes," she said, nodding slowly. "Every fortnight. Of course."

Cosima poured the water over her hair, making Vita shiver.

This was Vittoria's favorite day, no matter if it happened fortnightly or yearly or maybe only in dreams. No matter how much her stomach churned with nerves every time it arrived.

Cosima ran her fingers through Vita's hair, leaving behind traces of sweet-smelling oil. Vita's eyes slid shut.

"Will you tell me a story, Cosima?" Governess—whose name Vita could never remember, and so she could only call her Governess when she recalled the past—always told her stories as a little girl. She missed hearing the twists and turns that could only come from someone else's mind. Vita could never think up any story half so surprising that she shocked herself. She knew the ends before she even thought them.

"I don't know any good stories. You have heard my last one already."

Vita shook her head, somehow far too pleased at the way it made Cosima's fingernails scrape her scalp. She hated the thought of being touched, and yet each time Cosima arrived, she needed it a little more. "Then an old one, please. Or something funny that you heard. Or—"

"Very well. An old one."

Cosima told a story of a bear and a frog that always made Vita laugh. She knew the end to this story, but sometimes she could pretend to forget for the joy of listening anew. It was not quite the same, but Cosima's voice was steady, and she liked the rhythm of it.

"All done. Come; stand up and we will brush it out."

Vita's hair was very long now. They cut it only once or twice a year, and the rest of the time, it hung about her torso in golden tangles. Cosima was always kind enough to brush the wet strands and stoke the fire until it was warm on Vita's back.

When all was finished, Vita turned pleading eyes toward Cosima. "Must you go?" The dread of Cosima's departure made it difficult to ever truly enjoy their meetings. She never had anything that could not be taken away again.

"Yes. But not yet."

"Good," Vita said, nodding before laying her head in Cosima's lap, her shift sticking to her still-damp skin. She did not remember how this started. She did not remember the day that triggered it or Cosima's reaction to that first attempt at closeness. But now, Cosima only sighed and stroked Vita's hair. "Will you ask them if I might have another book? I would like to read something new."

"I will ask."

"Do you think they will say yes this time?"

Cosima said nothing. Vita did not remember the last time the family had given her something new to read. Had they ever? Or were these few books always here with her? Had they even been meant for her, or were they left behind by some other person, deemed so unimportant that even Vita would not get in trouble for possessing them?

"They always give you the materials you need for your

weaving," Cosima reminded her, nudging Vita's jaw lightly with her thumb.

"I would like to read a new book," she repeated.

"I know."

It was still light outside when Cosima was ordered to leave.

"I will see you in a fortnight," she said as she exited.

Yes. A fortnight. Vittoria could wait that long.

In the meantime, she would dream of her birds and nothing else.

Days passed, and Cosima visited again. And again. She cut her hair, and then she cut it another time. It grew down to her hips.

Vita forgot what *fortnightly* was supposed to mean. There was a part of her—a tickle in the back of her mind that she was certain touched upon old knowledge—that said it was fourteen days. Two weeks. But then again, that didn't seem right. Fourteen days was far too stringent. Fortnights must be like months, where some were shorter and some were longer. Some fortnights were fourteen days and some were twenty and some were so long, you could only cease counting until Cosima magically returned again.

Neda, the fifth crow, eventually began to show up with regularity. One winter morning, he was the first to greet her. One summer day, he let her stroke his wing with the gentlest graze.

In winter again, Zeda brought her a purple gemstone that reflected rainbows. It was very pretty, and Vita loved it with the same sincerity that she loved the plain gray pebbles the crows sometimes brought her.

She grew and grew until the servants were forced to help her make new dresses. They were sewn from a heavy brown fabric, and the hems were sometimes lopsided.

Vita treasured them. Something new, something just for her. Dresses that skimmed the floor when she spun instead of stopping at her knees. Some were so long she nearly got tangled in them and had to stop herself from tumbling over. Even better. It was like a game.

Days and nights and winters and summers and hair washes that felt as frequent as they ought as far as she was concerned. She recited poetry to her birds and read her books until she felt she could recite those too.

It was a simple life, and one that she might almost call happy, if such a thing was possible in so small a world. Any other kind of existence was difficult to fathom after all these years, and at least here, she was loved.

She no longer dreamed of her mother. Vita did not want to remember that place where she grew up.

But the staff still whispered sometimes. About a king. About her father?

"He's growing older," one of the servants murmured to another as they swept the fireplace.

Another night, she heard a guard outside her door say, "After all these years, there's still no legitimate son."

No one was supposed to mention the deaths of kings, like it was impossible that they should be capable of committing such a mortal indignity until one strange day they did, but here in Novogna, the distance made the people bolder.

There were only a bastard son and a daughter best forgotten.

Was that what her parents fought about? She could not remember meeting a brother, but she could not remember meeting a lot of people. Maybe she had been made to hold her mother's hand in the great banqueting halls and curtsy to her father's son.

Maybe no one had thought to tell her about her brother at all.

"Cosima, do I have a brother?" she asked on one of her visits.

"How should I know if you don't know yourself?" Cosima's fingers snagged on a tangle of Vita's hair.

"But does the king have a son?"

There was a pause, and then Cosima hesitantly said, "Yes."

"Is he young?" She tried to picture a brother. A baby, perhaps. A little swaddled thing with piercing, beady eyes like a newborn crow.

"Not so young. Eighteen, maybe? Twenty?"

"And how old am I?"

"I don't know."

"Older than him?"

"Yes, I believe so."

"How many years ago did the queen die?"

"Ten? Eleven? I'm not sure. Time seems to move so quickly these days. Eleven, I think."

Vita laughed, and the sound surprised her.

She was twenty, then, if Cosima's timekeeping was to be believed, and she was not sure how to be that. She only knew how to lay her head on Cosima's skirts and talk to birds and hide things in the back of her bed frame.

She only knew how to be a girl, wild and lost and forgotten by time.

When Cosima left and two servants came to bring Vita's meal, she watched them carefully. Their faces were angular and interesting. Both girls had their hair pulled back from their faces, but she did not think either had tresses as long as her own. After they departed, she pinched her cheeks and traced the lines of her nose and jaw. Did she look like them? She latched the window closed and stared at herself in the glass. Was she made up of those same graceful curves and barbed edges? Had the baby fat slipped off her bones like melting frost? She had spent so long within the same body that she forgot it changed over time. Even staring at her own reflection, she could not quite see beyond the girl she had once been. And yet, there was a reason they had to sew new dresses.

What would become of her in another eleven years? Would she still be here talking to Eda at the window? Would Eda still want to visit her after all that time?

At some point in the last decade, she'd stopped looking for escapes.

Chapter Four

"This is my life," Vita whispered to herself, patching a hole in her dress. "I have five birds for company and four walls for protection. Three meals a day. I am twenty years old. That is enough." The rest did not matter—could not matter.

She kept whispering it to herself as she opened the window to allow Eda and Zeda in.

"Where are the others?" she asked as she stroked Zeda's head. It was not uncommon for some of her flock to be elsewhere, and she rarely had all five in residence at once, but there were almost always at least three or four. This time, it was only Eda and her daughter.

She had watched Zeda grow up since she was a little chick who had only just learned to fly. Eda was Vita's first, but Zeda and her sister, Meda, were Vita's babies.

Eda paced back and forth across the windowsill, head perking up anytime she heard the slightest sound from the city. Even calm-natured Zeda seemed more on edge than normal, like she might fly away at any moment. Perhaps a storm was coming, though the sky was clear and sunny. Vita stretched her arms out of the window to feel the heat on her skin.

A woman below pulled her children out through the doorway

of their house, her hands clutching their collars to keep them moving. Vita smiled at the sight of them—so connected, so in tune—until she noticed the panicked way the mother ushered them down the street. The little boy, clutching a blanket, tripped, and the mother only stopped long enough to get his feet under him before they ran again.

The longer she watched, the more people spilled out onto the streets to do the same. No one carried more than a bag or two. Those who didn't leave peered anxiously out of windows like she did, watching as their neighbors disappeared. Some tried to nail planks of wood across their doors.

Not a storm, then. People, as a habit, stayed inside when the weather was unpredictable, like birds hunkering down in their nests.

A thunderous roar rolled across the city, chasing the people fleeing like scattered ants, but it didn't come from above.

Vita did something she hadn't done since she was a girl. Maybe she hadn't done it ever. She could not recall now with any certainty.

She walked over to the locked door and knocked.

"Hello? Hello? Please. I think—"

She did not know what the end of the sentence was, but the creeping dread seeped down into her bones. If everyone was leaving—everyone, even the birds—then she should follow.

"You have to let me out." She flattened her palm and beat it against the wood once, twice, and then in a terrified tattoo. She tried turning the knob, but it stuck. "You have to unlock the door."

There was no response. What if she was alone? Had the servants already fled with the only set of keys? Her hand ached under the force, but she hit the door harder, needing someone to hear her. "Everyone is leaving! You have to—you can't *leave me*—you—please! Let me out! Let me out! I haven't been bad! I don't try to escape! I don't want—"

She drew in a harsh breath.

I don't want to die here.

The awful sounds outside grew louder until Vita had to stop hitting the door to cover her ears.

I don't want to die here. Don't leave me to die here.

The room swam around her, and she slumped to the ground on wobbly legs. Pitifully, her hand thumped the base of the door a few more times, slow and sedate, as if these final attempts might be the ones to free her.

"Please."

She did not know how long she lay there. The sun peaked and began to descend again outside the window. Zeda flew away, but Eda stayed, coming into the room to nest beside Vita.

Earsplitting roars continued outside the window, far closer now than they had been, but Vita could not bring herself to stand up and look.

She was too big to fit through the window, and too frail to break down the door. It was solid oak with a series of complicated locks running down the side.

Whatever it was that troubled the townspeople would find her trapped, exactly as her father had left her.

She wanted to feel resentment or the raging inferno of hatred. Sometimes, they seemed almost to sputter to life in her, only to smother themselves again before anything could come of it.

Vita wished Cosima were here. She wished Governess were here. She wished her mother were here. Surely any one of them would know what to do far better than Vita herself did.

The bells didn't begin ringing until late afternoon. Once they started, they didn't stop.

Vita eyed the door again. Trying and failing would be better than giving up.

Screams echoed in the streets. Even with the ominous feeling that had lingered all day, the anguished cries below seemed to have come out of nowhere. One minute, it was fine, and the next, it was not.

"Help," she said, voice broken.

She pulled on the handle, jiggling it this way and that in the hope that something might miraculously spring loose. When that failed, she drove her shoulder into the wood, but it was useless. She would mutilate her body bashing herself against the door before she'd ever bust it down. She might as well smash the glass windowpane and cut off a limb or two to try to fit through the window.

Vita frowned. Would that work?

She dashed to the wardrobe, thinking perhaps that she could tie together dresses to help her climb down if she could squeeze herself out, but the inside was bare. Her three warm winter dresses had been packed away for the season, and the three linen ones must have been taken for laundering. All she had was the nightshift she wore.

Vita stared at the empty interior before shutting the door slowly.

Stupid, stupid, she was so *stupid*. If only she'd pushed herself to better remember all those poems and Governess's lessons and the myriad other things she'd been foolish enough to let slip through the cracks, then maybe she would be sharp enough now to come up with a plan. Maybe if she had really challenged herself from the beginning, she would've been smart enough to find a way out a long time ago.

Instead, she'd become passive and accepting, learning to love this place in her own way. The birds, the tapestries, the treasures hidden in her headboard, Cosima, the maids . . . Instead of learning to pick the lock, she'd watched almost gratefully as it clicked into place, knowing that it at least kept her far away from the things that frightened her most.

Now, she would never escape.

As if she'd summoned it with her own ill temper, the door banged open, swinging so violently on its hinges that it smashed into the wall on the other side. She had to stumble back several paces to avoid being hit.

An unfamiliar guard entered the room, hand on his short sword, though his armor sat askew on his shoulders, like he'd dressed in a rush.

"Are you . . ." Vita took a trembling breath. "Are you here to escort me out?"

He took unsteady steps toward her. "I'm here—I was ordered to—" He cut himself off, gaze drifting between her face, the nervous fingers she'd twisted into her dress, and the sword at his side. "They're taking the city," he said instead.

"But . . . you're not here to help me escape."

She watched his hand raptly, waiting for him to draw his weapon and strike, but he hesitated. "I have orders," he said, unable to look at her any longer as a tear ran down her cheek. His eyes closed, and they stood for several seconds in a charged silence, neither knowing what to do.

Vita nodded, wiping the tear away. Her father would have been foolish not to set a fail-safe in place: should anyone ever try to take Novogna, his daughter must immediately be killed so that she could never fall into the wrong hands.

Finally, he gruffly ordered, "Go. Soon it won't matter anyway." He did not wait for her response before running down the hall and toward the stairs.

Alarmed, she grabbed a blanket and a handful of her treasures. She urged Eda to fly away, and though the bird stubbornly refused at first, Vita's panic seemed to sway her, and she fled through the window.

"Wait! Wait for me!" she cried, running after the guard as though he hadn't come to her room to kill her. It was impossible to keep up with him now that he had such an immense head start. She hadn't had cause to run in far too long, and the burn that crept into her lungs after the length of a hall and a few flights of stairs was already unfamiliar. "Go *where*?"

By the time she reached the bottom, he was long gone. Vita glanced around, not knowing where to go. She wandered the halls, pushing open doors.

In the end, the exit was not hard to find. Though surely there were still people manning the walls in an effort to not let the castle be taken, whoever had used this door hadn't even closed it as they were fleeing, clearly too concerned with their own chance to escape the city to worry about the defenses of the building.

Vita wrapped the blanket around her shoulders. She did not have a coat or shoes. It was just barely spring, and it would be cold now that the sun was sinking low.

What was she running *toward* in order to run away?

She stepped out of the fortress and into chaos.

People darted every direction, and this time, when children stumbled, the parents did not always stop to help them. Sometimes, they kept running.

There were figures—huge, hulking figures with dark leather armor and helmets shrouding their faces. They ran through the street and cut people down in their doorways. Bodies lay in heaps on the ground. Some appeared to be whole families felled in a moment.

She did not know the fortress's purpose beyond housing a noble family and a single princess, but she was wise enough to know that she was not its only treasure. It might house any number of things raiders would want. And she was standing right in the entry, practically begging to be killed.

Vita dashed out into the courtyard before she could spend too much time questioning her choice. If she didn't flee, she would be trapped. She ran past ransacked homes. Inside one, someone screamed, the guttural kind of cry that had to be ripped from the throat, but Vita had no time to stop. She could not save anyone.

Shadows sapped all color from the scene until the world was gray and a horrible, muddied red. She dashed over bloodstained cobblestones, trying to keep her balance on the uneven path. Once, her foot almost slid out from under her, and when she looked down, entrails were smeared across the street.

Forcing back bile, she continued. Fires blazed in the distance. Perhaps the citizens had burned down the gate to get out of the city. Perhaps the invaders were setting houses alight. It was impossible to know.

A half dozen turns presented themselves to her, but Vita didn't know which to choose. Never, in all her life, had she walked the streets of Novogna. Her hand tightened around the pearl earring she'd grabbed from her collection, allowing the post to dig into her skin and ground her thoughts.

"Help! Help me!" someone cried. Vita's head turned

automatically, and she saw a man on his knees crawling toward her. His leg was badly injured, his hand raised to her in supplication. "Help. Please."

She opened her mouth, throat dry, but before she could say a single word, one of the raiders emerged from a nearby building. He raised his great sword and brought it down in a sweeping arc. It did not quite hit the man's neck, but the result was the same.

Vita stumbled back in horror. She was close enough that drops of blood spattered across the front of her nightshift.

She ran, and the attacker was either too invested in his kill or too distracted by some new target to pursue her, and for that she was grateful. If he tried to chase her down, he would win.

They are going to cut off my head. They are going to hold it up by my hair and parade it through the crowds. I have seen this all before. I have seen it.

She stumbled into an older woman who clasped her arms in distress, looking at her wildly in the hope that she would see some other girl in Vita's face. When she saw only Vita, she bit back a sob and shoved her away so that she might keep looking.

Vita reached a crossroads and turned left at random, trying to stay away from the smoke in the hope that she might avoid the worst fighting. At the next crossroads, for which each option posed equally unknowable threats, she did not choose at all. A boy sprinted right, and she followed.

Novogna was a foreign world to her, its twists and turns unforgiving. She would never be able to find a way out unless, like a bug, she got in line and followed those with an exit strategy.

The boy veered around corners and through the smoldering remains of what looked like a marketplace. In another lifetime, Vita might've stood at one of the stalls and purchased vegetables or chatted with the butcher's son.

She could finally see where the others were running. Just ahead sat the entrance to a tunnel. It didn't look like it was meant for everyday use—if there was one thing she *did* know, it was that cities liked to keep minimal points of entry. You would need to give your name at the gates before you could enter, even in times of peace. They could not let people come and go at random.

But there were always things that needed to be dealt with out of sight. Like here, where, based on the smell, they managed the bulk of the city's excrement.

People pushed and shoved each other to get through. The entrance was tiny, not even person-sized. Those who went in stooped low, and the crush to get in only made it worse. It was not meant as a point of evacuation.

Vita, unused to crowds, did not know how to get to the front. Bodies pressed against her from all sides as they angled to get closer, and it made her want to retch. The sweat and heat of these strangers touching her had her scratching at her skin until she was worried she'd draw blood.

The mob shuffled forward despite the fact that there was nowhere to go. A man with too-long legs nearly bowled Vita over trying to get ahead of her, and though she cried out, no one tried to help.

No one cared. If *she* made it through the doorway, *they* might not.

The mass of people before her was ten deep. As they trickled one by one through the opening, it dwindled to seven, then five.

"There!" someone cried from behind, and a horn blared. The beat of horse hooves on stone rang out across the crowd, and the crush transformed into pandemonium. Some tried to backtrack and run the other way, while those closest shoved people aside to get to the door. Vita, caught right in the center, could only try to protect her head as she was batted about. Her handful of stones and coins and old, chipped buttons spilled to the ground.

Men on horseback rounded everyone up, corralling them in until they could reach neither the door nor any other escape route. When a young man, hardly beyond childhood, tried to get away, a mounted warrior impaled him with his spear.

"You will stop fighting! You will do as we say, and go where we tell you! You will obey, or you will die. This is our mercy! Take it, for there will not be another chance."

A small legion of armed men ran into the passageway, and it only took a few seconds before the screaming began. Perhaps the very first people who went through the tunnel might have escaped. Might yet live.

The rest would not.

When the invaders pointed their weapons at Vita's group, she went where they told her to, marching through streets riddled with the dead.

At last, they brought her to a massive structure, dark and imposing in the dim light. Its slate-gray walls towered over the buildings nearby.

In a panic, she glanced behind her, trying to imagine an escape. There were only houses and small shops here, with their doors busted in and nowhere to hide.

It looked remarkably like—

Well, it looked rather remarkably like the view from her window.

She peered back up at the huge structure and saw, several stories above, a crow perched on a windowsill.

Chapter Five

The armed men marched Vita and the other prisoners back into the fortress she'd escaped from. She wanted to climb up a staircase—any staircase, it hardly mattered—until she found her way back to her room, but the guards did not give her the opportunity.

Instead, they descended.

She longed for her bed and her birds and the normalcy of a million other days. Until now, she had taken those moments for granted. Upstairs were the last little bits of *her* existing in the world, and as they ushered her into a cell and closed the door behind her with a loud *clang*, it became clear that she might never see them again.

Vita sank down in a corner, poking at the torn edges of the wounds on her feet. If she hadn't tried to run, they might've taken her from her bedroom straight to the cells beneath the keep, and at least then she would not be injured.

Vita's group was not the first to arrive, and they certainly weren't the last. Each time a new wave arrived, they would all have to shuffle back, pressing closer and closer against each other's grief.

Bile rose in her throat at the proximity. Sometimes, Vita

would purposefully touch a very tender spot on her skin just so that her focus could be drawn to a singular place instead of the whole of her overexposed being.

Determinedly, she steadied her breathing by not thinking the word *dungeon*. If she didn't let herself acknowledge it, it didn't have to be true. Dungeons were where traitors and enemies went.

Where mothers went and never returned.

People wept through the night. Vita stared at the ceiling, half reclining and half sitting as there was no space to truly lie down. It irritated her each time someone shifted, or tapped their nails on the stones, or sneezed. Someone's knee dug into her back, and a child slept pillowed on her thigh. Vita had to force herself not to shove them off, focusing instead on imagining a way out.

She used to love to imagine things. It was embarrassing that she could not do it better by now. There was no center to the maze that she could find with enough patience—there was only more maze.

She hadn't recognized this building on sight. She had lived in one small corner of it, but the fortress was huge. There was no path through it that she knew instinctively led to freedom. Even if she could escape the cell, she would inevitably walk straight into another trap.

Her cheeks burned in shame. What was she good for besides being someone's prisoner?

The only option was to get to her room and then try the same staircase as before. It didn't lead anywhere good, but at least she knew it led to an exit. Better to die trying than to wither slowly.

The people around her prayed that the Mother would give them strength and wisdom. That the Father would take away their suffering. Vita had not prayed in many years and just barely recalled the scent of their family chapel when the incense burned. She couldn't bring herself to try now, too afraid that no one would answer.

Guards swept through on a constant rotation, beating back anyone who tried to knock down the cell doors. A few prisoners were killed outright. Vita closed her eyes, forcing deep breaths through her mouth.

Night turned to morning, which turned to high noon. By the time evening approached again, the prisoners begged for food. For water. They did not try to bust down the doors anymore. Now they only wanted to be fed, to have sustenance for their children. How easy it was to bring a whole city beneath your heel.

It wasn't until another full night had passed that people began whispering about what the guards wanted. Vita closed her eyes as they spoke, trying to think only of the darkness behind her eyelids.

"They're looking for someone," said an older woman's voice.

"Does that mean—?" A young girl sitting nearby cut herself off, stifling her cries with her sleeve. "Will they let us go?"

"I don't know. I don't—"

The woman's hesitation dragged a nail against Vita's tenderest memory: her own mother's inability to give the answer that Vita needed to hear in a moment when the truth was so awful. She choked back a sob, trying to wash the fog of that conversation from her thoughts.

Because the truth that this mother knew was simple—they hadn't been captured because the invaders were looking for someone. They were captured because that was what invaders did.

"Maybe, my love. Maybe they will let us go when they have what they want."

Vita didn't look—didn't even bother opening her eyes, feeling too itchy—but she imagined a daughter curling into her mother's side, the older woman's nose buried in her soft hair. She would stroke down its length to calm her child, the action filled with unbearable love.

What was a touch like that worth? To be shielded from the harsh truths of the world by someone who would lie for you. Lie *to* you.

"But why do they need to move us?" asked a man on Vita's other side. "I can't stand on this leg."

"They are lining everyone up to check faces and take names. Don't worry—I will help you walk. It will be over soon." That was his wife, probably.

"Gia," he said, forlorn, "I am too big for you to carry. You can't waste what's left of your energy on me."

"If you can't walk, they will—" She took an unsteady breath. "It is not a waste to stay together."

"Everybody up!" roared a man outside the cell door. He beat against the cell bars with the dull end of a spear.

Groans rose around Vita as her entire cell filed out. Guards lined the stretch of hall, swords waiting at their sides.

They're looking for someone.

Vita should run. Run and escape or run and be killed—both were suitable options at this point. But she was a coward, and she could not bring herself to step out of line. She did not remember what it was like to think herself important in the world. To have others bow to her wishes. If they ordered her to walk, to line up single file, to face a man with a thick beard who looked her over like a prize cow—she would do all that and more.

They linked the prisoners together with cuffs around their wrists, and the choice was taken from her. It was almost a relief.

A guard walked up and down the line, grabbing chins and

pushing back dirty hair. First was a grandmother, withered down to nothing. The man skipped over the next three in line until stopping at a little girl, an old ribbon holding back her hair as she wept.

Women. They were only checking the women.

Before the man could reach Vita, he turned to his subordinates. "Bring the girl in. See who she recognizes. We don't have all day."

Another woman was escorted in with chains around her ankles.

"Which one is she?" asked the man commanding the room. "Do you see her? Remember what will happen if you are no longer useful."

The woman raised her chin and looked up and down the line. Her face was covered in cuts and bruises. Still, her eyes were visible through the grime.

I come every fortnight.

For a second, she could only watch Cosima watching her. Cosima's hands clenched at her sides.

"She is here," Cosima said. Those hands were the only ones that had comforted her in many years. "Fifth from the left." Vita had never let herself think the words, but Cosima had seemed almost an older sister to her these last eleven years. "Lady Vittoria, the king's daughter."

Men swarmed toward her. Desperately, she tugged at the chain around her wrist but only succeeded in pulling those on either side of her closer.

As they clicked new bits of heavy metal around her ankles and wrists, hands touching her in half a dozen places that she wished they would not, she could only watch Cosima through the gaps in the bodies. The woman kept her head low, unable to meet Vita's eyes no matter how hard she stared. Vita only needed one shared look to pass between them—something to prove that they *had* known each other, that Cosima *had* cared, that this was something she'd only acquiesced to on pain of death.

But Cosima would not look. Could not give her that last small moment of communion. And then, without warning, the sadness turned to rage. *I will kill her for this.*

Vita wanted to see her suffer just as she'd once wanted to hold Eda's dead little body in her hands. Just as she sometimes imagined what killing her father would feel like. If it would be freeing. She wanted to tear Cosima's throat out with nothing more than her fingernails, scratching and scratching until she could hold up the ribbons of her friend.

And still, she wanted to hug Cosima and disappear into a world where none of this had ever happened.

"Take her to the general," the leader said, gesturing to a few of the foot soldiers. "He has plans for her."

Chapter Six

Vita was paraded through various rooms as the soldiers gripped her chin and showed her off to anyone who might disprove Cosima's story. It seemed the only thing worse than not bringing the general a disinherited princess at all was to bring him an impostor.

The noblewoman who owned this fortress only yesterday—now bruised and weeping wretchedly—told them everything they wanted to know about Vita. Name, age, hobbies. How much money the king sent them each year to keep his daughter far from court. How Vita used to try to run as a girl, until one day she stopped and grew complacent.

Out the window, Vita saw the husband and one of the sons—now a man full grown—strung up in the courtyard, their bodies limp.

"They were supposed to kill you!" she screamed at her ward. "We sent the guard up to kill you!"

Vita shrank back as one of the soldiers moved to silence the woman.

They forced Vita down more unfamiliar halls, and she heard former servants speak with shaking voices of tending to Vita's hearth or filling her bathtub. No one lied for her, because she was not worth it.

Finally satisfied, the guards dragged her down the hall to a grand room she'd never seen before. Massive paintings and banners with the family's crest lined the walls, but blood and debris littered the floor, and she spotted a few places where swords or axes had hacked into the woodwork.

"General," one of the guards said as they brought her before him. Vita couldn't help squirming in their arms, her fear finally overpowering her detachment. When she refused to move her legs, they dragged her across the room and dropped her at the general's feet. "We've located her, sir."

The general was a tall, broad man with long brown hair, a well-trimmed beard, and a wound across his cheek. It looked freshly tended, sewn closed with black thread, but as he tipped his head to stare at her, a drop of blood spilled down and cut toward his jaw, leaving a red trail behind.

He was far younger than her father's ancient council members, their hair already streaked with gray if not gray entirely, but he was older than the young men who joined her father's household guard, starry-eyed and beardless for the first several years of their service. Having no other gauge by which to measure him, she could only place him at perhaps thirty or thirty-five.

Vita felt inconsequential before him. She was nothing, a girl in a soiled nightdress, and he was the man who had just taken a fortified city in a single day.

Wide-eyed, she watched him shift on the elegant chair, thighs spread and clothes covered in dirt and bloodstains.

There were a million questions she wanted to ask, but she couldn't make her voice work. Her throat bobbed as she tried to eke out a sound, and he smiled. That only made the wound on his face look worse, but his teeth were bright and the lines that formed around his eyes seemed almost genuine.

"Princess Vittoria. Welcome."

Vita still could not manage to speak.

She thought he might get angry, but he laughed. "Nearly escaped the city, I hear." He cocked an eyebrow at the scabs on her palms. "It's a good thing we found you in time."

"It—it is?"

He stood, stepping down from the dais situated at the end of the room. When his boots were before her, he extended his hand. "Please. You are not a prisoner. You will have to excuse my soldiers. They don't know how to treat royalty." Carefully, she put her hand in his, heart in her throat. The general helped her to her feet. "Amara," he said, turning toward a servant near the door, "you will get Princess Vittoria something clean to wear. And draw her a bath." Amara began to scurry off, and he shouted after her, "And the keys! For her shackles. Have them brought up from the dungeons so that she might be unchained."

He returned his attention to Vita. "Don't worry; I will make sure no one forgets how to treat you in the future. As soon as we realized you were among those captured, I put my soldiers to work finding you. They should have realized I did not wish for you to be in chains."

"I'm—"

Vita bit her cracked lip. Shouldn't she be out in the courtyard with the nobleman and his son? She was an almost useless game piece, but she wasn't yet unplayable. Better to take her off the board while he had her in his grasp, the way her father had failed to do.

"Sir, I—"

When she stalled again, the general brought her hand to his

lips, kissing the back of it. "You must call me Ardaric, Princess."

He looked at her expectantly, and though it made her tense with nerves, she nodded, repeating, "Ardaric."

"And may I call you Vittoria?"

Overwhelmed, she answered, "Yes, sir."

Amara slipped back into the room, and Ardaric waved her over. "We will talk later, Vittoria, once you have rested. Have a bath! After that, we will talk. There is much for us to discuss. Until then, know that you are safe here. I promise you that."

Dumbfounded, Vita allowed Amara to remove her shackles and lead her out of the room. She did not recognize any of the halls or staircases, but when they reached their destination, she was sure of one thing.

"Excuse me. This isn't my room."

"This is the room the general has allotted for your use, Princess. Can I get you anything to make you more comfortable?"

"Please, I want my room. I have a room here already."

"This is the room that the general allotted for your use."

They cycled through this same conversation three more times before Vita, close to frustrated tears, finally allowed Amara to coax her into the tub of water. It was as cool as all her baths, the chill stinging her open cuts and making her shiver miserably.

Amara did not wash Vita's hair with the same care that Cosima did. She missed Cosima, even if she wasn't sure that she was allowed to anymore.

Hand on the rim of the tub, she turned to Amara. "Do you know where Cosima is?"

Amara drew Vita out of the bath and strong-armed a slip over her head, never once asking Vita to do it herself.

Vita batted her away. No servant had ever dressed her before, and she didn't need to start letting them now. She walked to the dress that Amara had spread out on the bed, fingers going to the laces, but it took only a moment before she was hopelessly tangled.

Her brown dresses were all far simpler than this one. Had she ever touched something so fine? The green silk taffeta jacquard was far too elegant for Vita's use, stiff and heavy and impossibly beautiful.

Ardaric hadn't been dressed like this earlier. He wore the ragged, muddied clothes of a warlord, topped with leathers and furs.

"Allow me," Amara said when Vita's attempts became intolerable. It wasn't a command, but only just. She managed to get the hulking thing on Vita's body, including the sleeves that had to be tied to the bodice. She never could have managed this on her own. "I don't know where Cosima is," Amara finally offered. "I'm sure she's with the other prisoners until the general decides what to do with them. Likely they will all be made to swear oaths to him and pay a tax before they are sent home."

She is there, Vita thought. *And I am not.*

Cosima languished in the dungeons while Vita's feet were forced into dainty slippers.

"These shouldn't open up your blisters, but walk carefully anyhow," Amara ordered. "I will take you to dinner once we've fixed your hair."

"I'm not eating here?"

The dress should have tipped her off, but she always ate in her room. Even if this wasn't *her* room, she wanted to remain in its relative safety.

"No. You will eat with the general."

Chapter Seven

Amara led Vita to another room. It had once been sumptuous, apparent from the massive cherrywood table located at the head of the room and the tapestries covering the walls. Though she'd never seen them before, she quickly discerned that the story of King Catania the Merciful, a distant relation of Vita's, played out on one in incredible detail. Another showed what Vita thought was Odelina and Halse in the field of glass flowers from the old folk stories, though in truth, the threads were so faded that the scene could have been from any number of tales in Vita's book.

In all her years here, she had never been forced to attend a revel, either because she was not trusted to behave herself or because perhaps her father wanted to keep her whereabouts a secret to all but the most loyal. Still, sometimes in the evenings, she could hear the distant sounds of a celebration happening in the world beyond her room. Was this where they convened, with gossiping guests and flowing wine from the vineyards of Salajara? If she had been another girl—a daughter of the family, or betrothed to one of their sons—might she have danced here?

Like everything else in the fortress, it hadn't come away unscathed from the attack. Vita couldn't decide if this was the setting of the family's final stand or if Ardaric's men were taking revenge against Carcan artistry now that they'd won, but several portraits were slashed in two.

Fear had gnawed at her stomach all the way down the stairs, as she worried, based on her attire, that this would be a grand event to show her off as the spoils of war, but General Ardaric sat alone at the table. He grinned when he saw her.

"You look very well, Vittoria. The flush has returned to your cheeks."

She touched her face self-consciously. It felt warm. The bath had swept away the grime of the cells, though it could do nothing for her injuries.

"Come, sit." A place was set beside his own. "You have been hidden away for too long. There is much that you don't know, I imagine."

Stiffly, she took her seat. She could not force herself to look at him.

"I am not stupid, sir." She picked up her glass and took a sip. It certainly wasn't water, red as blood and tart on her tongue, but she swallowed it with a grimace.

"I didn't think you were," Ardaric reassured. "Only that your father wanted you locked away from the rest of the world for a purpose, and part of that purpose was that you never be educated enough on what is happening to stand as a credible threat to him. I would be happy to fill you in. It is important that you know the state of Carca. These are your people."

"My people?"

It didn't seem like they were her *anything* after all this time. They hadn't even tried to protect her from Ardaric, all too eager to trade information for their own safety.

"Yes. You are their princess. Most of them have no idea that you were imprisoned here. Some even believe that you were killed alongside your mother. In every city and town from Novogna to Messilio, there are people who have wondered what became of the king's daughter. After all this time, they've been made to accept the lie that there is no alternative to the king and his bastard son."

He paused, and if Vita had known he was doing so in order to force her to ask more, then perhaps she might have played her part. But Vita, who carried out most of her conversations with herself, continued staring at her empty plate and let the silence linger.

"*And*," Ardaric continued, "now that you are freed, we will make it clear that you are the rightful heir and always have been. You are their princess."

"Is that what this is, then?" She finally turned to face him. His eyes were a rich brown, and besides the wound, he was as handsome as any other man. His long hair hung down around his cheeks, looking freshly washed. "My liberation?"

She'd imagined freedom a thousand times, even when she stopped seeing her room as a jail cell, but it had never looked like this. It certainly hadn't included someone as dangerous as Ardaric as her rescuer.

"In a sense."

"What will you do with me, then?"

Ardaric gave her an intrigued look, like he was still parsing out the answer to that himself, but servants arrived with platters of food before he could say anything.

They heaped meat and potatoes onto her plate. Vita, who was half-starved from her time in the cells and half-starved from years of inconsistent bedroom meals, didn't even let them fully retract the serving spoons before she dug in.

Ardaric cleared his throat beside her, and with gravy on her lips, she turned to see him watching her raptly. The stinging chill of embarrassment swept through her. Her hands were covered in grease. Vita moved to pick up the knife and fork lying forgotten on the table.

Suddenly, Ardaric laughed. Loud and lively, like she was the funniest thing he'd seen in weeks. Before she could clean her hands on the tablecloth, he reached out and grabbed his food with his hands, too, discarding the utensils entirely.

Nervous, she returned to her food, picking it apart rather than inhaling it. He seemed more at ease now, and the tension drained away from her shoulders.

"We'll get married," he proclaimed.

The hunk of meat she was holding dropped back onto her plate. "What?"

He wiped at his mouth with the back of his hand. "You asked what I'd do with you. We'll get married."

"I don't—why?"

The pronouncement was so shocking—stated plainly as it was, like the wedding guests were waiting in the hall outside already—that she forgot why he might want to marry her. Forgot that she was the daughter of a king. Forgot that he could use her as a political tool. Forgot everything logical and could only settle on *Why would anyone want to marry me? Why would I want to marry anyone?*

"I don't wish to marry."

"Vittoria," he said, turning his body and leaning into her shoulder. He loomed over her like the curling moon. "What do you know of your mother?"

Flatly, she answered, "She's dead. My father killed her. What else is there to know?"

"Did you know she was Kasrian?"

He gave her a smug smile, like he'd been waiting patiently to tell her this.

It was strange, she realized, that she hadn't thought to ask what *he* was. An invader, certainly, and probably from one of the northern islands, like Kasri or Sopio. Carcan soldiers rarely decorated themselves in such heavy pelts. The summers were far too hot, and it was a foolish king who waged war in the Alstrin winters.

"And are you Kasrian as well?" she asked. There were, after all, three other northern islands where people dressed largely the same, but he did not look the part of either a Sopian scholar, a Tarlan farmer, or a Durbinian fisherman.

Two of her dusty history tomes bore beautiful maps of the many Alstrin Islands. Carca and Kasri, the largest two among the nine, had each been extensively described from the authors' travels. The Alstrins had a long history of trade and a longer history of war. Vita used to trace those maps onto fresh paper and annotate them with every detail that she could remember.

"I am. Queen Ana and I were practically kin."

No one ever told Vita her mother was Kasrian. No one spoke of her mother at all, as though she'd blipped in and out of existence with neither past nor future, but only the few glorious years that Vita spent at her side.

They didn't even speak her name—so hearing it now made Vita realize that she'd forgotten it.

"Truly?" She tried to picture her mother outfitted for half the year in heavy wool dresses with pelts over her shoulders for warmth, but it did not fit with the woman she knew, whose face always bore freckles and a slight tan from spending too much time outside in the warmth of Carca's summers.

He nodded. From a pocket, he pulled out a stained

handkerchief. Embroidered on it at one corner was her mother's falcon sigil. "Yes. And she was family in all but blood. Her father and mine were like brothers. They were the joint heads of the king's army back in those days. Her father was the king's younger brother, you know. He died when she was still young, but she was always another daughter to my parents. She was considered the king's most beautiful niece."

"Why did her uncle not fight to avenge her? When she was . . ."

Ardaric's smile melted away. "Both Ana's father and her uncle were already dead by that time. That's what finally prompted your father's action, I imagine—he knew there was less chance of retaliation. I'm sure Nicolo was truly fond of Ana once. But there's never been a man so changeable as your father."

"Why did he do it?" she asked. It was what she'd always dreaded knowing: what had caused her father to turn on them so suddenly. "What was her crime?"

They had been a family once. He used to chase Vita from celebratory feasts to her bedroom so she'd finally go to sleep. He'd laugh and lift his squealing daughter over his shoulder when he won the summer tourney like she was the prize. Perhaps if he'd always loathed that she was a daughter, Vita would be able to understand why he'd done it. But he hadn't. He'd loved her, and he'd loved her mother.

"The official story is that the queen was unfaithful. Multiple times, with multiple partners, including the Aligese ambassador." He did not explain what he meant, and it was only from those folktales of courtly love and Cosima's embarrassed explanations of the marriage bed that Vita understood his meaning.

"Surely it wasn't true!"

"It wasn't. Or, at least everyone who is not under your father's influence believes it wasn't. By that time, he and his mistress had already had a son who was only a year or two younger than you, and though there was no indication that another child with your mother was impossible, he seemingly gave up on that avenue. Elio was seven or so by then, old enough to be invested with titles of his own, but your mother stood in his way, reminding your father that *you* were his rightful heir. She would hear nothing of a bastard being placed before you in the line of succession, but if the king claimed his wife betrayed him, politically and intimately, then he could bend the law to his will. No one would want their queen giving secret information to the Aligese. And if his marriage to her could be dissolved, then you would no longer be an obstacle."

Vita sank back in her chair, cleaning her hands mechanically for something tactile to do. This was worse than no answer at all.

Ardaric cleared his throat. "Ana and I did not spend much time together when she lived at home. I was still young when she sailed off to be married. She was closer to my older sisters, all three of whom remember her fondly. But our families always swore to protect each other."

"So you have come in her family's stead? To avenge her?"

"Something like that. Her cousin took over after the old king's death, but he was mired in political scandals at home, on account of his having married two different women and no one knowing which was the true wife. Luckily one died in childbirth, or we could easily have had a civil war on our hands between the families of the two women. And after that, there was some fighting in Sopio to contend with. But things are settled enough now that your cousin could spare the effort of his army making such a journey to fight in Ana's honor."

"And you want—" Vita swallowed. "You want to marry me."

"You have a name, Vittoria. A name that, turned inward, threatens you. But if you let it shine outward, if you remind them who you are and what you are owed, it is a threat to *them*. Sure, you have no armies, no other potential allies." Ardaric shrugged. "You could run and hide and hope that no one finds you. Hope that your father's men don't track you down and kill you now that you're outside his power. Hope that someone with fewer scruples than me doesn't use you as a rallying point for a rebellion they aren't prepared to win, getting you charged with treason in the process."

Bluntly—for she didn't know how to speak any other way when she felt this exposed—she asked, "Do I get killed in all of your scenarios?"

"You will never be some nameless peasant girl, which means there will always be someone who wants you dead. Still, you've seen what my armies can do," Ardaric said, arms raised out as a reminder of his destructiveness. "You don't think I could protect you? Novogna has been in your family's control ever since the Carcans drove off Ravenna. And now it's mine, though I'm hundreds of miles from my own lands. We'll push across the rest of the island and take Messilio next. We'll depose your father."

"But—"

"He killed your mother. And he has killed many of his ministers. Killed peasants for breaking laws they have no choice but to break. Would kill you right this second if he saw us sitting together, plotting against him. You owe him no loyalty." Ardaric touched her chin gently. "The truth is harsh, but it is the truth, and I respect you enough to speak plainly. You are with me, Vittoria, or you are not. And if you are not, then I must treat you as I treat any other enemy. I know your value enough to recognize the danger you pose. So marry me and take your place as Carca's rightful queen, or I will give you the dignity of a quick and honorable death."

The blood drained from her face. He dropped her chin, and Vita focused on the wall as she fought to collect herself.

If her father hadn't sent her away, she would have been sold off into marriage eventually. Sent to Aligo or Durbina or Tarla. They would have promised her father grain or unencumbered trade or a few jewels to be spent on lavish parties and warfare.

It was hard to say if this was better than that, but it was at least no worse. She knew whom she'd be marrying, and she knew what the prize was at the end. She could return home.

Also, she had no choice.

It felt like the thing that made her *her*—the innate *Vitaness* inside her that kept her going through the loneliest, dreariest years—was leaking out through the soft shoes Amara had dressed her in, leaving an empty shell in the chair.

"I don't want to marry," she said blankly.

Ardaric tipped his head to the side, studying her. Apparently, he hadn't thought he'd be rejected when the options were so clearly weighted toward one response. "What do you want, then?"

"I want my room back."

"All right."

"I want . . ." She did not dare mention either her birds or her remaining treasures, those that hadn't been lost in the streets. "Books. More books."

"There's a whole library here that you can visit."

"I can?"

"As I said, you aren't a prisoner. If you marry me, you will be the general's wife. The king's wife. You will have whatever you wish."

"I—" She drew in a deep breath, closing her eyes to steel herself. "Then I will marry you."

"You're certain?"

If she was lucky, then maybe there would still be a chance of escape. They'd permit her to travel around the fortress. Perhaps they'd accidentally permit her to slip out of sight one day and never return.

And if not, *queen* seemed a step above *dead*, at least for now. The bodies hanging in the courtyard were proof enough of that.

"Yes." Then, hearing her own terror, she amended, "I will be. By the time we are married, I will be certain."

Ardaric took her hand, squeezing it comfortingly. "I hadn't thought to marry until we take Messilio and can be crowned, so there is time to find comfort in it. But I will announce our intentions soon. As I said, many people don't even know you are alive. You must be reintroduced to the public. Then, when we have our kingdom, we will swear oaths."

"Very well."

"Once I announce it, though, you cannot fail to honor your promise." He drew her face back toward him, forcing her gaze. "Do you understand? Can you commit yourself to me as a wife?"

"Um. Yes. I—yes." It didn't quite feel like the truth, but he had left her no room for uncertainty. She was not ready to die today.

"Good. That is all for tonight. You must be exhausted, and I have kept you too long. I will send for your maid." Her plate wasn't empty, but she had no further appetite.

He motioned one of the soldiers forward, listening intently as the man whispered something in his ear. Ardaric paused before nodding and giving a new order.

"Just one moment, Vittoria," he said as the soldier slipped out. Around them, servants removed food and refilled cups. The general drank from his while watching Vita over the rim. Now that she had sworn herself into this bargain, she didn't know what else to say.

Finally, the door that the soldier had disappeared through opened again. A girl walked in.

"Ah, Soline, come take the princess back to her room."

"Amara?" Vita asked, her mind just alert enough to look around for the familiar face. "Where is—"

"I'm told there was an accident earlier with your maid. Amara fell on the stairs and broke her wrist, but Soline has offered herself as a replacement."

The girl stepped forward. She was perhaps a year or two older than Vita, and several inches taller, though she carried herself with the willowy grace of someone who must have spent a lot of time around kings and queens. Her dark curls stuck to her forehead in the heat of the room, and her long matching eyelashes brushed her cheeks when she bowed her head. She wore a pretty yellow dress that only a woman of noble birth could afford, though it was stained a little along the hem, and no jewelry except for a dainty chain, the bauble at the end concealed under her clothes. When she raised her head to look Vita in the eye, the weight of her gaze pressed down on Vita, pinning her in place. It was commanding and difficult to look away from, lacking all of the fear that Vita herself couldn't escape. Vita swallowed thickly, staring back.

Soline was everything that Vita had once imagined herself becoming: a woman who would not look out of place dancing in a crowded ballroom with a dozen eager suitors or leading council meetings to discuss the business of state. Even standing alongside Ardaric's sheer bulk, she did not appear diminished—not in the way that Vita knew she herself must.

"Your Highness," Soline said. Her voice, by contrast, was honeyed.

No one had referred to Vita as *Your Highness* since the day that her life was stolen from her.

Broken and so, so lost in this place that had been her home for over a decade, Vita allowed Soline, with only two days' knowledge of the fortress's layout, to guide her back to her room.

It was the same wrong bedroom as last time.

Chapter Eight

The pitter-patter of dozens of feet passing the door kept Vita up all night, and by the time the thinnest predawn light touched her windows, she decided to do something about her lost crows. They would never know to look for her in this room, and the skinny slits of the windows sat too high to open easily.

Vita tried scaling the wall, fingers digging into the cracks where the mortar had chipped away, before losing her grip and dropping painfully to the ground. Brushing bits of rock out of her palms, she dragged the bed frame across the room and placed it under her. Then she climbed the wall again and again, dropping onto the mattress each time. Vita huffed, blowing stray hairs off her forehead as she pushed back the sleeves of her nightdress to try once more, shoving her toe into a crack halfway up to stabilize herself. Leveraging this new foothold, she just managed to stretch up and push the tips of her fingers against the glass. The squeaky hinges gave way before she fell again. Back flat to the lumpy mattress, she watched as the first gust of fresh air shifted the tapestries on the wall.

"Princess," Soline said, entering the room without knocking as Vita was pushing the bed back into its original place. Trailing behind her were a servant with graying brown hair and a gangly boy who looked nothing at all like Ardaric, though he had a sword strapped to his side and wore livery in the general's colors. When Soline saw Vita's state—hair plastered to her sweaty cheeks and her knees bruised beneath her shift—she raised her eyebrows. The other two dropped their gazes to the floor. "We're here to prepare you for the day."

"If you show me to my room, I will be happy to ready myself."

"I'm afraid there's no time for that this morning." Soline gestured to the maid, who was older and shorter than both Vita and Soline, reminding Vita a little of Governess, though she wasn't sure why. Governess was all harsh lines, and this woman was soft edges with a gentle, if polite, smile.

"This is Isotta. She will help me to take care of you, including dressing, washing, and maintenance. And this," she said, swinging around and hitting the boy in the chest, "is Marius."

"And what need have I for a Marius?"

Marius looked up, an argument in his own defense poised on his lips, but Soline beat him to it. "He has his uses. Passable with a sword if you require guarding, can help you write letters if you need, or act as your secretary." She shrugged. "I'm sure you'll drum up something for him to do."

"Very well. He will help me get my old room back."

"Certainly," Soline said, barely paying Vita any mind. "Marius, get out. We need to dress the princess."

"But I am supposed to—"

"Out," she repeated, shuffling him toward the exit despite his protests before closing the door summarily in his face. "Good. Now, breakfast."

Soline and Isotta dressed her like she was going to battle before marching on either side of her down the halls they'd already mastered. She expected to see Ardaric sitting at a table loaded with sumptuous foods too rich for the morning meal, but surprisingly, they stopped in a smaller chamber filled only with women.

All eyes turned toward her, assessing. Vita did not know what quality in her they searched for, and she could not have tried to act accordingly even if she could guess. Instead, she waited for a servant to bring her a plate of food before seating herself at the end of one of the tables, joined only by Soline and Isotta.

"Do they know?" she asked under her breath.

Soline's eyes narrowed. "About the engagement, you mean?"

"Yes."

Soline took a sip of her drink before nodding. "It hasn't been announced officially yet. But everyone knows who you are, and they can guess what it means if you aren't dead."

Isotta smiled at her kindly. She placed her hand on the table, not quite touching Vita's but close enough that it was a comfort. "They are grateful. You will help us to take Messilio when the time comes."

Nobody in the room save Isotta looked even close to grateful. How many of these women wanted to marry Ardaric themselves if it meant one day being queen of Carca?

Their eyes weighed heavily on her.

Soline tapped a steady beat against the table. "We should start preparing for—"

"It's too loud in here."

"What?"

"It's too—" Vita dropped her hand on Soline's fingers, forcing the tapping to cease. "I don't want to talk. It's loud." All around the room, the Kasrians were laughing and talking and saying her name. It was too loud, too bright, too *occupied*.

She pushed the food around her plate, too nauseated to eat.

Eventually, Isotta stood up and returned with some toasted bread for her to try instead. When she'd had enough to satisfy her minders, they escorted her back to the room.

Not *her* room, though.

She spent the rest of the day alone, repeating *Marius, Isotta, Soline* over and over again until her mind once again felt quiet.

"Marius, I need your help."

Being able to open her door was a luxury, even if it wasn't strictly speaking her door. Having guards standing outside at all hours wasn't reassuring, but that part was no different from her life before, and at least now she could poke her head out and ask for aid when she wished.

Marius scrambled to attention, eyes flicking to the other guard before returning to Vita. "Are you hurt? Should we send for the general?"

"No, no, nothing like that," Vita said, waving him in. "I can't reach something. Your help is most appreciated."

She'd returned from the library with three new books to a freshly closed window, and her hands were too raw to keep trying to climb up and fix it.

"There's a window up there. See? Would you help me open it?"

Marius stared up, gauging the window's height. He was tall, but even he would need a way to boost himself up.

"I can try. Why do you want it open?"

Vita gave him a small, pitiable smile. "I miss the breeze. My old room was a prison, but at least I could always open the windows. But here, when it gets stuffy, all I can think about is being locked away in the dungeons again." Her lip trembled on the last word, only half theatrically. "And anyway, it might be nice to leave out some food for the animals. Think about all they've been through recently."

"Of course!" he said, sounding embarrassed to have asked. "Of course we can open the window, Princess."

For the next half hour, she watched from the floor, eating berries that stained her fingers red, as Marius scaled the wall again and again. On what must have been his tenth climb at least, he managed to swing the window out of the frame.

"Finally!" he said, victorious on his perch.

"Don't forget the berries," she reminded him, squishing one between her fingers to watch the juice spill out.

"Oh, right." Marius pulled a handful of them from his pocket and stretched his arm practically out of its socket to dump them on the ledge. "Are you sure you want to be feeding the animals? Won't they try to come in?"

"Your army has scared off half the wildlife. And the squirrels around the fortress are quite friendly. It seems cruel to let them starve if I can share a bit of my own food with them. Don't worry; I won't waste much. Here, please—have a berry."

Marius dropped back down to the floor with a huff, his curly hair bouncing against his forehead. Then he folded himself down beside her and took the berry she held out to him.

"This isn't an escape attempt, is it? I probably shouldn't be caught in the middle of something like that."

"No, not at all," she said, intrigued that he would ask. It likely wasn't a secret that Vita had traded her hand in marriage for her life, but she doubted most people would be so casual about referencing it. Perhaps that was what she should do: find the most guileless of the staff and befriend them in the hope that they would not deceive her. "I appreciate your help. Really." A thought hit her suddenly, and she paused, head quirking to the side. "Should I be paying you? For your help?"

Marius frowned. "The general pays everyone under his command from the spoils, and my food and lodging are provided here in the castle."

"Yes, but . . ." Her mother's household was paid from her own purse, Vita remembered. It had engendered a sense of loyalty in the queen's staff to her above all others. It hadn't saved her in the end, but Vita knew that nothing short of the king's execution order would have ever made them abandon their patroness. Should Vita not do the same? If she was going to survive here—princess, prisoner, or pawn—she would need allies of her own. Marius did not seem like a bad place to start. He had a weapon he might wield in her defense, and at present, he did not strike her as having a fine, artful hand for politics, which was all the better. "You should allow me to pay you anyway."

Except that Vita didn't have money. She didn't even know what each coin was worth, having never had cause to spend any herself. Whenever she witnessed someone being paid by her parents' secretaries, the coins would be in discreet cloth pouches that jingled when dropped into the receiver's hand. Upon her twelfth birthday, she would have been permitted to join her mother's almsgiving efforts once a month, but she'd been sent away too soon. In Messilio, everything she'd wanted had been purchased for her, and since she'd come to Novogna, there was little enough that she was allowed to ask for.

"Just a moment," she said, standing up and wiping her fingers on her skirt before opening up the jewelry box sitting on the vanity. Ardaric had given her plenty of fine dresses and jewels as part of a collection overseen by Isotta, and they were the only things of value she owned in the world. Most of them were locked away, but a few remained in her room for daily use.

"Here." She thrust a silver ring out to Marius before he could object. It was too big for Vita's fingers and plainer than any of the other gifted pieces. It had probably been the nobleman's, left in the box with his wife's jewels for safekeeping and then given to Vita when the castle and all its belongings were seized.

"I can't take this," Marius said. He made to push her hand away and then thought better of it before touching her.

"Please. It will make me feel better about ordering you around."

"All I did was open the window."

"It can be an advance on your pay. It seems like you'll be stuck with me for a while."

Marius frowned down at the ring. "An advance? Like a bribe?"

"No!" She waved her hands, wanting to ward off that thought. "Of course not. Just an advance for general services rendered. I can't very well break the ring in half and give you part. Just take it, Marius."

"You're sure? I really don't need payment."

"I'm sure." She took his hand and pushed the ring into the center of his palm. "And when you get home, you can sell it. Or have it melted down and turn it into something else. Buy something for your family, or save it for your children. Whatever you like."

Finally, Marius accepted the ring, though he tucked it away in a pocket of his tunic instead of putting it on.

"Thank you, Princess."

Vita sat down again, going for the last berry in the bowl.

When she bit into it, a droplet of red spilled down her chin. "You can call me Vita."

She assumed he'd argue and they'd have to go through this whole conversation a second time, but instead, he looked at her, smiled, and nodded. "All right. Vita." Then his brow furrowed, and he backtracked. "Not even Vittoria? That seems a little more proper."

But nobody had called her Vita since her mother died. Not even the birds truly knew her name. "Vita, please."

And so that was what he called her, stretching his long legs out in front of him and answering all her questions about Kasrian winters.

Chapter Nine

Marius talked all day about home—about his baby sister, Stella, and the money he sent back to his family to care for her—and Vita sprawled out on the floor, only slightly jealous.

How easy it was to fall into the stories, imagining herself there with them in the heaps of winter snow as their whole town celebrated the darkest night of the year with a snowball fight, or standing alongside them, watching Stella saying her first words and learning to run.

"It sounds wonderful," Vita said, turning her head on the ground to look over at Marius.

He sat across the room with his back against the wall, like he wanted to be ready to stand up at a moment's notice but had grown a little too comfortable in the meantime.

"It was. The Kasrian countryside is the most beautiful place in the world."

"Do you want to go back? It seems a shame to be stuck here. We don't even get snow most winters."

"I miss my family, and I'd love to go back, but not until I have more to bring them. So not this winter, but maybe next."

Vita played with the end of her braid, dragging it back and forth across the pads of her fingers until it tickled.

There had never been anyone to miss her.

"Marius," she said, sitting up, "will you tell me more about my fiancé?"

"What do you want to know? I am not in the general's inner circle."

"What is he like?" Vita had struggled to get a read on Ardaric for days now, seeing him only at meals, where she largely went ignored in favor of discussing military tactics with his commanders. He appeared good humored around her, often laughing boisterously with his men, but this was a man who led armies and slaughtered anyone in his way.

"He's . . . passionate. Single minded. He wants the Carcan throne, and he will have it."

Vita searched for a response, but she had no idea how she was meant to feel. Ardaric's victory would require her father's defeat, and he would hold on to his throne until the bitter end. Thousands might die. Was that what she wanted?

Her mother deserved vengeance. Maybe Vita herself deserved it too. Her father had thrown away her birthright without a second thought for some bastard son whom Vita had never met. She forced the anger to drown out the terror.

"Well . . . good. I cannot afford to bet on the losing side."

Her father would never deserve a single one of Vita's tears, though he'd gotten enough of them already. Now she only needed to learn how to be a less disposable wife than she was a daughter.

And if she couldn't do that, she would have to think of an escape route from her marriage, but there was still time for that yet.

"You really want to see him dead?" asked a new voice. Vita jolted to attention, but it was only Soline at the door with a stack of laundered clothes. "He is your father, after all."

"Do you doubt my sincerity?" she asked, standing to look

Soline in the eye. Her hair was pinned in an elaborate bun, but strands had come free to frame her cheeks with dark wisps. "I have sworn myself to your general's cause, and that includes killing my father."

"No. But some people are sentimental about family."

"He is my father. And he killed my mother. Ripped me away from my family and the only life I'd ever known. If this campaign fails, surely he will kill me, though he must know I have little choice in abetting it. What use is sentiment to me?"

Soline set down the clothes and then, surprising both Vita and Marius, sat down on the ground. She removed the pins in her hair and let it spill out loosely around her shoulders. "Good. The general will be pleased to hear that."

Hesitantly, Vita returned to her spot on the floor.

They spent the rest of the night regaling her with stories of Ardaric's military prowess: from his successful campaign against the Sopians to the veiled threats he made to the Kasrian king that he would turn his army against their own ruler if he was not permitted the chance to claim territory of his own abroad. The army here wasn't fighting in Kasri's name or financed by Kasri's coffers—he'd proved to his men long before that he could win them riches all on his own. And as long as he paid homage to his king, the Kasrian court wouldn't stop him. *Couldn't* stop him.

And that was the man Vita was going to marry. A man with an army at his back so powerful that even his own king could not curtail his ambitions.

What had she done in agreeing to this? Perhaps she would have been better off accepting his offer of a swift death after all. The more Soline and Marius told her, the more nauseous she felt.

By the time Isotta brought them all food for a quiet dinner in, Vita could not settle her nerves enough to enjoy it.

Vita woke the next morning to a persistent nudging against her cheek. She tried to bat it away, but her hand met feathers instead of skin.

"Eda?" she whispered, eyes popping open. Vita rubbed at them, unable to believe what she was seeing. She'd barely slept since the night of the attack, but today she awakened feeling almost well rested. Maybe she was dreaming still. "You found me?"

Eda looked as pleased as a bird ever could, chest puffed out with pride.

Why are you here? the Eda in her mind asked. *You were supposed to flee the city.*

"I tried. Really! But I was captured, and a dungeon was involved, and now a warlord wants to marry me, and it's really a much bigger mess than I ever intended to get caught up in."

Eda flapped her wings twice before resettling, as though to ask, *Have you considered flying away?*

Vita rolled her eyes.

Eda bumped her head against Vita's hand as she stroked her feathers gently. Birds did not talk, and they certainly could not give advice, but they were still her most loving companions.

We've been worried about you, she imagined Eda saying.

"I'm—" She thought about the scabs that she kept accidentally tearing open before they could heal. How tender her feet still were days after being chased through the streets. All those bodies in the dungeon, bodies strung up in the courtyard, bodies in this castle that still wanted something from her. For her to fail or succeed or give her name to a cause she hadn't asked to be a part of but couldn't escape. "I don't know what to do."

Will you get married? Move to Messilio and be queen?

Vita hadn't mentioned Messilio yet, so even in her head, Eda shouldn't know to ask that. It wasn't how the conversation was meant to go. She tried to rewrite the dialogue, backtrack and start again, but kept finding herself at this same question. What now?

"I don't know. I don't know! No one cares what I want. I would run if I knew how, but there're too many guards, and where would I go? I don't know anyone beyond these walls."

But what would you want? If you could want things.

Now that she spent so much time talking to real people—people who did not understand that she had already scripted their next lines for them, and who instead veered off course with reckless abandon—she wanted to appreciate the ease of these imagined conversations more, but she'd forgotten that even when talking to her birds, she was beholden to thoughts she couldn't force behind the door in her head.

"Princesses aren't allowed to want things."

Eda stared up at her with beady eyes, waiting for a better answer.

"I want—" She'd never thought to ask it of herself before. Not seriously. Even when Ardaric had asked, she couldn't think of anything beyond a familiar room and books to disappear into. What did she want? "Ardaric said he can help me get revenge. For my mother."

But did she really want to marry someone to achieve that?

"I want—" A horrible, sweeping nervousness overtook her. "I want to stop being afraid. I want to stop spending every day wondering if this is when my father finally kills me. I want him to look into my eyes and know that I am going to be the thing that destroys him, because that is what he deserves. I want him to fear me the way he made me fear him. But—" Her voice, already low, dropped to a delicate whisper. "I don't want to get married, Eda. I don't. But there is no way to have both. And I want to be safe, so what other option is there?"

"Those are hardly your only two options."

Vita whipped around, nearly knocking Eda from her perch on Vita's knuckles in the process. There, ensconced in the doorway, stood Soline.

"You should knock," Vita said, her voice hard. The old serving girls never bothered to knock, because Vita never had secrets to keep, but as Soline was a *lady-in-waiting* and vehemently disagreed with being called a servant, Vita figured she could argue for a little more privacy.

"Noted. Next time, I will remember not to disturb you."

Vita wanted to ask how much she'd overheard, but she didn't want to call attention to Eda or the fact that their someday-queen talked to birds.

Instead, she asked, "What did you mean?"

"About?" Soline asked, shoving a bowl of breakfast into Vita's hands and moving to lay out her clothing for the day.

"When you—" Vita gestured toward the door but gave up when Soline's blank stare never wavered. "About having options. What did you mean?"

Soline stepped closer, holding a hand out toward Eda. Eda did not hesitate to stab at Soline's hand with her beak, and Soline barely managed to pull away in time. "I know that you convinced Marius to do your bidding yesterday."

"By asking him for help? Isn't that his job? Isn't that *your* job?" Even considering her eleven years of exile, Vita bore the highest status of anyone residing in the city. She was supposed to be able to issue commands, even if she wasn't accustomed to it.

"Yes, but you didn't order him to help you. You guilted him, toyed with his emotions, and made him think he was rescuing you in some small way."

"And?"

"And," Soline said, staring up at the open window, "you can get better at it with practice. Play the players. Make them want what you want."

"You want me to . . ." Vita couldn't think of an appropriate word for what she thought Soline was suggesting. "To . . . trick Ardaric? Your general? Shouldn't you be too loyal to tell me something like this?"

If Vita had been smarter, maybe she could have made Eda tell her this, but she hadn't been able to think so far ahead.

"I didn't say anything about the general. I would never speak against him," Soline said obediently. "If you interpret my words that way, that is your business, Princess. I just meant that you don't have to be some wilting damsel who has no say in her life."

"I am *not* a wilting damsel," Vita said petulantly, and Soline's raised brow made it clear that they both knew how untrue that was.

"Listen." Soline moved in closer until Vita was forced to take a step back if she didn't want to be nose-to-nose with her. Only Soline kept walking until Vita was trapped between her and the wall. They weren't quite touching, but Vita could feel the other girl's warmth through her dress. Vita dropped her gaze for a moment, trying to control the heat in her cheeks, before forcing herself to look Soline in the eye again. "Your bird seems great. Eda, was it? Bit of a strange name, calling her *first*. Does Marius know that's why you had him clinging to your walls for half the morning, trying to open the window?"

"More or less," Vita said, trying to sound unperturbed, though she wasn't good at disguising her fear. There was hardly a casual way to demand someone's silence without letting on too much. "But she's not important enough to mention, so let's not, yes?"

"I'm great at not mentioning things. And maybe, in return for not mentioning this in perpetuity, you could help me with something too." Soline smiled, brow raised.

Vita's eyes narrowed. "Are you *blackmailing* me, Soline? Couldn't I have you thrown out of my employ for that?"

Soline paused, watching Vita's face with careful attention. "You could. But what happens when Amara comes back? Or some girl you haven't met before, someone who might have her own interests? She might catch one glimpse of Eda and tell everyone who will listen, because she has no cause not to. Is that what you want?"

"I haven't decided yet."

"Very well. You might call it blackmail. I'd call it an equal exchange of services. Think of it this way: if you help me, and I help you, and the things we each need help with are not, strictly speaking, things we want to become public knowledge, then you can trust in my silence. In helping me, you reap your own benefit. I will swear never to mention Eda or any other birds you might have flying through the window. I won't mention friendly squirrels or rats or even a stray cat should one pop its head in. And in return, I only ask that you do one tiny little thing."

"And what happens the next time you need one tiny little thing done? Will you remind me again that you hold something over my head? How could I ever trust in your silence for longer than it takes you to want the next thing?"

Soline laughed, quiet and almost acerbic. Her eyes drifted around Vita's face like she was trying to assess the whole of her before saying anything else.

"You would have *leverage*, Vita. Is trust really what you want? Half the people in this castle would line up outside your door right now if they could to tell you a sob story so you'll help them. Maybe a few would be true, but most of them probably wouldn't be, and you'd still trust them because they would seem so *pitiful*. So good. I'm not offering you lies. I'm prepared to hand you leverage against me in exchange for your help, and you can't see how that would be better?"

Vita waited for her to continue, but Soline said nothing, still staring and standing far too close for Vita to properly focus. Worrying the fabric of her dress between her fingers, Vita said, "Fine." If nothing else, it was easier to rely on a person's own self-preservation instinct than their penchant for honesty. "What tiny little thing do you want?"

Soline leaned in, tucking Vita's hair behind her ear to whisper, "You're attending dinner tonight with the general and all his ministers, their wives, and the higher-ranking members of the army. It will be a huge feast celebrating their victory and officially solidifying your engagement. And I need you to listen to what they say."

Vita turned, their noses practically brushing. Her heart caught in her throat. "Your faith in them is shallow indeed if you want the turncoat Carcan princess to spy for you. What if I take this request straight back to the general?"

"If you do, then he will kill me or injure me or ignore me, or maybe he'll think you're lying or stupid or any number of other things." She stared down at Vita, though she was only a little taller. "Do you want to test it out? How well do you really *trust* the general to be taking risks like that when you haven't even heard what I have to say?"

"Then what do you want?" She tried to feign authority that she didn't feel. "I'm growing bored of this conversation."

"I don't care about most of what they'll say. They've taken this city. They'll take Messilio. None of this is news to me, and none of it is important. All I want is for you to listen for one name. Can you do that? Just one name."

Vita nodded slowly, watching as tension that she hadn't previously noticed around Soline's lips seemed to ease at her acquiescence. This close, she could practically count the freckles on Soline's nose.

"Good. Listen for the name Ivo. If they say it, I want to know why. I want to know who brought him up and their tone and what response they were given. That's it. Can you do that? And in return, I will take the secret of your birds to the grave if that's what you wish."

Vita let her head *thunk* back against the wall, staring straight ahead and avoiding Soline's piercing gaze. "Ivo."

"Yes."

"And who is Ivo, Soline? Is he a criminal?"

"No. He's one of the captains in Ardaric's forces."

"Will he be at the dinner tonight?"

"I imagine he will be, yes."

"And who is Ivo to you? Are you spying on him or spying for him?"

Soline stepped away, turning back to her work as if nothing had happened. "That hardly matters. As long as you listen for his name, that's all I care about."

Vita weighed her options, but in the end, there was no choice to be made. She didn't know what Soline was doing, but with any luck, her ignorance would help her should anyone ever take issue with Vita's hand in it. If she refused, who could say what would happen to Eda? "Fine. Ivo. I'll remember. Now if you don't have something for me to do right now, get out."

Eda had returned to the window, perched high above the scene between the two girls, but more importantly, her daughter Zeda was with her now. Vita wanted Soline far away from her family.

Soline kept working, moving by rote memory as she pulled out a dress for later. Then she stopped, staring down at her hands on the fabric. She turned over her shoulder toward Vita, opening her mouth and closing it once before finally settling on what she wanted to say. "Thank you, Vita. Truly. I don't want to be a damsel either. We all survive how we can."

Her name was said with such gentle confidence that Vita forgot that she'd bypassed both *Princess* and *Vittoria* entirely.

Not knowing how to respond, Vita could only match her tone and say, "You should go. I will call for you if I need anything."

Soline set the dress aside, giving up the pretense of working. "Must I? It looks like you have visitors"—she tipped her head toward the crows—"and as the only one who knows of their existence, you have no one else to share them with but me. I promise to be a suitably awed audience."

Vita watched her, waiting for the moment that something in her expression would give away the untruth. The malice. But there was nothing to find, and so, despite the distrust she still felt, Vita raised her arm out for Eda and Zeda to perch on. She never took her eyes off Soline.

Chapter Ten

No one in the castle was more excited for the engagement feast than Isotta, which was laudable, considering she would be stuck minding Vita all night.

Vita had hardly seen Ardaric since that first day. Though they'd been in proximity at a few other meals, Ardaric's attention was always stolen by members of his inner circle vying for his favor. Vita usually placed herself at the end of the long table and amused herself by watching Marius scanning for threats, as though someone was going to attack her in a room filled with the highest-ranking men in Ardaric's command.

This affair, though, would be a feast for at least one hundred of the men and women from Ardaric's troops, with lively music and drinking.

"What are you thinking to wear tonight, dear? Something blue to match your dress?" Isotta asked, digging through Vita's jewelry box.

"I don't know." Vita fiddled nervously with her hair. She didn't much care for the way the jewels felt on her, heavy and restrictive, but Isotta was convinced that Ardaric liked seeing her in his gifts. "Whichever you think looks best."

"None of that now," Isotta said, keeping her eyes on the box while batting Vita's hand away from the elaborate hairstyle she'd labored over earlier. "I know the perfect necklace." She rooted around for another minute, murmuring, "It must be in here somewhere."

"There are half a dozen blue necklaces in that box. I'm sure they'll all do fine. Don't trouble yourself."

"But I have admired this one many times, so it must be here. Only—" She turned the box upside down, having already laid its contents out over Vita's dressing table with no sign of the necklace she searched for.

"Maybe it was taken for cleaning. Come, choose whichever you prefer before I'm late." Vita dreaded having to spend the whole night surrounded by people, so she wanted to get there early and walk the room a time or two while it was still empty. It would calm her nerves to be able to count the wall stones in silence.

"Oh, very well," Isotta sighed. "This will look almost as nice." She fastened it around Vita's neck and turned her so they both faced the mirror. The necklace itself did little to bolster Vita's confidence, but Isotta's comforting grip on her shoulders somehow made all the difference. "There, dear. Now you look ready to meet your intended."

Vita stared at herself, marveling at how different it was to see her reflection in the ornately framed mirror instead of a windowpane. Dressed in such extravagance and with her hair styled like her mother's, she finally resembled the princess she'd once imagined herself becoming. She was taller than she'd ever properly acknowledged, dwarfing Isotta by several inches. The color of her hair was perhaps a little wan, not quite as golden as she'd remembered, but the length had allowed for Isotta to fashion it in a regal updo. Only the dark shadows under her eyes betrayed the vision.

"Thank you," Vita whispered, clasping her hands together to stop herself from reaching out to touch her reflection.

Vita pulled on Marius's sleeve until he was forced to bend down to her level.

"What," she whispered through a false smile, "is everyone doing here? The feast isn't meant to start for another half hour at least."

"Kasrians are very punctual. We are bordering on fashionably late as it is."

She took a deep, frustrated breath. "Wonderful."

The great hall was filled with at least a dozen long tables with benches running down their lengths to accommodate as many people as possible. It should have been enough space, but there were people sitting on each other's laps and others balancing with only half their bodies perched on the edge of the benches. Each person had a tankard, and judging by the sheen of spilled ale on some of the tabletops, they were drinking liberally already.

Marius led her to the head table, pulling out a chair at pride of place beside Ardaric.

Tonight, she told herself, *I am going to make this work. I will figure out how to fit beside him—figure out how to* stay *beside him when the conquest is over and I am no longer needed. I am going to do this right so that I can avenge my mother and not meet her fate.*

If Soline was right, maybe she could even learn how to sway him to want the things that she wanted.

"Vittoria!" Ardaric shouted too loudly as he pivoted to face her. "We thought you'd gotten lost again! I'd never seen someone need directions to walk down a straight hallway until I met you. Had you, Sorrel?" His glassy eyes focused on the man at his other side. Sorrel wore a dark green cape pinned to his shirt at the shoulders with bright gold clasps. His hair was salt-and-pepper gray, though he looked not much older than Ardaric in any other regard. Despite the several empty tankards littering the table in front of him, his expression remained uncomfortably stern.

Sorrel gave a response, though Vita's attention was stolen away as Ardaric's finger found a lock of her hair to twist around and around, tugging whenever Sorrel said something to make him laugh.

I will make this work. I will make this work. I will make this work.

"You look beautiful tonight. Like a doll. Blue becomes you."

Vita glanced down at her dress to avoid eye contact, her cheeks hot. Having had little occasion for compliments in the last decade, she found that she was terrible at receiving them now. She could not decide if it was genuinely meant or given by rote, and moreover, she did not know which was the better option. It would be easier if she could fade into the tapestries behind her and avoid being seen.

"When will you be announcing the engagement?" Vita asked. She did not want the attention of the whole room on her, but at least with that done she would be one step closer to retiring for the evening to the almost-quiet of her almost-room.

"Announce it? Everyone already knows. That is why they are here, dearest. To celebrate!"

"Oh. I didn't realize you'd made the official announcement already."

"News travels quickly among the ranks. But if you'd like to remind everyone of why they are drinking the best ale in the cellars—"

He stopped to grin at Sorrel before grabbing the back of Vita's neck and reeling her in for a kiss.

Vita didn't have time to close her eyes, forced to stare at him in shock as he pressed his lips to hers. She sat completely still, not knowing how he wanted her to respond when he kissed her again and then a third time, but Ardaric seemed unbothered by her lack of participation. She tried to pull away, a nervous laugh caught in her throat, but he pressed another kiss to her lips in front of the entire room before moving to smack a sloppy one on her jaw.

When she imagined the kisses in stories, she always assumed they would be less wet. Maybe it was a result of his intoxication.

Finally, he released her to whistles and shouts from the room. He leaned back, placing his hand on her thigh as he took another long drink. Even through her skirts, it was uncomfortably hot.

Across from them, one of Ardaric's other ministers raised his glass. "To victory!" he shouted, and the room echoed him, liquid sloshing out of tankards smashing against each other.

"And to the spoils!" Ardaric said before taking another long gulp. "Drink, Vittoria." He pushed her still-full cup toward her and watched without blinking until she raised it to her lips.

Vita took the smallest sip she could get away with before placing the goblet back on the table. She didn't care for the flavor of it at all—it tasted the way her mouth had once he'd released her. "To the spoils," she repeated, wondering if she counted among them.

Eventually, Ardaric lost interest in her again, speaking to the men around the table about securing Novogna and what all would need to be done before they could march on Messilio. Each of his effusive lectures could last upward of a quarter hour before someone else would manage to get in a response.

"Surely you'll want to wait until next spring," Vita said unthinkingly. Nobody had asked her opinion, but it slipped out anyway.

"Surely *not!*" one of the elderly men toward the end of the long table said. It was loud enough to draw everyone's attention to him. Nothing else he'd said all night had been noted, always overshadowed by Ardaric's closer confidants, but in scolding Vita, he would finally have the attention he desired.

Posturing—like a bird. Understanding men was not as difficult as Vita had imagined it to be, as long as she could view them like this.

She regretted speaking out, but the table's attention had returned to her, and she knew they expected a reply. "You will need time to establish yourselves in Novogna, yes? Repair the damage, secure supply lines, collect taxes? I know it is not yet summer, but there is only so much time before it will be cold again."

"Cold?" another man asked with a scoff. "Carca does not get cold. You have never seen a Kasrian winter, with gales of snow for months on end. We are made of sterner stuff than your countrymen."

Under her breath, Vita muttered, "Tell that to Villads the Terrible." As if the infamous Carcan king hadn't fought off nearly three times the number of invading Sopians—neighbors to Kasri and fellow stalwart northerners—by having the good fortune of an unusually early cold front pushing in and severely weakening the Sopians' numbers.

As befitted his name, Villads the Terrible sent the Sopian king's body back to his homeland one piece at a time, demanding an exorbitant ransom for each. According to legend, Sopio had never managed to buy back and properly bury the head.

"Don't fret," Ardaric said, squeezing Vita's leg. "We have

prepared for this moment for a long time. We brought the best of Kasri's army and several notable warriors from the other islands, all looking to reap the benefits of a victory here in Carca. We will leave Novogna well defended and still have more than enough men to travel to Messilio. By the time the Carcan cold rolls in, we will be safe and warm in your father's castle. Messilio will be ours before the Padrilux!"

The men at the table smashed their tankards together again with another triumphant cry that added to the din of the room.

"Padrilux is only a few months away." Summer would bloom soon enough, here and gone like the warm breeze, and then the Padrilux would arrive—the day with equal light and dark, where the Mother handed over the bounty of the year to the Father's wintry grasp. The holiday marked the beginning of the second season. There were rarely stories of wars waged after Padrilux in any given year because neither side wanted to lose half its army to starvation and hypothermia. Those who took the risk—like the Sopians all those years before—always made the history books, either for a stunning victory or for a horrendous, bone-chilling defeat.

"And we will celebrate it as king and queen. Now shush, Vittoria; you do not need to worry about our well-being. This is what men do."

Vita's mouth clicked shut, and she said nothing else for the remainder of the dinner as the servants added and removed platters. The conversation splintered into several smaller ones, and Vita was stuck listening to talks of Novognan grain stores and marching distances through the thick Carcan woodlands.

"Where is Ivo tonight?" someone whispered. Vita tried not to perk up at the name, tracing the quiet voice to two guests sitting diagonally from her who were using the merriment to cover their words. The speaker was a man with blond hair, who leaned carefully toward the woman sitting beside him. She was one of only three women at the high table, including Vita herself. The other was Sorrel's wife, who ignored Vita's existence entirely. The remaining women of higher rank were not army captains or members of Ardaric's inner circle, and they'd been placed at other tables.

Vita had to subtly lean toward them to catch what was being said.

"I told him to lie low," the woman said. "He never listens."

"I'm sure it will be fine. He's the reason for the celebration tonight, after all. He should receive a commendation."

The woman rolled her eyes. "Don't hold your breath. You know they're angry."

"They shouldn't be. He was tasked with securing the western quarter of the city without backup, and he and his men did it."

"You know that the general thinks it was weak to let the Novognans return to their homes after the fighting stopped. Ivo didn't even bring the ringleaders to the dungeons for questioning."

"The *ringleaders*," the man said, frustrated, "were practically children. It was a final stand. They could do no harm by that point, surrounded as they were. Better to send them home and not make a thousand more enemies here."

"*I* know that," she whispered. "I just know that the general doesn't agree. Ivo needs to stay out of his way for a while if he doesn't want his whole family to end up like Anselm. You know the general keeps a close eye on all of them, especially the sister."

The man said something in return, but it was drowned out by the sound of a drunk troubadour's rendition of the "Ballad of

Odelina" from the corner of the room. Dancers rose to follow the singer's lead.

Vita strained her ears in an effort to catch the rest of their conversation, but her window of opportunity had clearly passed. She surveyed the room in an effort to find Soline, but the girl was nowhere to be found, though both Isotta and Marius were stationed just behind Vita.

Vita tried to ignore the troubadour, the song agitating her mounting headache, but between his booming voice and the familiarity of the story, it was impossible not to follow along. He skipped over the part where Odelina's father invited all the eligible sons of the Alstrin Islands to Durbina, ostensibly to allow Odelina to choose a husband, only to refuse her choice of Halse so that he could instead betroth her to his ally in Tarla, a man nearly three times the princess's age. Instead, the troubadour jumped straight to the scene where Halse sailed to Tarla and walked across the field of glass flowers that Odelina's husband had planted to keep away rival suitors.

Vita's hair stuck to her forehead in the stifling room. She imagined Ardaric asking her to dance—putting his hands on her body, kissing her, leading her away to some room she'd never seen before—and suddenly she couldn't sit still another moment.

"I need to get some air," Vita announced to no one. Ardaric glanced over before waving her away, already returning to his conversation. She rose and grabbed Isotta's arm before she could be swept away by the revelers.

"How do we get out of here?" Vita asked.

Isotta dodged between dancers and wove through the crowd, dragging Vita behind her. They finally spilled out into a corridor where many of the women stood fixing each other's hair and whispering behind their hands.

"Can I get you anything?" Isotta asked. "You look flushed."

"No, thank you. I am well. I only need a moment out of the heat."

"Of course." Isotta moved toward a servant holding a pitcher in the corner, procuring Vita a drink. Thankfully, when she sipped at it, it was water.

She drew in several deep breaths, trying to settle her racing heart. Vita was going to marry Ardaric and avenge her mother. It meant letting him kiss her and dance with her and touch her. There was no way around that. She thought his hand on her thigh all through dinner had prepared her for the idea of more, but it was only in leaving that she felt any measure of relief.

If she knew the way to her old room, she would go there now and not look back.

Needing to find that sense of calm again, she listened to the conversations around her in the hope of hitting something innocuous enough to serve as a distraction.

Just beside Vita, a woman was extolling the virtues of finally sleeping in a bed again after months in her camp roll. To the left, several women were gossiping about one of the men in Ardaric's inner circle and the recent death of his wife, which had put him back on the marriage market. To the right, Sorrel's wife, Helka, a woman with golden hair and the faintest lines around her eyes, spoke noticeably too loudly about how excited she was to be invited back into the general's bed. Then she turned to look right at Vita and grinned.

If she was doing this to spurn Vita, she would have to try harder. Vita's breath settled for the first time in several minutes when she heard that someone else would be entertaining her betrothed tonight.

"You must be exhausted, Princess," Isotta said, petting her shoulder like Vita was a cat. "I sent Marius to ask Ardaric if you may be dismissed from the rest of the celebration. I'm sure he will understand that you are not yet used to such festivities."

"Thank you, Isotta."

They waited for Marius's return, and just as he came through the door, nodding his head to them, the bedroll conversation woman leaned close to her companion and said, "The bugs made me itchy all night. I'd hardly fall asleep before one of those bastards was biting me again!"

Whatever her companion said was lost to Vita, because the woman's words had given her a sudden burst of inspiration.

There was a lot to this new life that she had no control over, but maybe she could solve just one of her problems.

Chapter Eleven

Vita opened the door to her room and immediately slammed it shut again before she could pass through.

"Princess?" Isotta asked, almost walking straight into her. "Is something wrong?"

"Is there someone in there?" Marius whispered, hand already on his weapon. "Because I will protect you if—"

"No, no, there's no intruder," Vita said at a normal volume. "I just remembered that I'd like to ready myself for bed tonight." When neither of her attendants moved, she added, "Alone."

"Are you sure? That dress will be difficult to—"

"I'm sure, Isotta. Thank you for all your help. I don't want to trouble you anymore. We'll talk in the morning, yes?"

It took a minute more to convince them, but finally both Isotta and Marius retraced their steps back down the hall, whispering to each other.

With a sigh, Vita opened her door again and watched as Soline, Eda, and Zeda sat together by the dressing table and talked.

Soline talked, anyway, but the other two were excellent listeners. Whatever reservations they might have once had about this stranger, they'd warmed to her faster than Vita had expected.

Vita's own opinion on Soline was still undecided.

"What are you doing?"

Soline looked up from where she stroked Zeda's feathers. "Getting acquainted. What did you think we could get up to in a few hours? Are you concerned I'm already planning a mutiny against you?"

Vita rolled her eyes and tore at her updo. Half a dozen pins hit the stone floor with little *plinks*. She missed the days when nobody cared what she looked like and her hair was always unkempt.

Pettily, she wanted to shoo the birds away from Soline—or, truthfully, shoo Soline away from her birds—but she tamped down the urge.

"You probably shouldn't have made such a dramatic entrance," Soline said. She rose from her seat and batted Vita's hands away to pull out the rest of the pins. With a few gentle motions, Vita's hair spilled down again, feeling infinitely lighter. Then Soline unclasped Vita's garish jewels and set them on the table.

"It was hardly dramatic. I just didn't want them to see the birds."

"Of course. They'll wonder what you are hiding in here now, though." She turned Vita by the shoulders until they were face to face before wiggling her eyebrows. "A lover, maybe."

"You're ridiculous."

"Some handsome soldier with haunted eyes and a love for the language of flowers."

"I have more important things to protect than a soldier with haunted eyes." Vita loosened the ties holding her sleeves to her bodice herself, but she made no complaints when Soline helped pull them off.

"Oh, Vita, you flatter me." She grinned, eyes teasing and light for the first time, and it annoyed Vita immensely to see how pretty it made her look.

Scowling, Vita tossed one of the balled-up sleeves into the corner of the room. "I was talking about the crows."

"Naturally."

"They won't—" Vita paced toward the window and back, dress only half-deconstructed. "They won't really think I am sneaking a lover in, will they?"

Soline shrugged, reeling Vita in again to unlace the back of her dress. "Probably not. Marius and Isotta are too sensible—they have both seen how reserved you are. And they aren't gossips. But it would be good to start thinking of how the rest of Ardaric's court views you. It doesn't matter to them who you *are*, only who they think you to be."

"I don't care what they think of me." It was a petulant answer, and even Vita knew it. It mattered a great deal what they thought of her, because her status was the only protection she had.

"Losing favor with the court certainly didn't protect your mother."

"I—"

"Sorry," Soline said, placing a hand on Vita's shoulder to stop her from moving away again. "I shouldn't have said that."

"Tell me what you know of my mother and the Carcan court."

Eda leapt from the table, flying circles around the small room before landing on Vita's other shoulder.

"I wasn't there. I don't know what really happened."

"But you know something. Heard something. I'm sure rumors spread far and wide. Tell me."

Soline sighed, her usually perfect posture drooping. "In

Kasri, there were stories that your father turned the court against the queen. He told them that she was promiscuous, and that's why she couldn't have any other children—because she was being punished by the gods. That you weren't even his child." Vita made a sound of protest, but Soline shushed her before continuing. "And once she had lost much of her support, it was easier for him to act with impunity. Of course, kings make the rules; they can do what they please. But there will always be acts that push people too far. He had to be sure that killing his own wife would not enrage his people and lead to a rebellion in her name. In your name, even. So he laid the groundwork for his attack, and when the time came to see it through, there was no one willing to defend her."

That was much the same as what Ardaric had told Vita, but hearing it still hurt as though the information were brand new.

Vita pulled at the last few laces of her dress, until the bodice fell away and she could step out of the skirt. Wearing only her shift, she drew back the covers and lay down to stare at the ceiling.

She didn't want to talk about her parents anymore, or her old life, which felt like a dream.

"I heard them talking about Ivo," she said instead.

"Oh?" Soline sat beside her on the edge of the bed. "What did he say?"

"Not Ardaric. There were people at the end of the table whispering. They seemed like friends of his—of Ivo—and they were worried about him."

"What specifically was the cause of their worry?"

"They said that he was the one to lock down the last quarter of the city. And that he was more merciful to the Novognan resistance than he was ordered to be."

Soline cursed under her breath.

"They mentioned that Ardaric was keeping a close eye on Ivo and his family. Especially his sister. And that's why you weren't at the feast tonight, isn't it?"

Soline's hands balled up into fists, knuckles practically white, before she forced them to sit flat on her thighs again. "What?"

"You weren't at the feast because Ivo is your brother. That's why you wanted me to listen for his name, because you're trying to protect him, and he's lost the general's favor, right? I suppose Ardaric forbade you from attending the feast as some sort of slight toward your family."

"No," Soline said quickly, then paused to think through her next words. "Yes, he's my brother. No, I wasn't forbidden from attending. Ivo told me we should stay out of the general's way as much as possible for a few days, but he didn't say why. I thought avoiding the feast with every important member of his entourage and copious amounts of alcohol seemed wise, if only so I didn't lose my temper."

"Who is Anselm?" Vita asked, recalling the name the woman had mentioned. "Another brother?"

Soline stood so abruptly that the birds both flew up to perch on the windowsill high above, staring down at the pair. "No one. Anyway, it's late."

Vita rolled onto her side, curling up under the covers as Soline collected her things—a hairpin she'd probably removed hours ago, given the state of her dark waves; a pair of thin leather gloves; and the bowl that she and the crows had been eating from when Vita arrived.

"Good night, Soline," Vita said softly.

Soline hesitated, hand on the knob but not quite turning it. Instead of offering a polite farewell, she kept her eyes trained on the door and said, "Anselm was my brother. And Ardaric killed him."

Then she opened the door and disappeared.

Chapter Twelve

For the next several days, Vita tried to find a moment to speak with her again, but Soline stuck closely to Marius's or Isotta's side, mending clothes or whirling a knitting needle through the air with the skill of one clearly used to wielding a sword instead. Even when Vita tried to outlast the others, Soline would disappear before she could ever catch her alone.

She wanted to ask about Anselm—about how *exactly* Ardaric had caused his death and what she could do to stay far away from that future—but she instead had to focus on her other goal: training her birds to bring her a new kind of present.

"No, Meda. You're not supposed to eat the bug." Meda pecked at her fingers, confused at the command. "Stop. Ouch!"

She'd pried loose any stones in the wall that had the slightest wiggle, but she'd managed to find only three measly bugs. They weren't the same type, so even if Vita had weeks to wait for babies to be born, she thought it unlikely that there would be any coming.

"Bring me the bugs," she said, repeating the directive for the hundredth time. Though Vita was glad that more of the birds had returned to her and found this new window, she wished that it were Eda who'd joined her today. She would have watched Vita's movements with rapt attention and intuited her meaning as she always did. But Eda wasn't here, so Vita pointed to the window, then pointed to her own chest. "Like you brought me those presents. Earrings and rocks and old coins. Find bugs and bring them back." She looked to Meda, softening her words. "You understand, right?"

Meda stared at her blankly. Vita sighed, going through the request again, and then yet another time when more of her birds appeared.

By the fourth day, just as Vita prepared to give up and find another solution, Eda and Zeda each showed up with a bug in their mouth. Meda trailed behind, still looking confused, but when the others dropped their gifts, she didn't try to eat them.

"My loves!" Vita shouted, hands thrown up in the air. "You are so smart." She pressed a kiss to Eda's head that the bird suffered graciously. Only one of the two bugs was still alive, but that wouldn't matter much in the scheme of things. "Can you do it again? Bring more?"

After several more trips, she had a small jar of bugs, both alive and dead, covered with a cheesecloth to stop them from escaping.

"You little geniuses." The other three birds had eventually come to her aid, mirroring Eda's and Zeda's actions in return for treats. "You know, everyone in Ardaric's army thinks we're stupid. But you're going to outsmart them this time."

If she was going to build a life with him, maybe it was for the best that Ardaric underestimated her intelligence. Like Soline said—she could get what she wanted if she never made it known how badly she wanted it. Guide people in the direction she required them to go, and eventually they would think they chose it themselves.

When she heard Isotta trudging down the hall, she shooed the birds away and sprinkled the contents of the jar under her covers, behind her pillows, and in the cracks between the mattress and the frame. Then she fixed everything so the bed still looked untouched from when Isotta made it this morning.

Brushing her hands off, she looked toward the door and frowned when it didn't open, even though she could hear Isotta speaking just outside. Vita stepped closer, trying to catch Isotta's soft whispers.

"They turned my whole room inside out! I *knew* there were fewer than there ought to be."

"It'll be fine," came Marius's voice. "Maybe the inventory was a miscount after all."

"Well, they broke my nice teacup," Isotta huffed. "They should replace that."

They quieted, and by the time they finally opened the door, both Marius and Isotta had big smiles on their faces that gave no indication as to what troubled them.

"Is something wrong?" Vita asked, eyes narrowing as she watched Isotta ready her table for dinner. Most nights, when she wasn't needed by Ardaric's side, they ate here in her room, just the four of them.

It was nice. Like a tradition.

"No, dear. Now sit down. The servants will be up any minute with the dishes."

Soline snuck into the room just before the food did, and although Vita glared at her, Soline kept up conversation with Marius nearly the whole evening and paid Vita no mind. Vita kicked her shin under the table.

Isotta was stacking dishes for a servant to pick up later when the door burst open, and for a moment, Vita was once again the scared girl in a room upstairs waiting to see what might kill her first: the invading army, or the guard following her father's orders.

She clenched her fist to drive away the image as Ardaric and several soldiers stormed in. Everyone at the table rose, chairs clattering to the floor behind them. Marius's hand hovered over the pommel of his sword, as if he were unsure whether he was meant to be defending Vita or joining his commander.

Ardaric's men stormed toward the table. Vita held her hands out in front of herself, asking, "*What* is going on?" in a shrill voice. The guards paused at her interruption, but given an approving nod from Ardaric, they continued until they'd seized Soline's arms. She thrashed in their grip, trying to get away, but they held firm and dragged her across the room until she stood before Ardaric.

Frightened, Soline asked, "What are you—"

"Silence."

Vita took a tiny step forward. "Ardaric—"

"I said silence, Vittoria."

"But . . ." She swallowed. Soline hadn't given Vita great cause to trust her, but in truth, listening for Ivo's name hadn't felt as dangerous once she'd learned he was only Soline's brother and not some assassin or radical dissident. Her behavior was all otherwise aboveboard. Was Ardaric only acting now to punish Soline's brother, using her against him? "Soline is in my service and therefore under my protection. You must tell me why you are treating her thus."

Ardaric threw a bag on the floor, the drawstring at the top loose. Its contents spilled out, sparkling like dotted constellations in the sky.

"We had reason to suspect that someone was stealing from

you. From the gifts *I* gave to you. The guards searched all of your staff's quarters, and in her rooms, we found this. Eleven necklaces and four rings are in there. You may count them if you want, Vittoria. I will wait."

"Eleven?" Vita asked, dumbstruck. Then, perhaps a second too late, she added, "Of course. Eleven. And what of it?"

"A member of your staff is stealing from you. From *me*. I will not let this go unpunished. Thousands of people rely on me to see them clothed, housed, fed. If I allow one thief to get away with their crimes, then soon enough, we will be destroyed. You may balk now, a senseless girl unaccustomed to the necessity of violence, but someday, when you realize that showing mercy means death, you will appreciate this lesson."

"Wait—" Vita said, raising her hand.

Soline said nothing in her own defense, and Ardaric gave her no opportunity to speak. Her eyes never strayed from his own, but her hands shook where the soldiers held them.

"It must be done."

Needing no further instruction, the guards forced Soline's head down. She kicked at them, trying to escape, but there was nowhere for her to go.

Ardaric drew his great axe, and Vita panicked. "What are you—stop!"

"No mercy, Vittoria." He raised the axe high over his head, and Vita could see the arc it would take before it happened. The spray of blood. The *thunk*.

Unthinkingly, she bolted in front of Soline with her hands out, placing herself in the axe's path before she could consider the very real possibility that it would cleave her in two instead. "Stop! I said that she—"

"Vittoria!" Ardaric shouted, sounding truly livid now as he

swung wide to miss her. He moved in closer, towering over her and seizing the front of her dress, ready to throw her across the room if need be. "Get out of the way. We will discuss your behavior later."

But she couldn't bring herself to stop now. It was as though all she wished she could have done as a child on the balcony to delay her mother's execution came rushing out. "Please! You don't understand. I can explain—"

"Do you wish to be her intercessor? To argue that I commute her sentence? Perhaps you would rather see me cut off the thief's hands in order to spare her life. Is that the kind of mercy that would make you happy, Vittoria? Would you get on your knees and beg like queens are meant to do just to have the privilege of seeing her suffer? She is a criminal. Let it end here."

"No! No, I will not see her without hands."

"Then step aside."

"She didn't steal! She didn't. I gave them to her."

The room in all its chaos stilled. Vita could hear the incessant buzzing of a fly in the corner as her mind tried to catch up with her mouth.

"She didn't take them," she said, speaking slower now that Ardaric had stopped. "I gave them to her. They were gifts."

Ardaric closed his eyes before letting out a deep, beleaguered sigh. "You gave your lady-in-waiting—whose family is already compensated by our conquests—eleven necklaces and four rings in the few weeks that you've been under our care?"

"I didn't realize!" Vita said, latching on to any excuse. "I thought that it was standard! I haven't ever paid my own staff before, but my father—" She hit her stride, falling accidentally into the perfect answer. "And the family who used to live here! They were generous with their servants. They had so many fine things that they gave them away like treats from the kitchen. I just thought . . . that it was normal."

I just thought that you weren't cheap.

Of course, it wasn't the slightest bit true. Vita couldn't imagine any of the waiflike girls who used to tend her fires and drag the washbasin up the stairs fortnightly were getting diamonds for their trouble, but Ardaric didn't need to know that.

"I was just trying to do my duty. Trying to be a good representative on your behalf and to be generous with those who are loyal. And Soline is loyal."

Behind her, Soline huffed, like she really was a wronged, innocent victim. The guards looked to Ardaric, who gave a curt nod, before letting her stand up again and face them all.

"I'm sorry, sir," Soline said, brushing her hair out of her face. She looked entirely too calm for someone who would be dead by now if not for Vita's interruption. "I should have known it was wrong to take them. I thought it rude to refuse the princess more than once, but . . ."

Vita wanted to smack her shoulder but kept her face frozen in its embarrassed, pitiful mask. Of course the stupid girl trapped away for her whole life would make such an error. Of course only Soline's *kindness* would allow her to commit the obvious faux pas of accepting so many gifts.

"It's the truth. I gave a ring to Marius as well. A simple silver one, not worth nearly what his help is worth. And oh, I'm so sorry, Isotta. I was waiting until I found something perfect for you."

Isotta inexplicably blotted at her eyes, as though she were touched at the thought of being condemned to death by Vita's gifts. "Thank you, Princess. That is—"

Ardaric cut her off. "Marius, is this true?"

Marius gulped nervously, floundering before them. "Y-yes, sir. I'm sorry. I knew that I shouldn't have—"

"Enough. Give the princess her jewels back, and we will"—he stopped, forcing himself through gritted teeth to say words he didn't wish to—"forget this incident for now."

A complaint was poised on the tip of her tongue, ornery and foolish: *Won't you let them keep one each? For their trouble?* But Vita could not bring herself to speak the words. To draw his ire toward her again.

Better Marius have his life than that ring. And Vita did not owe anything to Soline after she caused this mess.

"Thank you," Vita whispered instead, sounding as weak as she felt. She'd done all she could to keep up some air of importance—that she was someone to negotiate with, to listen to—but she couldn't any longer. Her knees trembled. "Thank you. I am grateful."

"I will keep your gratitude in mind when I next ask something of you."

He turned to leave, gesturing for the guards to follow.

"Wait!" she said, already hating herself for stopping him. She needed to be far away from him now, where she could forget this horrible web she'd tangled herself into.

A single tear spilled down her cheek. She felt like a child, like she could not escape being that nine-year-old girl for long enough to help herself or anyone else.

Ardaric paused but did not turn.

Her voice wobbled. "My bed—" She choked on a sob, hating herself for this weakness and for going through with her stupid plan to begin with. She should have left well-enough alone. "My bed is infested with bugs. I—may I please switch rooms?"

The silence lasted long enough that Vita was certain she

should just give up, apologize for being bothersome, and agree to stay where she was rather than wait to hear his answer.

Ardaric finally deigned to look at her, perhaps persuaded by how pathetic she sounded.

Isotta, loyal to a fault, pulled back the covers on the bed. "Oh my." Bugs scuttled about in a dozen different paths beneath the blankets, a revolting tapestry.

Ardaric pursed his lips, perhaps finally regretting having allowed her to live at all. He reached out and grasped her chin between stern fingers, perhaps trying to see in her the outline of an unrealized wife the way sculptors see blocks of marble and imagine masterpieces. "Let me prove to you that I am what I claim to be—the man who will make you queen and be your ally. Take your old room, darling. But after this, I expect you to cause me no further trouble. Am I understood?"

"Yes, sir."

"Very well. Isotta, have the princess's things prepared to be moved. And, Marius, keep her door guarded at all times. Neither of you will accept any gifts."

They each muttered their agreement and hastened toward their tasks.

"And, Soline." When he stood in the doorway, it was impossible not to notice how massive he was. How easily he could cut down everyone in the room and be done with it. "You know I have always had great love for your family. The Iseldes are an ancient and revered house. See that this doesn't change."

He did not wait for a response before departing, and Marius and Isotta were quick to follow, each needing to elicit help from the staff to fulfill Ardaric's orders.

"Come on," Soline said, taking Vita's limp hand and giving it a tug. The room was empty now save for the two of them, the toppled chairs around the table, and Vita's infested mattress.

Not knowing the way to her old room, Vita allowed Soline to guide her, trying not to focus on the roaring in her ears.

When they reached the top of the last staircase and pushed through the unlocked door, Vita walked to the middle of the room, did one turn to take it all in, and promptly bent over to empty her stomach onto the stone floor.

Chapter Thirteen

Soline's eyes widened in alarm. "Vita?" She darted forward, entirely unconcerned about the mess separating them on the floor.

"Don't," Vita said, holding her hand out to ward off Soline's advance. It was too much—the overpowering smell, the acrid taste in her mouth, the sudden throbbing in her head, and the sweat and tears covering her cheeks. Vita felt like her skin had been removed and all that was left of her was an endless, bleeding void.

Soline stopped in place, staring at her with the wide eyes of a cornered animal. Nobody ever knew how to handle Vita. She barely knew how to handle herself. "Let me help."

"Don't," she repeated harshly.

Soline sank to her knees so as not to startle Vita before slowly shuffling closer, like Vita might not notice if she was sedate enough about it.

Vita curled her hands into fists and dug her knuckles into the floor, grinding them against it until the skin ripped. The feeling grounded her, steadying her erratic breathing the littlest bit.

"It's all right, Vita. You're all right. *I'm* all right. You saved my life." She let out a huff of laughter. "You even managed to get your room back somehow."

"I—" Her throat closed up, and she bent forward until her forehead was pressed to the cool floor, thankfully avoiding the mess, though she hadn't given it any thought. "I can't—"

With her eyes closed, all she could see was the glint of the candlelight from the dinner table on Ardaric's axe blade. The rush of blood in her ears became the roar of the crowd outside as everyone stood to laugh and jeer at the misfortune of the condemned queen.

Her hands clamped down on her ears as she tried to block out the noise. There was no escape, just bodies and bodies and bodies everywhere, all crushing in toward Vita, wanting to tear her apart until there was nothing left for the axe to mutilate— just like with her mother.

Something grazed her shoulders. At first, it moved up and down her arms, a gentle whisper that she could hardly focus on over the shouting in her mind. Eventually, it settled on her upper biceps and dug in almost painfully. The touch anchored Vita, pulling her out of the crush of bodies.

Soline's touch.

Vita drew in a painful, jagged breath, slumping farther into her curled-up position. Soline spoke, and though Vita couldn't make out the words at first, her voice was soothing, keeping Vita away from that imagined scaffold.

"He would have killed me," she rasped. Vita could never have promised him her undying love, but she had been prepared to try to be a wife to him. Prepared to do as princesses did, and marry herself to a man who could grant her the protection of an army. "He would have done it."

"Shh, Vita. He didn't want to kill you. Everything is all right. Take a few deep breaths, will you?" She slowed her own breathing so Vita could hear it. The crowd that roared in her head went silent, and when Vita allowed her eyes to peek, she recognized the familiar sights of her room: the tapestries she'd labored over for months on end hanging on the otherwise bare walls, the open window with its wide windowsill that she liked to kneel by, and the big wooden wardrobe that never held anything more than two or three dresses. She drew in a deeper, steadier breath this time.

Eventually, Soline helped her to sit up. With her sleeve, she wiped at the tears still running down Vita's face and the snot under her nose.

"See? It's fine now. Shh."

Before she could think better of it, Vita smacked Soline's shoulder. It was pathetically weak, but Soline still reeled back momentarily, then said, "I'm trying to help you."

"You nearly got me killed!"

Soline hummed. "You didn't have to step in front of the axe. Not that I don't appreciate the help, but—"

"You absolute idiot." She batted Soline's hands away. "What was I supposed to do? Let you get your head chopped off and then have Isotta ready me for bed?"

"With all the bugs?" she deadpanned. "Clearly not."

"What happened to *Oh, Vita, make them think they want the thing that you want. Lead them where you want them to go.* Was that your version of subtlety? Stealing from the general?"

"It could have worked."

"It didn't!" Vita threw her hands up. "And then I had to lie for you, and what happens if he finds out?"

"He won't. It was a good lie—playing into what he already thinks about you. The more foolishly you act, the less he'll suspect. Like the bugs in your bed. He didn't think that was you, because he can't imagine you scheming. You're the sad princess that he's saving."

Vita ignored her, needing to yell because somebody else should be hurting right now, and there was no one but Soline. "I suppose I have you to thank for that! *I'm sorry, General. I thought it the height of bad manners to refuse the sad, stupid princess more than once when she offered me eleven necklaces!*"

Soline's words came out in a harsh, whispered shout. "I did not call you stupid. And did you want me to tell him you were lying? How would that have helped? You gave me an out, and I took it. Now we're both here, both alive, and you're yelling like there's something we can do about it."

"Eleven! Necklaces!" Vita smacked her shoulder again with each word, but Soline captured her wrist to put a stop to it. Vita wanted to shake her off, to fight her again, but then she sagged. "Why?"

The girl laughed, letting her focus drift to the corner of the room. "What answer would please you? You're rich, even if you barely know it, and I'm a thief. Now dismiss me from your service like we both know you should, and we can be done with this."

Once, Vita had lived in a world seemingly devoid of lies. She'd believed everything she was told as a girl because there was no reason to question it. Her tutors taught her history, and it was the true history. Her parents told her of the strength, beauty, and goodness of Carca, and so it was correct—and she, in turn, was strong, beautiful, and good because she was a daughter of the land. Even after her disinheritance, she trusted that people like Cosima were telling her the truth. Cosima hadn't always been forthcoming, but Vita still believed her in all things, because

Cosima had been kind, and if she was kind, then it felt natural that she must also be honest and good.

It was clear now that Vita had been mistaken all along. Cosima had told her the untruths that the noble family of Novogna had wanted her to hear, muddling her mind until she could not even count the days. Her tutors had taught her of a kingdom so just and perfect that it could not possibly exist.

Her father had told her he loved her.

Vita had lied to Ardaric so easily, half convincing herself that the words were true. And Vita was certain now, listening to Soline's acerbic excuse, that she was lying too.

Because two things were true: first, that Soline wasn't a poor kitchen maid who would risk her job and her life for the chance to steal a lifetime's earnings from her employer. She wore fine clothes and existed within the general's inner, if not particularly intimate, circle. Her brother held an important position in Ardaric's army, having been the man to secure Novogna for the Kasrians. Ardaric had called her family an ancient and revered house. They probably lived on a massive estate without ever fearing for their finances.

And second, despite Soline's fortunes, she did not adorn herself in excessive finery. Vita watched as Soline twisted her simple golden pendant on its chain. It was the only necklace she ever wore: a circle with a signet design on one side and the letter *S* on the other. Each day, without fail, it rested beneath her collarbones, simple and elegant. Vita couldn't imagine Soline wearing the ostentatious necklaces she'd taken from the box, and nobody in Novogna was likely to buy one from her under the general's nose.

"You're lying." She dug the heel of her hand into her thigh, moving it back and forth, but she could hardly feel anything, as though it were being done to someone else's body. There was a weightlessness to it, a disconnect between the tattered edges of her mind and the physical world that still held the material shape of her. "This pact of mutual destruction is going to ruin us." Vita drew in a shuddered breath, too loud in the quiet of the room. "Why did you steal them?"

Soline sighed, then reached out to Vita, helping her up. "I will tell you, then, if you are sure you want to know. But first, let me clean this up." She ushered Vita toward her bed, sitting her there but not pulling back the covers. Vita kept her eyes on the far wall, staring at a crack in the stonework as Soline flitted in and out of view while cleaning the floor. Vita wanted to help—she'd been made to do so enough times growing up, nursing herself through her own ailments while locked in this room—but she couldn't bring herself to move from the spot she'd been placed in.

At some point, Soline must have stepped outside to order a bath be prepared, because a trail of maids arrived, carrying pots of steaming water and a grand copper tub.

When the room was quiet again and the bath was ready, Soline pulled Vita up from the bed and began removing her dress.

"Are you going to tell me now?" Vita asked, voice blank as she let Soline manipulate her body into whichever poses were necessary to disrobe her.

"Hush. I will. But I know you're exhausted, so get in the tub, and I will tell you what you want to know."

Vita did not argue, stepping into the water at Soline's bidding. At first, she couldn't feel it—could only understand the motion like it was happening to a girl in a story—but the unfamiliar heat began to sink into the skin of her legs. Soline guided her down into the water, and Vita drew in a ragged breath.

Her baths were never hot, not in all the years that she'd lived in this room. Yet this one was, and for just a second, the enveloping warmth forced her back into her body.

Soline wrapped Vita's hair around her palm several times, keeping it from getting wet as Vita laid her head back on the towel rolled against the tub's lip. "How do you feel?"

"Like I want to know what you planned to do with all those jewels."

"Vita." Vita's eyes, which had slipped closed in the warmth of the bath, opened again at the solemnity in Soline's voice. "Some things you cannot un-know, and once you learn them, you become complicit too. If I tell you things you do not wish to learn, we could both be in grave danger." She hesitated for just a moment before grazing her knuckles over Vita's bare arm. Vita tried to hold back a shiver, but it seemed impossible that Soline hadn't felt it. Goose bumps rose on her upper arms where the warmth of the water could not touch. "I will understand if you'd like to stay out of it. It's safer."

"No. I want to know. I can't—"

She cut herself off, staring at the wall ahead of her. Vita could never trust Ardaric now, not even as reluctant allies brought together by mutual ambitions. The man who wanted to help her avenge her mother was, at best, only a mask to get her to trust him. It was the cover that hid the rage of a warrior who won against every combatant he fought. The kind of man who could turn her bedroom into a battlefield.

Because why else had he chosen that place to execute his justice? Was Soline's crime so great that her punishment needed to be carried out feet from where Vita was meant to sleep? He would have killed Soline and forced Vita to build a home in the memory of it. To thank him for showing her the mercy in death.

So whatever Soline had to say—whatever was worth stealing and even dying for—she wanted to hear it. Because for every tale of courtly love Vita had read in the prison of this room, she'd spent just as long reading about the backstabbing of kings and generals and those who wanted power more than anything else.

She reached up nervously, settling her hand over Soline's where it still rested on Vita's arm. "I would have given you the necklaces if you needed them. I really did give Marius the ring, you know. You didn't have to steal."

"Then you're lucky this happened before Ardaric found out about that ring. He would have thought it was a *gift*."

"It was a gift."

"Not in the way he would have seen it. He would have thought you were sleeping with Marius and giving him expensive items afterward to keep him quiet."

"What?" Vita asked, half rising from the water. It sloshed over the edge of the tub, soaking Soline's dress, but she only moved her hand to Vita's shoulder to keep her seated.

Vita understood sex about as well as she understood anything in her life. It was something that her mother and Governess spoke around and alluded to without ever quite addressing. Only Cosima had ever bothered trying to teach her what any of it meant, and only because Vita had been so confused and inconsolable during her first bleed that the serving girls had been forced to send for Cosima at once lest Vita make herself ill. Cosima had tried to explain how it all connected to the marriage bed and child-rearing, first by harkening back to the folk stories that Vita knew and using mostly euphemism, but eventually she'd been forced to speak candidly. The whole discussion had disconcerted and alarmed Vita, and for once, she had been grateful to be kept far from her old life and the expectation of a political marriage.

In all the years since, sex was something Vita rarely had cause to think about. She was meant to live and die as a prisoner. It was only since agreeing to Ardaric's bargain that those old fears rose anew in her.

Never once had she thought of Marius that way—never even registered it as something she *could* think about.

"Never mind. I shouldn't have mentioned that. But it's lucky you gave me all those necklaces after all; don't you agree?"

"Yes, I'm so charitable," Vita said bitterly, settling back in the tub and letting it ease her irritation. "I would have given them to you. That's all I was trying to say. Now I want your honesty, considering that I saved your life tonight."

"I do not mean this as a threat," Soline started, voice wavering. "But as a reminder, we can mutually harm each other if required. I know about your birds, and you don't want him to know. So please remember that before doing anything reckless with what I am about to tell you."

Vita scowled but nonetheless said, "Very well. Continue."

Soline sighed. "What do you know about alchemy?"

Vita barked out a laugh so surprising that it temporarily overpowered her exhaustion before she caught Soline's pinched expression. "Oh. You're serious."

"I didn't think you'd appreciate a joke at this point."

"But alchemy is something out of a story." It was the kind of ridiculousness that let Odelina's husband turn all the flowers in the field around his castle into glass. It did not exist outside the troubadours' songs. Even Vita was not silly enough to believe in it. "That's what you almost lost your life for?"

"People think it isn't real because they can't do it." Soline picked up a bar of soap and lathered her hands with it before rubbing Vita's shoulders. "After all, what child hasn't tried for an afternoon? But when their attempts fail again and again, they assume it's nonsense and give up."

Soline's touch was more soothing than it ought to have been. "If alchemy were real, they'd fight wars with alchemists instead of soldiers."

Vita could list the number of soldiers lost at each Carcan battle going back a century. There were no such records for *alchemists*.

"When you don't want someone to have a power that you yourself cannot harness, the easiest way to keep them from it is to convince them they cannot use it either. That it cannot be used—that it was never real to begin with."

"All right. So how are the necklaces related to a power that no one can use?"

"Trade secret," Soline said. Vita huffed, and Soline poked her arm to settle her. "No, really. You're right that most people can't do alchemy. I'd wager almost no one on any of the Alstrin Islands can anymore. The knowledge was stamped out a dozen generations ago at least, and most people assume that it's a myth if they even know of it at all. If you can create from nothing, then what does that mean for the Mother? For the gods? You wouldn't need priests and tithes and prayers if you could will something into existence from your own desires. You could be your own king, your own god. And so all the books were destroyed, and anyone who tried to learn it was condemned. Not for practicing alchemy, of course—that would only bring further attention to what had once been a niche study unknown to the masses. No, they were killed for heresy. And how can a person learn it if they are never taught?"

"But surely someone must have taught you if you are considering it as a serious option."

Soline dipped her hands just below the waterline, eyebrow raised, but Vita took the soap from her to wash the rest herself, breath catching at the idea of letting Soline's touch progress any further. Shrugging, Soline let her fingers tap the rim of the tub as she spoke.

"If I'd been taught properly, I'd actually know what I'm doing, but I don't. My grandfather used to have a talent for it—like it came easier to him than anyone else, the way that some people are natural gardeners. I'm sure someone in our family must have defied the orders banning it, leaving something behind for him to study, but it's all gone now. If he'd lived longer, he might have shown me. My mother was too frightened that he would be discovered, and my brothers never bothered trying, because they were going to be warriors. And so the little remaining knowledge he had was lost to the world when he died. Grandfather tried to note down a few things—scattered thoughts that can't quite be distilled into words alone. It's just enough for me to try and fail at recreating it."

"Must you be born with the talent the way your grandfather was? Maybe the trait wasn't passed to you."

"People can be born with green thumbs, but those who aren't can still study gardening, can prune their roses diligently each season and learn the skill along the way. Alchemy should be the same. But if everyone who knows how to garden has died without sharing their knowledge, then who is left to show us the way?" Soline sighed. "I will try with his notes. That is my only hope now."

"And what will you do with it? If you succeed?"

Soline turned her head away from Vita, stilling her tapping fingers. "You can't expect me to confess everything. I must have some crimes that remain my own."

"Is alchemy a crime?" Vita's eyes drooped, and Soline took the soap from her, the backs of her fingers skimming over Vita's skin.

"To the church? To kings who could be destroyed if anyone knew its value? They wouldn't call it a virtue. Come; you're falling asleep in the bath. We will finish this conversation later."

Vita allowed Soline to help her out, water rolling off her skin in rivulets. Soline's touch was warm against the chill of the room. Vita was suddenly shy about being undressed, though Soline was the one who helped her change every morning and night.

"It's revenge you want, yes? For your brother—Anselm?"

Soline wrapped Vita in a towel before taking her shoulders and turning Vita to face her. "Revenge. Justice. You want it for your mother, and I want it for Anselm."

Vita nodded, yawning as she backed away and drew on a nightgown. "Then come," she said, pulling back the covers. They looked the same as they had the morning she ran, tucked by her own hand. The blanket that usually sat at the foot of the bed was gone now. "It's late, and your room is across the castle." Having never been to Soline's room, Vita couldn't say if this was true, but it was a good enough excuse to keep her away from Ardaric's men. To keep an eye on her so that she couldn't cause more trouble. "Stay tonight and tell me everything. I'm not too tired to listen."

Soline hesitated, glancing between the bed and Vita. "I should go."

Vita ignored her, blowing out the last of the candles before climbing in and scooting toward the wall to leave room for a second person. When Soline still didn't move, Vita reached across the open space to take Soline's hand and drag her closer.

Soline followed gingerly, and Vita smiled at her in

reassurance. She thought it would feel strange to have another body lying there, but it was comforting, even with all the space between them. Vita pillowed her hands beneath her cheek. In the dark, Soline looked softer around the edges.

Maybe trying to keep her out of trouble was all an excuse. Maybe she wanted Soline to stay just because she wanted her here, so Vita could feel the proximity of someone else in the dark, and there was no nobler reason for it.

"You've had a long day. You should sleep now."

"I'll rest my eyes," Vita said through another long yawn. "Now, tell me. Revenge. Justice."

Soline made a little humming noise but didn't offer up any explanations.

Which was just as well, since Vita was asleep only a few breaths later.

Chapter Fourteen

Vita woke to someone shaking her. Her eyes snapped open, and she expected to hear screaming from outside the window.

But the room was silent, and the only person with her was Soline, looking remarkably unrumpled where she crouched beside the bed, though Vita could tell from the divot in the mattress that she'd stayed all night, sleeping beneath the same covers.

"Wait," Vita said, rubbing at her eyes and trying to sound annoyed. "You let me fall asleep. We were supposed to talk."

"We will. But first, the general has asked to see you."

"He has?" The direction of the light coming through the familiar window indicated it was still midmorning, if a little later than she usually slept. Ardaric rarely called on her except for dinners. He had far more important people to meet with most of the time. "Now?"

"Yes. I'm to get you ready. Come on—the faster this is done, the faster you'll be back to get your answers."

Vita allowed herself to be dressed without complaint, but the thought of seeing Ardaric so soon after what happened made her heart beat too fast in her chest. She pressed a hand to it, willing it to calm, but it did not obey. How was she to act? She'd agreed to this marriage in the hope that their mutual goals would sustain their relationship long enough to protect her, or at least long enough to let her think of a new plan, but a man so quick to anger could never offer any kind of safety. In an effort to kill her father and escape his cage, she'd walked directly into another.

She was led out of her room to meet him at the foot of a staircase, and though Vita wanted to beg Soline not to leave her alone, Ardaric's nod of dismissal sent her away.

"Good morning, Vittoria." He took her hand and kissed her knuckles as though it were any other day. She forced herself not to draw back, though her stomach roiled.

"Good morning."

"I thought after the events of last night, you deserved some peace. Come. Won't you join me?"

"Where are we going?"

"It is a bright, sunny day, and there are lovely gardens nestled away inside the castle's walls. We will go out and laze in the sun today and finally get to know each other."

"Outside?" Vita asked. "Like a picnic?"

"Yes." He smiled, easy and affable, nothing like the man whose hand always seemed to itch to grab a weapon. Vita studied him, trying to see the mask, but he seemed earnest enough, as though everything he'd done last night were part of Vita's overactive imagination.

"But aren't you angry with me?" she asked before she could think better of it.

Ardaric frowned, but he took her question seriously. "There are crimes for which a leader cannot be lenient. Theft, for instance, which is why I took last night's discoveries so seriously. You will learn in time that my favor is conditional, even among my highest ranks. Even for your staff. There is never a person we can trust so well that they are above punishment. But you are still learning what it is to be my bride. I cannot promise you that I will always indulge you. In fact, it would be wise to not test the limits of my kindness, Vittoria. They are quite shallow, as they must be. But in choosing to marry you and take Carca together, I have made it my duty to turn you into the queen I require. You will learn your place."

The answer unsettled her, but it seemed to be as compassionate as he could manage. "I've . . . I've never been to the gardens. It wasn't permitted," she said instead. Vita hadn't thought to ask Ardaric if she was allowed out. There were some things in life that she didn't even remember were options until someone reminded her.

Once, she could recall loving the gardens in Messilio. But even those were faint and dreamlike memories now.

"Then allow me to be the first to show you. Come."

He opened the great wooden door, and light burst into the hall. She hadn't realized how dim and dreary the interior of the castle looked until it was strewn in sunshine. It almost blinded her.

Vita approached it how she imagined approaching a horse for the first time after so many years: a little fearful, a little entranced, but unable to keep entirely away.

Taking a step out, Vita regretted that she'd been made to put shoes on. The fresh scent of grass was far stronger than she'd expected, almost tickling her nose. She wanted to feel it beneath her feet.

Ardaric led her toward a bed of flowers that looked like they hadn't been tended in several weeks but grew wildly in spite of it.

A bee bumbled from flower to flower, and she traced its journey intently with her eyes. The breeze felt different on her skin when it wasn't coming in through her little window.

The whole experience was too much, her thoughts overfull with new information, and it all spilled from her mind like rain in the gutters during a summer storm.

She settled on the ground and then gasped. "The grass is wet." It dampened her skirts, and she ran her hands across the blades, trying to understand it. "It hasn't rained today."

"It's dew," Ardaric said offhandedly.

"I'd forgotten," she whispered, trying to reconcile this truth with her memories of the past. It must have been there all along, but she'd lost that detail along the way. Vita ran her hands over the grass again and again, wanting to imprint the sensation into her mind so that it could not be further misplaced. She hardly listened as Ardaric rambled on about provisions and how soon they could leave for Messilio and the lavish wedding they would hold when they were victorious.

"We will leave a small cohort of our army here in Novogna so that it cannot be retaken, of course," he said, snapping a flower's stem to hand her the bloom. "It's a beautiful city, though it is not the gem of Carca."

"I've never seen the city before." Vita twirled the flower in her hand back and forth so she would not have to look at him. "Except for . . ."

"When I am king, it will be made beautiful again."

Vita wondered what a warrior whose primary talent was destruction knew of cultivating beauty in the world.

"Might I see the city before we leave it? Just once. Perhaps I could attend Isotta on one of her shopping trips."

"No. It's much too dangerous. No reason to take the risk of sending you out into the streets. If you need something before we leave, you can send your staff."

"Risk? I thought the city was secured?" He'd talked about it at length, and she knew that Soline's brother had been integral to that process. "I would bring guards with me if it pleased you."

"Oh, Vittoria, you are so sweet. The truth is, securing a city is only half the battle. There will always be dissidents out there, no matter how well you treat the people you conquer. You are my fiancée and in my care. I will not have you put in danger now, when we are perhaps weeks from leaving for our final victory. We do not know the hearts and minds of every Novognan, and many of them would see you as a target to weaken me." He touched her cheek. "No, you will stay where you are safe. I would not see your brains splattered on the cobblestones out in the city."

She tried to blink away the thought. "And . . . when I am queen and the kingdom is ours? Will I have my own guards and freedom to move through Messilio? Surely my duties will require it."

"There is simply no need. We must be cautious with you. To the Carcan people, I will be seen as chaotic and dangerous, so I must have you to be my stability. The quiet grace of a queen. You will give the Carcans an heir to rejoice in someday—that is your role. To send you out among the people would only jeopardize that."

Dread budded like spring flowers in her chest.

He would lock her up as securely as her father had. Oh, he would grant her leave to walk the halls of the Messilian castle and enter the rooms he designated as accessible to her, just as he allowed her use of the library here. But it would never be her castle. Her home. She would always be a guest subject to someone else's kindness.

The closest she would ever come to freedom would be visiting these courtyard gardens, cultivated and contained like the flowers in their beds.

"My mother gave alms often in the city. It strengthened the people's relationship with the crown to see her out there helping them."

"I'm sure it did. But the current queen does not make such progresses, and she is safe and well still."

Vita's eyes narrowed. In all these years, she'd given no thought to her father's remarrying. Sure, he'd had a son with another woman, but Vita had always imagined him as the vengeful bachelor king, still harping on her mother's supposed betrayal—bitterly, yes, but in a way that felt a little like longing.

"Trust me," Ardaric said, leaning in close enough that she could feel the warmth of his breath. "It is my duty and my honor to protect you as a husband must. You will want for nothing." He kissed her cheek before turning her chin so she faced him and pressing another to her lips. Vita sat as still as a statue beneath his touch.

"Now, you must enjoy the food the kitchens have made for us. It is a fine day. I will tell you stories of your mother as a girl if you like."

Vita nodded, the lump in her throat too big to form words around.

"As I said, I was still young when she left Kasri, but she was remarkable. So beautiful that all the nobles' sons wanted to marry her. She was tall and lovely, but she was very strong too. She loved her horse and spent most of her time with him in the stables, and eventually she was the best rider of all her siblings. Nearly beat out her cousins—the king's sons—even."

Vita allowed herself to picture it: lush green hills, or perhaps snowy fields, and her mother on horseback in her huge dresses, tendrils of hair spilling into her face as she pushed her mount faster.

"I didn't know that. Her life must have been very different when she married my father."

"I'm sure it was. Ana knew she would have to give up some of her girlish pursuits and grow into her role once it was decided for her. She understood her duty to her husband, to her new kingdom, and to her homeland. How lucky you are to not be stuck between two places—Carca will always be your home."

"I would have liked to know that side of her. The one who was free." A girlhood like that was worth far more to Vita than jewels and tutors.

"She would be happy to know that you will don her mantle. That you will be the queen she always intended to be."

Vita placed her flower down, laying it beside the long handle of Ardaric's axe.

Her mother never intended for Vita to be meek, but she did want her daughter to survive. That was clear enough from the little that Vita could remember of the day that she died. Maybe giving in to Ardaric—marrying him and being obedient and unobtrusive—was how she would survive.

Even if it meant never getting to leave the castles he kept her in.

Ardaric continued, trying to distract her with more stories of her mother. Favorite things that she'd done and funny tales from her youth. Vita liked hearing them and pretending that she could be friends with this lively version of a woman whom she had once known so well, but knowing how her mother's life ended soured things.

He bit into one of the apples left by the servants, grinning as he seemed to recall another story. "As a very young girl, when she was allowed to run about her family's estate, she used to climb all the apple trees and pelt the boys at the bottom with them. She would perch at the top, eating her spoils and laughing as they all tried and failed to climb up beside her."

"Apple trees?"

"Yes. Her family spoke of those days often."

"Oh." After that, Vita remained quiet, letting Ardaric fill the silence. She traced back in her memory all that he had said about her mother, trying to find the jagged edges of lies.

Because if there was one thing Vita could remember about her mother above all else, it was that she was always, from her earliest days, allergic to apples.

"How did it go?" Soline asked, sitting in Vita's room with a needle in her hand and one of Vita's dresses laid out on the table, though it looked unaltered.

Instead of answering, Vita threw herself onto her bed, wanting to scream into the lumpy little pillow but too afraid that a guard outside would come running in and try to behead Soline for some undetermined crime.

"That well, huh?"

"Not now, Soline," she mumbled into the pillow.

Her life before was often a haze: part memory, part fantasy, and part dark cloud that obscured everything behind it. Details appeared and disappeared at random. Was she making these things up? Telling herself more stories for comfort?

Only she was certain that her mother never ate apples. She couldn't. Her father often told the story of the day he proposed, when he had all the apple trees in the gardens cut down and replaced with a variety of other saplings. At the time, it had seemed the height of gallantry to Vita—a love that inspired the growth of something new and safe.

No one was allowed to have apples anywhere in the palace, and they were especially not permitted anywhere near Vita in case she was allergic too. Her father had only one legitimate heir, and if she had a reaction more serious than her mother's, it could kill her in a few bites.

Of course, in the years since her imprisonment began, they'd fed her apples many times over. It no longer mattered if she died clawing at her own throat, and hunger eventually won out over fear. It was lucky that the affliction hadn't been passed from mother to daughter.

"Soline."

The woman looked up again from where she'd been frowning at the dress she still wasn't mending. "Yes?"

Vita bit her lip, uncertain what she wanted to say. In truth, she'd said Soline's name only for the moment of certainty it gave her; Soline was here, and real, and she'd stayed last night when Vita thought she might split apart into a thousand glass marbles and scatter to every corner of the room.

"I think . . . or maybe I just want to think, because I'm frightened and stupid and overwhelmed, and now I'm making things up in my head, or—"

"Vita. What do you think?"

Vita sat up. "He didn't know her. My mother. He told me we would avenge her together, but he didn't know her."

"All right. Is it important to you that he knew her? He still wants to kill your father, and so do you. Does that not make you allies?"

"If he never knew my mother, or never knew her well—"

It changed nothing material, but it changed everything to Vita. He'd claimed to be a family friend. Claimed that they were acting on mutual goals to avenge her mother's death. Of course, she'd realized a while ago that this was largely an excuse to declare himself king, but somehow it seemed all right if it was still in her mother's name. He'd been the last link Vita had left to that part of her own history, a boon after so long thinking that she would die having forgotten her mother's voice with no way of ever discovering more about her.

And to feed her stories that were likely lies, to confuse her and make her hope when her mind had already been muddled for eleven years by those who wanted to keep her vulnerable, was something that she could never forgive.

"I was doing this for her!" she said, angry. "Yes, I wanted to save myself. I wanted to see my father's reign end. But it was for her—to know her better! To learn her history and feel like—" She cut herself off, unwilling to give voice to anything more personal than that. "What is the point of any of this if none of it was true? Not the promise of security, or freedom, or even the chance to learn about someone I've lost. I could have consigned myself to a life at his side if I thought it was what she wanted, but *this*—you know I do not wish to marry. I should have let him kill me. At least then it would be done." Though she knew in her heart that she never would have been brave enough to accept death with grace, it felt good to say.

"What if . . ." Soline swallowed. She dropped what she was doing to join Vita on the bed, their knees touching. "So he didn't know her, and now you're stuck. But what if you could have power on your own terms? No father, no husband, none of it—just you. Would you do it? It's your title that holds meaning here."

Vita sighed, dropping her face into her hands. "Is this . . . the alchemy? You mean to kill him, then?" It was obvious, but it was the one question that hadn't been answered last night. The one truth she wasn't prepared to hear, exactly as Soline had expected. Soline wanted a death in retribution for her brother just as Vita wanted one for her mother. But the idea of the two of them managing to kill Ardaric, tall and broad and scarred by war in ways that only made him stronger, was ridiculous.

She couldn't help it—she laughed.

And laughed and laughed, until she had to practically smother herself to stop from crying. Vita tried to calm down, but it took another minute before the room was quiet again. Gingerly, Soline encircled Vita's wrist and drew it away from her face.

"And if that is what I mean to do? Would you turn me in?"

"I don't understand it. I know—I know you said he was involved in your brother's death, but . . . You followed him here. You left your home to come here to support his campaign to take Carca. Why?"

"My brothers are here, so I am here. My loyalty is to them."

Vita envied that level of devotion. There was no one left in Carca who would offer such loyalty to her. Not without being paid for it first.

"Only to them?" Vita asked, glancing down at Soline's hand still wrapped around her wrist.

"You know I would not betray you. Not now."

"Because I know too much? Because I could destroy you with what you've told me? That isn't enough, Soline. I cannot commit myself to . . . to *treason* on the premise of mutual destruction. If I choose to tie my ship to yours, I must know that there are no secrets between us. You will tell me everything—the whole truth and nothing less. I'm tired of waiting."

Soline said nothing for a moment before pulling Vita so close that their foreheads nearly touched, her whispered words a caress against Vita's lips. "Fine. I have three brothers. Ivo, Kellen, and Anselm." She stopped, face twisting. "Had three brothers. We were raised in the countryside most of the year, though my family was welcomed in the king's court. My brothers trained from boyhood to fight, and they were talented enough to make names for themselves when Kasri went to war with Sopio. Ardaric was in charge there, too, though he used to be more under the king's thumb."

Sopio, a smaller island off the coast of Kasri, constantly found itself caught in skirmishes with its neighbor. Land was exchanged between them frequently in the history books, but Vita had no idea who owned what now.

"They shouldn't have all gone off to Sopio—Anselm, at the very least, should have stayed home. But they went and left me behind. Our family was well off, but the last few winters have been harder on everyone, and they cannot all inherit our father's land. But soldiers on campaign, especially those serving just beneath the general, can amass considerable wealth."

"By stealing."

"Yes, by stealing. That's all war is, isn't it? Killing to steal. Land, money, food, power. And in a few weeks, we'll be marching again." Soline sighed before continuing. "They believed in Ardaric's abilities, and even now, I can't fault them for it. They were right. The general knows how to make a whole kingdom kneel. He convinced Kasri to finance what was essentially a test run of his ability to single-handedly dethrone a king."

"Is Sopio under Kasrian control again, then?"

"Yes. The whole island this time. Who knows for how long, but I don't think they'll regain power anytime soon, even with the general distracted trying to take Carca. Sopio was for the king, and Carca is for Ardaric. Technically if he takes the island, he will still owe fealty to Kasri, but I wouldn't be surprised if he never bows to the king again should that happen. Why would he? He has the men. The might. The proven capabilities. And if he takes the capital, he'll have a whole island under his thumb. And your cousin the Kasrian king knows it, too, which is why he did not stop Ardaric from coming here. He could either send his biggest threat away to claim his own lands and gain a Carcan alliance once the throne is won, or he could see Ardaric vie for the Kasrian throne. Neither option was ideal, but the choice was easy. The worst agitators among Ardaric's ranks would stay in Carca to enjoy the lands and titles taken from the Carcan nobles, and the rest of the army would return to their families in Kasri with their new Carcan money."

"And Sopio? What happened there?" Carefully, Vita put her hand on Soline's arm, letting her thumb drift back and forth across the same inch of skin. "What happened to Anselm?"

Soline turned her face away. "I wasn't there, but they told me enough. Enough to see the whole altercation like a play in my head. Anselm, my youngest brother—they are all older than I am except Anselm, who is—who was—who—"

"He was the baby."

"Yes," Soline said, laughing wetly as she wiped her cheek. "Acted like a baby about it too. Never let us forget that he was Mother's miracle child. If he hadn't had two older brothers to toughen him up into a warrior, he probably would have stayed at my mother's side for the rest of his life, cooking and laughing and gossiping and making the rest of us terribly jealous."

"You loved him a lot."

"I did."

Vita tried to smile. "He sounds wonderful."

Soline laughed. "Charming princesses even now. Typical. He used to bake treats for all the girls in town. He didn't realize until much later that they all wanted to be the only ones receiving his attention and were annoyed when they learned that they weren't. I don't think he was even trying to flirt; he just loved seeing people happy."

"What happened? To—actually, you don't have to tell me."

"No, I—it's okay. I want to. The general is temperamental—I'm sure you've seen that by now. He can be suave when he's in a good mood, and then it can all shift so quickly. On the battlefield, he's not trying to impress anyone with good manners. He's the best fighter because he's willing to do whatever it takes. And . . . there was a battle on Sopio. One of the most important, the one that they knew would either leave them victorious or stranded without a clear escape. It was tense, and Anselm was in the way."

"In the way how? Did he . . ." Vita didn't know precisely how to ask if he'd messed up so disastrously that the choices were either let him die or strand an entire army in enemy territory. Vita could almost understand making a decision like that if there were no other options.

"Ans wasn't the kind of guy who took risks. He followed orders and did what had to be done—he wasn't going rogue. He was never that kind of fighter. It was—Ivo, my eldest brother. He'd worked his way up to commanding his own battalion. Kellen had a leadership role, too, but it was over a much smaller unit, and—"

If Vita did not keep Soline's story centered, she would veer off in a hundred other directions, trying to avoid what she didn't want to say. "What happened with Ivo?"

"He had to retreat. The general wanted him to keep pushing forward. It would have meant the complete destruction of his battalion. Hundreds of infantry dead in a single push, with no guarantee of victory. Ivo decided to pull back and regroup. It was—they still won, in the end. I feel like that matters."

"Of course it matters."

"They still won, and hundreds of lives weren't wasted. And the other battalions managed fine, so it's not like Ivo saved his troops by condemning others. He did what he could in a bad situation, but he disobeyed orders. And the general, he—he gets into these *rages* sometimes. During battles, and then immediately after. He won, and he took the whole island for Kasri. But he still had Ivo brought to him in the aftermath, dead bodies littered across the battlefield.

"He screamed at him. Screamed and punched and made everyone stop to watch. And then, he had my other brothers brought out, too, to see Ivo's shame. To remind them and the rest of the commanders why they always follow orders."

Vita wiped a tear off Soline's cheek. She tried to pull away after, but Soline grabbed her wrist, pinning her there.

"Anselm tried to help Ivo when he was bleeding on the ground. I don't know if the general would have truly killed Ivo—he still needed the loyalty of his ranking officers if he wanted to come to Carca. But he wasn't afraid to hurt Ivo enough to be near death. And Anselm—" She stopped, trying to hold in a quiet sob. "He didn't like to see anyone suffering, especially not his family. So he rushed forward to check the wounds. I wish he hadn't."

"He was compassionate," Vita said. What she wouldn't give for a brother like that. She could imagine a whole lifetime of it, from children holding hands as they played, all the way through to adulthood, until one sibling brought their entire family over to the other's house for dinner, cousins playing and spouses chatting and, at the center of it, two siblings who always supported each other.

Soline had this kind of love and lost it, a part of her world winking out of existence in one moment.

But it made Vita grieve in her own way too. Compassion was a foreign thing to her, visible only in others' grief.

"The general didn't like that Anselm wouldn't suffer through it and watch like everyone else," Soline said, sounding distant now. "And then he . . . he just started swinging. Punching him again and again in the head. He didn't need his axe—he can cave a skull in with his bare hands, you know."

The detachment didn't stop Vita from imagining the scene in vivid detail, the same way that not being there didn't stop Soline. An enraged general, punctuating his every reprimand with another hit to a boy who had Soline's same curly hair and sharp cheekbones, mangling his face until it was no longer recognizable. Another boy, older and warier, sprawled on the ground in a bloody heap, pleading for the life of his brother, who was only showing mercy. A third brother forced to watch, held back by the men at his sides who did not wish to see him meet the same fate. One wrong step and their whole family might never see home again.

Somehow, she was sure the reality of that day was even worse than her imaginings.

Vita drew in a deep breath, holding it in for a moment to try to clear her head. This was the man she had to marry. Surely she couldn't stay with him—couldn't bank on his good humor to last even a few years, let alone a whole lifetime. What would happen the first time she displeased him after he was finally crowned king? Would she meet her mother's fate?

"I'm sorry. For Anselm."

Soline made a choking sound. Vita, unsure what to do to comfort someone, leaned in and hesitantly wrapped her arms around Soline. It was strange, but the longer Vita remained in the embrace, the less stiff she felt.

"My brothers couldn't get out. Oaths still bind them to the general's service. They don't care about this place—they just want to go home. They never want to see *him* again, but what choice do they have?"

"So you want to kill him and free your brothers from their oaths."

"I want justice. If he were anyone else, he wouldn't get away with things like this. But with an army at his back, he thinks himself invincible."

Vita thought of her father's crimes. Any other man who killed his wife went before the courts, but a king who killed his queen was beholden to no one except perhaps her family if they cared enough to put up a fight. And clearly, Vita's maternal relatives did not. They'd forgotten her the way that everyone else had.

"If he were anyone else," Soline said, "you wouldn't have to marry him."

Vita pulled back from the hug, startled.

"I could have said no."

"That's not true, and you know it. It was never a choice. And you cannot rescind your acceptance either. He will never allow that. Even if he miraculously doesn't kill you, he will revoke every small privilege he's granted. You will be nothing more than his hostage. You'll never see your birds again, and I know how important they are. If he dies, you are likewise freed from your oaths."

Grief and something warmer swirled within her, tangled so wholly together that she could not begin to unpick them in her mind.

Because Vita was never going to be allowed to choose a

partner for herself. She'd been destined to be married off in the service of Carcan interests, with only her father's word holding any true weight. There was no freedom for girls born just the littlest bit too close to power.

And now there was Ardaric, and nothing about him was a choice either.

"So then, all that's left is to make sure that he dies before he can take the whole kingdom for himself," Vita said dispassionately.

Soline shook her head. "It was wrong of me to bring this to your attention. Not if you aren't prepared for what it will mean."

Dungeons appeared in her head, inescapable and terrifying. The scene morphed from the one beneath the fortress into another set hundreds of miles away that would never stop haunting her.

But what good was trying to avoid them now if she would spend the rest of her life with the same fear? That at any moment, he could send her there and she would have no way to stop him?

She did not need to be queen. It would afford her neither power nor safety. She just needed a chance to run, to make something of herself far from here where no one knew her.

She could go back to Kasri with Soline and her brothers. She could change her name and start over. All she had to do was get rid of Ardaric.

"I could be . . . swayed. If you promise not to abandon me here when it's over."

Soline stared at Vita through bloodshot eyes. "You want to leave Carca?"

I don't want to be alone. "What has Carca ever given me? If I can bring my things, we will run together, and you can take me someplace safe."

Vita expected Soline to ask a dozen questions at least about this plan, up to and including how she was meant to harbor a political fugitive for the rest of Vita's life, but instead, she nodded. "You help me kill him; I help you escape. It's a deal."

"But you must consider what comes next, because we are trapped in a city run by Ardaric's army without any way to get out. If he mysteriously dies, we will have to act quickly. Especially when my father could easily retaliate against a fractured enemy."

"Ivo can get us out. I'm sure of it, Vita. Even now, after all that has happened, he has the respect of his troops. He would do whatever was necessary to get my family out of this mess. And I will make sure that you are with us."

"Then it's a deal."

Soline wiped her tears and left soon after, needing to return to her work.

Vita spent the rest of the day alone, praying not to the Mother and the Father, but rather to her own mother. Asking for forgiveness. If she killed Ardaric before they reached Messilio—perhaps the only time they could do it relatively quietly, given that it would only become harder once he was the reigning monarch—then they would never avenge her mother.

Knowing that she would not blame Vita was the only thing that allowed her to accept this plan. Her mother would want her to stay safe, even if it meant letting Vita's father rule for many years to come. That was someone else's fight.

Don't worry, my Vita. All will be well.

Chapter Fifteen

Two weeks later, Vita walked through the halls with her hand pressed to the stone, trying to imprint the twists and turns into her mind in case she had to escape in a hurry tonight.

She should have known from the moment Soline said, "All right, so here's the plan," that it would be the worst idea imaginable. Considering she also thought stealing eleven necklaces would go unnoticed, her scheming skills were clearly suspect.

Isotta trailed behind Vita, politely bemused but refusing to comment on Vita's attempt at mapping the castle one more time. It had become something of a joke within Vita's household that she could get lost three doors away from her own, and no matter how long she spent trying to acquaint herself with the halls, the farther she walked, the more she forgot, the directions leaking away like water held in her palms. No matter how much she tried to refill them, there was only so much she could hold.

At least Isotta couldn't be implicated in any of this if it all fell apart tonight.

Soline and Vita had argued in her room for hours the night before, trying to come up with the best plan.

"We can't exactly take a dagger to his throat and expect it to work," Soline had said, whispering emphatically. "Unless you think you can take him down in a fistfight, in which case, be my guest."

"I'm not saying you're wrong. Only that I thought you knew a little more about your grandfather's alchemy when I agreed to this."

"And I told you, I can figure it out. We need a catalyst—an item of great value. You can't create something from nothing, so we'll get our hands on one nice bauble or another and make it work. Not the necklaces, but something comparable."

"And then?"

"And nothing. We have to do this part first, and this is the part you can actually help me with, so focus on that."

"No. I need more information. What happens after we have a catalyst? What does it do? Is it like wishing?"

Vita made a lot of wishes in her first year locked up in Novogna. She would sit by her window and try to think up things to wish on. *Catalysts.*

A shooting star? *I wish they would bring me something other than lumpy porridge for dinner.* A storm with lightning but no thunder or rain? *I wish I could grow wings and fly out the window to play with the children in the street.* A night as bright as a summer afternoon? *I wish my mother had taken me and run.*

Most or all of those things probably couldn't grant wishes, but they had seemed strange enough to try at the time. Vita gave up on such childish fancies long ago.

"It's not at all like wishing," Soline said. Vita waited for her to say what it *was* like, but they sat in silence before Soline continued. "Alchemy probably could have done a lot of things in the past. Most of them I will never know. But my grandfather used it to make potions. Different ones could do different things—small things, mostly centered around healing. One made my mother's broken arm heal faster. Another saved Kellen as a baby from a fever. They were never miracles . . . but they helped."

It sounded more like a physician's tonics than alchemy.

"Well, unless you want Ardaric to live fifty years more—"

"Luckily," Soline had continued, "I think I can reverse one of them to do the opposite."

Which had led to a whole argument about Soline's ability to make the inverse of something if she couldn't even make the something itself.

Vita shook her head, trying to prepare herself for dinner with Ardaric. More and more evenings had been taken up with feasts, as though his men had nothing to do but rest on their laurels here in Novogna and eat their way through the fortress's larders.

She knew this wasn't true—they spoke often of ensuring there were more than enough provisions for their march on Messilio in the coming weeks. But it seemed like all anyone did anymore was drink and dance and eat everything they could find.

The feasts kept Ardaric's highest-ranking captains happy to serve, at least, as they vied for his attention at the head table. Perhaps they thought he would dole out Carcan estates by order of sheer proximity, with some beleaguered servant pulling out a ball of twine to measure exact distances.

Vita forced a smile as she sidestepped between two exceptionally large warriors. Even the guards along the walls were sneaking drinks, and the floor was covered in spilled beer. Hopefully it was the same downstairs, everyone trying desperately to taste life before the inevitable battle arrived. Then she and Soline would have a chance at not dying tonight.

Isotta pulled out the chair at Ardaric's side for Vita, but he didn't look up when she joined him, too engrossed in his conversation. All the better, considering her stomach felt full of lead. She imagined she must look milk-pale compared to everyone else.

Behind her, Isotta joined Marius and Soline against the wall, waiting for Vita to need something. Soline, who held a wineskin, shot Vita a pointed look.

She had one job tonight, and one job only.

"Did you know your family used to live in this castle?" Soline had asked the night before, when they'd paused long enough in one argument to start pursuing another. "Not recently. Not even within the last hundred years or so. But once upon a time, this was the main seat of the Carcan court."

"Vaguely," Vita said. It had come up a few times in her history books, though Vita always assumed it was a copying error when they said that the Carcan kings were in Novogna instead of Messilio.

"It was gifted to the Poletta family a while ago now, and so they closed down the mint, but—"

"Who is the Poletta family?" Vita cut in.

"The family who lived here. Did you not wonder why they call it *Castel Poletta*? Or why your coins are called pola? Although I think the coins came first, actually."

Vita had never noticed anyone calling this place Castel Poletta. It was always just *the fortress* in her head, the same way Governess had no other name.

"Will you sit?" Soline asked, reaching out a hand from where she knelt on the ground to try to catch Vita's arm. "You're pacing again."

Vita frowned but did as Soline asked, coming to rest at the base of the fireplace too. It remained unlit, and in the ashes,

Soline had drawn up what she considered tactical plans, though as they looked like neither words nor a map, Vita couldn't figure out what she was meant to be reading in them.

"I'm sorry for being short with you. I promise I will know what I'm doing before we put ourselves in too much danger."

"All right." Vita wanted to say she was sorry for doubting her, but she wasn't sure it was entirely true. Most of Vita's bravado had ebbed away since making the declaration that they would escape together. Marrying Ardaric was dangerous, but this was no better. Every possible future unrolling before Vita made her want to be sick.

"You can trust me, Vita. There is a way out of this—a way where we both get what we want. Revenge. Escape. All of it."

She squeezed Vita's hand, and Vita squeezed hers back. She wanted to believe it was all possible, and so she did.

"What about the mint? If it's been closed for decades, I doubt it'll be any use to us."

"Ah, see, that's the thing. Sure, most of the mint's work moved to Messilio, but now we are here. Ardaric did quite a lot of looting since leaving Kasrian shores, including all that he took from the Novognans. From this castle, even. Coins, jewels, candelabras, you name it. He's got people trying to catalog it all, but they've amassed a lot, and it's all stored away in the mint until it can be dealt with. It would be impossible to have perfectly accurate numbers already, and they wouldn't know if we took a few things."

Vita had sighed but acquiesced. "Fine. How do you intend to sneak me in there?"

Soline laughed, the sound so loud and unexpected that Vita had worried the guards would barge in. "You're not going in. You're the distraction. I'll only have to evade a few guards if we're lucky. Your going would be too noticeable. Everyone knows that you are the general's intended. You would get caught, and then he would kill you for sure."

This all led to another argument. Vita wanted to slip away while everyone was certain she was somewhere else. Soline could vouch for her, and if they timed things correctly, they could send Isotta or Marius out of the room on a task just before Vita escaped and time it so that she was back before they returned. Then they could faithfully state that they'd spent a long and quiet evening with Vita in the library, or the garden, or some other innocuous place. A few minutes away running an errand would hardly seem suspicious given all that they did for her each day, and it would appear like they were leaving Soline in charge of Vita during that brief window. This way, whoever was with them wouldn't have to know anything of the plan but could still serve as a secondary witness should questions arise.

"You can't be the one to go to the mint," Vita had reminded Soline, "because Ardaric already tried to kill you once, and we don't need to give him more reasons to doubt your loyalty. Let me do this."

It was, in truth, the bravest Vita had felt since those first failed escape attempts she'd made as a girl, when guards routinely had to haul her back to her room like a kitten held by the scruff.

"But if he still doubts me, then I cannot be your primary witness, and Marius or Isotta alone will not be enough without my statement, because I would be the only one with you the whole night. Plus, what will protect you if you are caught? You barely know your way around the castle."

"You could teach me." She hadn't always been so easily lost, and surely orientation was a skill that she could relearn in time.

"Trust me; sending you is not a good idea. I appreciate that you're trying to protect me, but that plan only leads to one or both of us dead. If I go, we still have a chance." She'd patted Vita's knee. "And if it fails, I won't take you down with me; don't worry. You can try again if you want, or you can marry him after all and hope that his offer of protection is good." Soline shook her head. "I won't begrudge you that."

"But if you go and something happens—"

Her mouth had shut with an audible click before she could say more, not certain where her sentence was going but sure that something stupid would come out if she continued.

Now, sitting at the table with Ardaric sucking grease from his fingers before going back in for more food, Vita knew what the end of the sentence was meant to be.

If you go and something happens, I will have to watch you really die this time.

Just as she'd watched her mother die. Could she really bear it again? She picked at her cuticle until it began to bleed, knowing that acting against Ardaric could only end two ways, and one of them certainly led to Soline's execution. Probably to her own too.

Her mother's death had broken something in Vita, and it had never managed to heal itself. It was like always walking on a fractured leg; eventually it became stable enough perhaps to bear weight, but it could never be what it once was. It was misshapen and painful, even over a decade later.

And Soline, for all her bad plans and angry retorts, was the closest thing to a nonbird friend that Vita had since Cosima betrayed her to Ardaric.

What would be left of Vita when everyone was gone? Would Ardaric take Marius and Isotta from her, too, slowly stripping from the world anything that bore Vita's mark of affection?

She had agreed to Soline's ridiculous plan in the end, if only because thinking about it any more made her head spin. And now all that was left was to grab and hold the attention of the room.

Soline slipped away from her spot against the wall, coming to refill Vita's untouched cup. "Any day now," she whispered.

Ardaric had his entire body leaning over the table, yelling to a man three seats down about *that time in Talme that you almost got me killed*, but at least he was grinning. He wasn't paying any attention to Vita.

"I don't think we should do this anymore," Vita hissed out from behind her smile.

Soline ignored her. "Once people start leaving, we have no chance. Some of them are still pretty good with swords when drunk, and I can't dodge all of them. It has to be now."

"Soline."

Soline pinched Vita's arm through her dress, as though that might spur her into action.

"Just pass out, fall into Ardaric's arms, and draw a crowd. It's not difficult."

Ardaric was busy waving around a hunk of meat to accentuate his storytelling. Vita could probably keel over and not draw a single eye.

Vita shoved her away. "When you get killed, I'm not forgiving you."

But when Soline returned to her spot next to a servants' entrance, Vita found that she couldn't make herself do anything. Her mind whispered, *Now. All right, now. No, now. Now. Now.* Each time her muscles tensed to act and then just stayed tense, unwilling to follow orders. *You're wasting time. They will all look at your distraction if you would only start. Do it now.*

Soline's glare bored into the side of her skull.

For the rest of the meal, she sat with her hands under her thighs, trapped on a precipice and uncertain if she would jump. It was ridiculous even to consider going through with their half-baked plan, and the longer she let that thought consume her, the farther away from the cliffside she felt. Soline could glare as much as she wanted. There was a better way to do this than to send Soline down there with no real understanding of how to get in or out.

Eventually, Vita rose from the table and bid Ardaric a good night.

"What game are you playing?" Soline asked, spinning around as soon as the door to Vita's room was closed behind them. "He has already ordered a small dinner with just a few confidants for tomorrow. Who knows how long it will be before we have another opportunity like this one, where everyone is drunk and not paying attention?"

"I'm sorry," Vita said, pulling off her jewelry in a huff. "But you're being stupid, and I was being stupid going along with it."

"What do you mean? Are you backing out?"

Surprisingly, there was no anger in Soline's voice. She sounded instead like she was worried.

"I'm not backing out. But I'm also not a thief."

"If you're prepared to—" Soline said, glancing at the door and avoiding the word *murder* just in case, "then I don't think being a thief is too morally bankrupt."

"I don't mean I'm too good to be a thief. I mean that I'm *not* a thief," Vita said. "I can't plan elaborate heists and watch as the dominos fall one by one. And clearly, neither can you." They were two women barely out of girlhood trying to undermine a tactical genius. They would not win this way. "But I am a princess. Why are we bothering to break in? Are they using the mint to create coins?"

"I—yes. I think so. Like I said, there are quite a lot of bigger pieces, so they've been melting some down and turning them into coins. Easier to dole out and spend that way," Soline explained.

"All right, perfect. Let me do this my way."

Chapter Sixteen

Soline's plan had been *too* simple, leaving out any explanation as to how it was supposed to work in practice, which was how Vita knew it wouldn't.

But her plan was just simple enough, a plan that looked like no plan at all, which was how she knew it would work.

"It'll be easy," she said, explaining it to Soline while they passed a cup back and forth between them. Soline had refused any water, but as soon as Vita filled her own glass, she stole it off the table to take little sips as though Vita wouldn't notice. "I'll ask to see the mint and all the new money that my fiancé is creating for his war. And I will act suitably impressed by his efforts and the hard work being done to fund our attack on Messilio, and then perhaps they will gift me a few coins in celebration. Unlike priceless jewels, Ardaric will not care where a small handful of coins ends up."

Soline frowned, and Vita snagged the cup back from her hand, triumphant.

"Admit it. It's a better plan because nobody has to risk anything. No sneaking around, no stealing, nothing that we can be punished for."

"Fine. We'll try your way."

Vita felt the same sense of victory when she left the mint three days later, the pockets of her skirts heavy with coin.

She'd begged Ardaric to allow her to begin preparing for her life as a general's bride, and after a morning visiting the armory to marvel at sweaty chain mail and the practice field to receive congratulations from sweaty men, she managed to direct them toward the mint.

"All these years it has languished, wasted by my father and the Polettas. I know you will not make the same mistakes when you are king." She brightened her grin as she said it, so saccharine it made her cheeks ache. "I would love to see the gold that will win us our kingdom."

It took only a little more fawning for him to agree to bring their growing entourage to the mint. They were joined by Soline, Marius, Isotta, two of Ardaric's guards, three of his servants, and even a few of his captains, all eager to be closest to the general and his bride.

Ivo was there as well, noticeable because he had the same curly hair and olive skin as his sister, along with an identical pair of brown eyes. He was quieter than the others, deferring to Ardaric's every word. Vita could not decide if he was in league with his sister and keeping his head low, or if he was so caught up in trying to survive that it was impossible for him to consider acting against Ardaric.

The skin of his face was largely unmarred, but the bone structure seemed off. A broken nose, a slightly sunken cheek. All the men here had battle wounds, but the longer Vita stared, the more obvious it became that he'd been badly beaten. The bones had mended, but the injury remained.

The workers in the mint bowed to her repeatedly, clearly unsure what her exact title was—did a princess outrank their general, or did being disinherited mean she wouldn't have a true position until Ardaric chose to show her pity and give her a crown? They erred on the side of deference. One older man with gray hair and arms like tree trunks kissed her hand four times in a row, too excited to consider the impropriety.

"It took us many days to get the forges working to melt down the gold! And then many days more to create and engrave the dies for striking the coins! Oh, we could have left them as blanks. Or, I suppose if there were dies with the old king's face, we might have used that for now. But to have our general's likeness on the pola was very important to us! Carca will celebrate the day that he is king, but in the mint, we must celebrate now and be ready for when the day arrives. We are the grateful subjects of King Ardaric already."

Vita didn't know exactly how to feel about her father already being *the old king* when he still sat on the throne. Losing one city did not mean the forfeiture of his crown. It happened too frequently to signify defeat. He could still win. Could easily live long enough to see his daughter dead and buried in an unmarked grave.

She laughed anyway, begging him to show her how he struck the impressions of Ardaric's profile onto the coins. Charmed by her excitement, he brought her over and turned a blank coin into a minted *Ardaric* right before her eyes.

"How marvelous! Can you do it again?" He did. Then, "Oh, can I keep these? As a memento of such an exciting day?" The man granted exuberant permission, warning her to wait until they were cool enough to touch. Then, "Might I try? Perhaps there's a future for me in the mint."

She looked to her fiancé. Ardaric, wanting to look both invested in the work being done by his staff and charitable toward his silly, half-feral bride, nodded obligingly, already turning away to speak with one of the men beside him. They all largely ignored her—all except Ivo, whose narrowed eyes followed her as she worked.

She messed up the first three, because striking a coin was not as easy as it looked. Then she messed up a few more for good measure, since everyone seemed mostly amused by her childish ineptitude.

In the end, she left the mint with almost twenty coins. Though some were horribly misshapen by the time she was done, what mattered most was that they were gold and precious and lining her pockets, and no one would come looking for them.

"Soline, Soline, Soline," she said, spinning around her room in excitement once they'd returned. "I *knew* we wouldn't have to steal. It was so easy! They all thought I was foolish and let me do whatever I pleased."

"In that case," Soline said, counting the coins, "you have my blessing to keep being as foolish as you wish."

Vita joined her, counting them over Soline's shoulder. *She* did this. *She* got them what they needed from right under Ardaric's nose. Soline even looked impressed, though she gamely tried to hide it.

"I'm so glad," Vita said, apropos of nothing.

Soline turned toward her, their faces close. Vita steadied herself with a hand on Soline's shoulder. "That you got the coins?"

"Yes. And . . ." Buoyed by her victory and sudden certainty that Soline was the key to her escape from Ardaric, her father, and Carca entirely, she allowed herself to be honest. "I'm glad we are friends."

"Friends?" Soline asked, surprised. "Yes. I'm glad we're friends, too, Vita."

Soline paced the floor, pulling at the tangles of hair falling across her forehead. She'd ruined her tidy bun hours ago. "I just don't understand what I'm doing wrong. We have the gold. We have the nettle, the marigold, the mint. We've swapped in lavender and rose hips based on the consistency. Tried it with oil, tried it with water, tried it dry. We've made it powdered, made it soupy, made it with big lumps. We're not even hoping to kill a human yet! Just a bug, and somehow we still cannot manage that! *Vinegar* can kill a bug!"

For weeks, they'd tried everything they could think of to make the alchemical reaction occur, working through a lengthy list of ingredients in the process. Soline scoured every bit of marginalia left by her grandfather. They tested adding clippings of Soline's hair to bind her to the spell and, on one less than pleasant attempt, managed to get hold of one of Ardaric's toenail clippings after his servants had been around for a trim. Neither worked, and Vita wasn't keen to try anything quite like that again.

They even sent Marius out one day to hunt for frost laurel and spoolwood, claiming they were little-known ingredients in a remedy for the aches that came with women's monthly bleeding. Both herbs were difficult to find in the Carcan countryside, but even after Marius's escapades in hunting them down, there was no change. Soline threw the book aside, knowing those were the last two plants that her grandfather had included in his notes.

But they were running out of chances to try. After the first attempt, which had created a brown sludge that smelled of smoke and sewage and could have only killed someone by being so foul that they chose to die to escape its presence, Vita had forced back the bile in her throat to pull out the gold coin and try again. But no matter how much she rooted around, there was nothing in the bowl to latch onto. Finally, in utter bemusement, she'd dumped the muck out onto the stone floor to see where the coin had gone. But it wasn't there. Vita had stared at the refuse on her hands for several minutes, trying to understand where the coin was. For all her efforts, she hadn't really believed in the idea of alchemy. She was sure that all any of this would amount to in the end was a poison tonic, no magic required. But the coin was gone, eaten away in the reaction, the price paid for whatever it was they'd concocted.

When they'd tried again, the result had been an almost powderlike substance. It did nothing of consequence, not even to bugs. At one point while Vita was distracted by Soline forcing yet another test on a beetle, Meda got too curious and stuck her head in the bowl. Vita had grabbed her in alarm, trying to brush the powder away as fast as possible, but Meda only stared up at her blankly. They'd watched her for a full hour, concerned that the results were delayed, but nothing ever happened. Meda spent the whole night enjoying being doted on.

The next morning, when she could finally again focus on the concoction, Vita was certain the coin would be waiting there at the bottom of the bowl this time, unable to have melted away. But again it was gone. Every subsequent failure ate another coin, stealing what remained of their hope.

She could understand now why Soline had been foolish enough to take eleven necklaces.

"We're down to four remaining coins, and there's been no progress! So what's wrong with me?" Soline kept patting her pockets, digging her hands into them as though they might reveal more gold if she tried long enough. Her pacing led her to bump into Vita's dresser more than once. Vita winced each time she heard it bang against Soline's hip bone.

"There's nothing wrong with you. You will figure it out."

Soline's head whipped around. "No, I won't. All this wasted effort, and we have nothing to show for it."

Having seen that Soline was right about the possibilities of alchemy, despite all of her initial doubt, Vita now had entirely too much faith in what Soline was capable of doing. "We will. You'll see. You will figure it out. Who knows how long it's been since anyone has even gotten this close. It's progress."

And if they couldn't manage it, then they would figure something else out. Maybe she could flee while they marched on Messilio. Maybe she could get really close to Ardaric's friend Sorrel's wife, Helka, in the hope that ingratiating herself would offer protection.

Or maybe Vita would be killed in the battle, or by Ardaric, or by her father, and none of it would matter anyway.

That wasn't what Soline needed to hear, though, so Vita remained loudly hopeful.

Soline sagged. "What happens when we run out? Your trick with the mint won't work twice."

"There must be someone else we can schmooze for an item of value. Or we start using the necklaces and hope we get close enough to your solution before anyone notices they're missing."

Vita wasn't certain what Soline was trying to make. It seemed to shift depending on Soline's mood. Some days, it was a death tonic that would leave no trace on a person's lips, too powerful even for the antidotes that Ardaric's healers carried. Others, it was a powder or a vapor.

Some days, it was hardly more than a thought. A wisp that

flew through the air and stole a soul from a body before anyone even knew it was there.

Some of them frightened Vita more than others. They were nebulous and wide reaching and prone to disaster. Until Soline could make any of them a reality, though, Vita tried not to let it worry her.

"I wish I knew more." Soline sat on the bed, anger burning down to defeat. She dropped her head into her hands. "I wish I could make this easy. We deserve one easy thing, don't we?"

"I'm not sure what we deserve," Vita said honestly. What had she done in this life to warrant anything being given to her?

If she wanted a new life, she would have to take it for herself. No one, save perhaps Soline, was going to give her anything for free just because she thought she deserved it. And even Soline's plan came with a hefty price if they were discovered.

That thought followed her through the next week. They used a coin, then two, then three, until Soline refused to try again with the last.

"I will study more, and then next time, I'll be ready. I'm sure of it."

Vita smiled. "Of course. I have faith in you."

But Soline didn't try. Not that week, or the next, or the next.

Eventually, Vita stopped counting the days.

Chapter Seventeen

"Bring her in!" Ardaric called from the next room. "I have news!"

Ardaric's guards threw open the doors to reveal the wide, bright space beyond. Soline had tried to explain exactly what a solarium was, but until now, Vita couldn't properly imagine the amount of light that could filter into a room made entirely of glass.

One end of the huge space was filled to the brim with budding flowers of every color, nestled into beds of greenery. They were grander even than the garden flowers, suspended in a captive summer. On the other end stood a cluster of the men and women in Ardaric's innermost circle.

Ardaric moved through the room like he walked on air, so unlike his usual lumbering tread. "Vittoria, my dear!"

He took her hand, and her breath caught as he held it up over her head and twirled her around like a figurine in a music box. Once, twice, until she felt again like the little girl who would spin for hours in her room alone to pass the time. He reeled her in, resting a hand on the curve of her back to steady her dizzy form against himself. His other hand still held hers as he stepped backward, pulling her along, before moving forward again into a turn.

Dancing. Ardaric, the man who had killed Soline's brother in a fit of rage, the man who had taken Novogna in a day, was dancing. He grinned as he guided her through the steps. In spite of herself and all her fear, she smiled a little. It wasn't as bad as she had feared at that first feast.

When Ardaric was in a pleasant mood, it was so pervasive within the room that it was almost possible to forget all the terrible things he'd done. He had a loud, booming laugh and a wide grin that belied the warrior within. There was a magnetism to those good days that made Vita see why people were still willing to follow him into war.

But Vita could not bring herself to forget, so though she enjoyed the dance itself, she did not let him use it to sweep away the things about him that frightened her.

"I have news I would share with you." The onlookers didn't seem at all confused by Ardaric's behavior. In fact, they smiled without cruelty, the sparkles in their eyes showing their own excitement. It was that, more than anything else, that allowed Vita's shoulders to relax.

"News?"

"And a gift. You might consider it a betrothal gift, even."

"You have given me too much already, sir," she said, feeling it was better to humbly decline than to ask too much. When his face twitched into the beginnings of a frown, she quickly amended, "But I'm sure this will be the greatest gift yet. I simply would not wish to grow spoiled."

"This one is the most important." He pulled her closer to him, their movements tighter as they danced only within the same few feet of space. He spun her again. "But first, the news. You have long wanted to escape this castle, and now I can finally make it happen."

"Truly?" she asked, the excitement unmistakable in her words. "I might go out into the city now?"

"Better." Ardaric drew to a stop, cupping her cheeks and pressing a kiss to her lips. "The last of our preparations are complete, the wagons are loaded, and we march on Messilio tomorrow."

Dread flooded in to fill the places that the buried laughter had vacated. Despite all of Ardaric's grand plans and even Vita's own hopes, part of her had thought she would live and die in this castle.

Vita looked over Ardaric's shoulder to where Soline stood against one of the glass walls, haloed in golden light rushing in from behind. Vita could not see her expression, cast in shadows as it was.

"Are you happy?" Ardaric asked, kissing her again and again, each one a short, joyous peck.

"Oh." She tried to smile. "Yes, very happy. Will we really leave tomorrow?" Vita's voice caught, thinking of all she would need to do before then. They had given her no time to prepare. How would she have enough time to say goodbye?

"Our troops are ready, our coffers are full, our supplies are prepared, and our victory is imminent. There is no reason to delay. I have promised you that Messilio will be ours before the Padrilux, and I intend to keep my word."

"So soon? That is . . . most impressive, sir."

"It helps that your father is so obviously terrified." Her face twisted up, and he laughed. "Don't fret, my Vittoria. You will have your vengeance soon."

"Has he sent word to you?"

Had he asked after her? Did he even know she was still alive?

"He sent a messenger. Asked if we couldn't come to a deal—I'd pay him some money for the pleasure of keeping Novogna, and we'd all leave happy."

"And that means he's scared?"

"It was a very low price. Practically asking me to take his own city off his hands for him, which is exactly what we've already done."

"Oh." Vita understood that well enough. Though she hadn't been tutored in leadership since she was small, she'd read several books that alluded to the subject, hidden in fairy tales and tucked between the lines of histories written to impress whichever king had commissioned them. "So he is worried that you're coming for Messilio, which you are, and he wanted to give you legal means to keep the city you've already taken as a pacifying gesture. You get Novogna, and he gets to pretend it was all a business arrangement, and maybe that will be enough to keep you from pushing on."

"Exactly," Ardaric said, patting her temple with his thumb like she was an impressive pupil or a particularly well-trained dog. She flushed. He wasn't testing her intelligence. No one here cared what she thought. They only cared that she was the king's daughter and their general's fiancée, and her job was not to mess either of those things up.

"But you've rejected the offer."

"We have not come here to take a single city. We have come here to depose a king. I do nothing by halves. Well—" He grinned again, and the people around him tittered. "Some things I may do by halves. Like your gift."

With one hand holding hers and the other on her back, he escorted her to the front of the room, where a serving tray sat, a domed lid resting over the top of it like it held a steaming meal that the kitchen wanted to keep warm.

"Will there be a final feast before we leave? Is that my gift?"

"No, Vittoria." Smile lines deepened on his face. He was, in spite of everything, a man who smiled often enough for wrinkles to form there. "Your gift is far better." He lifted the lid. "It's the messenger."

Vita bent double, her stomach trying to expel her breakfast before she could understand what she'd seen. The boy's face was pale and a little blue. The place where the neck had been severed from the rest of his body was in tatters, as though it had been hacked off.

Her fiancé's gift to her was a head. The head of the boy who came to Ardaric from Messilio to broker a deal.

A hand rested on Vita's shoulder, pulling her up. She felt queasy. Vita had to keep her eyes on Ardaric to avoid seeing that horrible thing resting on the tray like an offering. "Vittoria. This is a gift." The smile lines remained though the smile was gone. "The first kill of our final battle, an undertaking my men assume in your honor. You must accept it graciously."

She slapped a hand over her mouth, trying not to vomit all over his shoes.

"There will be more like this. Many more. You are the promised bride of a conqueror. This is what victory looks like."

Quietly, like the words were a failure of courage, she whispered, "I do not want a boy's head. I—" What else was there to say? *I saw my mother's head like this once. I heard the stories even from my secluded tower of how her eyes continued blinking after it was cleaved clear off her shoulders. I would never accept such a thing as a gift. I do not have the stomach of a warrior.* "I—"

Her throat closed up, and she didn't know where to look. The room of shimmering sunlight was suddenly too bright, too blinding.

Ardaric stepped closer to her, his torso pressed against her back. He angled himself and Vita until they had no choice but to stare at the horror etched forever on the boy's slack face. "Look at him, and then thank me for it," he murmured into her ear. Their audience could not be confused about their conversation, and yet Ardaric kept the words quiet, a threat just for her. "Most warriors would have to go out and make their first kills themselves. This is our way, Vittoria. We've been kind enough to bring you this one already dead. Thank me for it."

She was small and hopeless and powerless against him. The room closed in, and she could not see Soline poised against the wall behind them.

"I have done this for you. I have spurned your father to continue my quest toward Messilio so that we might avenge his slight against you and your mother. So thank me—that is your place."

The fear of being Ardaric's enemy was like a storm, lightning flashing on another atrocity before there was time to process the last. Soline with the axe against her neck again, face tear stained. Marius's and Isotta's heads on two gleaming silver trays. Vita conveyed down the endless path to a platform, until there was no place she could turn that did not lead to the executioner's block.

He leaned in closer to kiss her cheek. "I am not cruel; I told you that it was my job as your intended to teach you how to be queen—this is how. You are to be gracious. Your victory comes at the expense of thousands of deaths, and it would not do to pretend otherwise. You cannot turn away from this truth. When we leave Novogna, there must be no more outbursts like that night with Soline. I have forgiven you for that, as I said in the gardens. But you must not forget again—we will be dealing with far more serious things out there, things that will get your troops killed if we are not careful. Do you understand? My word is law, and my word protects you. You must always listen to me. I doubt you will forget this lesson again. Now, we are meant to be celebrating, Vittoria. Today is the first day of our triumph. Thank me so that we might move on."

"Thank you," she whispered, trying not to cry. Then, louder, "Thank you."

The boy was already dead, and she could not save him now. She forced a smile and said her lines again and again until she was sure everyone had heard her. They did not care if the words were false, only that she was conquered. "Thank you for my gift."

"The boy's hand and the note it bore will be redelivered to your father in due time," Ardaric said. "You should take the head to your room tonight. As a reminder. When we leave the safety of Novogna, people like this boy will be dying in your name."

Stoically, she picked up the tray. The domed lid had long since been whisked away, and Vita could not hide from herself what she held.

It was not her head. It was not Soline's or Isotta's or Marius's, but that was the coldest comfort.

Her fingers trembled with fear, with rage, with an unnamable thing as she carried it across the room, footsteps echoing in the silence as everyone watched. The doors opened for her again, and Soline hurried after her, taking up her place behind Vita before the guards could separate them.

Halfway through the labyrinth of staircases and narrow halls, Soline whispered, "It will be okay."

Vita said nothing, focusing on keeping her hands steady.

Soon enough, it would be their heads. Whether Vita rebelled or stayed the perfect devotee, she could not stop him from taking whatever he wanted. From using and discarding her.

She burst through her bedroom door, and Soline barely

managed to scurry in before it was slammed again in its frame by Vita's firm kick. The locks were on the other side, but Soline wisely shoved a chair beneath the handle before turning to Vita with a wounded look.

Vita wanted to climb into the wardrobe and hide in the dark behind the dresses. She'd always done that as a girl. When her life was small, reduced to a single room, it seemed the only way to protect herself when she became overwrought was to make it collapse further in, pressed from all sides by the heavy oak and the scent of tallow soap on clothes.

Instead, she thrust the head into the bottom of the wardrobe and shut it away before she could be forced to spend a single moment more looking into the boy's milky eyes.

"I will not have him," she said, moving like a flurry through the room. She fetched herbs from her dressing table.

Vita wasn't sure if she meant the boy or Ardaric, but Soline didn't question her. "You must have him."

"I will not. I'll escape."

Soline tried to move closer, hand outstretched toward Vita, but Vita brushed her off. "Right now? How will you leave when there are guards on the door?"

Vita screamed, picking up ingredients and then tossing them aside when they weren't what she wanted.

"Who needs the door?"

"How else do you intend to escape?"

"Somehow. It doesn't matter how. I'll figure it out myself. No one else is going to save me."

The drawer squeaked as she pulled it open, revealing the final coin. Vita grabbed it unceremoniously, ignoring Soline's cry of alarm.

She tossed herbs into Soline's mortar at random, grinding

them just enough before burying the coin in the center of the pile. Gesturing for Soline to come closer, she ordered, "Say the words."

"Which words?"

"I don't care which words. You've tried them all." There had been nearly twenty failed incantations. It didn't matter which she used now. "Pick some or make them up! I don't care. Just *say them.*"

"Maybe I was wrong," Soline said, looking scared of Vita for the first time since they'd met. "I shouldn't have mixed you up in this."

Vita ignored her, stirring the herbs like they were in a magic cauldron. "I'm already here. I'm mixed. I want out. Now say the words."

Soline gave in, murmuring words too indistinct for Vita's ringing ears to catch. A wisp of smoke curled up from the bowl, and Vita said, "Good. Again."

Soline continued chanting until the wisp disappeared. Vita dug through the herbs, frantic to see something at the bottom of the bowl. The coin at the very least, or—if she was lucky—something with which to kill her intended. But though she searched, she found nothing but the crushed plants.

"No. No!"

She crawled toward the headboard with its hidden trove of goods. The hollow contained little of value, but surely there was something.

Vita drew out the single pearl earring that she'd had in her hand when she fled the castle on the day of the attack. She'd been certain it had been lost with everything else, but later a laundress had found it dangling from the torn remnants of her nightdress.

It was chipped in several places, with only the littlest bit of gold for the hook, but it didn't matter. It was going to work because Vita would force it to.

"Keep going. Do not stop."

A tear tracked down her cheek, but as Soline resumed the words, Vita dropped the earring into the mortar and covered it in herbs, holding her hands there like it was a seed she could press into the earth to create new life.

Then, unthinkingly, she added her voice to Soline's chant, saying words she did not know. They fell from her lips like a foreign lullaby. Like the magic was clay and she could mold it in her hands. She imagined destruction—the kind that a woman like Vita could not wield on her own. She saw the chaos of the attacks on the city and wished for a tenth of that power to be at her disposal now. The terror and the anger and the flames that engulfed the world.

A curl of smoke rose again, and Vita doubled her efforts, voice broken.

He will not have me.

"Stop," Soline said, breaking the incantation, but by now Vita knew her lines. She could carry the cadence on her own. "Stop! Vita, you have to—the bed is on fire!"

Vita's reverie shattered, and it was only then that she smelled the smoke. Her bed linens were swallowed by flames, and already they were leaping up and up, trying to climb the nearest tapestry.

"Vita. We have to get out!"

She drew her hand back as the flames tried to lick at her skin. "I have to get my things."

Even during the attack on the city, she hadn't left it all behind. She would not leave it to burn now either. Her gifts from the crows were the only items that mattered to her in the world. Thousands of hours' worth of tapestries could burn, and Vita would not mourn, but she could not lose the pebbles and broken pieces of jewelry and half-copper coins that she wasn't sure would even pass as proper pola.

She got as close as possible to the bed frame, reaching her hand in to remove what she could. The flames rose tall above her as they jumped from the tapestries to the wooden beams of the ceiling. Soline dashed across the room to her dressing table and picked up the pitcher of water sitting there. "Here," she said, upending the pitcher and dumping its contents onto the flames edging toward Vita.

When the water touched the fire, it did not sputter out or shy away. Instead, it roared closer, forcing Vita to scramble back on her hands and knees so that it did not burn her fingers clear off. All of her treasures scattered around her to be consumed by the flames.

"Gods," Soline whispered. She tossed the empty pitcher to the side before hauling Vita up. "It's going to bring down the ceiling and destroy the whole room. We need to get out."

Smoke coated the inside of Vita's lungs, but she still tried to fight against Soline's pull. "These are my things."

"It doesn't matter. Either it burns through everything, even us, or we escape without them. Choose."

Even us. "You should go, Soline. Don't wait for me."

"We're both going. Stop being an idiot."

Vita could make no further arguments. As the fire grew, leaping toward the wardrobe still holding the boy's head and Vita's clothing, Soline strong-armed her through the door.

Smoke poured into the hall, and guards could be heard racing up the staircases, but as soon as Vita was clear of the worst of the fire's effects, she slumped to the floor and wept pained, blackened tears.

PART II

There Can Be No Peace

Chapter Eighteen

"I have been exceedingly patient with you, Vittoria."

Ardaric's hand spanned her jaw, forcing her head up so that she couldn't look away.

"I have promised you a crown of your own. I have outfitted you like a queen, with the finest dresses and the grandest jewels. You are to be my wife. I have never mistreated you, even if sometimes it has been made clear to me that your neglected upbringing has done you no favors. You see punishments everywhere, and yet I seek only to instruct.

"But this—and on the night that we celebrate our campaign toward Messilio. Did you burn your room down to scorn me? Did you destroy *everything* I have given you to prove that you are no more than a petty child?"

"No," Vita forced out, staring right at him. His eyes raged like the fire.

She had no tears left in her to dredge up. She didn't feel the bravery that came before the spell anymore—she only felt tired. Resigned. The fire had cauterized everything else.

"You didn't burn your room down like a child?"

"It was an accident."

"A carelessly knocked-over candle," he said, repeating the lie she'd first told when the general's harried servants arrived. "Which burned so furiously, it could only be put out by smothering."

A dozen soldiers had injured themselves trying to stop the flames. Her room was isolated from much of the castle, so there was little threat of its spreading, but they couldn't be too careful.

They, too, had learned the hard way that this fire loved water just as it loved straw and wood and fabric and skin.

The room, as far as Vita knew, was still a smoldering pile of ash.

"I don't know what happened."

Ardaric raised his brows, and his grip on her cheeks tightened, crescent nails digging in. "You are not a good liar."

"I don't know what happened," she repeated, an honest vehemence in her words. Vita did not need to lie: she did not know what had started the fire. Not really.

Soline had spent weeks trying to distill that alchemical spell down into something that would bring about death, but it was never meant to be so unwieldy. So chaotic and destructive. If they could only create fire, then they had nothing.

No way to stop him.

"You didn't like my gift, though it is only a reminder of what we go to do in Messilio, so you went upstairs and decided to destroy my castle. You're lucky it was confined to your room. Less merciful rulers would not suffer such an act of defiance, not even from you."

Ardaric shoved her away, and she stumbled, falling to the floor.

"Instead, I will have the heads of all your father's army. Heads, arms, hearts, whatever my men can take. And then I will be king. You will not be the omen that stops this from happening— do you understand?"

And what will I be? she wanted to ask, but she could not bring herself to say the words.

"I have tried to be kind to you in spite of what you may think. But if you cannot behave, then I will have to garner your obedience through other means."

He beckoned a servant forward.

"I have no interest in idle threats, Vittoria. I do this only to remind you that I have tried to play nice, and that if it is cruelty and punishments you expect, then I can give you those too."

When the servant finally stepped out of the thick shadows cast over the general's private office, Vita saw what he was holding: an ornate wrought-iron cage, slightly too small for the creature inside to perch comfortably.

Eda.

"Your bird will remain with me until I can trust you to behave. If you do not give me a reason to mistrust you, I will return it as a wedding gift. If you cannot manage that, then I will pluck every feather from its body before roasting it on a spit."

Vita gasped, trying to reach out toward Eda, but the servant stepped back until he was out of reach.

"Now get out of my sight, Vittoria. Preparations have been underway for weeks, and we ride out tomorrow morning whether you burn down this castle or not. If your maid cannot find something to dress you in, you will go in rags. Or naked and covered in soot. I really don't care. Until then, find somewhere else to be."

Vita took one last mournful look at Eda before running toward the door.

"Did you tell him?" Vita asked again, crying pitifully into Soline's shoulder where they lay squished in Soline's tiny bed. She already knew the answer, had heard it half a dozen times from Soline's own lips, but she could not resist asking again, if only because she could not face the truth.

"No, Vita," she said with the same patience as all the other times they'd gone through this. "I didn't tell him or anyone else about Eda. You know that I could not for my own safety, but also . . . I would not. Not anymore. You have allowed me to know them, and I could not betray them now either."

Vita had already sobbed through the whole retelling of her conversation with Ardaric, and though Vita wished she could blame Soline for what had happened, she knew that it was her own fault.

She'd been so angry after receiving the boy's head, and she'd wanted to believe for just a moment that she could actually do something about it. But her actions had done nothing to protect her, and now Eda would pay the price for her foolishness.

It was careless to think that all the guards in the castle and out in the streets would not notice the birds coming and going from Vita's window. That they might not hear her greeting them and see her sneaking them food. They did not need Soline to tell them—there were more than enough ways to learn this information all on their own.

When the silence had gone on long enough, Soline let out a huff. "Well, I suppose there's nothing to be done about it now," she said lightly. "We'll have to run away and change our names."

Soline made it sound far too easy, her hand stroking Vita's hair. Vita didn't care how small the room was; she was just grateful that it was private and that she could lie down to cry without anyone's scrutiny.

"And go where?" she asked, smearing tears across her cheeks as she tried to wipe them away. "Kasri?"

"No. Ardaric might not be the king of Kasri, but he has too much sway there. It would not be safe while he's still alive."

Vita laughed hopelessly. "And we can't stay here. Soon he will be king, and then there will be nowhere to go."

"But you would be queen if you stayed, and that is something."

"Is it?" Vita buried her face in Soline's itchy blanket. What use was a crown when she would wield no power? When she would have no say over anything that happened to her?

Soline shifted, squirming her way beneath the covers. "No, you're right. That won't do. Back to running, then. We can go to Aligo."

Vita peeked out from under the blankets. "What would we do in Aligo?"

Soline frowned, perhaps recalling that they had no valuables left to trade, and they could not use sympathy for Vita's plight to gain allies. Vita's true identity could never become known no matter which island she found herself on. If the Aligese learned that they possessed a foreign princess—one caught in the conflict between a father who would surely want to kill her and a general who wished to use her—then they would try to strike a bargain with whichever of them would offer the better price.

She was nothing to everyone, and yet somehow she'd become a central piece in a game she'd never wanted to play.

"I suppose we would walk until we reached a convent and then ask to join the order."

Vita pulled back, staring at Soline's wide eyes shining in the darkness. "And become nuns? Is that what you want?"

She tried to imagine Soline cutting off all of Vita's hair before

Vita turned and did the same for her. Tried to imagine feeding the hair into the fire and praying for the Father to take away their vanity.

At least the Aligese seemed kind to their nuns. It did not go so far as veneration, like some kingdoms venerated their priests, but the role of a nun was sacrosanct. Noble, even, as far as callings went. Far better than somewhere like Durbina Minor, where, at least according to the history books that had burned in Vita's room, a radical sect had taken to worshipping only the Father. It was decided that if the Mother hadn't given the world disease and famine and death, then the Father would never have had to take. They'd even burned down their convents with the nuns still inside.

Aligo would be better, far from the shores of Durbina's anger, but it would be a false safety.

Soline turned onto her back with her hands folded over her stomach, a soft smile on her face. "Not in the slightest. Do you think I've spent a single day of my life on my knees in prayer? Everyone I know who claims devotion does so only to look pious in front of others."

"Is there no other option for us but feigning piety for the rest of our lives?"

Soline slid closer under the blanket. "If we took vows, we'd have new names. We'd fade into a sea of boring, devout women who do their work and pray for the souls of the dead and never stir up trouble. The sisters would protect us."

Vita's crying stopped, and she wrinkled her nose. "It sounds . . ."

Vita had spent her whole life hidden behind thick walls. Those in power wanted her to remain unseen, unheard, unknown. The people she'd once watched in the streets each day going about their lives probably had no idea that she existed.

Could she do that again? Don a new name and hide herself from view? She wouldn't be alone this time, and she'd never dreamed of power the way Ardaric did. Ardaric and then Soline had both swayed her toward vengeance, but she wasn't sure that was what she needed. The desire still burned somewhere in her chest, a small flame that no amount of smothering could put out, but fear kept it small. Contained. She was a good girl, like her father and Governess had tried to teach her to be. She did not complain. She always waited for Cosima's visits, even when they felt a lifetime apart. She did not stir up trouble.

Trouble would get her killed.

But trouble—like magic, like fire, like hope—was more than a little intoxicating. Shutting herself away for the rest of her life would be safe, but it would not mean freedom.

And if she were going to give up the only freedom she'd ever tasted, it would have to be for the assurance of safety. But no one could swear to her that what had happened in Durbina would never come for Aligo. At least here, she knew her enemy's face.

"It doesn't matter," she finished finally. "If we run, Ardaric will kill Eda, and then he will find us. We have no way to buy passage on a boat and no knowledge of the ports' schedules. If we run, we won't make it out of Novogna much less to an Aligese convent. He will tear apart the kingdom before he will let us go."

"So we march, then."

"Yes."

"And we'll figure it out as we go." Soline rolled so that her cheek was smushed against the top of Vita's head. The warmth was grounding.

"Yes," Vita whispered. "I want to know what went wrong with the spell. I thought—I thought it would be different."

"We could . . . try again?" Soline offered. "It's never worked at all before, but this time *something* happened. There have to be some alterations we can make. Maybe *you* are the answer, Vita."

"Absolutely not," Vita said, imagining an entire army encampment set alight and Ardaric's men—both the good and bad among them—screaming. That would leave her with less than nothing to show for her pain. She would have no path back to Castel Poletta. Her father would reclaim her, and then, seeing the damage one man had caused when he had her in his keeping, the king would have her killed so as to never be inconvenienced again.

Soline sighed. "If you're sure."

"You can have your revenge in time if that's what concerns you. But if we try again, we will only bring destruction."

"I'm not only concerned for revenge. We must keep ourselves safe too."

Vita closed her eyes, unable to resist the wave of exhaustion. "If you stay away from me and keep your head low, you should be safe. I know the same cannot be promised for your brothers, but we will do what we can for them."

"Vita," Soline chided, voice soft. "I'm not going to leave you on your own to deal with him."

"You should. There's no sense in wasting your time worrying for me, Soline." Then softer, one foot already in sleep, she mumbled, "Soline, Soline, Soline," the name like a song.

"Why do you do that?" Soline asked.

"Do what?"

"Repeat my name when you're falling asleep. I've noticed it practically since we met, but especially when you're upset. You've done it with Marius's and Isotta's, too, but mostly mine."

Vita let out a little hum, shifting closer to Soline's side. Had she been repeating names while drifting off? She couldn't remember doing so, and it certainly hadn't been intentional. "It's probably"—she yawned—"probably so I don't forget it. I'm always . . . doing that. You know . . ." Soline's warm palm came to rest on her cheek. "Forgetting things I want to remember."

"Like what?"

Vita wanted very badly to sleep, but she dredged up an answer for Soline from the murky depths of her mind. "I had a governess growing up, but I cannot recall her name, or the exact color of her hair, or how her voice sounded. A whole childhood spent with the same woman—she was practically another parent to me—but all that's left is a blur. And in my first months in Castel Poletta, I tried to befriend a maid. I think she may have even played with me two or three times, but then she disappeared without a trace. I cannot recall her name either. And . . ." Tears filled her tired eyes. "Until Ardaric reminded me, I'd forgotten my mother's name. Ana. Queen Ana."

There had been all the shadow puppets she'd made friends with when she was first brought to her tower room, each given a name now lost to her, like they had never existed at all. Once, she'd named the children living in the street below her window, creating whole stories for their lives, but soon enough she could not recall if the boy was Parick or Aldo or Leon, though the options sounded nothing alike.

The crows were easier; it would take Vita a long time to forget how to count. But Marius, Isotta, Soline . . . they could be lost to her in a matter of weeks if she wasn't careful. She even recited as many of the names of Ardaric's lackeys as she could, and on a few occasions, Soline's brothers' names.

Eventually, she would forget enough of the people around her that Vita herself might disappear too.

"Vita," Soline whispered, her voice cracking, but whatever pity she was going to offer, Vita was mercifully too close to sleep to hear.

Chapter Nineteen

Seeing the cavalcade of riders, carts, and infantry preparing to leave for Messilio made it obvious that everyone else had known for a long time just how imminent their departure was. But even before the fire, no one had come to pack up Vita's things or prepare her to travel.

It was lucky that Isotta had taken several of her dresses for laundering only hours before the stunt in the solarium and its aftermath. Because of her, Vita still had enough to wear, though most of the space in her trunks was reserved for the books that Vita begged Marius to steal for her from the Polettas' library.

Ardaric, in his magnanimity, even gave her a few pairs of britches to ride in, though a scowl marred his face when he handed them off to Isotta.

"But I don't know how to ride," Vita said, staring at the britches in alarm. When she was a child, servants used to lead her pony around the courtyards inside the castle walls, praising her as a future warrior-princess. But it had been over a decade since anyone had let her near a horse, and even seeing them lined up outside frightened her. Why did they have to be so tall?

"No time like the present to learn, I suppose. If I can ride, then anyone can." Isotta laughed, but Vita did not. She'd probably been riding since birth. "Don't worry; there will be plenty of people around to teach you, and many days to get it right. You'll only be sore for the first week or so."

"Oh, good," Vita said, forcing levity into her words. "Thank you, Isotta. For your faith. And the clothes."

"If you want to thank anyone, Your Highness, it should be Helka. She graciously gave a few of her own dresses over for your use when she heard about the fire. I was terribly worried about what we'd do with only five dresses and a war to fight, but Helka came right up to me and insisted that you take some of hers. They might not be what Ardaric has made you accustomed to, but they are still fine things indeed, and very warm."

Head poking through the shirt she was putting on—and arms still uselessly tangled in the sleeves—Vita peered out the window again to where she knew Helka would be. She always stood beside her husband, Sorrel, and Sorrel was always standing stoically beside Ardaric. There was no singular man who had more sway over Ardaric's decisions than Sorrel Aventicus.

Helka looked up toward the window of Soline's room, where Vita was preparing for the journey, and made direct eye contact. Vita wanted to flinch back. Helka was wealthy and well connected and sure of herself in a way that Vita could never be. Helka did not wilt beside her husband. The pelt that she wore, slightly too heavy for the southern heat, was probably from something she'd hunted and skinned herself.

Helka nodded to Vita, and Vita returned the gesture. The clothes, at least, would be appreciated, even if she knew nothing from Helka and Sorrel could ever be free.

Vita finished dressing, and then a harried Isotta conveyed them both downstairs before they made everyone late.

Vita hadn't seen the rest of the birds all morning, perhaps

scared off by Eda's capture or else beaten away by Ardaric's staff. Vita could only pray—to whichever god might hear her, the Mother, the Father, or some other entity entirely—that they would be safe. Selfishly, she wanted them to follow her to war like she was their nest, but she knew that it was best that they didn't.

It was better for them to find some new home far away from Vita. Far from Ardaric's cages and her father's army and out-of-control alchemical fires.

"Goodbye," she mouthed, staring up at what had once been her window. Even from her vantage point, there were visible scorch marks on the stone.

To leave felt like being ripped from the earth, uprooted from all she knew. A garden could be a prison in its own way, but if it was the only place anyone ever watered you, it was hard to leave the safety of its soil.

"Come, Your Highness," Marius said, taking her hand. "I'll help you onto your horse."

"No need." Ardaric's voice boomed out over the procession of servants and soldiers eager to march. "She will need time to adjust to sitting a horse again on her own. Until then, she will ride with me."

Marius smiled, though it looked a little tight. He handed her off to Ardaric before mounting his own steed.

Soline was several rows back, but she dipped her chin when Vita looked toward her.

They could have run—even if it meant a swift death—but Vita chose this path for them. It was too late now to turn away.

Ardaric lifted her onto the giant warhorse's back, and she had to dig her fingers into the creature's neck to avoid slipping off when he mounted behind her.

"Careful," he chided. "You have a habit for destruction,

whether you intend it or not. But I will have no harm come to Magritte."

Petulantly, Vita wanted to ask why he could protect his Magritte but she had to watch her Eda suffer, but she supposed that was the point. He did it because he could.

"Magritte? Your warhorse is a girl?"

"I keep several horses for battle: mares, stallions, and geldings alike. They all have their uses. But today, we ride Magritte."

His hands rested on Vita's hips as Magritte took her first steps, the rest of the grand parade falling in line behind them. For the first time, she was grateful for his touch, if only to keep her balanced. It was a long way to fall.

"You will be sore soon, but we will not stop."

Vita nodded, staring ahead. "I understand."

"Isotta and Soline will help you this evening. I am not so unkind as to deny you that."

Strangely, in some ways, she believed him. Or, more importantly, she believed that he believed his own claims. He did not think himself bad. He maimed, and he killed, but such was the life of a warrior. When you saw the horrors of war as merely another step in a grander plan, was it any surprise that the heads of messenger boys became gifts? Did it make him worse than anyone else? Worse than Vita, who would see him dead if she could? He would fight to protect whatever he deemed valuable enough to keep. If he would bind himself to her in an unbreakable, magical oath of protection that he could never forsake, perhaps she would forget all his transgressions and marry him gladly, if only so that she would never have to worry for her safety again.

It was only that she could never be sure of his mercy. To him, kindness was weakness. He believed that he was helping her by not relenting. Eda was proof of that.

"How long will we be traveling?"

"Our company will move slowly so we aren't separated. If the weather is fair and the roads are dry, it will take two or three weeks to reach Messilio."

Vita glanced up at the sky. A few clouds streaked across the expanse of blue, but they were bright white and spoke only of much-needed summer shade. No rain in sight. "And if the weather turns?"

"Then we will be a miserable bunch with a month or more of travel ahead of us."

The threat of a month riding Magritte made Vita eager to become an expert horsewoman.

Once the cobblestone streets of Novogna were behind them, all that was left was forests and farmland. Vita could not recall ever seeing so much green. Great lemon trees bloomed along the road, their scent filling the air and covering the odor of thousands of unwashed travelers.

The first night, when Ardaric finally helped her off Magritte and the others tore through vineyards in search of as many of the fattest grapes as they could find, Vita lay on her camp roll and tried not to wish herself dead.

In a show of what was either kindness or pity, Ardaric gave Isotta an ointment to rub into Vita's sore muscles.

"It will not be this difficult forever," Isotta said from their place in Vita's tent, where she was manipulating the ointment into her legs. "Eventually, you get the knack for it."

"But not by tomorrow," Vita groaned. The thought of getting back onto a horse made her sick.

"No, not by tomorrow, but I'm sure the general will be accommodating. It was good of him to send you this salve."

"Yes." She wondered at the delivery of it. Ardaric's moods were often hot and cold, but Vita thought she almost understood him now. He was the hero of the story—the Halse, the savior of a lost princess—but he could only play the role in the way he understood it. He was a warlord, and he operated in blood. He could not learn a new language now, so he would use the one he had. And he refused to compromise, because he knew his way was best. That was the thing about those old folk stories; they worked so well because the women did not dissent. It wasn't Vita's place to buck tradition, and so he would do what he needed to bring her to heel. "Yes, very good of him."

The next morning, when he made to boost her up onto Magritte again, she said, "Thank you, Ardaric."

He watched her for a moment, she atop the horse and he standing beside it, before giving a single sharp nod in response. He climbed on silently behind her.

It was several hours into their ride, when the burning in Vita's legs was nearly unbearable, that she decided to distract herself with conversation.

"Is this what it was like when you marched across Sopio?"

He did not say anything for several long seconds, only letting out a small hum, as if lost in thought. "Yes, though the army was smaller in Sopio. The weather was not so nice. But the rest of it—the pace, the orderly lines, the encampments at the end of the day—that was all the same."

"The army was smaller? Was that not the king's army, though? I was under the impression that this was more of a volunteer mission."

He laughed, and it was much quieter than the usual booming

sound she heard at the feasts. "I suppose you might call this a volunteer mission. There are some who have sworn oaths to fight with me, and so they remain. But as for the rest . . . I have made a name for myself, and many Kasrians who did not have to come decided to find their fortunes with me anyway. There are also others among this army—a few loyal Sopians and some enterprising Tarlans and Durbinians. Winters in the north are hard, and between the chance to make money here and to potentially stay in Carca, there were many willing to swear their allegiance to join."

"Could you not have overthrown your own king with such a fighting force? It seems the men already respect you far more than they respect him. Why bother with Carca?"

"Because I, too, have sworn oaths, and for as long as I count myself among the Kasrians, I will not break my word. I am not without honor, Vittoria, in spite of what you may think."

Ignoring this comment, she instead asked, "Will you still consider yourself a Kasrian when you are a Carcan king? Will you still owe the Kasrian king fealty?"

"No. Kasri will always be my homeland, but it will not force my hand any longer. When I am king of this country, I will owe fealty to no one. That is the way of conquest."

Vita ran her fingers through Magritte's mane. "And will you take Kasri for yourself someday? When you are no longer bound by your oath?"

"I'm not sure, honestly," he replied, his voice lilting in a way that showed genuine interest in the question. "Maybe, but not immediately. Life is long. There will be time."

For the rest of the day, they existed in a strange truce—she was not unruly, and he was not cruel. Sometimes, he would point out things of interest along the road: an old, burned-out watchtower that had once been part of Carca's defenses, a monastery miles off in the distance that they could see clear across the hills, and even some of the island's animals. In return, Vita recited one of the poems that she'd managed to retain all these years. It was a famous story about two Carcan lovers caught on opposite sides of a civil war between noble houses. Though both characters were only distant relations of the two families, it was not enough to allow them to escape tragedy in the end.

Vita didn't focus on the words as she regurgitated them by rote, instead letting the rhythm lull her. Ardaric never interrupted.

On the third day, when they had once again gone silent, the stretch of road offering no distractions for him to comment on, she said, "I hear that I have Sorrel's wife to thank for providing me with dresses." It was perhaps an unwise thing to say, drawing his attention back to the fire that had destroyed a considerable amount of her own wardrobe, but there was something she wanted to know. Needed to know, really.

"Helka? Yes, I heard that she'd come to your aid."

"That was kind of her," Vita lied. "She must respect you immensely to offer her own fine things to your intended when there will be no chance of her replacing them for some time."

"I'm sure she does," he said noncommittally.

"You are . . . close?"

"Yes, Vittoria. Sorrel is my second-in-command, as you know."

"Only"—she swallowed nervously—"I had heard . . . heard from *her*, actually, that—"

"You are asking if we sleep together?"

"Yes," she said, coughing to hide her embarrassment.

"We do. It is of no consequence to you, really. She is married and cannot be queen, and you are marrying for political purposes. You will be my wife; you will bear my children. It will not be a passionless marriage. I will have you just as I have had her, and I will not forswear myself to purity and faithfulness. Does this upset you?"

The only part of his statement that upset her was the reminder of her obligation to give him children, but she could not say that. "No, sir. I know my duty."

"As long as you are faithful, Vittoria," he said, kissing her cheek, "we will have no issues."

By the fourth evening, Vita had to implore Marius to teach her to ride when they made camp for the day.

Though her working truce with Ardaric had given her a lot of new information to think over, she could not bring herself to stay pressed up against him all day after their discussion about Helka and the marriage bed. Vita knew that this was the future that loomed over her: sex and childbearing and being kept inside, away from all dangers, for the health of an heir that was not even a person yet. The knowledge sat uneasily. Even mistresses would not save her from this, and she could not let them. Not forever. If she did, he might decide one day that he'd rather have someone else on the throne beside him, and then she'd be in the same position as her mother.

For now, though, they were still just engaged, and if she could learn to ride on her own, then she would have that small freedom at least. She needed to clear her head and consider what other options might still be open to her, though every day seemed to bring her closer to that looming future.

Soline, Isotta, and Marius had taken to entertaining her in the evenings before the camp settled down to sleep. They had already shown her the wonders of the forest: the rings in tree stumps and nests in high branches and which berries they could eat, letting bright juices spill down their chins. Marius had even tried to explain what exactly dew was and how it formed, questions she'd been pondering since that day in the garden, though she wasn't sure she'd understood his answers well enough to repeat them back.

This march had allowed her to see so much of the world that had been stolen from her, but it wasn't enough yet. Vita needed to learn more if she was ever meant to truly live in it.

"Please, Marius," she asked for the fifth time at least. "Just a few laps around the camp—nowhere far. I have to get better at riding somehow."

Marius poked carefully at their tiny fire until it grew to a respectable size before pulling out their rations. He should have been allowed to sit with his company, but instead he stayed with Vita, Soline, and Isotta, knowing that it was his duty to protect her.

There were a dozen other guards stationed nearby, men bigger and stronger than Marius, but he was the only one who remained at her side.

"The horses need to rest before we march again in the morning. Don't worry. You will adapt in time."

The excuse made sense, but if Vita could not practice tonight, then the same went for every night of their campaign. The horses would always have more to do in the morning.

"Can you give me advice, then?"

It started off simply enough, but the more involved the advice became, the more Vita needed to imagine with her body what he meant, which led to her straddling a fallen log and pretending it was a great beast. Marius tried to help, but eventually Soline's laughter grew too loud.

"No, no, hold your reins like this," Soline said, pantomiming teasingly.

"That looks exactly like what I'm doing. There's no way that I'm doing *that* part wro—"

"Actually," Marius cut in, looking sheepish, "she's right. You want your thumbs to be upward. And elbows in toward your torso."

"Yes," Soline said, tossing her hair. "Now kick her up to a canter."

"What?"

Soline clicked her heels together twice before moving to Vita's side and tugging at her shoulder, trying to bounce her up and down.

"Stop," Vita laughed, swatting at her. "You're not helping."

"You have to get into the rhythm, Princess. This is expert equestrian training you're receiving."

Even Marius grinned, but outside their circle, others glanced over in bewilderment. It took another moment for Soline to notice, but when she did, she awkwardly bowed her head, muttered a *Your Highness*, and stepped away from Vita.

On the sixth morning, Ardaric permitted her to ride with Isotta, who was, exactly as Vita had assumed, an accomplished horsewoman.

"You've made remarkable progress, you know. Soon you'll be itching to race out ahead of the whole army."

"Maybe. I'm not sure I'll ever ride as well as you, though. Marius told me you beat all the men at a joust during the Madrilux celebrations when you were a girl."

"Well," Isotta said, drawing out the word, and when Vita turned back to look at her, she was grinning with enough pride that it could have happened only yesterday. "I'd had a lot of practice."

Vita never stopped feeling the ache in her thighs, but eventually it dulled, and by midway through the second week, she was told that the next day she'd be given her own mare to ride.

"If you can't keep up," Isotta said, still sitting behind her for the rest of the afternoon journey, "then we'll have the groom ride her again until you're ready. Don't worry if it doesn't go perfectly on the first day. It will come."

"Thank you, Isotta. You have been very patient with helping me learn."

Isotta drew in a deep breath, and Vita waited for her response, but the woman hesitated.

"Vittoria. Princess," she said finally, like she couldn't decide how best to address her.

Out of the corner of her eye, Vita spotted a crow that looked an awful lot like Meda, with distinct streaks of white in her feathers. But from so far away, Vita couldn't be sure they were identical markings.

Distracted, half her attention on trying to track the bird, she asked, "Yes?"

Isotta's posture was far stiffer than Vita was accustomed to after so many days riding together. Pulling her eyes from the trees, Vita glanced over her shoulder.

"I want . . . to be of use to you. If I have something to teach. Or advice that I might give you."

"I would like that. It has been a long time since anyone has bothered to instruct me."

"But I worry," Isotta continued, ignoring Vita's words as

though to stop talking would mean losing whatever courage she'd mustered up, "that you will not always like what I think is most important to tell you."

Isotta's hand rested on Vita's side, more to anchor Vita than for any need of her own. Unthinkingly, Vita placed her own hand over it. Isotta's skin was worn, starting to fade into something papery. Still, though Vita couldn't feel them, she knew the opposite side of Isotta's hand bore calluses that she was proud of. There was a full life written into the lines of her body.

"Even if I do not like it, I can promise to hear what you must say."

It was silent between them for a moment, the sounds of thousands of marching men leaking into the peace of their conversation. Finally, Isotta said, "I think you should be careful."

"I will. I know I have gotten into a few too many scrapes recently."

"Be careful," Isotta cut in, repeating herself. "And . . . maybe. Well—"

"Yes?"

"It might be wise to stay away from Soline."

"What?" Vita jerked her head around so quickly that she nearly overbalanced and fell off Isotta's horse. "Forgive me. I meant—why? I know that she has been under the general's scrutiny recently, what with that mix-up with the necklaces, but that was my fault."

"It's just that . . . I think it would be prudent. I have seen how you are with her."

"How I—?"

Vita thought Isotta might say something truly damning, like *You are too trusting.* After all, Vita *was* too trusting with Soline, considering how they had met and all the foolish attempts at treason that had passed between them in the time since. But that wasn't what seemed to be troubling Isotta.

"It would be prudent not to grow too attached. You do not walk an easy path. It would be . . ." She paused, looking for the right word. "Messy. Deadly, maybe."

"Deadly?"

"Yes. You know how people get when they're jealous."

Vita laughed in disbelief. Jealous? Ardaric jealous that Vita didn't stick to his side like a prickly bur and waste all his time when he had mistresses he'd rather entertain, or Soline jealous of Vita's future status as queen? Neither seemed likely.

"Thank you for your warning. As Ardaric gave her to me as a companion, I'm not sure that—"

"I don't mean that you cannot have a companion, or even that you cannot have *her* as a companion. But simply—no more than that, if you are protecting yourself. More will only bring trouble."

More. Vita swallowed the lump in her throat.

More looked like nights spent curled near each other. *More* felt like a warm hand pressed to a flushed cheek.

More of Soline was something that Vita did not allow herself to imagine for fear that thinking the words would etch them on the lines in her palms like Isotta's wrinkles until even Ardaric could read them. Instead of giving her a ring on their wedding day, he would chop off her treasonous hands and hang them above his throne for all to see.

Here are the hands of Vittoria Marsisco, daughter of King Nicolo, the girl who dared to ask for more.

How much of *more* was obvious to Isotta, when Vita didn't even understand it herself?

Vita nodded, grateful that sitting chest to back meant that Isotta could not see her expression.

"I'm sure you're right."

That night, when Isotta slept to her left and Soline to her right, Vita tried not to feel like the world—bigger and brighter than it had ever been—was closing in, waiting to crush her lungs.

Chapter Twenty

On the morning of their arrival, a full seventeen days after leaving Novogna, they rode past the hastily evacuated ghost towns on the outskirts of Messilio. All of those people would have been welcomed inside the city's walls, not for their protection but so that her father would have more bodies to defend him. Men of fighting age or with particular skills. Women who could cook or tend wounds.

Hopefully they'd brought as much food with them as they could carry. There were still unripened lemons visible on the trees.

Some of the farms looked like they'd been abandoned mid-task. Vipsania, the horse she'd been given, trod over a little straw-stuffed doll lying abandoned in the road. One of the button eyes was missing, and the line of stitches attaching the head to the body was coming apart.

The urge to climb down and pick it up was strong, but Soline shook her head when she noticed Vita looking at it. The lines of horses and marching soldiers would not stop for Vita's whims.

"We will reach Messilio within two or three hours. This will be over soon."

Vita nodded, but she craned her neck and watched the scrap

of fabric as it was kicked around from the horses to the infantry. She only refocused when it was long out of sight.

When the city walls were still only a speck in the distance, Ardaric doled out orders. Men to take the left flank and men to take the right. Men to start digging trenches and men to protect those who were digging. Men to set up the catapults and the command tents. Men to scout the surrounding forests for game, and men to double back toward the abandoned farms and take whatever they could find.

As Vipsania marched her closer to the home she hadn't seen in over a decade, these groups peeled off, moving with expert precision. Before she knew it, thousands of soldiers were each following their own captains to different places around the city.

"What are they all doing?" Vita asked, guiding Vipsania until she was trotting beside Magritte. "I've never seen a battle before."

"Does it matter what they're doing? I will win you Messilio."

"In the books I've read, they always describe war so . . . generally. *The armies fought at Tarvere, and the invading Kasrians beat the Sopians.* Hardly any details."

Ardaric broke into a grin, and Vita hid her own. The example was a true one from her book, but she'd chosen it specifically. Though the Battle of Tarvere occurred long before Ardaric's time, it was a point of pride for the Kasrians. One that, even today, he was likely still emulating in his own conquests, considering the last thing he'd done before coming to Carca was reinstate Kasrian control in Sopio during the Battle of Talme.

Tarvere created folk heroes, names that were still sung in drinking songs and invoked in prayers, and if Ardaric wanted to be remembered, he would need to win an equally memorable battle.

"I'd like to learn. I will never be a warrior. I don't know if I could even lift your axe. But I want to understand how you will do it. How you will steal a whole city and the crown of a king."

"The numbers alone don't favor us. Our army is large, but so is your father's, and they have the city walls to protect them. They will wait to see what we do. If he has called for reinforcements, they should not arrive yet for at least three or four weeks. And if he didn't call for them as soon as he knew this was coming, still hoping his offer to keep Novogna would persuade me, then they will take considerably longer. But once they come, we will be entirely outnumbered, so we must take away his advantage in the meantime."

"I thought that sieges were mostly about waiting for them to starve. Will you knock down the walls instead to speed things up? That is why we brought the catapults, no?"

Finding a favorable spot to stop, Ardaric dismounted from Magritte before helping Vita down from her own horse. He stood beside her, and the two of them watched as hundreds of people all around ran from task to task like ants.

Like this, standing above them all and watching them run, Vita could almost understand why Ardaric could kill his own men and not feel guilt. They followed his every order, and when they listened, he won. It did not absolve him, but now she knew where in his heart the impulse grew. The more power he gained, the more of it he wanted, and the more humanity he lost along the way.

"Trying to destroy a wall is not the only way to win," he said, holding his hand out in front of them and mimicking running it over the wall like he could touch it for real. "Sometimes it does not even mean victory."

He moved behind her and pointed to a section of the wall

from over her shoulder. "Here, you see. If we destroyed that bit of wall right now, what do you think would happen?"

Vita paused, trying to picture it. The wall blown to bits, with a big chunk missing in the middle. She could not see much behind it—the houses were all too short—but the great cathedral's spire and the castle itself poked out proudly.

It seemed like an easy answer. "You would send your men inside to slaughter them. Like you did in Novogna."

"Ah," he said, chidingly. "In Novogna, the gates opened for us. We killed several of the city officials before anyone knew there was an army to fear, and once we showed up outside the walls, there was enough panic among the nobles that it only required taking a few prominent figures hostage before their families were clamoring for the gates to be opened. Novogna's army met us outside the walls, trying to take back their sons. And they did not win. From there, it was easy to get inside."

"Oh."

"If we had destroyed the walls, my Vittoria, you would have known. Now tell me. What would happen if we brought down Messilio's?"

Destruction. Chaos. The things that haunted her nightmares still.

She forced the thoughts back, trying to think more practically and see the situation as he did. "Oh," she repeated, understanding now. "Rubble. You would not be able to run in and fight, because you would have just knocked down a whole section of stone wall."

Ardaric nodded. "It would take a long time to clear a path. Soldiers can be incredibly brave when they are motivated, but sending them into certain death is not wise even if they are willing. Especially because tearing down a wall creates a bottleneck. Only so many of my men can make it through at a time, even if the way is clear. Two, three, ten. Depends how wide the hole is. But your father can have his entire army positioned and waiting on the other side, and then they can pick my men off a few at a time until there's no one left."

"So, what then?" Vita asked, trying to piece together his plan. To beat Ardaric, she would need to understand him. "How can you win if you cannot break through the walls and take the city, and you also cannot afford to wait for reinforcements to arrive?"

He ran a hand across the horizon, from one side of Messilio to the other.

"I don't need to break through his. I will build walls of my own, and then we will see who can outlast the other."

No matter how many times Ardaric explained it—only once, as he was then pulled away on an urgent task—or how many times Marius explained it—thrice, though the first two tries were exceptionally poor, given that he was trying to construct Vita's tent at the same time—Vita struggled to visualize the plan.

"So there is Messilio's wall," she said, drawing a circle in the air with her finger, ringing it around her closed fist. "Which is the only wall currently. But then we will build a new wall around theirs." She drew a second circle, wider this time.

"Yes," Marius said, being far too kind given how distracting she was being. "Not right up against their wall. There will be a gap of a few hundred feet. A trench in between. And then yes, a wall of our own, wide enough for archers and, in some places, mounted catapults. Ten feet tall minimum, though taller in other areas. It's called circumvallation."

It sounded like a massive undertaking to build a wall sturdy enough to bear the weight of catapults. "Won't it just stop us from getting in?" Vita asked.

"There will be hidden ways in that we can use when required. But that's the point; they have secret exits too. We need to trap them inside." He anticipated her next question before she could ask it. "Messengers. Hunting parties. Assassins. Anyone who can improve their odds will be sent out if we don't prevent it. With our wall in place, they won't be able to do any of that. No contacting their allies. No sneaking food into the city. They will have to survive on what they have. If any other kingdoms send troops to help, your father will have no way to coordinate with them."

"And our camp is outside our wall, meaning that we can hunt and travel and send letters."

"Yes. Ardaric will have hunting and raiding parties out more than he will have anyone firing on Messilio. We will win by being better provisioned than they are."

"Because," she said, doing her very best to follow his logic from the last time they'd gone through this, "we're then going to build a *third* wall. And eventually wall ourselves in."

"If we have reason to believe that the others will send troops, then yes. We will build a third wall."

She pantomimed the third and final circle, widest of all. "And if aid comes, *we* will be under siege. While we are laying siege to Messilio."

"Exactly. Which is why we need to be ready. Because then we will have to live on the food we have on hand. We have no idea how long something like that could last."

"Then why are we doing this? I thought you carried out a siege when you knew your forces on the outside could last longer waiting than the people trapped inside. But if another army can come up behind you and trap you in, too, then you're the one waiting, and they have plenty of land still to steal from. They can outlast you."

"It's a risk. But anyone who comes to your father's rescue will likely do so begrudgingly. Even among Carca's allies, the king is not well regarded." Then, as though switching from military man to Vita's bumbling friend, Marius said, "Sorry. No offense intended."

Vita shook her head. "It doesn't offend me. My father hasn't done much to make himself popular with his allies *or* his daughter. Do you want me to help with that?" she asked, pointing to where Marius was unloading her heavy trunk of books.

Marius waved her away. "Probably never thought he'd need to. He deeply offended the Kasrians with your mother's death, and yet they did nothing for over eleven years. Carca is the largest of the Alstrin Islands. No one except Ardaric is bold enough to try something like this. But that's why it will work. Your father is a king with a massive army who need never fight, and—"

"They've grown lazy," she interrupted. "They've indulged. They've begun to think that they are safe, because no one has challenged them."

That was it, then. For all these years, they'd had the illusion of safety.

The world had chipped away at Vita's illusion for so long that there was nothing left of it. Her bastion against her fears— her room—was a scorched ruin back in Novogna. Eda had been taken from her, and with any luck, the rest of her crows were safe at home or off in faraway places that Ardaric could not reach.

She wasn't safe; Soline wasn't safe; Marius and Isotta weren't safe. At any moment, her father could send men out to fight with Ardaric's army and keep them from building their walls. She could be dead in an hour, or taken hostage by her father, or fall victim to some new horror that she didn't have time to consider.

But finally, her father's illusion of safety was crushed too.

"And now," Marius said, "we will win you back your home."

The sword at his side had never seemed so conspicuous, but somewhere under all of this was the boy who had told her excitedly about his little sister. She supposed that the two Mariuses weren't so different—bound by loyalty and deeply caring—but one would soon cut men down.

"We will be here for a long time, right? Weeks. Months."

"Hopefully weeks, but yes. It'll take a while just to complete the walls. They won't let us trap them in without a fight, and it's miles of construction. Even with tens of thousands of men, it won't be quick. But if they aren't properly prepared for a siege, this could be over sooner than you think."

"Queen by Padrilux," she murmured without any excitement. "When you have time, will you teach me to use a weapon? Just in case." Around them, shouts rang out, the men yelling tasks to each other as they dug into the earth. Only a short walk away, a half dozen men constructed the general's command tent. "There can never be any guarantee of safety here, so I should know the basics."

Marius agreed, though neither knew exactly when a free moment might arrive. The first days would be a constant struggle of guard shifts and building and cooking and hunting. Everyone, from the lowest born to the highest, would do their part.

Eventually, Isotta fetched Vita so that they could help deal with the food stores. There were other women, the ones with their own swords strapped to their backs, who dug trenches beside their brothers and husbands.

But for Vita, it was enough just to sort through rations.

They worked in contemplative silence for several hours, which was only occasionally broken by Isotta jumping into the telling of a story from her life in Kasri as though they'd been talking the whole time. When Vita's head began to ache, Isotta passed the work off to another group of women and led Vita back to her tent. On the way, they passed Ardaric and Sorrel speaking to each other in clipped tones, and Vita slowed down to listen.

"Have they readied any of the catapults yet?"

"A small one, sir. The rest will take longer to reassemble."

"The small one is all we need." A servant arrived, carrying a box. Unlatching it revealed the decaying, blackening stump. It took several beats before she realized it was an arm. The arm, she imagined, that was once attached to the same body her gifted head came from. The messenger boy.

Vita drew Isotta to a stop beside her.

Ardaric smiled, and it only grew wider when he saw her watching him from the center of a flurry of people. Uncaring of how foul the appendage looked, he picked it up out of the box and waved it at her. It looked waxy, like they'd tried to preserve it for this moment. Along the length of the arm, someone had carved the words *No Hope*.

They calibrated the catapult and added the payload, then sent the arm soaring over the wall for someone in her father's employ to find.

Vita spent the rest of the day thinking about that inscription as she organized her tent. *No Hope.* There can be no hope.

There was a saying that all Carcan mothers repeated to their children. Even Vita's mother would say it to her when she was disobedient. *Where the Mother weeps or the Father plays, there can be no peace till the end of days.* It was a cautionary message; if you upset the gods or your hubris caught their attention, then you would never know peace. Whole cities were destroyed in the earliest years of their history—in Carca and across the Alstrin Islands—because people tempted the gods' wrath. Now, kingdoms would do all they could to portray themselves as being divinely favored, building grand cathedrals and waging war in the gods' names only.

Those who did not worship piously had always been under threat, and conversely, if someone was under threat, it must be because of some fault of their own that had forced the gods' hands.

Vita had been appropriately religious as a child, though those days felt distant now. Since she'd been taken to Castel Poletta, no one had cared to continue her religious education. She had not seen the inside of a chapel or cathedral in years.

As she awaited sleep that night, she tried to reach out to touch something on the other side of eternity. Something beyond the beyond, where only the divine could live.

But even in earnest hope, part of Vita recoiled at the thought. She did not want to find any gods on the other side of the sky, watching and judging them. Vita hadn't known peace in many years, and she didn't think any of it would have been different if she'd said a hundred prayers a day. Piety would not have saved her.

In Carca, they said *There can be no peace* as a reminder. Do your chores. Obey your parents. Be a good citizen, and if everyone does their part, only then will there be peace.

On some of the other islands, they exchanged the word *peace* for *comfort*. There might be peace, but it would be hard won. It would be painful and ugly. Where you disgraced the gods, you would always find struggle.

The Kasrians were of a third attitude. They, too, did not use the word *peace*.

Instead, they said something more dismal still: *There can be no hope till the end of days.* This was the message that they sent to her father.

Chapter Twenty-One

It took three days of everyone holding their breath before the Messilians finally sent out their army to stop themselves from being trapped. Just before dawn, screams rose up from the northwestern side of the city walls.

"Come," Soline said, pulling on Vita's arm where she stood stock still in her tent. "We're no help to them. Let's go into the woods. Hunting might do you good."

That shocked Vita out of her stupor. "Hunting? Me?"

The idea of being anywhere near weapons and massive wild animals sounded more than a little ridiculous to Vita, but Soline was insistent. With an encampment of tens of thousands of men, it wasn't difficult to stay away from the chaos, but when Vita stood on her tiptoes, she could still see the men on horseback charging toward each other, weapons drawn. She could not make out the details, but it was easy enough to imagine the bloody scene.

Soline tugged on Vita's arm again. "Yes. Hunting. All of your father's army is either fighting against our line or behind their walls. We've seen no signs of aid coming yet, and the woods are constantly surveilled by the watch. It's the safest place we can be."

Vita could think of at least a hundred reasons why that didn't seem true, but she settled on "I don't know how to hunt."

Soline rolled her eyes. "Isotta is saddling Vipsania now. Don't worry; Marius will be there to protect you."

For the first time since they met, Soline covered herself in weapons: a dagger sheath belted around her waist, a tiny knife strapped to her upper arm and another flush against her ankle. If they'd been in the palace, massive skirts would have covered it, but here most of the women, Vita included, wore sturdy trousers when they could. They were always getting mud-splattered. Soon, probably, it would be blood and entrails and vomit.

"Don't worry," Helka said, her stallion sidling up to them. "This skirmish is nothing exciting. We are not yet prepared to carry out the worst of our destruction, and they are not yet desperate."

"But if we are truly to starve them out, this is the strongest they will be. Couldn't they destroy us now and be done with it?"

"They will try," Helka said, caramel-colored hair blowing around her cheeks where it had escaped her braid. "The general knew that, though. It was only a matter of when. He was prepared for this. We will push them back behind their walls and close them in, and then it is a waiting game."

"I'm surprised you're not fighting," Vita said honestly. Helka was not one of the wives who hid herself away. She was always adorned in weapons, even in Castel Poletta. She and her husband each commanded troops under Ardaric.

Helka laughed, guiding her horse toward the forest. Over her shoulder, she said, "I don't waste my time on anything but the really nasty battles. Come along, Princess." Then her horse disappeared in the foliage.

"It will be fine, Vita," Marius said, helping her up onto

Vipsania's back. He patted her knee once before his brow furrowed and he pulled back, clearing his throat. "The general is very good at what he does. The real problem will be the waiting, but we will keep you distracted."

"Thank you," she said, removing her foot from the stirrup to gently kick the toe of her shoe into his side. "I'm glad the rest of you are all so assured."

"We've all done this before," he reminded her. "And when you are safely behind Messilio's walls, Queen of Carca, most of us will probably do this a time or two more. Generals who become kings rarely forget their bloodlust."

She waited until he saddled his own horse, a mottled brown thing that looked a little too small beneath Marius's lanky frame but nonetheless ran faster than anyone else's, before saying, "Like Queen Vitenya."

Marius grinned, and when he did, his face lit up beneath the flecks of dirt on his cheeks. It reminded her a little of the way Soline's whole face seemed brighter every time she laughed—even when she was laughing at Vita's expense.

"Exactly. Tell me what you remember."

After raiding the library for all of Novogna's history books, Marius and Vita had taken to discussing their favorite kings, queens, and heroes to pass the hours on the road, and she knew it impressed him how much of the books she could quote at random.

"Vitenya was never satisfied," Vita said, repeating the phrase that the historians always used. "I'm not even sure she died happy, though she ruled Tarla, Durbina Major, and half of Durbina Minor by the end of her life. Probably would have turned her sights on Kasri next if she hadn't slipped away in her sleep one night." Some doctors had blamed poison, and others thought the cause was a plate of bad seafood. No one knew for certain what had finally felled the great queen who had always seemed indestructible.

Cries of pain rang out from over the hill, and Vita's good mood shifted. "What a way to die. It's strange how people can seem so big, and then one day they're just . . . gone."

Vita's own mother had been like that—so very *there* for so long and then gone in an instant. If she'd lived, Vita's life would look unrecognizable. Ana could have helped her learn what it meant to be royalty. Or if her father was still set on seeing them gone, they might have run away and lived other lives, always together. Might have become nuns like Soline suggested, or met a kind farmer and learned to milk cows. Or something. Something that wasn't found at the sharp edge of the executioner's blade.

"I was named for her, you know. *Vitenya* and *Vittoria* are distantly related, at least according to the genealogists and historians and priests who advised my father. *Vitenya* is your northern version. They thought it was a good omen: a warrior-queen who fought bravely and died old and at home after a successful reign, clearly favored by the gods." She pursed her lips, letting her eyes drag over the wide expanse of green forest rather than look Marius in the eye. "It seems funny now to think of how much trouble they went to."

"Maybe one day you'll understand why it was a good omen after all," Marius said. Vita did not know how he found endless reserves of optimism. Even she, used to imagining her own joy into existence, could not live off empty hope forever. But somehow, Marius never seemed truly troubled. "Vitenya was never satisfied, and I imagine the general will be the same. The two of you could do great—"

"Oh, the general is *never* satisfied," Helka said, moving her horse closer to Marius and Vita as they rode through the woods. Soline and Isotta were up ahead, practically racing, and the rest of the hunting party trailed behind. "You know how men like that are. Absolutely insatiable."

Then, looking right at Vita, she winked.

"Truly?" Vita asked flatly, her intonation making it barely a question.

She assumed Helka was expecting jealousy, but even feigning it seemed impossible. She neither desired Ardaric nor wanted him to desire her. If Helka could keep him occupied, then he would stay far from Vita. And for as long as Helka's husband lived, she was no great threat.

"Oh yes," Helka said, drawing the word out with false intrigue. "I'm sure he'll die as Vitenya did: in bed."

"It's treasonous to speak of your king that way, you know," Vita said. "We aren't meant to imagine them as fallible."

Eventually, Helka grew bored of trying to needle Vita and rode ahead again with the others. She wore a bow strung over her shoulder, and she alone seemed eager to actually return with game.

For the rest of the afternoon, though they could hear the distant clashing of metal, they kept their eyes focused on the wide expanse of forest. Most of the fruit on the trees was barely half-ripe, but Vita collected whatever she could find, leaving anything that Marius shook his head at. Helka brought down two great deer, which she butchered immediately. "Easier not to drag whole bucks back," she said as she tore through fur and gristle to separate the meat from the bones. Helka loaded it all into the hunting bags of the women attending her.

"How much longer, do you think?" Vita asked when she was riding between Soline and Marius, a fair distance from the others. It wasn't asked out of any true desire to return to their encampment. The whole place reeked of sweat even before the battle, and her tent, which was the nicest of anyone's save Ardaric's, was still only a tent. But the thought that she would have to remain constantly in motion to avoid the battle behind them seemed no better.

"They probably won't bother to fight through the night," Soline said. "Once it's dark, nobody has an advantage, and even desperate people aren't willing to lose whole contingents like that. They will regroup and then perhaps try again tomorrow."

"Tomorrow?" Vita sighed. War seemed at once both terrifying and utterly boring. "Did you feel like this when you were waiting to take Novogna?"

"Restless? Sure, I suppose. Everybody likes to think that war will be quick. There comes a point where the songs you sing on campaign to keep you excited no longer do the trick. You can watch the life drain from a person's eyes weeks before they are finally cut down. But eventually it ends, one way or another. If you live, the spoils make many greedy enough to do it all again. I think some people force the bad so thoroughly from their minds that they go into each campaign like it's brand new. Eventually, they'll all remember. You'll see it happen."

"Soline," Marius chided, "don't scare her."

"I'm being honest." Then she turned to Vita and took on a kinder tone. "Sorry. It can be difficult; that's all I'm saying."

"I'm not afraid," Vita said, and it wasn't entirely untrue. "I'm more . . . tired. Already—and we've barely begun."

They fought again the next day, though it ended far earlier. The third day, it seemed half-hearted at best. It was uncertain if that was because her father was already conceding that his army would not be able to stop the walls being built, or if he had reason to hope that help was coming and wanted to reserve his troops for a greater offensive move.

After that, nobody bothered to make Vita go out into the woods. Instead, she took to doing chores obsessively. Isotta tried to stop her, pulling laundry from her hands whenever Vita began to help, but eventually she relented. Vita needed tasks to keep herself busy.

On the fifteenth day, when some stretches of the wall looked almost complete, the Messilians attacked again. They tried to get through one of the weaker, unreinforced sections, but that was exactly where Ardaric expected they would target, and his men were ready to beat them back.

"Come, Vittoria," Helka said, flipping loose hair over her shoulder. "There is simply too much going on today for us to be of any use. We should get away so that we might return in better spirits."

Vita tipped her chin back to look at Soline, who was perched behind her, braiding Vita's endlessly long hair. She did not need to ask the question for Soline to see it on her face. *Must we?*

Soline only smiled sardonically. Once, Vita might not have known how to interpret such a look, but now she was well versed in the thousand things a smile might mean. Soline made for an excellent case study.

"Yes, I think getting away might be for the best," Soline agreed. When she reached the final inches of Vita's hair, she added a piece of cord to two of the sections and braided it in to secure it. After neatly plaiting the ends, Soline used the tails of the string to tie the braid off. "Come, Princess. I'm sure we can make better use of our time elsewhere."

On their last few trips into the woods, Soline had begun looking for the herbs that had created their single successful attempt at alchemy.

"We can't stop forever," she had reasoned. "We need something in our arsenal, even if it is a very small something."

"Fire," Vita had responded, feeling like her feet were buried in the earth, "is not a very small something."

"If we hone it in a manageable way, it may not present as fire. It may become something else. That is the thing about alchemy—it can be very precise, and yet we do not know the measurements. If we change a detail, we might end up with something different altogether."

Vita hadn't responded.

She didn't want to try again so soon. What could another fire do to all this wood and fabric and human flesh?

And yet, more than anything, part of her did long to try. To feel the power she'd felt speaking something into being where there had been only a trinket and a bit of plant dust before. She wanted to believe that somewhere in the marrow of her bones, she could call to destruction, and it would answer her.

In all her life, Vita had never needed to be brave, and she'd never truly thought herself meek either, because there was nothing to compare herself to. She simply existed, floating aimlessly between days until whole years brushed past her like a gentle eddy. Or maybe a maelstrom.

Now she did not know which was better. To submit and pray for safety, or to lash out and perhaps burn it all down, herself included. What life was there in either?

They rode out into the forest, and when Soline jumped down from her saddle to look for specific plants growing in the brush, Vita stayed atop Vipsania.

"I don't know what they look like," she reasoned, the same excuse as every other day. It was the truth, and it was also a crutch. If she looked, if she found them, then would she still have a choice?

Soline knelt on the ground to cut away a sprig of spoolwood. The flowers were tiny, and you needed quite a lot of it, so Soline was always looking.

Vita reached down, prepared to take the sprig from Soline and stow it in her saddlebag at least, but something up ahead caught her eye. A bit of darkness perched in the bare branches of a dead tree, marring the bright blue of the sky.

Vipsania dashed forward before Vita could recall digging her heels into the horse's flanks.

She wanted to shout Meda's name, but it escaped as a surprised whisper.

Her beloved fourth crow—Eda's daughter, who'd come to her as a little hatchling fresh from the nest with what Vita had thought was a broken wing. The poor thing couldn't fly, and Vita had nursed her back to health right there on the windowsill. She had been Vita's sweet and silly companion for all the years since.

She stopped Vipsania at the bottom of the tree. Filled with a sudden desperation to be closer to Meda, she considered trying to stand on Vipsania's saddle and hoist herself up into the branches, but before she had cause to, Meda flew lower, perching only a few feet above. When Vita stretched her arm, she could run a finger over Meda's wing. The crow seemed to nuzzle into it.

"You're here," Vita said, tears in her eyes. "I've missed you."

She had followed Vita all this way, far from their home and protection. Surely that meant Meda had missed her too.

"Are the others with you? Are you here for your mother? She is safe. I swear that I will free her."

Meda toed at her fingers, scratching the skin in an almost delicate manner.

"They followed you?" Soline asked, riding up behind her to look into the trees. "I hadn't thought they left Novogna much. It is not as cold here as it is in Kasri, where the birds must migrate."

"I don't think they've ever left Novogna. Most of them were with me often enough that I'm not sure when they would have gone."

She imagined them flying away from all that they'd known. Neda, cantankerous but devoted, like an aggrieved uncle. Zeda, the first of Eda's two hatchlings that Vita got to watch grow up. Jeda, the father to the group, who protected the younger crows as fiercely as Eda herself did. They were Vita's family—her devoted flock that had kept her company for all these years.

If she could, she would scoop Meda right out of the tree and squeeze her to her chest.

Tentatively, like she heard Vita's thought, Meda stepped onto the back of her hand. Vita was careful not to startle her away.

A fast, vicious *swish* cut through the air, and then Meda's tiny weight was gone. For a moment, Vita could not work out where she had disappeared to. Flown away to find the others, or frightened by a girl who no longer sang to birds in windows?

But then Soline gasped, and another voice cheered as a horse clopped toward them. "A difficult shot!"

Meda's eye was still wide open when Vita finally turned. An arrow stuck straight out from her head, pinning her to the tree behind. Numbly, Vita reached out and touched the entry spot. Her fingers trembled. Blood seeped out onto Meda's dark feathers. Her whole skull had shattered beneath the force of the arrow.

Helka grinned. "An excellent find, Princess. I will have to commend you to the general. Perhaps you will be a huntress yet."

The words were mocking—Ardaric would never willingly arm her with a bow and arrow and release her into the world—but Vita could not focus on them. There was a steady, engulfing ringing in her ears that she could not escape from. It felt like the time that she decided to hold her head under water for too long in the bath.

Marius jumped from his horse and came to stand at her knee. "Vita."

"Meda?" she whispered. The bird made no sound. "I—"

"Here," Helka said, inching closer to the tree. "I will have the spoils."

"No!" Vita spit. Despite the urgency of the word, her motions were slow as she pulled the arrow from the tree in horror and cradled the limp body in her hands. "Leave her alone."

"Vita?" Soline asked, trying to catch her eye. When Vita made no reply, Soline turned to Marius and began whispering.

Tears streamed down Vita's face the whole way back to camp. She did not lead Vipsania; Marius had to walk beside her and guide the horse along. It was enough that Vita managed to stay upright on the horse.

The rest of the group followed behind, a stony silence permeating the air.

People passed her by in blurs when they returned. She could not make out anything about the scene other than that, as far as she could tell, the battle appeared to be over. She wouldn't care if it wasn't.

Ardaric ran toward her and plucked her off her horse before she could even rearrange her face into something human. He held her shoulders, steering her around and up a tiny staircase. She nearly tripped, body disconnected from her thoughts, but instinct made her climb up when he pushed her.

He positioned her proudly on the top of the siege tower for all to see, his hand on her back.

"We have won again," Ardaric shouted, seemingly taunting her father, though she could not imagine how he would be heard across the hundreds of feet of distance between them.

Still, through her tears, she could make out the blurred image of a figure standing on the opposite wall. Ardaric's men did not shoot at him, and in turn, the figure did not order his men to shoot at Ardaric, though it would have been easy enough to hit either one with both so prominently displayed.

"We have won. Our wall is complete, and we will starve you out until you beg me on hands and knees to let your people live, Nicolo."

Ardaric's men cheered loudly, a horrible, grating din.

"We have your daughter! Little Vittoria Marsisco, abandoned by her father!" Then, whispered only to her, he said, "We must get under his skin, you know. You are excellent as both a bride and a hostage."

Turning back to his opponent, Ardaric taunted, "Will you save her, Nicolo? Will you surrender now to protect your daughter? Your only legitimate heir? You can have her if you open the gates."

From his place behind her, Ardaric put his hand on her neck, forcing her chin up so she had no choice but to stare at the little smudge that was her father. She knew what he would say, knew that no man who locked up his heir could ever consider that child a worthy successor in the first place.

Vita stared ahead, the corpse of her bird still puddled in her cupped hands, and listened as her father's distant voice cried, "Let there be war."

Chapter Twenty-Two

They pulled Vita down from the siege tower at the first sign that her father might send a volley of arrows their way. Hands covered her body, tugging on her heavy cloak and scratching her skin in an attempt to protect Ardaric's precious commodity. Touches—dozens of touches from people shouting loudly enough to disorient her—made her stomach heave. She couldn't beat them back without losing her grip on Meda.

"I'm fine," she said, feet on solid earth again. The harsh *thwack thwack thwack* of a hundred arrows hitting no-man's-land filled the air. "I'm fine. Stop touching me. Stop—get off! Stop!"

Dozens of warm hands moved her through the crowd until finally she was passed off to someone at the edge of the melee who guided her back to her tent.

"Are you all right?" Marius asked, one hand on her arm and the other on his sword, ready to swing at anything she commanded him to.

"All right?" she asked, confused. "No, I—" She couldn't hear her own voice over the cacophony around them, but she could taste it on her lips.

"Go in," he said, pulling open the flap to her tent. "I will keep watch."

She ducked inside before he could say anything else.

Her old wardrobe in Novogna was the only place that the world ever fell silent for her, but it had burned down along with everything else. She searched out the next best thing, eyes landing on the worn trunk full of her clothes in the corner.

Isotta kept the trunk meticulous even now, clothes clean and neatly folded, ready for wear. Rather than pulling anything out, Vita carved a space in the center to cradle her and then climbed in, letting her mind go blank and dark and silent.

"Telling me you lost our princess? Where could she have—?"

"She was in here. I swear! I don't know."

"The general will have our heads for this. Father, spare us! Oh, don't cry, Marius. That won't help at all."

"But I—"

The voices sounded like a distant dream. Vita's eyes opened lazily, only a small crack of light managing to illuminate her hiding space, before she nuzzled her cheek into the shirt beneath her and let them close again.

"Both of you, out. I'll handle this."

"Soline—"

"Stop fretting, Isotta—it isn't helping. Marius didn't lose her, and we're not going to be executed. She's still here. Just go; I'll deal with it."

The other two voices grumbled before disappearing.

Vita liked the silence. Liked feeling encased—held by the world and yet lost to it.

She imagined the tapestry of her existence, faded and

moth eaten around the edges, forgotten in an attic that no one frequented.

The trunk opened, and daylight rushed in. Vita drew in a gasping breath.

"Vita," Soline whispered, and the weight of the world pressed down on Vita with that single word.

Vita had forgotten that she'd brought Meda in with her, and the dead bird now lay stiffly beside her. Carefully, Soline reached in, removing the crow and one of Vita's shirts to wrap the body in.

"Don't take her," Vita said, voice raspy. "Please."

"We can bury her. When you're ready. Or burn her, or anything else that you prefer. But for now, let me wrap her up for safekeeping."

Whimpering like a child, she said, "I want to go home."

Where was home exactly? Was it Castel Poletta, where she could be the ghost haunting another family's life? Was it here in Messilio with her mother, her father, and her governess?

Wherever it was, her birds would be there with her. No one was captured. No one was dead.

"I want it to be over."

"I know," Soline said, digging through the rest of the clothes in the chest. "It will all end soon. We will make another place home. Wherever that is. A castle. A nunnery. A hovel in the woods." Eventually, her hands stilled. It took a moment before she ran the backs of her fingers along Vita's shoulder. "I would join you in the trunk, but there simply isn't room. So either budge over, or let me help you out."

"Soline—"

"I know," Soline repeated, squeezing Vita's hand. "I know. I'm sorry. This is all I can give you."

She helped Vita into a seated position before extricating her from the trunk. Vita moved lifelessly to the little lump of a bed in the corner.

"Lie down," Soline commanded, and Vita, grateful to have someone else making decisions for her, obeyed. Soline gathered more blankets, perhaps from the same trunk, and then tucked them around Vita as if she were a girl again in need of tending.

Brushing her hand over Vita's temple, Soline said, "I know you will not believe me today, but one day, it will be easier."

She lay down behind Vita, bracketing her body as though to hold her together. The touch felt like fire, so hot that it burned and made Vita want to tear at her skin, and yet she could not bring herself to move away. She liked it and she hated it. Craved more despite how exposed she always felt the second someone got too close.

"What will be easier?"

"All of it. Living. Hoping. It will be easier because the parts of you that are most broken will have healed into something functional again, but also . . . It will be easier because one day, it will not be like this. He will not always have control."

"They all have control. All the time. My father. The Polettas. Ardaric."

Soline buried her nose in Vita's shoulder. "They do. For now. It doesn't have to be forever. That is the hope you hold on to."

The canvas sides of the tent were awash in brilliant reds and oranges as the sun began to set outside. Vita closed her eyes against it. "Is that what you tell yourself?"

"Yes. And then I met you, so already I have been proven right."

"I have given you nothing of use. You are no closer to your goals."

"In some ways, things are harder than before. And in some ways, they're easier. Better than I might have ever expected when Anselm died."

"I'm sorry. I'm not—"

Vita did not know how to express what she meant. In spite of how hard she tried to adjust to a new life with people who were all normal and knew how to handle battles and friendships and all the things that Vita couldn't, she didn't know what it was to be *like* them. To watch a brother die. To even have a brother whom she knew beyond rumor. She could not picture these things no matter how hard she tried. The next best thing was to imagine it some other way. Vita pretended, for a moment, that Marius was her brother. It would be difficult to lose him even though she'd known him for only a few months. A whole lifetime would be altogether worse.

"It was different for you. Anselm was your brother, and Meda is just—" She cut herself off. "They are not the same."

The words felt like someone else's. Like something Governess would have instructed her to say long ago. *You are a princess with all that this world can afford you. You do not know hardship, and it is unbecoming to throw fits.*

Soline squeezed her so tightly that it was almost painful. "Don't say that. Birds and brothers are not so different when they are the ones you love most in the world. They are your family."

"I couldn't save her," Vita said, eyes brimming again.

"No. None of us could have stopped Helka. But we will do what we can for Eda and the others. I promise. If revenge is still what you want, if revenge is what will make it easier one day, then you will have it. I swear. And if it's not . . . we will find another way."

Vita turned over in the bed, her face close to Soline's. "What of *your* revenge?"

Soline shrugged, her hand running up and down Vita's arm. The rustling of her clothes sounded almost like soft rain. "If we take my brothers, if we run away and live well . . . that could be enough for me."

Vita ducked her head under Soline's chin, saying nothing more. That Soline would give up all her grand, foolish plans if Vita asked meant everything. How could she allow them to try to kill Ardaric again, knowing that she might have to witness Soline's death if they failed?

"Sleep, Vita." So very gently, as if Vita were imagining it, Soline brushed a kiss along her hairline. "I will still be here with you in the morning. You aren't alone."

Chapter Twenty-Three

Vita returned from the murky dreamworld with her face pressed into the curve of Soline's neck and her arm draped across her torso. Outside, campfires still crackled in the night, and men laughed as they discussed their kills and their bright futures in Carca. Somewhere, there must be people in mourning, preparing the dead for hasty funerals, but their voices were lost in the merriment. Daybreak was hours away, and until then, these soldiers did not need to concern themselves with anything but the thrill of war.

Vita tuned them out, focusing on her hand on Soline's waist. Soline was alive against her in a way that nothing and no one had been in the whole of Vita's life. She wanted to scream and to weep and to rage for things stolen from her, and yet, at that moment, Vita could not even consider moving. Perhaps her final act of defiance would be to fuse herself in this moment with molten gold and magic until there was no princess left for anyone to steal pieces of.

Delicately, for fear of waking Soline, she drew back. Dark curls spilled over Soline's shoulders, and Vita brushed them away, breath caught in her chest. Even with the sounds of the camp outside, it seemed that a single too-loud inhale might ruin the quiet darkness of the tent.

Leaning in again, Vita pressed her lips to the jut of Soline's cheekbone and held them there. She had never kissed anyone willingly before. Never considered how sensitive lips were.

"Vita?"

Soline's voice was threaded with sleep as Vita drew back, wide eyed, to stare at her in the dark. A gentle hand brushed Vita's hair behind her ear.

"I was dreaming of you," Vita said, the answer to a question neither had asked.

Soline's lips curled into a tiny, lazy smile. "Good. It's only fair. You've been causing nothing but trouble in my dreams for weeks now. Since long before we left Novogna."

An owl hooted outside. Men deep in their cups sang a rousing chorus.

"Truly?" Vita whispered, sitting up and shifting back on her heels.

Soline followed, each watching the other in the shadows. "Yes." A stuttered breath. "Yes, truly."

Vita pictured herself walking through Soline's dreams and curling up there like they were a warm patch of sunlight on the floor.

"What . . ." She swallowed, trying to force the question past the lump in her throat. "What do I do there?"

"Sometimes you coat your mattress in bugs again, and I tease you as I pull a stray beetle out of your hair. I remind you that I am *not* your servant and that you're going to have to clean this mess up yourself, and you smile before threatening me with a handful of mostly dead bugs." Soline reached out, cupping Vita's jaw. "Sometimes you weave at your loom, and I can't help but watch for ages as whole scenes appear from nothing. Scenes of your life, and mine, and all the places we might go after. You work for so long that I have to pull you away because night has sapped all the color from the design."

"Oh?" Vita asked, breathless. Soline's dreams were so ordinary, and Vita loved them for that.

"Yes. You want to complain because, though your fingers are aching, you've forgotten the pain entirely, too absorbed by your work. But I pull you in and—it's easy enough to make you forget why you wanted to argue."

Vita did not need to hear the rest of the dream to know how it must have ended. Her shaking hand touched Soline's cheek, and Soline smiled.

"That's the cheek you kissed."

Vita felt her face flush at the mention of it. "Well, you kissed my forehead before I fell asleep," she whispered, as though it absolved her.

"Yes," Soline said, unrepentant. Her eyes twinkled in the darkness. "I did."

Vita slipped her hand back into Soline's hair, admiring her curls, but she was too hesitant to do anything else. She didn't want to shatter the moment, but before she could overthink it, Soline leaned forward and pressed her lips to Vita's.

Vita wasn't sure exactly what to do. It was different in every way from the kisses that Ardaric had stolen from her—softer and sweeter and far more pleasant—and she wasn't sure how to respond. She could feel the precise moment that Soline began to doubt herself, and before she could pull away, Vita drew her closer, setting aside her cluttered thoughts and allowing herself to lean into the kiss to discover what felt right.

It was strange to think you could feel a kiss in your fingertips, in your stomach, in your tiniest toes. If someone had written about love like that in a book, Vita would have considered it poetic nonsense. But she felt it now. A shiver ran up her spine.

Romance in all its forms had seemed so alien to her, a thing that she could understand in theory—in stories and songs and as something that happened to other people—but never in practice. She did not dream of being rescued like Odelina and carried off by a handsome prince. She hadn't even really permitted herself to imagine what it would be like to kiss Soline before tonight, though she'd found herself stuck between the urge to get closer to her and the urge to remain as far away as possible. The want had existed, but she hadn't been able to put a name to it.

Now she knew exactly what it was. It was just as the stories explained, that intangible, immeasurable *truth* between two people who lowered their walls for each other. It was desire, and the thing that shocked her most was that desire was *joyous*.

She allowed Soline to guide her backward, pressed between her and the thin camp mattress. Vita was grateful to let her take control. She'd always imagined kissing like worship, the way the devoted spoke of their gods. Experiencing it now, it felt exactly like that—awe-inspiring and transformative and too big to fit in her human form. Soline guided her through it, never allowing her to get lost.

Vita's free hand ran down Soline's back, dragging her down the rest of the way so they were pressed together in every sense.

"Did you dream this?" Vita asked, breathing raggedly. Her nose skimmed against Soline's before Soline smiled and nipped at her bottom lip.

"Yes. Often. Too often."

"Too often?" Vita arched her back as Soline pressed a kiss,

warm and soft, to the column of her throat. "I think—I want to dream of it more. All the time."

Soline laughed, and it sounded like sunlight dripping down windowpanes the way fat raindrops did. Vita wanted to collect the sound in her palms and carry it with her as she moved through the world. "Then I will do all I can to inspire you."

Vita slept that night curled in Soline's arms. They giggled until exhaustion stole them away from each other, all the while pretending that there was no reality in which the harsh morning would ever greet them.

Chapter Twenty-Four

Vita buried Meda's body outside the camp limits the next morning. Isotta, Marius, and Soline joined her, and though Helka tried to follow, Vita glared until Marius was forced to send her away on a made-up task.

Isotta watched the funeral rites with barely disguised confusion, though she laid a sprig of holly on the mound of dirt all the same. Marius, who'd never interacted with Meda until her death, wiped away a stray tear when he thought no one was watching. It might have seemed for show if Vita hadn't seen him capture and release the spiders hiding in the corners of her room. Vipsania stayed pressed to Vita's side like a sentry throughout, her steady breathing keeping Vita almost calm.

Finally, Vita stepped forward and knelt to lay down a flower, tears dripping onto the overturned earth. She did not speak, possessing no words to express her guilt or how adrift she felt now that Meda's innocent joy was lost to the world forever. The others waited in silence until Soline came to stand at Vita's side.

She leaned over, adding her own flower to the grave before taking Vita's hand to help her to her feet. Vita carelessly swiped tears off her cheeks as Soline led her back toward camp.

Isotta and Marius trailed behind them, the latter holding onto Vipsania's reins.

"I swear," Vita whispered as they trudged through the tall grasses, "that I will never again bury one of my birds until both my father and my husband are dead. This is my home, and it will be theirs too."

Soline drew her toward the center of camp, which was quieter than the two edges. Having completed the first wall going around the city, half the army was laying the foundations for the one that would encircle their own camp from behind. Soon, Vita would not even be able to escape into the woods without permission.

The other half of the men spent the morning loading huge stones into a catapult to be shot into Messilio. Nobody cared much where they landed as long as they caused damage. If innocent people's homes were crushed, then they were acceptable losses to the Kasrians.

Or maybe they would destroy the tall spires of the great Messilian Library, famed for holding some of the rarest books in the Alstrin Islands. Vita used to stare out at the spires from her bedroom window as a girl. And if they spared the library, then perhaps they would turn to rubble the famous Messilian marketplace that she'd always longed to visit. Churches, hospitals, the guildhalls . . .

Even if the Kasrians won, what would be left of the city to own?

"Perhaps you'll get lucky, and you'll bury a fiancé instead of a husband," Soline whispered, careful not to let anyone overhear her words.

Vita glanced at Soline's soft face before forcing herself to stare ahead again. She wished that they could share one more kiss, but the happiness that she'd felt in the safety of the dark had washed away with the rising sun. "I'm sure I've already used up my lot of good luck."

Instead of wallowing like she wanted to, Vita pulled Marius away from his tasks to beg him to finally train her. After more than twenty years being the helpless pawn of others, she wanted to know that she was capable of defending herself. Even if she would never beat someone like Ardaric in a battle of brute strength, it didn't mean that she shouldn't learn basic techniques.

"We're in the middle of a siege," she reminded him. "No matter how close you stay to me, I'll never be completely safe."

"I don't know," Marius said, eyes trained on the tent that Ardaric had gone into with his advisors. Ardaric always said that Vita need not trouble herself with any of their strategy sessions, but both she and Marius wanted to be in that tent listening.

At least training would distract them from what they were missing.

"A Messilian could sneak through the wall and kill me. Or my father's allies could come and take me prisoner. I know I will always be at a disadvantage, but I'd rather die defending myself."

She took his arm, leading him toward the makeshift armory. Most of the soldiers kept what they needed with them at all times, even while they slept, but the armorer did all he could to service the weapons and reassign those that were taken from the dead.

"Help me pick a sword from the leftovers. You will have better knowledge of what I need. The weight is important, isn't it?"

"Gods, not a sword. Don't touch that!" Marius swatted her hand away from the one she reached toward. "A dagger will do for today." He led her to a corner of the armory, where only a few remained. Some, Vita could tell, were in poor shape, and even the armorer could not do much by way of repairing them here.

Marius sorted through them, picking a few up and testing their balance before setting them aside.

"Here," he said, taking her hand and placing one in it. "Try this. Does it feel right in your hand?"

Vita wasn't quite sure how she would know, but she held it aloft and slashed at the air a few times, attempting to get a feel for the balance. She felt stronger just for holding it, like Marius had handed her a wisp of freedom. "Yes, this will do."

She tricked him into many days of lessons by doing something just wrong enough at the end of each session that he felt honor bound to continue the next day so she wouldn't injure herself practicing alone. Under the hot Carcan sun, now edging into full summer after many weeks, he led her through stances and techniques. Around them, the outer wall grew taller and longer, until it snaked away behind the city.

"Do you suspect help will arrive soon?" she asked, practicing one of Marius's moves in slow motion. He kicked at her foot until she moved it to the proper position. He often complained that she made herself too small, and it left her open to all sorts of attacks.

"Keep your stance wide," he said. "Someone could knock you over with a gust of wind." She tried the move again, and he nodded approvingly. "Truthfully, yes. We weren't sure at first. It seemed equally likely that the other kingdoms would let your father flounder and try their luck making treaties with a King Ardaric once this whole business was finished. Most of them are on good enough terms with the Kasrians that it wouldn't be troubling to them to see your family fall from power."

"But now you've had information suggesting that they might come after all?" She swiped a stray, sweaty lock of hair off her cheek. Marius attacked her slowly, exaggerating his movements and letting her get a feel for how she must evade. They had long since moved to using sticks, too worried about the loss of the princess's fingers.

"There are spies in all the courts. Ravenna's spy raised alarm bells to us in their last letter, and since then, we have heard nothing. No letters, no contact. If they have rallied an army, they could already be en route. We can send scouts out to keep an eye on the main roads, but realistically, if they come, we will have little warning. We can't surveil the whole island. Even if we mobilized the troops we left behind in Novogna, it still wouldn't be enough."

His stick hit Vita's wrist again, and he smiled wanly.

"That would've been a bad one. I'm not feeling too confident yet about ever leaving your side."

"I'm getting better," she groused, though her mind was stuck on the Ravennans. "Don't they hate us? Ravenna."

Marius did not correct her use of *us*, for, of course, the hatred they felt toward the Carcans did not include him.

The Ravennans had once conquered the whole of Carca as Ardaric wanted to do now. It had taken nearly one hundred years for the Carcans to wrest back control, culminating in the great Battle of Coressina. It was how Vita's family—the Marsiscos, a minor branch of the original royal house—came into power. Without that conflict, the Marsiscos might only own a country estate somewhere far outside Messilio, forgotten by their more powerful relatives.

Governess had only covered the battle once in their studies, sweeping over the finer details, but her father boasted about it all the time. It was the pride of their family. Later, even when she hated him, she read that chapter of her history book over and over again until the pages were as thin as spiderwebs.

Vita frowned. "It is Aligo and Salajara that everyone should be worried about. Ravenna would not help my father."

"There are no treaties between Carca and the Aligese or Salajarans. But the war ended with a treaty of mutual protection between your family and the Ravennans. Perhaps they will honor it after all. It would be the least they could do, since the treaty was far kinder to them in defeat than it should have been. Your ancestors might have taken over their island otherwise, but they showed mercy."

"It won't be Ravenna," Vita said, blocking Marius's next strike. Even a decade removed from the world around her, she thought it seemed the obvious answer. How many years had she spent at Governess's knee, learning about the deep distrust that existed between the two lands? How many other treaties had been signed by both kingdoms and then forgotten, left for scholars to argue over as though they carried any real weight with kings who could not countenance the idea of mutual trust? Her father used to go on long rants about Ravenna's foreign policy, and he was harsh to an almost troubling degree with the Ravennan diplomat who lived with them at court. Could all of that change in only eleven years? It seemed impossible. "Unless my father can pay them vast sums up front, why would they come? I would sooner fear the Aligese, and considering that Soline told me their diplomat was sent home in disgrace after my mother's death, that's saying something. Aligo can be bought with much lower sums. Ravenna's pride has always been expensive."

Marius shot her a curious look, and she used his distraction to go on the attack, though he was quick to focus his attention back on her stick. "We've stopped any incoming letters from reaching your father, even by bird. They're shooting them right out of—uh." Marius stopped, looking embarrassed to have reminded her of Meda's death. Vita's face hardened, and she rapped his knuckles with her stick in a move that was probably ungallant. "Well. He has no way of receiving any communication, so if help is coming, hopefully it'll be a surprise to him too."

"Have you heard from your spies in Aligo? Or Salajara?" Of all the Alstrin Islands, only these two and Ravenna were physically close enough to send aid quickly. The others were too far north. With the potential for seasonal storms out on the waters, it would easily take any of the northern islands weeks to reach Carca, and that was only if they'd already spent all spring and summer mustering their armies and readying their ships.

"From Aligo, yes. There is no cause for alarm there. And we've always struggled keeping reliable contact with Salajara."

A catapult launched a huge stone from behind them, and then another followed. Vita let her stick drop to the ground. Everyone cheered when the payloads landed, and in the distance, she could hear the screams that came from the people who couldn't escape the destruction.

It was all too easy to imagine herself in their place now, running from street to street in a dirty nightshift and trying to find the one exit that someone might not have considered. These people did not even have that hope, and they'd been living with the threat for weeks now. Weeks without a chance to leave. To find food. To trade.

If help came, this would be Vita soon. No amount of food would be enough when they were trapped between two walls with no way out.

"I really don't think it will be Ravenna. Trust me. Tell the general to check in with your Salajaran spy if you must. I'm going to wash," she said.

Marius blushed, though he'd been nervously guarding her bathing time since they'd first arrived. He gathered their practice sticks and trailed behind her without complaint.

Vita spent her days training with Marius and her nights lying beside Soline, close enough to feel her every movement without ever quite touching.

She leaned in close once, finally ready to try again, but Soline held a hand up between them.

"We shouldn't."

"We have already. It's too late to go back."

Soline shook her head, thumb pressed to Vita's lips as though she could stop her from saying anything she couldn't bear to hear. "I know. But Ardaric has spies. We shouldn't."

The kiss had answered a question Vita hadn't known she'd been carrying with her since those first days in Novogna, but it had destroyed something between them to know it. Soline still brushed her hair. Vita still instinctively grabbed Soline's hand when the catapult was put to use. But some days, they could barely hold eye contact.

Another week passed in that manner, with Vita caught between wanting and having, and then two, three, four, until she ceased counting. The punishing heat was already waning, and the bugs had stopped biting at every inch of Vita's exposed skin. Her cheeks were aglow with freckles that she'd never seen during her years in Castel Poletta, and when Vita was close to sleep, she would feel Soline tracing her fingers across them, though it was something they never spoke about.

Over four months of the siege were complete. Soon, even the

second wall, significantly wider in circumference, would be finished and ready to withstand attack.

"Not a moment too soon either," Soline said, biting into a dark red berry. "Your father's aid is coming after all."

"Really?" Vita set aside the dagger that she meticulously tended to every night. "What have you heard? Is it the Salajarans?"

"Did Marius tell you already? He said they've been spotted near the coast. Huge army. They'll arrive within the week, probably."

"Marius? No, I've hardly seen him all day, but he didn't need to tell me. *I* told *him* that the Salajarans would come."

"How did you know? Even the general was surprised. I heard he's been in meetings about it all day. They all thought it would be Ravenna, and apparently, he's not very happy about it. Ravenna's general is seasoned but predictable, and Salajara's is all but unknown to him."

Vita shrugged. "My father could never work with the Ravennan king, and the Ravennan king would only come to his aid if he could steal the throne back for himself at the end of it. I wouldn't be shocked if my father didn't even request aid from him. The only greater indignity than being conquered by Ardaric would be being conquered by the Ravennans again. I thought it was common knowledge. Why didn't Marius mention this to me if he found out hours ago?"

"It's still deemed *need to know* information."

"And you needed to know? I didn't realize you sat in on the general's strategy sessions." The words should have been biting, but instead, Vita moved in too close, resting her hand a hairbreadth away from Soline's on the ground.

"No," Soline said, huffing out a laugh. "I threatened to beat

Marius up if he didn't tell me what he knew. He was practically bursting with it."

Skeptically, Vita couldn't help but ask, "And that worked?"

"Of course. We grew up together. It would not be the first time I've beaten Marius up."

"You did?" Vita asked, interest piqued. She imagined the children in the street below her window, playing with dice and racing each other down to the last shop and back. "You've never told me that before. What was it like?"

"It was only when our families were at court, but we spent many years being tutored together. It's just as well that he's found a place in the army, because I can say with some certainty that he'll never be a mathematician."

"By the sound of it, he won't be the future ambassador for Carco-Ravennan relations either."

Soline rose and left to fetch Vita's dinner long before Vita could muster up the courage to cover Soline's hand with her own.

The following days hummed with tension, the last gasps of summer making the heat stick to them like honey. Everyone worked vigorously in spite of their exhaustion and injuries.

Vita could be found working side by side with Isotta, which under normal circumstances would have been pleasant. These days, though, the older woman muttered under her breath, speaking of destruction and terror and all manner of things that set Vita on edge.

"I've been meaning to ask you," Vita said, abruptly changing the subject so that she could stop Isotta's rambles. If she heard one more thing about the Salajarans coming to cut them all down, she would have to lock herself in the chest again just to breathe.

"Yes?"

"Your warning. About Soline. I don't understand why you wanted me to stay away from her."

"You know the stories, right? Had all those books in that room of yours." She paused, then amended her words. "I'm sure you've read all about knights and damsels and the Alstrin tales of courtly love."

There had only been one such book, but Vita had read it front to back a hundred times at least. She could probably recite Halse and Odelina's story from memory. *Both* versions—the one where Halse successfully rescued Odelina from her husband and carried her across the meadow of glass flowers to freedom, and the version where the glass had damaged his feet so badly that he stumbled and cut his own throat on a fresh bloom before he could ever get to her, though his final words reached her window.

"Yes. I know a few."

"Husbands have been reaping the benefits of those stories for years."

"Reaping the benefits how?"

"Well, think about it. How many of those stories teach young girls about the gallantry of men? About how a man will pine away for the love of a woman until at last he defeats whatever foe separates them and they can be together. And if he cannot win, then they perish for loving each other. But it's not like that. Not really. Except who is going to tell you that when you're just a girl enamored by the idea of it all?"

Vita thought back to those tales, where the men always fought with honor, and when they made mistakes, they atoned. Where the women waited and pined until their love returned.

None were like the men and women she knew. Men wasted no time on true honor, and women fought back until they couldn't. There wouldn't be queens like Vitenya or even her own mother otherwise. She doubted that her mother had spent a single day pining after her father's return when he was away, too busy relentlessly carrying out her duties.

Stories like Odelina's were for girls like Vita, left behind with no recourse but to wait.

"You're right," she said. She'd hardly expected her marriage to be anything like the stories, after all. "Men aren't like that at all. They're cruel."

"Well, I won't speak ill of the general, but husbands are all the same, really. It's the first lesson a girl learns after she is married. Very few learn it before."

Vita frowned, looking over at the woman and her graying hair. Even now it was pinned perfectly into place. "Were you ever married, Isotta?"

"I was," she said, and the smile was not gentle. "And now I am not, gods rest his soul. The Father needed him, and it seems there is still more for me to do here."

"Do you . . . miss him?" Vita asked, trying not to seem indelicate, though Isotta's tone was too chipper for the subject at hand.

"There's a truth no one tells maidens that I will tell you now, Princess." Isotta ducked her head close. "Maids are happy in their innocence, and then they become wives, and much of that happy innocence is lost. But the happiest women across all the Alstrin kingdoms are the widows."

"The widows? All of them?" Maybe no bride ever left her wedding feeling like her story belonged among the great romances.

"Every marriage has its own secrets. Its own rules. But though they play out in a thousand different ways, they look nearly identical for us. There are many things we don't discover until it is too late. And even if we knew sooner, like I'm telling you now, it wouldn't fix anything. It doesn't mean we can say no. No girl can escape the fate of marriage unless she is called to a convent. And only widows, if they have the money to support themselves, have authority over their own lives. I have that now, and I wouldn't trade it for anything. Even if it meant I got to live in a palace instead of this muck."

"And you recommend widowhood?" Vita asked, voice quiet and eyebrows raised. "As a matter of course?"

There was nothing duplicitous in Isotta's eyes. Just an openness, like a mother trying to counsel her daughter on what was to come. Surely she wasn't indicating that Vita should wish an early death upon her fiancé, but she didn't seem inclined to lie about the beauties of the marriage bed.

"Now, Vita," Isotta said, exaggeratedly huffy. "You are going to get me in all sorts of trouble. I only mean to say that it is not always pleasant, though it doesn't have to be terrible either. But for many, marriage is . . . confining. You have experienced life as someone's daughter, and it has not been kind to you. Life as someone's wife can be equally challenging."

"It can't be bad for every wife. I think Marius's bride will be happy enough one day."

"Yes," Isotta conceded. "Whoever she is, she will have a very good chance of happiness. Maybe in the end she will make him miserable instead."

"Well, I will hold out hope for him. Someone should get a happy ending."

"Oi! I have a happy ending now," Isotta reminded her.

"Then I am pleased for you too," Vita said, jostling Isotta's shoulder. There was no telling how long it might take for the golden years of widowhood to present themselves to Vita. For all she knew, Ardaric might already be planning for his years as a widower, the sole inheritor of his dead wife's throne.

Her original question popped back to the front of her mind, and she couldn't help but ask again. "What does Soline have to do with it, though? It sounds like you should have been warning me away from Ardaric, and it's far too late for that."

Isotta stopped her work to pat Vita's hand reassuringly. "You are more obvious than you think, dear." Vita blanched, and Isotta added, "Don't worry! Or don't worry yet, at least. It's as I was saying—marriages are all unique, but most of them still follow patterns. You are not the first to become close with a friend who can understand you better than a husband ever could."

"Really?"

The fear of what she and Soline did—what she wanted to do again—ate away at her until she often felt sick. If they were not alone in this, then someone could advise her. Isotta herself, even, if she knew so much about the subject.

"Of course not. It is easier with women," Isotta said, voice low and halting. "They understand. They bring comfort. The maidens from the stories all fall in love with the knights, but in real life, the idea of a princess and her servant makes far more sense for plenty of women who have seen the other side of marriage. But they're not the ones writing the stories."

"Do husbands know of this?"

Isotta laughed with her whole chest, head thrown back. Suddenly, the wrinkles around her eyes looked like scars from a battle that brought her the ultimate prize: joy. Freedom. A future of her choosing. Whatever had come before, she had seen it through and made it out alive.

"Some might know and choose to look away. It isn't the same as being set aside for another man. There is no threat to his lineage. But most men have no idea, and wives are smartest when they keep it that way."

"So I don't need to avoid . . ." For some reason, though Isotta already knew, she couldn't bring herself to say Soline's name again to implicate her. "I don't need to avoid *her* as long as I am careful."

Isotta's laughter cut off, and her face sobered. "You are a different matter. When I cautioned you to stay away, I said it in good faith. It isn't that you don't deserve something of your own. It is only that your intended is so different from those of other girls. You put yourself in greater peril."

"And do you . . . Do you fear him?"

Isotta drew in a deep breath, taking a moment to consider the question. "I respect him. He will win this war, and he will be king. I don't think men become conquerors unless they command respect and fear in equal measure. I believe my life will be better here than what I could have hoped for in Kasri. Even esteemed widows do not have all doors opened for them. It is difficult in the world for women, and I made a choice to do what I had to. But part of me will always wonder if following him on this journey was right."

"But you suspect that I am in particular danger."

"Dear, you've always been in danger. You know that as well as I do. If you keep your head down, you will survive the siege and see yourself crowned queen. After that . . . I don't know. Hopefully there will be a role you can establish yourself in. You will bear children, and the mother of the heir is often a more important role than the wife of the king. That will keep you busy enough, and you can see that your child protects you one day as you protected him."

"It doesn't sound like much of a life," Vita whispered.

"Sometimes it isn't. You have to hold out long enough for the day when it is again."

Chapter Twenty-Five

The next morning, the archers and crossbowmen received a rude call to arms when, without any warning, people began streaming into the no-man's-land between the Messilian and Kasrian walls.

"Aim!" Ardaric shouted, voice booming down the line. Vita bolted out of her tent, watching as everyone stood poised to shoot on the general's orders.

Foolishly, Vita elbowed her way through the gawping onlookers toward the wall. She managed to get a line of sight through an unpatched hole left from a recent battle. It was only large enough to peer through if she pressed her face against it.

"Vita," Soline warned, voice clipped as she tried to pull Vita back. "What are you doing? It'll be just your luck if a Messilian archer takes your eye out."

Vita shook her off, focused on what she could see of the people coming toward them. Even with her limited scope, one thing was clear.

"Sol, they're all—"

"Hold!" Ardaric shouted. She tore her gaze from the people to look up at Ardaric standing on the siege tower, just barely protected from being shot himself. Unlike Vita, whose stomach was churning with a new kind of horror, he looked entirely unfazed.

"Sol," she repeated in a fervent whisper. "They're not coming to fight. They're all . . . they're children."

"What, all of them?"

Vita looked again, cataloging the hollow cheeks of a little girl holding her mother's hand, toddling across the stretch of land while her mother carried a bundle in her arms. Tear tracks cut through the grime on the mother's face.

"Mothers and children. All too skinny." There were women with head coverings to protect against the sun, but those who didn't wear them had far less hair than any woman Vita knew. Not in the length but the thickness. Whole patches appeared to have fallen out.

"Let me see," Soline said, bumping shoulders until she could peer through the gap. "Surely they had rations ready. It's not like the king didn't have reason to believe we were coming, even if he did try to make peace. Weren't they prepared? It's only been a few months, and this is the capital of one of the richest kingdoms. It should have taken longer to starve them out."

Many elderly people, men and women alike, traveled with the mothers and children, but there were no men of fighting age. After about age thirteen or fourteen, the men disappeared entirely until they were gray and stooping over.

"What are they doing?" Vita asked, though she could already guess at the answer.

The Kasrian camp was silent as the Messilians approached their wall. Bows remained drawn, but no one moved to shoot.

Ardaric looked down upon the first few dozen Messilians who came to stand before him as more streamed in behind them. "Why have you been sent out instead of your cowardly army?"

Some of the older boys, angry on behalf of their fathers and their king, squared their shoulders. Mothers laid steadying hands on them, knowing that they would never, ever win.

A woman in her midfifties, her brown hair gray-tinged at the temples, emerged at the front and looked up at Ardaric without fear.

Then, in a careful display of subservience, she bowed her head.

"Our king requests that you let us through the walls. Among us are the weakest in the city, who will likely not survive the coming days if we cannot get food. We are none of us soldiers—certainly no threat to your forces. We ask only that you grant us the chance to live."

There was something in her voice—perhaps unsaid by the woman, perhaps only imagined by Vita—that sounded like *And if you are to be our king one day, what mercy might you show us now? What kind of leader will you prove to be?*

"These are your children?" Ardaric asked, waving the point of a dagger between two young kids standing behind the woman. They weren't the closest to her—she was surrounded by other adults ready to plead their case. She'd probably warned her children to stay back in case things got ugly. But somehow Ardaric picked them out immediately. The older girl, wearing a dirtied pinafore over a moth-eaten dress, clutched her younger brother to her side. The boy, only perhaps four, looked up at Ardaric with wide, terrified eyes and bit down on his fist to keep from crying.

Their skin looked gray, and they were so thin that even Vita during her days in captivity could have beaten them both in a fight.

"Yes," the woman said, resigned. "They are no harm to anyone. Please, sir, we beg of you."

"Your king begs it, though I don't see why. I know what

Carca can withstand. I know how long starvation takes to set in and how much food the city was capable of storing year to year. He could have fed you if he wanted. He made his choice, and you, your elderly parents, and your children, have become his sacrifices."

"You could save us. We would never forget your mercy."

He shook his head, and a more forgiving person might think he looked almost sad. "I am not your king. I am not equipped to feed hundreds of extra people in our camp. You will be left wandering the Carcan countryside. Most of the closest towns are abandoned, and no inhabited town you reach will be able to do more than perhaps give you water and a day's worth of bread. If you arrive as a whole group, the safest way to travel, you would overwhelm them. You'd have to try to steal what they have. If you're too moral to steal, you'd have to keep walking. Walking and walking as more of the children succumb to their hunger. To disease.

"No," he said conclusively. "You are better off convincing your king for aid. You are his people. You pay your taxes to his granary each year, and yet you see no benefit now. Return and bid him to do what an honorable king owes to his people."

That this would starve the whole system out faster, forcing a surrender, went unsaid in his explanation. Six months ago, Vita might not have heard the subtext, but she did now. She could see her father's desperate ploy and Ardaric's counterstrategy.

Some of the people, especially the older boys who felt it their duty to protect their mothers and their sisters, began to shout and bray for release, but Ardaric boomed out over them, "Return! Or I will order my bowmen to shoot."

From atop the wall, they could pick people off one by one. They could destroy the whole group—hundreds of people easily—in a matter of minutes.

"Nobody is getting out," Ardaric said, and though the people were disappointed, they took the hands of their children and the arms of the elderly to walk back across the expanse of still-green grass.

"I bet you the bastard prince was hidden in the group so he could go for aid," Marius said across the dying embers in their firepit. "And that's why the general couldn't let them out. Of course, the king would want to use this as an opportunity to get his son to safety."

"I wonder if they know somehow that Salajara is coming," Soline said, still peering through the hole as if there was something to see. "Maybe information slipped inside after all. If those people could get to allies on the outside, they'd survive."

"How long do you think they have?" Vita asked, picking at the skin around her nails to avoid looking at anyone directly. "Some of those children were so thin. I knew this was part of the siege, but . . . I didn't realize what it would look like."

Vita's life had been so intensely sheltered. She'd missed the joy of the world—grass beneath her feet and the experience of shopping in a busy, lively market—but she'd also missed much of the pain. She'd witnessed the death of her mother and then nothing else. No one died while she was with the Polettas. Every day was the same. Even as she grew, taller and taller until her dresses hit her knees instead of the floor, her life was untouched by desperation. She'd been hungry, but they'd never let her starve.

Her father would watch his city slowly perish if it meant saving himself the indignity of surrender.

Would she be brave enough in some far-off future to lay

down her life so that her people wouldn't waste away? Could she claim she was any different, or did his selfishness pass to her like his eyes had, a tragedy of birth?

Soline sat beside her, taking Vita's hand. "Some of them will likely last a few weeks more. People get inventive when they are hungry. There may be things yet that can sustain them."

"Yes," Marius muttered, moving to look through the hole himself. "Like their shoes, if they still wear any."

"Shoes?" Vita asked, trying not to cry.

Marius, eye glued to the hole, started blindly reaching for Soline's arm. "Come here. Look, look. They're—I'm not imagining this, right?"

Soline took his spot, and it wasn't long before the whole camp watched the guards on the wall drawing their bows again.

"They've come back," Soline whispered.

Vita nearly choked on her own spit. "Back? But—"

She rushed toward the hole, needing to see for herself that it wasn't true. The same woman, who had to dash the tears off her cheeks to remain calm before her people, came again to face Ardaric.

"General Ardaric, we—"

"You've returned," he said, cutting her off. "And yet my answer will not change. Go home. Be with your husbands until your king sees sense and ends this siege."

"Our king has refused us reentry into the city."

At this, Ardaric's stern facade finally yielded. His forehead scrunched as he raised his brows, and he asked, almost benignly, "Oh?"

"He sent us out here to be rid of us, apparently. And your refusal has not changed his mind. You must let us through. We cannot get home."

"Must I?"

"Please, sir. Our children will die here." The kids wailed, though it was unclear how much the youngest understood. Perhaps it was enough to sense how desperate everything around them felt. "You are our only hope. We are prepared to pledge our loyalty to you."

"You will pledge loyalty to my cause and my army when we seek to destroy your own? You would see us kill your husbands and sons inside?"

The woman swallowed thickly, hands clenched into tight fists at her sides. "What other choice is there? The Father takes. We are asking that you act on behalf of the Mother and grant us our lives. If that means we owe you our devotion, you will have it. We understand what it will cost."

Ardaric did not look pleased by her words, and he did not look swayed. He shook his head, grave more than anything else. "Return to your king. Bang on the gate if you must. He will see sense."

Chapter Twenty-Six

The king did not see sense, and the cries continued long into the night. They were the wails of the children who wanted to be in their homes. Wanted a hot dinner, or any kind of dinner at all. Wanted anything but to feel the cool night air robbing them of their warmth.

Her father's aptitude for cruelty couldn't surprise Vita anymore. Once, she'd tricked herself into thinking that he'd sent her away out of some sense of protection. After all, her mother was convicted of treason against him, and that meant Vita lived with a stain on her too. Though she always believed in her mother's innocence, she knew that the opinions of others would spread. The court could easily have been a dangerous place for a fallen child.

It had been many years since she'd entertained such fanciful hopes. Vita knew now that he did not send her away to help her, just like he did not send his weakest citizens outside to give them a better chance of survival. He simply wanted them gone.

Her nose tingling from the effort to hold back tears, she asked, "Won't his army revolt? He is intentionally stranding their sick and starving children with no provisions."

"He may have chosen them specifically." Soline spoke softly, distracted by petting Vita's hair where they lay in bed. It was the first time they'd curled up together properly since the night of the kiss. "Widows, maybe, so they have no husbands to defend them. Orphaned children. Elderly people whose sons have predeceased them. Perhaps . . . well, perhaps his army is grateful. It means longer before their own families starve."

The group had gone back and forth until the moon was high in the sky, begging the men on either side to relent and let them through. They would have sworn any oath, paid any price, to not be trapped in the empty space between two disparate kingdoms.

Sorrel, standing at Ardaric's right hand, had snapped that he would shoot the next child who disturbed his wife's rest, but that had been hours ago and the wailing hadn't stopped, so either he wasn't permitted to follow through on his threat or else he was too lazy to bother. Maybe he secretly reveled in their agony.

"I can't sleep. I will never sleep again."

"You will," Soline whispered consolingly. "You will. It will not always be like this. I told you that, and I meant it."

Vita grabbed Soline's wrist, desperate to feel something human. "Is it my fault? Did I make him like this? If I had been a son, if I had been smarter, if—"

"No, Vita. You didn't do this. You cannot fix men like that. Sometimes all you can do is hold them back from their cruelest instincts for as long as you can."

Vita buried her head in the covers. "Are we meant to listen to them slowly starve to death?"

"I don't know. But I know that I will be here with you through it all."

In the darkest hours of the night, Vita disentangled herself from Soline and went outside to sit near the wall. The moon was just a sliver above her, newly born and already witnessing human callousness.

The guards on patrol left her alone, more concerned about the imminent arrival of the Salajarans than about one restless girl awake after dark.

Peeking through the hole in the wall again, she could see very little. There wasn't enough light to distinguish anything beyond the dark mass of people huddled together, but she could still hear them. A mother shushed her child, but it did nothing except make them cry harder. Another woman hummed a lullaby that Vita recognized.

If she were braver, she would slam through the wall and free them. Were these not her people? How did their king and the man who wished to become their king each care so little? She wanted to throw her own food over the wall, but she knew that would certainly get her into trouble with the guards. Insubordination against the general's commands was a far greater crime than sleeplessness.

Useless. That's what she was to them. Utterly useless. She slumped down against the wall and sat at its base, eyes closed. She'd almost managed to clear her head, needing to figure out what her plan was now, when she was interrupted by someone shifting beside her, sitting just to her right.

"Go away," she muttered, knowing Soline must have noticed her absence.

"No."

Her eyes flew open at the sound of Ardaric's voice. "Sorry! No, I—" Taking a deep breath, she tried again. "I thought you were one of the servants come to drag me back."

"Alas," he said, legs folded like hers, hands resting on his knees. It made him look smaller. Almost human. "Just me."

Vita kept her eyes trained forward, watching the embers of a dying campfire two dozen paces away. "Why have you come?"

"The guards informed me you were here. You should be in your tent, Vittoria."

Her head thunked back against the wall, and she allowed her eyes to slip closed again. If he wanted to punish her, he would.

"I cannot sleep when I can hear them crying."

"Then it will be a long few days," Ardaric said, somewhere between humor and pity. "I can let Sorrel shoot them after all, if it will please you. He'd enjoy carrying out that order."

"How can you sleep?" she asked before he could set that plan in motion. It didn't matter that the question was impertinent. "Knowing they will die out there. Slowly."

When she peeked an eye open to glance at him, Ardaric wore a small smile. "I sleep soundly knowing that this wasn't my doing."

"You could fix it, though. They need not pay the price of my father's crimes."

He shook his head. "That's the thing you don't understand yet, Vittoria. It's not about faults or punishment or justice. It never is. They are the enemy. Your father could have protected them, but he chose to send them out with the false promise of freedom and then locked the door behind them. If they get out, he wins. Surely someone in the group will deliver his message to the Salajarans. And if they never leave the confines of our walls, he still wins. He needed to get rid of them, to cut down on the mouths he has to feed, and he has. That was his choice, not mine."

"If you saved them, they would owe you fealty," Vita reminded him. "You could take my father's own citizens from him.

You could be the merciful liberator come to kill a king who does not care for them."

"How many kings have *the Merciful* after their name?"

Vita racked her brain, imagining the pages of her history book flipping quickly behind her eyes. "King Catania the Merciful. He ruled three kingdoms simultaneously because of his birthright. Carca, Ravenna, and Aligo."

"And remind me, how did Catania the Merciful die?"

"He was . . ." Vita frowned, remembering the passage at the bottom of a page. "He was killed by the nobles when he tried to make reforms that were unpopular within his inner circle."

"But those reforms would have helped his people, yes?"

Vita swallowed. "Yes."

Ardaric leaned his own head back against the wall, far too languid for a general-king sitting on the ground in the middle of the night. Once in a while, the shadows of the guards above would pass over them, but their footsteps made only the faintest sounds.

"So you see how kindness can be its own curse. By your measure, he was trying to do the right thing, but Catania's land reforms never saw the light of day. No one benefited. If he'd walked a middle ground and kept the support of his nobles, he might have done more good in the long run. But then Villads the Terrible took over and undid everything. Is that better?"

Hesitantly, she asked, "No?"

"No," Ardaric agreed. "Having power is no simple thing. There was only one king styled *the Merciful* because there is no room for endless mercy in ruling. If you want to be a queen who survives her throne, you will learn this lesson. Sometimes you grant clemency. Most of the time," he said, tilting his head toward the sounds coming from beyond the wall, "you let the mistakes of others play out as intended. Your father's mess is not mine, and it's not yours. Soon, it will solve itself, and their cries will not keep you awake anymore. And then one day in the future, when the cries are different but the pain is the same, you'll realize that you've tuned them out entirely."

Vita drew in a ragged breath, trying to understand how he could care so little. It wasn't a surprise—not after the messenger boy and Eda—but she didn't know how to find that well of hatred in herself and let it consume all else until she could turn away from suffering. From her own humanity and hope.

"So nothing I say will ever convince you to take them in or let them pass."

"No. Our men on the northern edge of the camp are already seeing disease spread among the ranks." Ardaric held up a hand when Vita tried to cut in, stopping her. She hadn't known about any disease. Nobody on the southern side of the camp, nearest Messilio's main gate, had mentioned any such concerns. "Don't fret. It will pass soon enough. But you can see why we can't afford weakness. Why there is no room for excess mercy."

"What of Magda the Merciful?" she asked suddenly. "In Aligo. You asked for kings, but what of her?" Queen Magda had almost slipped Vita's memory, but she recalled the story now. A daughter born to a king whose five male heirs all died tragically young. When her father finally passed after naming his daughter as his successor, the councillors tried to install a cousin to the throne instead, and it sent Aligo into nearly ten years of civil war. But in the end, Magda took power, and she spared the lives of those who betrayed her. Even her cousin was merely exiled to Durbina Minor.

"Magda?" Ardaric laughed. He uncurled himself from the ground and pulled Vita up beside him without warning. Still holding her hand, he led her through the alleyways of tents and sleeping bodies. Vita could barely keep up.

They stopped in front of his own tent, grander than any other, and he gestured her inside.

Though Vita wanted nothing less, there was no one around to deflect his attention. No one to say that she had some other important task to do. No escape route. Nervously she walked in.

At the front of the tent, instead of a bed, there was a long table of solid oak. Had they brought that with them as they traversed half the kingdom, or had someone built it from scratch in the time since they'd arrived in Messilio?

"Surely you know the end of Magda's story, sweet Vittoria. Everyone does."

Magda the Merciful had lived so long ago that some weren't sure she had lived at all. The civil war was what stuck out most in Vita's memory, though, so she shook her head.

"No one calls her Magda the Merciful anymore. They call her Magda the Murderer. Funny how that happens."

Vita paused where she had been walking the length of the table, hand dragging over the top. It was unpolished but still expertly crafted.

"I'd forgotten," she said, though the story came back to her now in a rush. Magda the Murderer. Magda, whose cousin tried to return with an army to reclaim the kingdom years after she'd been anointed as queen. Magda, who rounded them all up and watched them hang one by one down a line that spanned the length of the city.

Maybe Ardaric was right. Maybe mercy only got you so far. Magda had tried to be gracious, and in the end, it only led to more deaths. If she had killed her cousin at the end of the civil war, there would have been no one for all those soldiers to follow. No reason for them to die.

But Vita still could not reconcile this truth with the starving families inside. They did not choose any of this.

There was no one to save them now. Vita was nobody's hero.

"Your education has been woefully neglected, but that's all right," Ardaric said, walking closer. When he stood directly in front of her, he tipped her chin up so that she could not avoid his eyes. "I have sworn to protect you, and I will do so. You will not be unprepared for your role by the time you take it. I will teach you."

He spoke in a benevolent tone, perhaps imagining a future for Vita sculpted entirely by his hand. He could make her something simultaneously more deadly and more docile. To others, she would be a force to be reckoned with—a queen worth fearing. But to him, she would be akin to a well-trained pet. There seemed to be no world in which he would view her as an equal.

He was wrong, though. Vita wasn't unintelligent, even if she had lost out on eleven formative years of her life. In spite of all the ways her father tried to ruin her, she knew the names of a hundred kings who had lived and died in the time since Magda supposedly reigned. She could tell you all about their faults and virtues. She could pinpoint the exact moments in their lives when their decisions had cost them victories.

For the first time, she permitted herself to admit that she wasn't stupid. She was the one who knew that the Salajarans would answer the call for aid, not the Ravennans. She was the one who saw her father as he was, not as people wanted him to be.

Vita was clever in her own way. Admitting this made her feel older, and finally, she could sit with that truth. No longer was she the girl who jumped from shadow to shadow down her father's cold stone halls with a barrage of tutors traipsing behind her. That innocent girl was all but dead. Even if she could go back, she would never again belong in that world.

She was a woman now—one who wanted things and who knew how to get them. For all that life had stolen from her, she was capable. She would see her father's kingdom taken from him, and then, when the time was right, she would steal it for herself.

Whatever future her mother had imagined for Vita was gone. Moreover, whatever future Vita had tried never to imagine for herself and that had crept in through the cracks of her anyway—a future of hope and peace and gentleness—was gone too. Perhaps she could fashion it herself, but only through bloodshed. There was no version of Vita now who would not know loss.

"And you will teach me to be like Magda?" Vita asked, trying to sound young and frightened.

Ardaric laughed, and then, without warning, leaned in and pressed his lips to hers.

He didn't move them against hers or pull away, more a mark of ownership than a kiss. Uncertain, Vita put her hands on his shoulders, knuckles white. She refused to back away this time.

"We will be Magda and Villads both," he whispered. "The whole of Carca will obey us unquestioningly because they will know the consequences of disobedience. Do you understand?"

"Yes."

"I will make you a happy queen, Vittoria," he said almost whimsically as he touched her cheek. "As long as you are good. Listen to me now: the people outside will die. They will be the first truly innocent victims of your father's war, but certainly not the last. And when the Salajarans are outside our walls and you taste the horrors of a siege for yourself, you will understand why this world does not reward compassion. *There can be no hope.* Do you understand?" he repeated.

"Yes," she murmured, the word sucked up into the silence that permeated the air. The cries, the crackling fires, everything seemed to have hushed the closer he stood.

"Good." Ardaric's eyes were drawn away from her face, and she caught him looking over at his bed on the other end of the tent, huge and covered in a dozen furs though it was not yet cold enough for so many. A spike of fear lanced through her, and she tried to come up with any excuse to leave.

But when she turned to look at it fully, she realized that it wasn't empty. In it lay Helka, shifting in her sleep at the sound of their conversation.

When Vita looked back at him, Ardaric was smiling. "Run along back to your nursemaids, dearest. There will be time for your duties later."

Trying not to feel sick, she scrambled out of the tent just as a sleepy Helka sat up in bed and beckoned Ardaric to her side, eyes on Vita the whole time.

If it hadn't been for the pin digging into her palm, Vita might not have managed to keep her focus. The pain centered her.

Later, safely returned to her own tent with a nervous Soline fussing over her, Vita uncurled her fingers.

Cupped in the center of her palm was the jeweled cloak clasp that Ardaric had been wearing all evening, lost to him during those horrible moments of their kiss.

The next day, like the punch line to a terrible joke, the Salajarans arrived under the command of General Drusus Dubrivae, boxing them in.

Ardaric was right. There was all the time in the world now for Vita to learn the horrors of a siege.

For Ardaric's forces, it meant a two-front war. It meant a battle that very night, fought under the limited light of a waxing moon.

For Vita, it meant hiding in her trunk, trying to tune out the sounds of war on one side and dying children on the other.

The fight lasted for three days before Drusus stopped trying to breach their walls. He didn't have the luxury of waiting if he wanted the Messilians in the center of the mess to still be alive when the dust settled, but he could put the same pressure on the Kasrians. Now they were the ones without continual access to the outside world. The camp shrunk down to the space that existed between the two walls.

After the third day, the cries from the Messilian children ceased.

By the sixth day, Vita was sure there was no one left living in that horrible stretch of empty land. It hadn't rained once.

Twenty days after that, they marked the Padrilux.

"King by the Padrilux indeed," Vita groused into her porridge. Another cart carrying the bodies of fallen Kasrians was dragged to where they were being buried.

The winter chill would set in soon, and they would have none of the Mother's warmth to bolster them. There would normally be a celebration of the harvest and a huge feast for the town, but instead, everyone would be counting their rations.

When Soline had first shown her tree rings, she'd thought they were beautiful. Now, living in the midst of a city-destroying tree ring, she could feel how encasing they were. How one version of the tree would be subsumed by another, stronger and better, feeding from the inner until it could no longer see the light at all.

"Come on," Soline said once Vita had finished eating, guiding them through throngs of people with faces caked in dirt. She shoved a grown man aside when he blocked their path. "Isotta stowed away a Padrilux treat for us."

Marius trailed behind them, following until they were huddled in the empty space near Vita's tent. For fear of what Ardaric might do if something happened to her, no one else came close to it, which meant that their fire was always the least crowded.

Isotta did have a treat for them—dried berries that she'd likely spent far too long trying to preserve.

"There aren't many," Isotta said, tugging at a tendril of hair that had escaped her usually perfect coiffure.

"Thank you, Isotta," Vita said, patting her shoulder. "These might be our last strawberries for a long time."

Vita tried to savor each bite, making them last longer than they should. Soline handed Vita one of her own slices with a smile, and Vita took it gratefully, though she knew she shouldn't. Strawberries were something that she'd never had until recently, and it was difficult to imagine living without them again.

When they'd polished off as much of the food as they dared, they leaned back in the dirt and watched the clouds overhead. There had been no skirmishes today—all three of the kingdoms marked the Padrilux, and all tried to celebrate it as best they could. The farther inward you went, the more austere those celebrations became.

Vita chirped out a little tune, and one of the birds she'd seen flying overhead—a small blue thing that looked nothing like her crows—flew down to perch on her hand. Vita ran a gentle finger over its feathers.

"Does she always do that?" Marius asked Soline. "I didn't think that happened outside of stories."

"Pretty standard behavior for her," Soline said, eyes so focused on Vita that it made Vita's cheeks heat. "She's got a way with them. Some extra sense, perhaps."

"Not even that," Vita said. "It's just kindness, and a lot of patience. I've always thought that birds have a good sense of who is trustworthy. Anyone could do it."

"But not anyone would," Soline reminded her.

Marius watched Vita for a moment before regretfully saying, "You should send the bird away before someone tries to make their own Padrilux feast."

Soline eyed the tiny bird before scoffing. "Not much of a feast there."

"Depends how hungry you are."

Vita pressed a soft kiss to the bird's head before releasing it so it could fly off. Marius was right. Eating the bird would save no one in the long run, and she couldn't watch another creature who trusted her die.

Eventually Marius was called away to a meeting with Ardaric, and Vita scooted across the ground so she could whisper in Soline's ear. "I stole the pin days ago. When can we try again?"

"You were the one who didn't want to try again at all," Soline reminded her, staring at the limited strip of grass between them warily, like it was a danger to her.

"I've changed my mind. Ardaric was right about one thing, and that is that there is a time for mercy. Mine has run out."

Soline shook her head, already frustrated. "But maybe you

were right before. What happens if we set the whole camp alight? There's nowhere to escape except the river, and the Bestino will drown us if we try to swim in it. Even then, the water probably wouldn't help anyone already on fire, given what happened in your room. We'd be lucky not to set the whole river ablaze!" The rant died off as Soline blew a fallen curl out of her face. "What good does it do us to kill him when we're trapped? We need him to take Messilio. After that, we can reevaluate."

"But we could learn how to control the alchemy. Last time, I was . . . I was so angry, so . . . afraid, and then suddenly there's an angry, unquenchable fire burning down the room. Surely those details are connected. This time, we'll be more careful."

"You have no idea if those two things are connected, and even if they are, you expect me to think that you, with the font of mercy you were just bragging about, are capable of being careful and patient and methodical right now?"

Huffing, Vita whispered, "Of course I can be methodical!"

"Methodical about what?" asked a deep voice. Vita nearly flew off the ground in her attempt to turn and face the speaker, not wanting an enemy at her back. To her surprise, it wasn't Ardaric.

The man's face was the same as when she'd last seen it: slightly misshapen, like it had never healed right, but strong and sturdy in spite of it all. His jaw was covered in stubble, so he'd shaved much more recently than anyone else in the camp.

The resemblance between brother and sister was obvious.

"Ivo," Soline said, her whole face brightening as she stood to greet him. "What are you doing here?"

In the time since they'd made camp outside Messilio, Vita had sat across the fire from Kellen to eat more than a few times, but she'd seen little of Ivo since that day at the mint. Sometimes when Vita was occupied with helping Isotta or training with

Marius, she'd catch a glimpse of Ivo walking beside the inner wall with his sister, but he never seemed to visit when Vita was free the way that Kellen did.

Though the general had lost much of his faith in Ivo after the day when Anselm died, Ivo had steadily worked his way closer to Ardaric's confidence again. Ivo was too talented a strategist to be ignored.

He returned Soline's hug, but as soon as they separated, he looked right at Vita with narrowed eyes and asked again, "You can be methodical about what?"

"Nothing," Soline said immediately. Then, as if realizing her mistake, she twisted her fingers together in some complicated-looking knot and said, "Stop worrying about us."

"Now you have to tell me." Though nothing in his face visibly softened around his sister, it was clear how fond he was of her. How protective.

Ivo had once watched as his youngest brother was beaten to death for the crime of trying to defend him. If Ivo hadn't disobeyed Ardaric, his whole battalion might have died, but Anselm would still be alive.

It was the kind of guilt that ate away at the edges of a person until they frayed, pulled and pulled so many times that the shape of a human was reduced to a pile of indistinct thread.

"You should focus on your troops and not on listening in on girls' secrets," Soline said. "We're fine. Really."

"Really?" he asked, decidedly unimpressed. Vita nodded stiffly. Moving closer to Soline, he whispered, "Because no matter how many times you tell me that the fire was a coincidence, I know it was you, Sola. And I know that *you know* you aren't supposed to be trying to do that anymore."

"I have no idea what you're talking about."

Ivo ignored her, frustrated in a way that seemed uniquely familial. Turning to Vita, he said, "You too. You are going to get her killed, and then I will have to get vengeance on her behalf, and it really isn't going to be pretty for anyone."

"I wouldn't," Vita said, breathless.

He glanced around, then smiled and laughed loudly, jostling Soline's shoulder until she laughed too. Everyone nearby turned to watch them, but when nothing happened, they returned to what they were doing.

Careful not to attract further attention, Ivo whispered, "There are better ways to get what you want, if you're sure that you want it. *Safer* ways." He said it to Soline, a promise, but at the end of the sentence, he turned his focus to Vita, eyebrows raised.

Vita kept her voice carefully neutral. "What kind of ways?"

"Ways that take far more planning than whatever you two are cooking up."

"But we could help!"

"Is that really what you want?" His gaze pierced through her, testing her mettle. Nobody saw Vita as a threat.

"It is."

When Soline had first offered her freedom in exchange for Ardaric's life, she'd been frightened. That fear had colored everything she'd done. Looking back with a clearer head, she could feel now how that terror had even tainted the alchemy. How it had spread through the concoction like alcohol, turning a flame into an inferno. It wasn't science, and she couldn't prove that it was true or quantify the feeling, but she was sure somehow that her emotions had heightened the reaction to an unmanageable degree.

Now, she wasn't afraid at all, even as she admitted her near treason to a man who only knew her through his sister. If he could turn Vita in to save Soline, perhaps he would. It wouldn't stop Vita from finally admitting what she knew was true. "It is what I want."

If Magda the Murderer had killed her cousin in the first place, no one else would have needed to die. Now, two men stood between the Messilians and mercy. She was no soldier, but someone must wield mercy like a punishing sword.

Ivo monitored the others around him, smiling and laughing again when someone walked too near. Vita joined in, trying not to make her laugh sound stilted.

When they were alone again, Ivo bit his lip before saying, "There are others. People who are . . . similarly inclined."

Hope perched itself in her chest. "Are there? Tell me more."

"I cannot. But you need to listen to me when I tell you not to act." He looked between Soline and Vita, his gaze stern. "You will only get yourself and my sister killed."

"Ivo," Soline chided.

Vita took a deep breath, trying to force the worry away for long enough to ask what needed to be asked. "What is their plan? Will it be soon? And what about—"

Ivo shushed Vita before she could finish the question.

"But surely there *is* a plan?"

"Well, there's—"

Soline cut him off. "There's a plan, right? Tell me someone has a plan."

"When we aren't trapped between two enemies who both want us dead, then there will be time for a more thorough plan. Until then, my chief concern is not letting you two get yourselves killed. Really, Sola, you'd think you wouldn't want to put our mother through this again."

Soline's face fell, and for a moment, Ivo looked as though he might take it back. Instead, he sighed.

"Sorry. I only meant . . . I don't want anything to happen to you." He rested his hand on her shoulder, squeezing it softly. "I need you to stay alive. And Vita—"

He pursed his lips, like he wasn't quite sure where the sentence ended.

"I suppose everyone else needs you to stay alive."

Chapter Twenty-Seven

I suppose everyone else needs you. I suppose everyone else needs you. I suppose everyone—

The words refused to let Vita sleep.

For just a few moments in Ardaric's tent, she'd finally believed that she was capable of more than what people expected of her. Vita wanted to feel that way again—to believe in herself in an entirely unfamiliar way. If she could drape that assurance over herself like a mantle, perhaps she wouldn't be so frightened anymore.

More than anything, though, Vita didn't know how to be needed.

She rolled over, nudging Soline's shoulder where she slept only inches away. "Sol," she whispered, voice raspy in the night.

"Hm?" Soline rubbed a hand over her eyes, staring up at Vita. "Is something wrong?"

Everyone might need Vita—need her to live long enough to outlast Nicolo and Ardaric, to rise to the occasion of her birth and fix the mess created by her father and worsened by her fiancé. But there was only one person that Vita needed, and she could be honest enough with herself about it now.

Even in the darkness, Soline's curls cascaded down her body

like spilled ink. Vita reached out to touch one of the coils before allowing her fingers to trace the neckline of Soline's shift.

"It's been weeks," Vita said, skimming her fingers back and forth over Soline's collarbone. "It's been weeks, and all you've said is that we can't. We shouldn't."

Soline's eyes followed Vita's movements. "Because we shouldn't."

"Because I'm the princess? Because of Ardaric?" Vita leaned closer, hand coming up to cup Soline's jaw as her own long hair spilled down around them, a curtain keeping out the rest of the world.

Soline swallowed. Her tongue poked out as she licked her lips nervously. "Because it's dangerous."

"I know," Vita admitted. Isotta's warning lingered in her mind. "I know. I'm sorry—I shouldn't be putting you in this position. It's only going to get you hurt. But I can't . . . I can't *forget*, and I don't know how you have."

Soline's hand came up to Vita's hip. She readied herself to be pushed away, but Soline only held her there, thumb circling her hip bone through the cotton.

"I know this is my fault," Vita continued. "If I were someone else . . ."

"Your fault? I'm trying to protect *you*, Vita. Not myself," Soline whispered, barely making a sound.

"Me?" Vita squeezed her eyes shut, trying to suppress the swell of wanting that rose up in her. It was so foreign and overwhelming as to almost be frightening, and the few weeks that she'd dealt with it were not enough to acclimate. Strangely, the fear did not temper the want. "I don't think you *can* protect me. What is coming will come. I just want—" She licked her lips, nervous. "In the meantime, while there's still the chance, I—"

Soline dragged her down before she could fumble through the rest of her thought, fusing their lips together with a little groan that Vita tried to capture and stow away.

"I know it's unfair of me to ask," Vita said when she pulled away enough to form words, but Soline rolled them over, pinning Vita beneath her and kissing her again. Her lips were warm. Vita had spent so long trying to recall that first night that she'd worried she might have accidentally mythologized it.

But no. It was as wonderful—as sensuous, as bittersweet, as devoted—as anything her imagination could inspire.

All those years of going weeks without another human touch. Of begging Cosima to visit her more often, until she realized that pleas would get her nowhere. And now she had Soline's hands weaving themselves into her hair to keep her as close as possible, as though a single breath between their lips meant they were too far apart.

"Everything's unfair," Soline murmured, bringing her lips to the column of Vita's throat. "But I still want you. I can't stop."

"Then want me," Vita said, slotting her leg between Soline's. Everything else could be taken from her, but no one could ever steal away this decision. It was hers to make no matter the consequences. "Please. *Have* me, and let me have you." Then, quieter—a hymn she couldn't stop herself singing even when she knew it was ridiculous, even when she knew she could never forget this woman's name—she whispered between kisses, "Soline, Soline, Soline, Sol—"

It was only Soline's kiss that could silence the litany.

Later, when sleep found them with the rising sun, she could only think, *She is my one good thing. They can have me if I can have her.*

The chill of the second season set in as the number of infections mounted. Already they'd had to section off the areas most heavily affected by disease, but the wall still required patrols, and raids from both camps needed to be fought off, so there was no way to slow the spread.

As promised, Ardaric summoned her to his tent for lessons, making her one of the few people to still see him now that he refused to hold large council meetings. All decisions were made with only the help of his closest confidants. He carefully balanced his concerns, aware that he could neither afford to appear daunted nor risk getting sick.

Some days, he instructed her in strategy. Using the little figurines on the table, he reenacted his past battles for her, and Vita asked just enough inane questions to distract him from how her eyes drank in the information.

More often, he ranted almost incomprehensibly. He threw the figurines that represented the placement of various armies, dashing them against the table or the canvas of his tent. Sometimes he shouted at Vita until she ran from his quarters without a goodbye.

And occasionally, on the days when things looked better for their cause, he spoke to her like a person. Imparted bits of wisdom that had Vita itching for an inkpot and a piece of paper to take notes.

It was impossible to know which version of him she would get until she arrived, but in no position to turn away insight freely dispensed, she returned each day.

He complained about keeping the wealthy lords on his side

and putting up with the peacocking captains. She studied the careful balancing act that he seemed to be attending to at all times: when to turn aside and when to show no mercy. Ardaric explained the rations and the way they related to taxes. He spoke of Kasrian laws and even Carcan ones, though often only to criticize them.

Vita wasn't sure if he realized she was there half the time. He seemed to simply enjoy talking for the sake of it. Lecturing to the room kept him occupied while the Salajarans outside refused to fight.

After dinner, if there weren't more important things for him to be doing, Marius still trained her in the basics of fighting.

"You're doing better," he said one evening, wiping sweat from his forehead. It was unseasonably warm that day, the last gasp of heat for the year.

"Not really. I could never hold my own."

Marius narrowed his eyes, assessing her like an opponent. "I wouldn't recommend picking a fight. But if you were attacked first, you could hold them off better now than you might have a month or two ago. That's not nothing."

Vita sheathed her dagger. She wore it always now, even around Ardaric, and he never tried to stop her from having it. Its weight at her hip was a reassurance.

"Thank you, Marius. I don't think I've said it enough, but I really appreciate your help." There were a million better ways he could spend his limited free time, but he never shirked what he considered to be his duty to protect her.

"Happy to help," he said, grinning ear to ear. He slung an arm around her shoulders like Kellen sometimes did to Soline.

"Should we go again?" she asked, glancing up at him.

Before he could answer, another soldier shouted his name

across the camp. The soldier jogged toward them, putting his head beside Marius's ear to whisper urgently. "It's getting worse," he said. "Too many to bury."

Marius sheathed his own weapon and handed her the flask of water that they'd tossed to the side. "I'm sorry. I have to go."

Chapter Twenty-Eight

It only took another two days before everyone in the camp seemed to bear the same sweaty, greenish faces of the plague-ridden. The Kasrians called it the strangers' sickness—because, as Isotta had told her, no island would admit that they had caused the initial spread of it over one hundred years before.

Vita had never seen anything quite like it, having been kept away from the public for the whole of her life for one reason or another. Whenever she had gotten ill in those years, it was always the kind that passed within a few days.

There was hardly anyplace left to sequester the sick, but they tried to keep them toward the northern and eastern sides of camp, nearest the river, as if that would help.

"Won't that be where the Salajarans aim their next attack?" she asked as she sat at Ardaric's table. He paced the floor in front of her, having spent ten minutes raving about all the forces acting against him. The Carcans, the Salajarans, and even the gods were his enemies now.

Ardaric paused at her words, giving them a real moment's consideration, before his feet picked up their ceaseless motion once more. "We have kept the severity of the disease quiet for as long as possible, and so far, they don't know the extent of it or where we're keeping the infected. And anyway, it hardly matters. If the disease spreads, we will wipe ourselves out long before they ever need to. It is this or destruction. We'll put the sick where the wall is most naturally defensive so we won't need many guards there. The rest of us will manage."

"I'll help, then," she offered. "With the relocation. It will take some time to move the tents and set up what they need, and they won't be able to do it themselves." Already she was rolling her sleeves up her forearms, concerned by the sheer volume of people who needed assistance.

"Absolutely not. In fact, you've already been around them too much. If they die, they die. You still have a role to play."

"But I could—"

"I will have the women organize the relocation. They will manage fine without you."

"I must prove myself to them," she said. "That was one of your lessons. *A ruler must ingratiate himself with his people and establish his competence.*"

"Vittoria," he said, slamming a goblet down on the table. Wine spilled over the side, and the ravenous part of her imagined how many people in this camp would kneel at the table's edge and lick it up gratefully. How much longer could she last here before she, too, felt that same hunger? Isotta still did all she could to give Vita one hearty meal on bad days and two on good ones, but half the time it was no more than thin porridge. "Enough. Stay in your tent. We will sacrifice every woman in this camp before I let you waste your title on saving the condemned. This does not concern you. Your job is to marry me. The women will serve the cause I command them to."

"And the men?"

"They must remain healthy for as long as possible. It is for men to win wars."

How many men across history had said that to their daughters, their wives, their mothers?

How many more times would Vita have to hear it?

And, worst of all, how many more times would the same logic be used for whatever purpose he required? *It is for men, for me, to decide where you live. It is for me to decide how many children you bear. It is for me to decide that you are no longer necessary for my political agenda.*

"Of course. I'll return to my tent." Vita stood and gave a quick curtsy, ducking her head so that she would not have to look into his eyes. "Good luck with your plans."

"Here you are," Isotta said, ladling porridge into a bowl to hand to Vita.

Vita didn't reach for it. "But that's the whole pot. Save some for yourself, Isotta."

"Nonsense, dear. This is for you." Isotta took Vita's hand and, squeezing it once, turned it over to balance the wooden bowl atop it. "You need to eat. You've grown far too skinny here."

Vita's head ached, and she didn't want to fight. "Do you have more for yourself?"

Isotta's smile was small, tender, and a little sad. "Don't you worry about me. I will find something elsewhere. What remains of this food is for you, and we have to ration it as such."

"Take some. Please, or I will give it to Vipsania and then we will both be hungry."

"Please don't feed this to your horse," Isotta chided. "They are the only ones of us not yet starving."

Despite scoffing at Vita's lackluster threat, Isotta did steal a few spoonfuls, and the two ate together in the safety of Vita's tent. It didn't take long to polish off their portions, but there were others who were already scrounging. The general and his commanding officers would all be fine. Vita would be too—Ardaric would give her more if she asked for it. But she couldn't help but wonder how Ardaric was any different from her father in this situation: choosing who was worthy to eat and who wasn't.

Soline arrived shortly after they'd polished off their meal, and Vita looked down at the dregs in the bowl and felt terrible. "I'm sorry," she said, tripping over her words. Her tongue felt heavy in her mouth. "I'm sorry. I should have waited. Or saved you some. You must be hungry."

Soline shook her head, laughing in spite of the gray day. "Not at all. I ate with Kellen and his men. I'm sorry—I should have told you not to worry."

"But we didn't save you anything," Vita babbled. "It was wrong to eat it all. Now what will you do? I wasn't thinking." She rose to stand again, teetering as she tried to catch her balance. "I'll have to find something else. Isotta will help me, won't you—"

"Vita! Vita," Soline said, trying to stop her from destroying their food stores as she pawed through them. There wasn't much there, the rest was kept with Ardaric's under armed guard. "Stop. I told you—I'm fine. I don't need anything more. Kellen fed me. Vita."

Vita was barely listening, her head filled with crow feathers, and she needed to make sure Soline was fed. And what of Marius? Who was feeding him? The only option was to get more food.

Vita exited the tent and darted across the camp before realizing how unfamiliar everything looked. Turning in place, she tried to find the food stores, but it wasn't long before she grew dizzy. A hand reached out to stop her. Vita nearly tripped into Soline, and the other girl had to wrap her arms around Vita's waist to keep her upright. People around them had stopped to watch.

It didn't deter Vita from wanting to lay her head on Soline's shoulder and cry.

Marius ran up to them, rattling in his chain mail. They must have stuck him on patrol. "Is everything all right? You look—"

"Where is the food? I have to—I *have* to—"

"You have to sit down," Soline said gently, placing a hand on Vita's forehead before jerking back. It was only a moment before she laid her palm there again, icy against Vita's face. "Marius," she said, something false in her voice. "I think we should take the princess back to her bed. She's tired."

"Of course," he said, taking Vita's arm and dragging her back when Vita's feet refused to cooperate.

"She hardly slept last night," Isotta said from behind them. "Surely that's all it is."

"No," Vita said, shaking her head until she couldn't any longer. "I slept through breakfast, remember?" In a camp as loud as theirs, only the deepest sleep could last that late into the morning.

Marius guided her through the camp, past makeshift stalls for horses and campfires with meager meals cooking over them. She had to close her eyes and rely on her companions when the throbbing in her head refused to lessen.

It didn't matter where they took her. They could walk her up to the top of the siege towers and straight off the other side if it pleased them.

When they reached the tent, Soline tucked her into bed. They didn't remove her dress or her shoes, and Vita was too exhausted to care. "Sol?"

Soline stared into her eyes, measuring something that Vita could not see. "Yes?"

"Will you leave when I fall asleep?"

"Do you want me to leave?"

"No."

Soline took her hand. "Then I won't."

Tears spilled down Vita's cheeks, shockingly cold. Soline wiped them away with her thumbs, murmuring softly.

"Shh, Vita. Go to sleep. I'll take care of you."

Chapter Twenty-Nine

Vita fumbled in the dark, fighting her way out from the blankets encasing her.

"Help them; help them, someone—someone has to help them."

She freed her arms and bolted upright. A head popped up from where it had been resting by her hip. Blearily, the person said, "Vita. Stop; you'll hurt yourself."

"You have to help them. Please. Don't leave them there."

"Help who?"

Vita touched a hand to her nose and realized gratefully that it was still on her face. There was a pool of snot beneath it, and her cheeks were wet. Through her tears, she said, "The people. The ones outside. They're starving."

Soline grabbed her hands, forcing them back to her sides before she could start scratching at her skin. It was sweaty and grimy and too hot. She wouldn't be able to cool down until she'd torn it open.

"It's okay, Vita. You were dreaming. There's nobody out there."

"No! They're screaming. I can hear them out there. They need our help."

A dark figure loomed just outside the tent, and Soline glanced back at it before shaking her head. The shadow stepped away, disappearing again.

"Help them. Please."

Soline squeezed her hand. "They aren't screaming. Nobody is."

"I can hear it. I'm telling you—they're *there*."

Soline pursed her lips for a moment before she whispered, "Vita, those people . . . they're dead. They aren't screaming. They died a long time ago. I'm sorry."

Vita shook Soline's hands away and clutched at her skull, leaning forward until she was bent double, forehead to the bed. "They're so loud. Why is no one helping them? They're not dead."

"Then we will help them," Soline promised, rubbing circles on Vita's shoulder. "Drink this. It will make you feel better, and once you feel better, we can help them."

"Promise?" she asked, head shaking back and forth so that the bedclothes scraped her forehead.

"I swear. Here, let me help you."

Carefully, Soline sat her up, and though she did not like the way it made her skull ache, Vita drank her tonic and wept silently as good daughters should. When Soline laid her back down again and stroked her hair, Vita grabbed her wrist.

"Do you hear them?"

Soline shook her head. "I can't. But I'm glad you can still, even if it's hurting you."

"I want to help them," she whispered. "I wanted to help them."

Leaning close, Soline pressed a kiss to Vita's forehead like a brand. "I know you did."

Mornings and evenings and nights blended together. Her lips tasted of the sleep tonic that Isotta made from their hidden bundles of valerian root and spoolwood.

Sometimes Vita could not remember Soline's name, could not remember meeting her, could not remember why she was not in her bed beside the window where the birds came to sing.

Sometimes when she woke, she asked the girl beside her where Eda was. Sometimes she asked why the children were still crying outside. Sometimes she stared lifelessly at nothing, too hot to be certain if the faces staring down at her were nightmares or not.

She awoke one night trapped in the in-between with those children, banging on walls that would never open. She cried and screamed and begged for her life. Eventually, her raw, bloodied hands dropped to her sides, staining her nightshift red.

Always a nightshift, perpetually a little girl, with her hair unbound and feet uncovered, running through city streets slick with blood.

A horrible grinding noise sounded, and Vita swiveled to face it. Messilio's massive gates opened, and a lone rider perched atop a stallion appeared, backlit by the sun.

He rode toward them, and like a spell had been cast over her, Vita walked closer, the sea of starving children and sick mothers parting to let her pass.

When at last she stood by the horse's forelimbs, she looked up at the man in wonder. Eda sat perched atop his shoulder, her talons welded to his armor so that she could not fly.

"Have you finally come for us?" Her voice was as soft as a song.

"I will always come for you, Vittoria. You are mine. Always."

The man removed his helmet, revealing a face almost lost to her memories. Almost, because she would never forget that day on the balcony.

He was her mirror: older and crueler, perhaps, but his face was still her own.

King Nicolo. Her father.

"Always," he repeated, before raising his great sword and swinging it through her neck.

Vita gasped, throwing herself out of her bed.

"Vita!" someone shouted, coming over to her where she was crumpled on the floor in a heap. Soline, probably, though Vita did not open her eyes to check.

It was a dream. It had to have been a dream. She was seeing things, fever bubbling and boiling until apparitions appeared before her.

She had cried so much already, weak as she was. Still, with no tears left to dredge up, she dry sobbed into the floor. For all she knew, this respite was the dream.

"Come, let's get you back into bed. Marius, help."

Vita did nothing to aid them, though they eventually maneuvered her where they wanted her.

A hand touched her cheek before it opened her mouth to try to spill water into it.

"Swallow, Vita. Please."

She coughed it back up.

"He wants to move the wedding forward," said a deeper voice. Marius, then.

"What? How could he? She's so ill; she won't be able to stand for a ceremony."

"He sees it as a precaution. In case . . ."

"In case she dies."

"Yes. It wouldn't give him the same legitimacy, but he's claiming by right of conquest anyway. The wedding was always just extra insurance to lend him credibility. If she marries him and . . . and dies before the takeover, it would be nearly as good. He would retake the city in her honor."

"Please, Marius, don't let him do that. She needs to rest. She will not get better if he drags her around for some farce of a wedding."

"Nobody *lets* the general do anything. You know that."

Soline's voice cracked when she said, "I know. I know, but still. We could try. *You* could try. Otherwise, I'm afraid she—"

"Soline," he said, sighing. Then there was a hand in Vita's hair, distracting her, a thumb resting on her temple. "You should prepare yourself. If . . ."

"Vita will get better. She's young and strong."

"Young and strong men have been dying in droves for weeks. It's going to get worse before it gets better. I'm not saying it's impossible; I'm just saying . . . I just want you to be prepared. If."

"If," Soline repeated.

"I'm sorry."

"I'm sorry too. We all love her."

Silence. Silence so long that Vita thought she had lost her connection to the world again, so deep in the dark that she would fall right through its center.

Then: "Yes. But you especially."

A sniffle. "Just. Just speak with the general if you can. Try to change his mind. Tell him to leave an offering instead. It'll mean the difference between some chance and no chance."

"Tell him," Vita croaked, voice so hoarse that it sounded

nothing like her own, "that I will swear an oath not to die if he gives me back my bird."

Eda had haunted her from the edges of every nightmare, waiting to be rescued.

"Vita? Gods, Vita, are you awake?"

Vita pursed her lips and groaned, but that was enough for Soline, who threw herself across Vita's chest and held her close.

"Go tell him," Soline said, ordering Marius around again. "The bird in exchange for Vita's oath."

"I'm not sure that will mean much to—"

"Tell. Him."

Vita lost the thread of conversation after that, slipping again into night terrors, but later, she felt tiny talons digging into the skin of her shoulder and knew that Eda was home.

Chapter Thirty

Vita awoke with a shiver, the sting of the morning air noticeable for the first time in days.

Snuggling into the blankets wrapped around her, she turned her head on the pillow to see Soline poking a needle haplessly through a scrap of fabric.

"Sol?"

"Oh!" The fabric was tossed aside as Soline dropped down from her chair and knelt beside the bed. "You're awake."

"Yes."

"You aren't hallucinating this time? Nobody else is in the room with us?"

"I—no. I don't think so." Vita glanced around, taking in the tent. "Should someone else be here?"

Soline's hand shook as she slid it across the bed to hold Vita's. "I was so afraid for you."

"Was it very bad?"

She knew the answer, but she couldn't stop herself asking. After all, Soline was *afraid* for her. When was the last time someone truly worried on her behalf?

"Yes. Even Ardaric was concerned, in his own way. It's why he gave in so quickly on Eda."

Vita turned to look, and sure enough, the crow slept perched on Vita's other wrist, talons digging in but not uncomfortably. Stranger still, Zeda was also there, staring at Vita.

In all the time since they'd left Novogna, Vita had yet to see Zeda anywhere. Had they all followed? Was it safe for them to be around after what happened to Meda?

"Hello," she whispered, grateful for their company. Eda would not sleep so close to Vita if she did not still trust her. "I've missed you both so much."

Though Zeda could not smile, she tipped her head to the side, and Vita pretended it meant that she missed Vita in return.

"Why did he give Eda back?"

"You asked for her in exchange for your survival."

Vita's brow furrowed, though she did vaguely remember making such a pronouncement. "And that worked?"

"It was his offering. You're lucky you asked when you did—he might have given something much less meaningful otherwise, and then who knows where we'd be."

"His offering of what?"

"His *offering*. You know. For you." When Vita shook her head, Soline continued. "Do you not give offerings here? When someone is . . . is dying, we leave a gift at their bedside. Something important to them, or something important to you. It's a gift to that person to entice them back, but also . . . I think people hope that if they leave an offering in exchange for the person's life, the Father will take that instead. Of course, it doesn't always mean a person won't die—it's tradition, though, so everyone does it anyway. And since the Father rarely comes to collect, the items become yours if you survive."

"Huh." Was that a Carcan custom, too, or was it something

that only northerners did? Vita had never sat vigil by a deathbed. "So he gave me Eda?"

"Apparently, he really didn't want you to die."

Vita remembered her dreams. The people screaming and the way they had echoed in the recesses of her skull. For as long as she lived, she would never forget those horrible visions, and she would never forgive Ardaric for putting them there.

"I hope he suffered, then."

"Oh, he has. Marius said he's been unwell, too, only he won't admit it. He's ranting and raving, but what can anyone do about it? No one will tell him to rest. One of the men tried to eat his own horse, and the general nearly took his head off."

Vita's eyes widened in alarm. "Eat? His horse?"

"Half of the sick won't eat. We could barely get you to take a few sips of water each day. So they haven't been sending much food up to the quarantined areas. It was deemed a waste of resources. But, of course, some of the sick are hallucinating, and they're hungry. The man snuck to the stables and killed his own horse."

"And what will happen to him? If he was not of sound mind?" The warhorses were a finite resource. Until things became dire, killing them was a capital offense.

"It remains to be seen."

Vita sighed, shifting in bed and accidentally waking Eda. "How much longer can we live like this?"

"However long we must. Something will have to give soon. Either Messilio starves, or we do. We cannot be far from someone's surrender."

"What . . ." Vita swallowed, clearing her throat. "What happens if it's us?" No one ever considered the possibility of defeat out loud. She didn't know what would become of her if they waved the white flag, enemies hemming them in. Where would she go?

If her father wanted her dead, she would have to die killing him. It would be a hollow victory, but at least she'd know that the people he sacrificed were avenged.

Soline gave no answer, perhaps knowing that they were well beyond reassurances now.

"I saw horrible things when I slept. Things I don't want to see for the rest of my days."

"I know," Soline whispered. "You cried in your sleep."

"Please." She turned Soline's hand over like she might read the future in the lines of her palm. "I know you don't want to try again. But what's left for us otherwise?"

"You heard what Ivo said—"

"And I know that waiting means nothing if we're only going to starve to death or be conquered by Salajara while our general loses his mind trying to pretend that he isn't unwell. Does my father really think they're here to liberate him? That they won't see our troops *and* Messilio's equally weakened and try to seize power? We'll be carted off as prisoners of war, and they'll use us however they please." She squeezed Soline's hand with all her waning strength, wondering if it was enough to hurt. "*You* wanted to kill him. *You* brought me into this. Now please—help me finish it, and then Ivo or someone else can take charge and win this war."

"I know that I started this," Soline said, her face crumpling. "I know! And I want to do it still. But how am I supposed to—" She stopped, forcing herself to take a deep breath. "It was easier when I only had to worry that I would die. I shouldn't have gotten you involved."

Vita pressed her lips together. "If you can't bring yourself to try again, I will do it alone."

"Vita, you've been in bed for a week. You're not strong enough to walk to the river, let alone to do alchemy that might set the whole city and three armies ablaze."

"I'll figure something out," Vita said uselessly. What could she offer the world but the little she had left of herself? "I can't not try. Not now."

"I'll speak with Ivo. Try to learn what his contacts have in mind for getting out of this mess."

Vita lay back down, staring at the ceiling of the tent like the answers to all her problems might be hidden there. "Fine."

Before Soline could say anything else, either to console Vita or to snipe at her in return, a scream pierced through the camp.

Vita rolled out of the bed, still woozy, her legs tangling in the blankets as she rose.

"Stay," Soline ordered, finger raised pointedly. "I will go see what's happened."

But Vita could no longer be still. For the whole of her life, she'd let people decide for her. She would not cower now.

"I am the princess of Carca, and I will go where I please."

Soline looked stricken. "Vita—"

"Sol," she said, softer now. "I have to know." Then, on wobbly legs, Vita staggered out of the tent and into the chaos.

A crowd had gathered, making it impossible to see what they were looking at, but Soline ran up behind her and, sensing that Vita would not back down, helped shove people aside. Soline shouted Vita's title to get them to move, either because of her status or because her illness had been well known and they did not wish to get sick too.

"Stop *stealing* from me!" Ardaric shouted.

His eyes were bloodshot and bulging, and instead of wearing his customary fine leathers, plated mail, and giant furs, he stood shirtless in the middle of the autumn day. His whole torso was covered in the sheen of the sick, though his grip on his great sword looked as strong as ever. He waved it around like a toy, and anyone standing too close had to jump back for fear of losing their limbs.

"No, no, I—it had to be cleaned!"

Sprawled out on the ground, blood already running down the side of his head, was Marius. He held no weapon, and his hands were raised in fear. Vita was on her tiptoes, nearly hopping off the ground to see over the jeering onlookers.

"I was taking it to be cleaned. I haven't stolen. I swear—please, General! Please."

"You're a thief," Ardaric shouted, swinging wildly, though luckily high above Marius's head. "My cloak clasp, my money, my armor! Where have you taken them? Tell me!"

Vita's eyes widened in alarm. She knew nothing of stolen money, and presumably the armor really had been taken to be cleaned. But the cloak clasp . . . *She'd* stolen that before falling ill.

She fought her way forward, but the burly men standing closest to the action refused to let her pass.

"I must get through!" Her words were lost in the melee. "Please, you must let me—I demand—"

"General," Marius choked out, and finally Ardaric's swing hit its mark. The flat of his blade struck rather than the sharpened edge, and it was lucky he wasn't wielding his axe, but the blow still made a loud cracking sound. "Please," he whispered, low enough that Vita had to read it on his lips.

Marius was so lanky that sometimes she could almost forget he was strong. That he'd been chosen to protect her. But at Ardaric's feet, he looked entirely defenseless. No one would stand up for him, and even against an unwell opponent, Marius could not win. He wouldn't even be permitted to try. The crowds, filled with the horrified and the excited alike, would never let him kill their leader.

"Ardaric!" she shouted. "Ardaric, stop!"

She wasn't sure what she meant to say or if she would implicate herself, but she knew she couldn't let him kill Marius. Crouching, she shoved between two soldiers' legs before flinging herself against Ardaric's side, grasping his bulging sword arm. The fingers clawing at him were thin and frail, but he still turned toward the interruption.

"Please. Don't kill him. I'm sure it's a misunderstanding." Then, quieter, mindful of how great men always loathed to be reminded of their own faults in front of others, she whispered, "You are not well, sir. Please let me take you back to your tent so you may rest."

He hesitated, glassy eyes bouncing between the different parts of her face. She took a deep, steadying breath before laying her palm on his cheek.

"I will take you to rest, and tomorrow you will feel better. I will find your pin and the missing money in the meantime." Remembering what Soline had told her, she added, "I will give an offering for your health, and when the gods have accepted it, we will be stronger. Your victory is only days away, but you must allow yourself to heal."

He looked entranced, like her words were a witch's spell and not frenzied half promises.

He brought his free hand up to cover hers on his cheek, turning his face so that he could kiss her palm. "Marius has stolen. I will have justice."

Before Vita could consider or refute the outrageousness of the claim, Ardaric stepped away, sword swinging.

"No!"

The last of Marius that she saw was his terrified eyes as the sword bore down, smashing through the center of his skull like it was a war hammer.

PART III

There Can Be No Hope

Chapter Thirty-One

Vita could not bring herself to leave the crimson-stained patch of earth until long after the crowd dispersed and Marius's body had been carted away. She'd tried to fight them for it, knowing that he would not receive a proper burial, but Soline held her back and reminded her that she was still unwell. She cried as the body was removed, and afterward she refused to follow Soline to the river to clean the spray of blood off her cheeks. Vita wandered listlessly around the camp instead.

All she could think about was Marius's body, his mangled head in her lap as she begged him to come back.

Despite the burn in her muscles, she didn't stop walking until the sun had set behind the distant hills. Moonlight guided her back to her tent.

"I'm doing it," she whispered as she reentered. She focused on removing her boots, unable to look Soline in the eye without her nose tingling. "Warn Ivo to be ready. I don't care how. I'm not waiting again."

Soline drew back the covers from where she lay in Vita's bed, and stood. "Vita—"

The soft sadness in Soline's voice made Vita turn to her in anger. "He's *dead*. Dead just like Anselm, and neither of them deserved it. So are you going to help me or not?" Soline said nothing. "How many more people should I let him take? Should we let him kill Isotta? Or maybe he wipes out the rest of your brothers just because he can. Marius—" She gasped, a sob wrenched from her chest. "Marius was the closest thing I've ever had to a brother. And now he's gone because of me. Will you make me watch him kill you next?"

"I'll help you. I just don't want—*Vita*." Tears leaked silently down Soline's cheeks, and she cradled Vita's face in her hands. "Don't you see? He'll never risk killing you in a blind rage, but it won't stop you from being executed for treason. He just *beat Marius to death*, and I can't let you get yourself killed too!"

Eyes on Soline, Vita took her hands and drew them down until they were pressed to her sternum. "This is how we live. This is how we find our own freedom. Otherwise winning this siege will mean nothing."

"The timing is all wrong. What about the Salajarans and the Messilians? We could be condemning everyone here."

"Talk to your brother. Tell him to prepare however he must, and I'll handle Ardaric."

Soline gave a somber nod, dressing again to escape for an audience with Ivo.

Vita pulled out the small bundles of plants she'd hidden in her satchel weeks before. She didn't remember every detail about how she'd done this the first time, but that was okay. She didn't need a forest fire—she just needed *something*.

She crushed the flowers and roots until there were enough to bury Ardaric's clasp beneath them. Then, like a birdsong, the chant she'd used before but never understood rose unbidden in her mind. She whispered it and imagined hope, fragile and berry sweet.

Soline didn't return until it was nearly dawn. The bowl was empty, having taken that last gasp of hope with it.

"Ivo cautioned us to wait but said he would make his people aware in case things change. Is that enough for—are you all right?"

Vita stared down blankly at the bowl, unable to swallow the lump sitting in her throat. "The clasp was the only thing I had to give, and it didn't work."

Marius lost his life because she stole that clasp, and now it couldn't even avenge him.

"I don't have anything else. All the jewels we had access to burned in the fire, and the rest of the items Ardaric took from Novogna are locked away for safekeeping. There's no way to steal them. No one to sweet-talk or lie to or . . ."

Soline crouched beside her, placing a hand on Vita's knee as she studied the empty bowl. "What if . . ." She paused, lips pressed into a flat line. "What if it's not about their worth in gold? We gave nearly twenty coins to the spell, and not a single one worked."

"Why did it work with the fire, then?" she rasped. "Do I not want it bad enough now? I don't think I could want anything in the world more than this. What more does it want from me?" Her voice cracked, and she dashed the bowl against the tent wall. It bounced off the canvas and landed on the ground, not even having the dignity to break.

"Shh," Soline said. "It's okay, Vita. It's okay. Last time, you used an old pearl earring, right? It had its own value, sure, but that wasn't the point, was it? It was something important to you. Something sentimental that you'd carried with you for years."

"My birds gave it to me," she whispered. "I was carrying it when I tried to escape Ardaric's attack on Novogna. I dropped everything else, but the earring post stuck in my skirt, and it was the only thing that came back with me."

"You offered something of sentimental value, and it worked. That's the difference. The clasp, the coins—they meant nothing."

"But what do I have left to give?" All of her precious belongings had been destroyed in the fire, and the only things that mattered to her now were her friends and her crows. She would never sacrifice those.

"Well . . ." Soline walked over to the rickety little table that stood near Vita's camp bed. On it was a pitcher of water and a few trinkets that Vita didn't recognize. "There's this."

Soline handed Vita a gold ring. Confused, she tried it on, though it was so tiny that it only fit on her smallest finger. "I've never seen this before." How could she have a sentimental connection to a ring that she didn't own?

"No, I suppose you wouldn't recognize it. You've never met the girl who used to wear this ring."

"And who was that?"

Soline took Vita's hand and held it up, letting the light from their candle shine over the gold. "Marius left this for you when we thought you were dying. It was his offering. He said it belonged to his little sister, and he always wore it into battle on a chain around his neck. Marius . . . he was meant to bring it back safely to her when this was all over, but he gave it to you in the hope that the gods would grant you your life."

"He gave this to me?" Her heart felt heavy in her chest. "Even though . . ."

"He loved you, Vita. The way he loved his sister, or the way Ivo and Kellen love me. You were family to him."

"But I am the reason—I'm—it's my *fault*."

"It wasn't. Ardaric did that, not you. You would never have hurt Marius."

Vita drew her fist up to her sternum, her other hand covering the ring, as though protecting it would somehow protect Marius too.

This was all she had left of him. Vita should keep it and return it to his sister as promised, even if it would be a cold comfort coming from anyone other than her brother.

"You think I should use this?" Vita asked, voice shaking. "It's all we have of him." They'd probably dropped his body into some mass grave already, another anonymous face among those who had died of the strangers' sickness.

"He gave it to you with no expectation that you or the gods would give it back to him, and here you are. Give it in his memory, and maybe we can kill his murderer."

"I thought you didn't want to do this."

Soline bit her lip. "I don't know. I don't know anymore. Being here, trapped and agitated and crazy, is making it hard to decide. I want him gone. I want us safe. I'm not sure we can achieve both."

"We'll never be safe unless he's gone," Vita whispered.

"Maybe there's no world where we're safe, and I just have to accept that. Only . . . I didn't ever know I could be so afraid. Everyone I love is trapped in this forsaken wasteland, waiting for death or victory, and I . . ." Soline brushed the tears on her cheeks away with an angry swipe. "There's nothing we can do about it now. The only way out is to keep going. I thought we should wait until this campaign was won before we did anything drastic, but the general is sick. If he's no longer an asset in this war, then he's a danger to everyone. So if you want to do it, then . . . Ivo and the others will be ready. They will pick up the pieces, and they will win the war for us. They can. I know they can, because what other choice is there?"

She sounded like she was trying to convince herself, but Vita nodded anyway, not wanting to talk her out of it.

"So I have to destroy the ring. For Marius."

"For Marius," Soline agreed. "If you don't . . . maybe none of us lives long enough to return it to his sister. Better to use it in his memory. He would like that."

Vita nodded and took a deep breath before removing the ring from her finger. Soline was right—though Vita had just learned of the existence of this ring, it was already more important to her than anything from Ardaric. Losing this would be a true sacrifice.

She reset the needed ingredients, grinding herbs and nestling the ring inside them.

"I feel like once the ring is gone, then it's really over. He's dead."

Soline knelt next to Vita, both girls staring down into the bowl. Then she laid her hand on Vita's shoulder and said, "He is gone. He's gone today, and he'll still be gone tomorrow and next week and next year. But he swore himself into your service to protect you, and he would want to do the same now. For you and me and Isotta and everyone. He wouldn't want you to carry him so close to your heart that you miss the chance to save yourself from the same fate."

Vita imagined all those days of learning to fight with Marius. All those times his hand had instinctively gone to the hilt of his sword when someone got a little too close to her.

"All right," she whispered. "I'm ready."

When she chanted the words, she did not see great walls of

flames and destruction. Instead, she imagined poison traveling through the body and turning everything it touched black.

When the spell was done, the bowl was not filled with sludge. It was not on fire.

Instead, it was filled with a lilac-colored powder, crushed far finer than Vita had managed to crush the herbs.

"Do you think it worked?" Vita asked, staring at it in wonder.

"There's only one way to know."

Vita laughed, a little hysterical. "But it looks like it worked, doesn't it? The last powder we made was just crushed herbs, but this turned *purple*. And that means that you were right about personal connection. I didn't get lucky with the fire, and you didn't fail with the coins. We just didn't know the recipe."

"You think I could do it too, then?"

"Why not? You will be the heir to your family's legacy, after all. As soon as we can, we'll test it out."

Soline's hand went to her neckline, under which Vita knew sat the pendant she always wore, like she needed to check that it was still there and not lost to an alchemical reaction. "It'll have to wait a while." She stared at the bowl for a second longer, throat bobbing as she swallowed. "Do you think it'll set fire? If we combine it with water?"

Vita wasn't keen to set herself alight, but she was curious. Taking the smallest pinch and putting it in the center of the tent with nothing around it, she dipped a clean finger in the water pitcher and flicked it at the little speck.

Nothing happened.

"Oh, thank the gods," Soline murmured. Then, as though

seeing it as an asset and not a threat for the first time, she asked, "What is it, then?"

"I'm not sure," Vita said. "I was trying for poison, not fire."

"Then maybe it's—don't try it!"

"I wasn't going to," Vita retorted, though she had been letting her fingertips touch it again in wonder.

Vita stood, finding in her belongings a little pot of beeswax salve. Sometimes she coated thread with it when she sewed. Increasingly, she used it on her cracked lips, trying to protect them from the harsh winds.

She scooped out a glob and, with markedly little care for her own well-being, mixed the powder into the wax.

"We can paint it onto his lips while he sleeps. Or slip it into his food. Or—"

"How will we get that close to him?" Soline asked, eyeing the concoction. "If anyone sees you too near or has reason to suspect you . . . There are many who will still fight and die for him."

"Don't worry," Vita whispered, moving to take Soline's hands. They shook in Vita's, so she rubbed gentle thumbs across the backs. "I am not as frightened as I once was."

Discretion was not difficult when the man she wanted to murder was already throwing himself about in rages like a lunatic. All it took was visiting him for another afternoon lesson and listening to him shout about the insubordination of some of his men.

She knew he counted Marius among them—Marius, who was innocent of all crimes and would never have plotted against Ardaric any more than he would have hurt Vita—and it hurt her to pretend that she didn't care.

Often, she mumbled soulless platitudes about Ardaric's intelligence and fortitude. His eyes were glassy, but he listened to her compliments like they were water and he was dying of thirst.

"I knew you would come to see things my way, Vittoria. I knew it." He paced the length of his tent, waving around a sheathed dagger. "I knew from the moment we met that you would be a good wife. Brave but obedient. Any more obedient and you would not have run out from the fortress that first night. Any braver and you might have escaped successfully. But no, you were just right. The perfect amount of each, my Vittoria."

She wanted to place a hand on his forehead and see just how fevered he was. Perhaps he would not even need poisoning. His body was already trying to shut down. She could wait. The last decade had taught her patience.

But his lips were chapped and bleeding, so before she left, she swapped his pot of beeswax for the one hidden in her skirt pocket and prayed that nobody would notice the faint purple cast. If she was especially lucky, they might even feed some to him in the hope that it would make him feel better. Soline had done the same for her only a few days prior.

With a smile and a curtsy, she left Ardaric to his fate.

Please, Mother, she prayed, uncertain if she was entreating the Mother goddess or her own mother. *Please give him exactly what he deserves.*

Chapter Thirty-Two

In the months they'd spent at war, Vita had learned many valuable things, but the most important lesson was this: no matter how awful things are, keeping up the appearance of an inevitable victory saves you half the battle.

Surely her father had spent these besieged months trying to convey that same illusion of absolute and unquestionable triumph to his people. The floor was crumbling beneath him, but he could never let it show.

Ardaric taught her this, and it was no surprise then that he followed his own rule book.

The attendant arrived at her tent two days later. It was his fierce, whispered argument with Soline that startled Vita from her fitful sleep.

"It's the middle of the night, and the princess is *sleeping*, sir. I'm sure your message can wait."

"It most certainly cannot," the man spit out, though the outline of him was thin as a reed and hardly resembled a soldier prepared to force his way in if she refused. "Wake her up. Now."

"I'm awake. What is your business?"

"Princess," the man said, voice still acidic. Then, realizing whom he was speaking to, he softened his tone into something closer to feigned deference. "Princess, I have news of the general. It is . . ." He blinked, looking between Vita and Soline several times before deciding this was as private an audience as he would likely get. "Urgent. It's urgent."

"Tell me," she commanded, recognizing him as the man with ink-stained fingertips who lived perpetually in Ardaric's shadow. He bowed his head, stepping into the tent. When she nodded for him to speak, he obeyed.

This was what it meant to be respected, she realized. To have the command of even one man who would listen to her whether he liked it or not.

If she went outside while Ardaric lay dying, could she command a hundred men? A thousand? Could she lead battalions and win a war?

Vita knew too little of the world, but she would learn—would consult the best advisors and consider the ramifications of her every decision. She could be a leader that people would want to listen to.

If they gave her a chance, she could do it. Before, this had caused her anxiety, but here, with this man moving to kneel at her feet, she saw a future where she still wore a crown on her head and no shackles on her wrists.

"Your Highness, the general is very ill. He took a turn for the worse this morning. Sorrel, his second-in-command, you may remember—"

"Yes, yes," she whispered, waving a dismissive hand. "I know Sorrel." Horrible, awful Sorrel who didn't care about killing children and was married to Meda's murderer.

"Sorrel is commander in the general's absence, though he hardly fares better against the disease. He may soon become incapacitated himself."

Vita did not bother feigning maidenly distress. A good commander would not do so, and she did not care for either man, so it would be wasted effort. "What of Ardaric's health, then? Do his healers anticipate recovery? The Salajarans will surely try their luck again soon."

"His well-being remains uncertain. The general does not wish for rumors of his ill health to spread. He did not even wish for us to tell you, but it is a matter of grave concern that the people not feel abandoned."

Certainly Ardaric must have a chain of command that extended beyond Sorrel, but wasn't this what princesses and wives were for? To be the beautiful thing that people looked to in times of trouble? To be the thing they blamed later when it all went wrong? She would make an excellent distraction.

"What would you have me do . . ." She left the end of her sentence hanging, gesturing toward him to prompt for a name.

"Ferra, Princess."

"What would you have me do, Ferra? You are the general's secretary, yes? You must have a recommended course of action."

"I would . . ." He paused, pursing his lips.

With far more censure than she felt her once-meek voice could carry, she asked, "Have you not a single thought on the matter, then?"

"No, Your Highness. That's not it at all."

She understood what went unsaid. He did not give opinions, because no one usually asked them of him. But he had plenty— perhaps even in excess.

"I would like to hear your suggestions, sir."

"I think it best to be seen more in the next few days. The general's absence has been noted, and it will become conspicuous in a day or two, especially in light of recent events. We don't have time to lose morale among the ranks, you understand."

"I do. And I agree." She held out a hand to him, helping him up. "Thank you, Ferra. I will call upon you again if required."

She did not go back to sleep, instead dressing for the day. It took longer than usual, as she was still weakened from her time spent bedbound, but with Soline's help, she looked the part of a leader.

When the camp rose for the morning, Vita ventured out to a fire where men and women with deep lines of exhaustion marring their faces awaited breakfast, and instead of standing silently on the outskirts, she joined with a small bit of honey to add to their pot.

They tried to wave her off, but she said, "Please. I would like you to have this."

"In that case, won't you stay and eat with us, Princess?" asked one of the men, however reluctant he felt at sharing their food with another mouth. She smiled and sat beside a young woman with her long hair braided back from her face, but Vita only took the smallest portion when they offered it to her.

At first, they mostly ignored Vita's presence among them, listening as one of the older soldiers finished a story that he must have started the night before. Then a younger man chose a story, telling it with elaborate hand gestures. He had to double back each time he forgot an important detail, and his performance had the whole circle, Vita included, in much better spirits by the end.

Emboldened, she chimed in with a tale of her own, memorized years before in her tower room.

At first, the circle quieted, unpleasantly reminded of their interloper. But when Vita got to the part of the story with the hedge witch and her golden chicken, everyone laughed at the ridiculous voice she put on. They were a far more engaged audience than her crows had ever been. It didn't take long after that before the girl beside her was smiling and the man who invited her to sit was smacking her on the back like she was his old friend.

At lunch, she joined another fire. Then she wandered from group to group until dinner, smiling and listening to war stories and pretending that meeting so many people wasn't at all overwhelming.

"You're good at this," Soline whispered two days later. As they walked through the camp, people at various campfires waved her over to join them. Her presence was coveted now, not tolerated.

"I'm trying very hard not to puke," Vita admitted, feeling nauseous from all the touching that people did when they wanted to be your friend. "But I'm going to be good at this no matter what it takes."

Vita would become the thing that brought them joy in a hopeless situation. She would make them love her.

And for the next several days, she kept to this plan, watching as Sorrel glared at her with lifeless, sunken eyes until eventually his hand shook so badly on his pommel that he had to hide it in his coat.

By the time he stopped showing up in the mornings to police Vita's every move, hardly anyone noticed at all.

Vita noticed.

Chapter Thirty-Three

"Archers! To your defenses!"

A horn blared so harshly through the once-calm morning that Vita spilled hot water all over herself, scalding her fingers.

"What's happening?" she asked, silently to herself at first and then again, louder, to Ivo as she ran toward him. In the absence of both Ardaric and Sorrel, Ivo had run into the center of camp and made the call to arms. "Tell me what's happening."

Ivo had armed himself with as many weapons as he could carry. "An assault. The Messilians inside and the Salajarans outside, both attacking the weak points to the northwest. There was no warning."

"Both at once?" she asked, surprised.

Grimly, he nodded. "Yes."

Vita curled her fist around the dagger at her side. With his ring lost to magic, the dagger that Marius had selected for her was the only thing she had left of him. "How would they have coordinated the simultaneous start? They have no way to communicate."

Ivo shook his head, dark hair falling into his eyes. Though he was far older than both Soline and Vita, he looked strangely like a boy in that moment, as though neither pain nor age had touched him until now. Rationally, Vita knew it wasn't true. He'd seen war. Seen his own brother slaughtered by the man he was still forced to serve. But when she saw through the facade of strength, he looked as innocent as Vita had once been.

"No time to worry about it now. You are safest here, as far as possible from both walls. Tell Soline where we have gone and not to worry for us. I will make sure Kellen makes it back safely."

"And you," she said, laying a hand on his arm to stop him from rushing off. His leather pauldron was not even fully buckled onto his shoulder, hanging off him like a wilting flower. "She will not forgive either of us if you are hurt."

Though Vita knew little of harnessing armor, she fiddled with the buckle until it seemed tight enough.

"When you return," she said, offering him no other option, "we will discuss what must be done now that half the chain of command is not of sound body and mind."

Ivo bit his lip before tersely nodding. "Yes, Your Highness."

"May you be granted swift victory," she said, stealing the last line of another leader's famous battle speech.

"There can be no peace?" he asked, using the familiar Carcan words.

"No." She smiled grimly, feeling, for perhaps the first time, more like a Kasrian warrior-queen than a Carcan princess. "No. Today, for our enemies, there can be no hope. Do you understand?"

He nodded again. This time, though his hair still fell into his eyes, he looked ready to carry out that order. "Yes. I understand perfectly."

Vita ran to the western side of camp, watching the fights taking place on both walls. She should have followed Ivo's instructions to stay away, but she couldn't spend the day wondering if their camp would be taken over. Better to be killed quickly, in that case.

By the time the Salajarans withdrew to regroup, the sun was already setting and Vita had bitten her nails down to the quick. The Messilians pulled back shortly after.

Kasrian soldiers poured off the walls, weary and bloodied. Some were pulled down like limp sacks of grain, and it was clear that nothing could be done for them. No poultice or tonic or magic could bring them back.

Lacking any place better to convene, Ferra allowed Vita to host a meeting of the general's remaining council in Ardaric's tent. In the back, closed off by a curtain, Ardaric still grunted and groaned in his sleep, fighting to stay alive.

Vita rather enjoyed the gentle chorus of his agony, and she doubly enjoyed watching all of Ardaric's remaining supporters listen to him die while trying to plan for the battle that surely awaited them on both fronts again tomorrow.

"And where is Sorrel Aventicus?" Vita asked, tracing her fingers over the line of the outer wall drawn on the table. "Surely he was not lost in the battle. I wish to hear his report."

A man with deep wrinkles lining his face shook his head. He appeared far too old to still be besieging castles, but he was one of the few who didn't treat Vita like an imbecile as she played at commanding them. "He did not fight at all, Your Highness. His illness grows worse."

"Hm," she said, finger tapping against the side of her face as she thought. "How unfortunate for him. Then who took command? I only know of Ivo making the call for the archers. Surely you had contingencies in place for this. The illness's spread is certainly not news. Sorrel's own second-in-command has been sick since I was, and his third is dead."

"I did," the man said, bowing his head with no small degree of pride. Was he the type of man to envision himself as a Carcan king should Ardaric die? Many things dwindled with age, but rarely ambition. "Aart Svaldalur, ma'am."

Vita ran her tongue over her teeth before saying, "Very well. And what of the cavalry, Svaldalur? I noticed they were not engaged today."

"We have made a concentrated effort not to use the cavalry since the Salajarans closed us in, Your Highness," Svaldalur said. Ivo, sitting one seat to her left, nodded in agreement. "To make proper use of them, we would have to be outside the walls, engaging the Salajarans on an equal playing field. The wall has thus far been to our advantage."

"And you expect it will stay this way?" she asked, genuinely curious. Walls, Ardaric had taught her, could be formidable allies. It was for that reason that they hadn't knocked down the walls around Messilio already. But if the Salajarans could not waste time starving the Kasrians out, then they would find a way in, whether over the walls or through. The Kasrian defenses, put up as quickly as they were, would not hold up to the same attacks that Messilio's could. Eventually, given enough time, the Salajarans would break through.

"No. I think—and the council agrees—that, should another attack come tomorrow, we will need to be ready to fight them out in the open. They have done considerable damage to the fortifications."

Vita stared at Svaldalur, trying to measure some unnamable thing within him. "Ready how?"

"We did not barricade ourselves in without escapes, just as Messilio did not build its own walls without hidden routes. Tonight, we will sneak our cavalry out under the cover of darkness using the southernmost exit."

"Straight into the Salajaran camp? To be slaughtered?"

Svaldalur grimaced. "With any luck, no. We will need them if we are to survive."

Ivo laid out their plan, moving pieces around the table to show where they would target.

"We will send the cavalry out through this exit point, and they will sneak behind the Salajaran camp here." Ivo tapped the place marked by a Salajaran standard. "They will not act until morning. Then, when the sun rises, the infantry within the walls will split to fight the Messilians on one side and the Salajarans on the other, as we did today. But the Salajarans will not expect to be overtaken from behind too. They will be focused on the wall, and that is when the cavalry will ride in and cut them down."

"And you believe this plan is achievable even in the absence of the general? You believe yourself up to this task?" Vita appraised Svaldalur. He was old, and his breathing noticeably wheezed in the quiet of the room.

"The Salajaran numbers are much smaller than we first assumed," Svaldalur reassured her. "This was likely a voluntary mission. Maybe even a full contingent of sellswords. Either way, they are not defending their own lands, and they may choose to flee if they see us as a formidable threat."

"We only have to even the playing field," Ivo said. "The siege could be finished by the end of the week. Maybe the end of tomorrow."

"You think that if the Salajarans flee, then my father will concede?"

"I think he will have no choice." Ivo's voice was strong and sure. "His army is on its last legs. His people are starving. Without outside support, he will not be able to continue."

Vita opened her mouth to ask another question, but when she looked around at the assembled group, she realized that they weren't asking her permission to execute this plan. Of course not. They weren't even truly asking her opinion. They were simply informing her, in the absence of some greater authority, so that, should Ardaric recover, their efforts would not seem like a coup.

She nodded, unwilling to call attention to what everyone already knew about her status in this room. "Very well. We will send the cavalry out tonight. There is no encampment by the intended exit?"

"None that we can see, Your Highness," Svaldalur said. "Our exterior wall is miles long, and there aren't enough Salajarans to do more than standard patrols. In the dark, we should be able to time it so that even the horses can escape undetected."

"And will the cavalry be prepared in time?"

"They've already received their orders," Svaldalur assured her.

"Good. And what would you have me do? I was useless today, but I would not like to find myself that way again. In the absence of the general and Sorrel Aventicus, there must be some way to utilize me."

Svaldalur smiled, but though his words were as kindly spoken as everything else he'd said thus far, his expression felt gently patronizing, like she was a small girl asking how she might best chuck dolls at the enemy. "Your safety is our greatest asset. If we lose you, we lose the general's mandate for restoring your rightful claim to the throne. Staying out of the way is how you can help."

Being summarily dismissed was not unfamiliar to Vita, but this time, it stung.

She was no fighter. Had no talent with a bow or a sword. Was nothing like the women who donned their own leathers and painted their faces.

But she would not be forgotten again. Would not be left to gather cobwebs.

"You're all dismissed. May we be granted a swift victory."

If the councillors were surprised with the abrupt send-off, they did not argue.

As they cleared out, she followed after Ivo.

"Not you," she ordered.

"What?"

"Why will they give me no role? At the very least, they could use me to rally the troops. Purely ceremonial. I'm not unaware of my limitations."

They stood in the threshold of Ardaric's tent. Ivo glanced around at the soldiers slumped beneath the open sky, sleeping as close to the fires as they could. Each of them still wore their boots and leather armor. They could be ready to fight at a moment's notice, crust still clinging to their eyes. "They are worried."

"About what?"

"Plenty of things. They don't know enough about you to trust that you can handle taking on more."

"And?"

"And what?"

"If that was the main issue, they might have just said. It is not news to me that I am young and inexperienced. There are other reasons."

"Fine. The Messilians, for a start."

"What about them?"

"How did they know where the Salajarans would attack? How were they able to coordinate so precisely?"

"That's what I asked you."

"That's what everyone is asking, Princess. Forgive me, but there are a number of people who saw a concentrated attack by two sides with no clear mode of communication and began to draw their own conclusions."

"And what? They think—" The words were on her lips before she could fully understand them, and when she finally did, she almost had to sit down. "They think I was the link? An informant?"

"Some might. You are a Messilian princess. No matter how poorly you have been treated, there will always be those who wonder if you aren't secretly on your father's side."

"His side! Are they—how could they think that?" To avenge her mother and see her father finally brought to justice, she had signed away the rest of her life to a man who would bleed her dry of any usefulness she had left. There were a lot of things she was willing to do—up to and including killing Ardaric—but she certainly wouldn't spy for her father. She did still want the Kasrians to win in the end.

Although, all things considered, that likely wasn't an exonerating argument.

"Until tonight, I did not even know what our army was doing. How do they think I could be an informant without information?"

Ivo rolled his eyes, pulling her closer in an effort to keep her quiet. "They don't. None of the saner ones, anyway. But some of the foot soldiers won't care about how implausible it is, and some of the captains and lieutenants don't care if it's untrue.

The Messilians could have released a bird that we didn't manage to shoot down. A message could have been sent downriver in a bottle and made it into the right hands. But none of that matters when there's someone easier to blame. The general is dying—might not live long enough to see our victory. They are all vying for power, and you are in the way, neither fully Carcan nor Kasrian. You're easily disposed of if one wants to try."

Though Vita's hands shook, she clasped them together in front of her and forced them to be still. "Then I will make myself indispensable."

Chapter Thirty-Four

Vita dressed in her finest clothing by candlelight.

Despite the early hour, Isotta had hunted down a white dress that had been tucked away in an unopened trunk since they'd left Novogna. It had fine brocade detailing all along the bodice, and the heavy fabric of the skirt concealed a pair of equally white trousers. The sleeves were stiff around her upper arms but draped down at her elbows, long and elegant. If she'd been planning to carry a sword, they would have hindered her, but this was strictly about pageantry.

With the chain of command still muddied, Isotta had also managed to get into the guarded jewels and withdraw several pieces. There were a necklace of bloodred rubies to hug Vita's exposed collarbone, a ring that resembled a proper signet, and a golden diadem. These pieces were earmarked for Vita's use only after she was crowned queen. Having never been entrusted into her care, they were spared the fate of the jewels that burned in the fire.

Vita adjusted the diadem as Soline fiddled with the long, intricate braid she was weaving down Vita's back. Her fingers were uncommonly clumsy in the dark.

"Stop worrying," Vita tried to order, though her voice was

both too soft and too fond for the command to bear any weight. "All will be well. I swear."

"Are you sure you want to do this? You're not a fighter."

Vita scowled. She loved weaving and reading and sewing. She loved poetry and birdsong, and truthfully, she'd never taken to having a dagger in her hand no matter how hard Marius worked to make it feel natural. She wasn't a fighter and had no wish to be.

But it stung some buried part of her to know that if she'd been a son, warfare would have been her birthright. They would've given her the finest instructors from boyhood and taught her to protect her kingdom as it deserved to be protected.

"I'm not a soldier. But there are many ways to fight for something, and I owe it to myself to do what I can."

"What about what Ivo said?" Soline asked, having heard the whole story upon Vita's return. "They don't trust you, Vita. You aren't safe."

"Some people don't trust me because of wrong conclusions. If I'm ever to have a future here among these people, I need to prove them wrong. And I will."

"And if you die?"

Vita laughed mirthlessly. "We might all die. We're trapped between two enemies with no clear escape. If this goes wrong, it won't matter where I've hidden myself."

Soline sighed, dropping her forehead to Vita's shoulder. "I don't like to imagine you dead."

"Then imagine me alive and happy. That's how I always imagine you," Vita said, running a hand through Soline's hair. Weapon strapped to her side, Soline was dressed for combat, but her hair still hung loose around her shoulders. "We'll win; Ardaric will finally choke on his own vomit, and we'll take Messilio. No one is going to hand me something good, so I must take it for myself."

"But will we be happy?"

"Yes." Vita turned and pressed a kiss to the top of Soline's bowed head. "I always thought I could only have little dreams. There's never been room for anything bigger until now."

"And what is your big dream? A crown? A kingdom?"

"All of it. A crown, a kingdom," she confirmed, "and you."

"And me," Soline whispered.

"Yes," Vita said, voice shaking as she smiled. "And you."

The candlelight made Soline's face look gaunt, but she tried to smile. "Okay. We will win; Ardaric will die; and you will take Messilio. Ivo and his people will ensure it."

Vita laughed again, this time less jaded. "I don't think Ivo trusts me very much."

"Ivo doesn't trust anyone very much," Soline said, pushing Vita away teasingly, "but he's smart enough to fight for you. Ardaric will destroy us all even if we do win. It's only a matter of time. And even if he dies, his inner circle is no better."

"But Ivo barely knows me. Does he really think I'm the best option?"

"Ivo knows *me*, Vita." Soline drew her in for a gentle kiss. "And I trust you."

Vita hiked up her skirts and mounted Vipsania before letting them drape over the horse's flanks. Soline stood at her right knee, and together they watched as the first tendrils of light sprung forth on the horizon. Eda sat perched on her shoulder, dark and imposing as her beady eyes flicked back and forth, making Vita look far more wild than Ardaric's careful cultivation of her appearance ever permitted.

Soldiers were stationed atop both walls, ready to fling projectiles and shoot arrows and defend themselves until there was no one left standing. The rest of their troops, huddled masses bearing any weapons that were still serviceable, looked up at her as Vipsania forced her way through the horde to its center.

"My *amardinnen*!" Vita called. The word caught their attention. It was a colloquialism local to Kasri used for those closer than friends; it was spoken only between comrades bonded by the specter of death. No other island in the Alstrins had even a cognate of it, and though Vita could understand its meaning logically, she knew its greater effect was lost to her. It was entirely their own. "We face the gravest day of our campaign yet, where sickness has beaten us down and hunger has left us weak!"

Soline had urged her repeatedly not to harp on the bad—to do so, she said, would never motivate anyone—but Vita could not imagine ignoring the truth. The people *were* tired. They *were* hungry. They *were* fighting against starvation and disease with everything they had. Each day they'd been here was a battle.

There was a pain in them that Vita could not ignore.

"The Messilians and the Salajarans are prepared to use these weaknesses against us. They wish to tear through our camp and leave nothing behind but ashes.

"They believe they can do this because they have never seen the Kasrians fighting at full tilt. They have never seen the valor of every person here who will choose death before dishonor! They have only ever heard of warrior-queens in stories—today they will meet one! Today they will bow before one or die before one. Those are the only choices for those who seek to quell our advances. This is *our* fort! These are *our* walls! And by tonight, Messilio will be *our* city! We will fight to the last to see Carca freed from a tyrant king!"

She didn't know if they truly thought her father a tyrant. She didn't care. After all, Vita had never seen the Kasrians as liberators. What mattered was the way they cheered for her from all sides as she shouted the words. That they convinced themselves that there was still a reason to fight.

"We have faced setbacks, and now we will have our reward! Today—victory! Tomorrow—our spoils!"

Swords and axes and spears were raised high into the air around her as the crowd roared. Those closest to Vita reached out to touch her feet in the stirrups. Eda let out a piercing caw before launching herself off of Vita's shoulder and into the sky.

"You know your roles. You know how to win. I will be right there with you all, ready to die for this land. For Carca!"

And in unison, thousands of people who hadn't been born here—who had no family buried in this soil, who responded best to northern phrases over local ones—shouted out, "For Carca!"

Chapter Thirty-Five

While everyone else fell into position, Vita joined the few remaining cavalry stationed near the hidden exit in the wall. The rest of their party had slipped out hours ago, but those who remained would be the distraction that would thrust the whole morning into battle.

There was a man toward the back of the party, short and ruddy-cheeked but marvelously brave looking atop his horse. Hands shaking on her reins, Vita steered Vipsania to his side.

His eyes cut over to her from where they'd been staring at the wall, perhaps hoping to spy a glimpse of his future. He swallowed slowly. "Your Highness." He dipped his head in a respectful bow, and Vita returned the gesture.

"Sir."

"You gave a wonderful speech."

"Thank you. I was nervous," she admitted.

"I suppose we all are now that it's here. You didn't look it, though."

"How did you end up as part of the charge?" she asked. Vita knew they had scrambled to coordinate the final details last night, but it was unclear how these riders were selected. Their job was the most dangerous of all.

He pressed his lips together before taking a deep, calming breath. "I volunteered."

"You're very brave, then. Braver than my father. Braver than any royal, perhaps."

"No, no, not at all, Princess."

Vita laughed, watching the way orange streaked the sky above them. For how many people would this be the final sunrise? "Trust me, you are. I've met kings and commanders and all manner of people. Anyone who chooses to charge into battle first is braver than any nobleman who hides behind the line and pretends at his own importance."

The man looked askance, uncertain if agreeing with her was tantamount to treason against his own general-king. But if Ardaric lay dying, did it really matter? Vita stood here before him, flesh and blood and ready to commiserate.

Finally, instead of rebuffing her, he bowed his head and said, "Thank you."

Vita held Vipsania's reins in iron-tight fists but did not direct her away, even as plans were disseminated among the riders to ready for the charge.

"What is your name?" she asked.

"Berimund." His voice was a choked whisper.

"Do you have family here, Berimund? Or people waiting for your triumphant return at home?" For some reason, the fear that this one man—this stranger—might die alone in a foreign land made her want to tuck him away. She couldn't save all of them, but maybe saving Berimund would be enough.

He smiled. "My wife volunteered as well. She's up there by the wall, finalizing the last of our orders." He pointed toward a dark-haired woman at the front with fierce lines of black smudged across her face. Despite the gravity of the orders she received, she caught Berimund's eye, and her lips quirked up at the corners.

"You've both chosen the front lines?"

"I was sick during the first wave. We didn't expect I'd survive, and then when I did . . . I thought I would never get out of here. I could have gone with the rest of the cavalry and been out already, but I was afraid that once I got free, I'd just keep riding and never come back," he said, admitting freely to his worries the way she had earlier. What harm was there now that they'd reached the end? "And I couldn't do that to my wife—couldn't let her face the dishonor. I knew she would have followed me, and I knew that she didn't deserve to be called a coward too. So when they asked for people to stay and cause the distraction, even knowing it meant almost certain death, I just . . . needed to prove to myself that I was brave enough."

"And your wife?"

Berimund laughed, and his whole face changed with it. Suddenly his rounded cheeks glowed, and a spark lit his eyes. "She's the better fighter. Volunteered to protect my sorry ass, she did. I tried to convince her to join the others in the Salajaran camp, but she wouldn't have it. If we make it out of this alive, she's never going to let me forget that I wanted to send her away."

Vita smiled, imagining a home filled with Berimund's laughter and his wife's passion. "Then I pray you have many years of being suitably berated."

"Thank you, Princess."

The man beside Berimund started teasing him about his wife, and then a woman a few people over joined in, and suddenly everyone wanted to tell Vita about why they themselves were here. The families they had at home or the people they'd lost or what it meant to them to start again someplace new. Some of them had relatives in Carca and roots they wished to return to. Others felt they had no place else to go. A few reached out to touch her hand as she listened, as though it were its own kind of blessing to be in communion here with her.

Though many had shining eyes, the joy of remembrance on their faces as they spoke was real.

"Tomorrow," she said, trying to sound half as brave as they did, "after we've secured our victory, we will all celebrate together."

When at last they were called to order and the wall was opened, the cries of their charge were buoyed with new hope.

It took mere moments before the clamor of steel striking steel rang through the air. Vita did not usually pray, but she prayed for them.

Then, she turned Vipsania around and rode for Soline.

The catapults began firing to her left, huge stones sailing over the no-man's-land and into the city. Soldiers stationed at the inner wall ran through an opening to meet her father's army in a great clash. They would fight on the bones of those children who had perished so many months before.

She hoped her father was afraid.

"There you are," Vita shouted over the din, pulling Vipsania to a quick stop as she spied Soline with her own massive sword in her hands. "Where are you going?"

She dismounted, cutting Soline off before she could break away.

"Kellen is outside the walls already, and I can't help him." He'd been in command of one of the first battalions to sneak out the night before, and by now they might already be attacking the Salajarans from behind, splitting their focus. "But Ivo and his men were assigned to the Messilian attack, so I'm going to join them there." Then, more quietly, she said, "Don't ask me to stay behind and hide when I haven't asked it of you."

Though Soline had never been in Ardaric's army as a soldier, she had trained with her brothers long enough to stand her ground. Still, Vita's breath caught in her chest as she imagined Soline in the thick of it.

"I will come with you, then."

"Vita," she said chidingly.

"I know. I'm not a fighter. But I can still do something. Here," she said, handing Soline the reins. "Take Vipsania. You will have greater use for her. Protect your brother, and she will do what she can to protect you. And so will I."

She pressed a lingering kiss to Soline's cheek, the pandemonium around them the perfect cover. Then, squeezing her shoulder, she said, "Go."

Vita watched her ride away before running toward the line of catapults.

"I can help," she said to the first person she saw. The boy was young and clearly struggling to roll a massive stone by himself.

He looked up from his task before shooing her away. "I don't think—"

Vita looked down at the white dress she still wore. When she'd chosen it, she had done so thinking only of the speech. But now that the battle had begun, she could not bear to wait it out in her tent when she'd sworn to the soldiers that she would be with them. Her words had been symbolic, and they likely had all known it, but what good would she be if she abandoned them all now?

Drawing her dagger, she made quick work of cutting off the excess fabric of the drop sleeves. The skirt was simpler—it detached from the bodice with easily severed ties to reveal the riding trousers beneath. "There. Now show me how to help."

He pointed wordlessly toward their pile of projectiles and didn't try to stop her from helping roll one toward the massive bucket. Those in a group farther down the line were loading theirs with dead bodies. When the boy and Vita had theirs ready, he muttered a prayer.

"Careful," he said, pulling her away so that it could be deployed.

The stone sailed beyond their walls until it disappeared from view. Over the cacophony of battle, she heard it crash somewhere in the city. How many people had she just killed? Vita would never be able to keep a tally.

Maybe it was for the best.

"Down!" someone shouted, and the boy instinctively threw himself and Vita to the ground, though the wall had been protecting them well enough. A split second later, she heard dozens of thwacking sounds as arrows pierced the ground a few paces behind them. One of the men operating the smaller catapults atop the wall screamed as an arrowhead embedded itself in his chest. He stumbled over the edge before landing beside Vita and the boy.

"Still want to help?" the boy asked, trying not to look at the dead man.

The boy was older than Vita first thought—perhaps her age. His hair was blond and curly, though even in the cold morning it was damp with sweat.

"I do. Let's reset the bucket."

They rolled another stone, panting beneath its weight, and watched as it made its curved arc across the sky.

And again. And again.

Something landed on her shoulder, and she jerked back before realizing it was Eda. "There you are," she said, relief coating the words. "You should get out of here."

Eda squawked out a horrible noise, and Vita had only a moment to consider what it meant before she was diving to the ground again, a wave of arrows hitting just behind where she had stood.

She took several shallow breaths, trying to steady herself. "Thanks for that."

Eda headbutted Vita's ear.

"Oh gods," the blond boy whispered, staring back toward the outer edge of camp.

"What?"

"Where is everyone?" he asked, climbing up for a better view. Vita scrambled behind him. The cavalry was busy outside, but the outer wall itself looked empty of those meant to be defending it. Where had the archers and swordsmen gone?

Their camp was still relatively untouched by the battle, sandwiched between the two walls protecting them. But if the Salajarans breached that final defense, everyone inside would die.

"What can we do?" she asked, already brushing off the knees of her trousers in preparation to stand and fight however she could. He put a hand on her shoulder, keeping her down behind one of the barricades.

"Nothing. We're on catapults. Since they won't help us maintain our defenses, all we can do is keep trying to bring down the city. I'm sure they have contingency plans out there."

"We can't wait. We have to help somehow."

"What are *you* going to do? Man the wall on your own? Do you even know how to use a sword?"

She touched the dagger at her hip, frowning. "No. But someone has to try. We can't—"

Before she could finish her thought, they watched as a lone rider burst across their nearly empty camp, heading straight for the wall.

The boy gasped. "Is that—"

"Ardaric?" Vita said, brow furrowed. Surely he couldn't have survived the poison. He'd been gasping with each breath just last night, and everyone had carefully avoided calling it what it was: a death rattle.

That's when she knew, with frustrating certainty, that the pot of beeswax with its faint purple cast must have remained untouched. He hadn't been dying because of her—he hadn't been dying at all. He'd been deep in the grips of the strangers' sickness, but evidently he'd been *recovering*. Now there was no hope that he would slip quietly away.

He looked tall and poised atop Magritte even from so far away, his head held high. Ardaric carried his axe like it was weightless, and as soon as he passed through the wall, he swung his weapon and decapitated a Salajaran trying to get in.

Vita gasped, staring at the detached head, only a dot in the distance. Just another body to add to the piles.

"Come on," she said, forcing herself to forget about him for now as she returned to the ground. "The general has it in hand. Let's reload."

Chapter Thirty-Six

Renewed Kasrian battle cries rang out behind them intermittently for the next several hours. She and the boy climbed up again to use one of the smaller catapults mounted there to shoot burning payloads into the city. Anytime Vita permitted herself to look back toward the Salajaran fight, she saw Ardaric cutting down his enemies in huge swathes, rarely slowing between kills.

Awe in his voice, the boy said, "They're scaling the wall."

"What?" she asked, shocked. The Salajarans could be at their throats in minutes if they were climbing the defenses.

The boy shook his head. "No, there," he said, pointing ahead. "Our people are scaling the Messilian walls."

Vita turned, taking in the bodies strewn across the open field. In the distance, she could see the little ant-like figures climbing ladders they'd lined up along the Messilian curtain wall.

"It's over. It's over—we won."

"It's not over," Vita said, watching as desperate Carcan soldiers dumped anything they could find on the ascending Kasrians. "We don't know if they'll succeed."

"It's only a matter of time now." Someone tumbled off the ladder when he was pelted with stones, landing in a broken heap on the ground. Three new ladders materialized against the wall, and there was no shortage of people ready to take the dead man's place climbing. "Their army is destroyed. This is a final act of desperation. It won't stop anything. Eventually, someone will get in, and more will follow."

"Truly?" she asked, hands clenched in her lap where they crouched and watched the scene. The catapults no longer fired. "It's over?"

Tears sprung up behind her eyes as she struggled to picture the months of torment finally ending.

They'd won, but Ardaric was still alive. Hale and healthy and once again a war hero.

"It is," he said, putting a hand over hers to still their shaking. "It's over."

Swallowing thickly, she wiped grime off her cheeks before straightening the diadem still braided into her hair. "Do I look all right?"

He barked out a laugh before realizing she was asking in earnest. "Um, yes? Or . . . you look battle hardened. And that's better."

"Good. Yes, that's good. Then I need to go down there."

"Down? Why? They'll be done soon—you can wait here until it's over."

Vita shook her head, rising to tidy her hastily cut-up outfit. Dirt and blood stained the white, though she'd remained as far from the actual bloodshed as someone could. He was right, though—if she showed up looking as pristine as she had this morning, no one would respect her. This was better.

"Ardaric is still outside, fighting off the last of the Salajarans. I'm sure they'll flee once they realize that Messilio is falling. But until then, I need to be down there."

Before he could offer a rebuttal, she started climbing down.

Then, not wanting to forget, she poked her head up over the side of the wall again. "You fought very well. Thank you for letting me work beside you."

The boy—the man—offered her a genuine smile. "It was an honor, Your Highness."

"What is your name?"

"Winnog."

She nodded. "Winnog. Good. I'll remember that. Winnog." She made to jump the rest of the way down, before remembering to add, "I'm Vita. Pleasure to meet you."

With Eda still on her shoulder, she marched across the muddy ground that had once been empty, staring straight ahead at the massive city gates. They were closed, but soon they would creak open in triumph. The Messilian archers were all dead.

Off to her left, skirmishes were still petering out, but Vita didn't bother unsheathing her dagger. If they wanted to kill her, they would.

She stopped in the shadow of the great gate, a lone figure waiting. The Kasrians manning the ladders paused to watch her before sending another volley of men up. Vita kept her chin raised and her fists unclenched at her sides as the wind blew tendrils of hair across her face.

"There you are," Soline said, riding up beside her on Vipsania. Though Vita released a deep breath at the sound of her voice, she did not turn away from her goal.

"I'm so relieved that you're okay," she said under her breath. Vita shifted her eyes to the side, Soline in her peripheral vision. She looked bedraggled but bore no visible wounds beyond surface scratches, and Vita released a sigh. "I worried for you."

Soline grinned. "And I worried for you, but here we both are."

"Yes. And Ardaric too."

Soline inhaled sharply, and Vita returned to watching the wall. "Ardaric?"

"Yes. Went to fight the Salajarans. He still lives. Without him, the outer contingent might have fallen."

"Then the army owes him this victory," Soline said solemnly. "Yes."

"You should ride Vipsania in," she said as she dismounted, handing Vita the reins. "Here. So you will be more visible."

Vita climbed atop Vipsania, comforted by the animal's presence. If it all went wrong, maybe she and Soline could make a run for it with Vipsania and Eda as guides.

"Are we making a mistake?" Vita asked. "Should we be trying to sneak away in the chaos?"

"I think it's been too late to run since before we left Novogna. So we'll just have to figure out a new plan before everything falls apart."

Vita nodded, watching raptly as the Kasrians chased off the last of the guards on the wall. They would have to first raise the portcullis and then open the heavy wooden doors, but judging by the sound of metal scraping metal, it would only be a few minutes at most.

Kellen rose up to Vita's other side, sword drawn like he was her guard. Out of Soline's living brothers, he was the one who looked most like her, and though he was several years older, they might have been twins. He had her same sharp features and dark, canny eyes. "Ivo says they will be ready soon."

"Good," Vita said, then softened her voice to add, "I'm glad you're safe, Kellen. I know Soline worries."

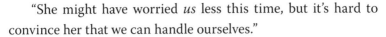

"She might have worried *us* less this time, but it's hard to convince her that we can handle ourselves."

Soline let out an aggrieved huff.

Ahead of them, Ivo coordinated the opening of the gates, commanding all those on the wall. The portcullis clicked into place at the top. "How are your men?" Vita asked.

Kellen grimaced, but he didn't look stricken. "We sustained heavy injuries in the fight against the Salajarans, but I think that many will recover if they're treated quickly enough, which is all we can ask for. The sooner we can take the castle and move them inside, the better."

"Isotta has been taking care of them back at camp, I think," Soline added. "The way she works, the whole of the army will be ready to fight again by dinner."

The doors groaned open, and before she could second-guess herself, Vita prodded Vipsania forward.

She expected to go through alone, uncertain what dangers would await her on the other side: desperate soldiers, raging fires, piles of debris. As they proceeded, though, dozens of worn-down Kasrians flocked behind her horse, following her like she was their king.

Nobody stopped Vita as she processed through the city, tracking her way down the wide streets toward the castle ahead.

It took until they were in the courtyard itself for Ardaric to catch up to her.

When he did, sitting atop Magritte, a long gash in his leg and scratches all over his cheeks, he pressed a kiss to her cheek and whispered, low and almost menacing, "My Vittoria. My little warrior-queen."

Vita couldn't force herself to meet his eyes.

Chapter Thirty-Seven

By the time Vita was permitted to set foot back in the home of her childhood, dozens of guards had already run inside in squadrons, weapons raised and prepared to cut down the last defenders of the king.

She didn't know how many people bothered to keep fighting at that point, knowing all was lost, but as she walked through the castle, it seemed remarkably untouched by violence.

"Your father will be transferred to my custody," Ardaric said, waltzing through the halls with the arrogance of a man who knew he now owned the place. "We need only uncover him."

In spite of her concern that a desperate soldier might appear at any moment, Vita sagged against one of the cold stone walls. Everything about this was wrong—here with her father and her fiancé in a place that held such terrible memories—and yet the safety of a fortress was all she'd known for so long. The built-up tension from months of sieging finally ebbed away.

They'd won. They'd taken Messilio—whatever that meant for the future.

"What of Drusus?" she asked. They'd known so little about the Salajaran general's fighting style going into the battle, and yet she'd heard no mention of him since.

"Oh, he was easy to kill," Ardaric laughed. The whites of his eyes looked bright and manic against his war-splattered cheeks. "I didn't even have to dismount Magritte to cut him down. Barely put up a fight. And to think—that is Salajara's best!"

They congregated in the throne room off the great hall, waiting for updates. It took only minutes for a boy about Vita's age to be marched in wearing heavy chains. His head was bleeding and his eyes looked glassy, but he walked with minimal assistance.

"Ah," Ardaric said, taking the boy's chin in his hands and turning it back and forth. "Vittoria, meet your brother."

His hair was a few shades darker than hers, almost a light brown, and Vita tried to see her cheekbones, her eyes, her mouth reflected in him. There were similarities there, but the more she looked, the more a stranger he became.

"Elio the Bastard! Your father left you to be captured by the enemy but hid himself away?" He offered his bride a smile, gesturing her forward so that the siblings might meet each other face to face. "And you thought you were his only unloved child, my dear, but today we learn that this is simply his way. All of his heirs are disposable."

The boy glared. "My *father*—"

"Will be executed in due course, as will you," Ardaric cut in. "Do you have anything to say to your sister before then? This will be your one chance."

Elio pressed his lips together, glaring at her with a visceral, seething hatred.

"Very well, then. Take him to the dungeons." The guards at Elio's side dragged him out again, the clattering of his chains growing more distant. Then, Ardaric clapped his hands together. "Are you pleased, Vittoria? Your long-awaited family reunion and the promise of vengeance. Now all we need is to unearth your father, and this can finally end. Do you know where he might hide? A place known only to your family?"

Reports had already come in, informing them that his office and chambers had been ransacked, with no sign of the king. And though it was deemed unlikely, both her mother's rooms and Vita's from her childhood had been searched too.

His new wife was found dead in Vita's mother's bed, clutching a bottle of poison.

"I don't know anything of his habits," she said, stepping away from Ardaric to pace. Vita rubbed the heels of her hands into her eyes to clear away the fog of the day. How could Ardaric have been all but dead to her only this morning? How had meeting Berimund and his wife been hours ago, and now nobody knew if they were dead or alive?

She needed to sleep, but no one would allow that until her father was captured.

"But you have guesses?"

She stopped in place, staring at the ground for a moment before nodding.

"Then lead the way."

It would take Ardaric's men hours to search every room in the castle, and if her father was on the move, he could evade them for longer still. But in the back of her mind, there was only one place she could picture him waiting for her, despite how little time he'd spent there in her childhood.

When they exited the great hall, her feet took her immediately to the right, and then down a long hall and up a set of stairs. Vita didn't have to think about it; she'd been so lost in Castel Poletta, but she knew the exact route she needed now, like her mind had always been trying to take her down this path. The major arteries of her home were scarred into her memory.

She rubbed the stitching on the side of her trousers as she walked. Ardaric's heavy gait remained always two steps behind.

There was a small wooden door hidden in a dark alcove. She pushed it open, the latch on it a heavy, rusted iron. It used to be kept locked, but the last few months must have made it less of a priority. Sunset cast the whole of her family's private gardens in brilliant oranges.

The flowers were all dead for the season. Couldn't this small patch of land have been used to grow food through the summer before the cold swept in? How many of the gardens had been left overgrown and untended while people starved?

She shook her head against the thought, focusing instead on the hedge maze at the center of the garden.

"Ah," Ardaric said. "Not the wisest hiding place, but one that would require enough time to be frustrating."

"Not for me. I know this maze."

She followed the turns easily—a right, three lefts, another right, then the center path. They moved through several twists that never gave her a moment's pause. Eventually, they reached the point from which every subsequent turn was a left, a joke conceived by the ancestor who had commissioned the maze, and she knew then that they were close.

The scene at the center was expected and unexpected at once: part of her had thought her father would run, using some hidden tunnel or secret door that had never been divulged to her. But he was there, sitting on the fountain's rim like he was waiting.

The fountain was off, the water drained and the pool filled with fallen leaves and debris. It was easier to focus on that than on her father, who looked a good deal older than she remembered him in his patched finery.

"Vittoria," he said, with the same lilt of condescension that

Ardaric always used. "I knew it would be you to find me."

The skin around his eyes looked bruised, probably from sleeplessness rather than any fighting. In all these months, never once had the Carcan army been led into battle by their king.

"It was an odd place to pick," she said, voice flat. "You rarely joined us in the gardens. Mother was the one to teach me how to find the center of the maze."

"That's true. But that window," he said, pointing up to one of the squares on the east wall that overlooked the courtyard, "leads to my private office. Sometimes I would watch you playing out here while I worked. And that one over there on the north side—that is the dressing room in my chambers. I came here because I knew that eventually, so would you."

Vita could recall seeing many faces watching her at the windows, but never his. Still, she faintly remembered her father pinching her nose teasingly when she'd been naughty and saying, "Be good today. I am always closer than you think."

It used to be a comfort. Now it sounded like a threat.

"And that was her room," she said, pointing to another set of windows. Vita smiled sadly, because she *could* picture a face gazing down from that one. Now it was tainted by the knowledge that his new wife had slept in there. Had died there, even. "Do you regret it?"

His brows jumped up on his forehead. "Do you want me to regret it? Will it make you feel better if I do? Make my death a kinder thing to witness if I go to it remorsefully?"

"No," she said, and the answer surprised her more than it should have. "Your regret, if you have it, is your own. My mother might deserve it, but I want only your honesty. Remorse won't save you, and it can't give me peace."

"I regret many things that led me here, but I've never regretted that," he said.

"You knew, though, didn't you? You knew that those charges against her were false."

"Of course I knew. They were my invention."

"So why, then? If she hadn't been unfaithful, if she hadn't shamed you in your own court, why did you risk everything to kill her?"

He crossed his legs, leaning back to look her up and down. "She would not agree to be sent away to a convent so that I could marry Elio's mother. I promised that if she went quietly, if she let me acknowledge my son and his mother, then I would allow you to remain at court and still make a good match for you as the king's beloved bastard daughter."

"I was *not* a bastard. I was your lawful child and heir."

"If I could have declared my first marriage void, you would have no longer been lawful. But I would not have been cruel to you. I swore that to Ana. And despite her choices, I have kept that promise. Do you know how many of my advisors told me to kill you and be done with it? How often Elio begged me to not keep you around as some contender to his throne? But I never hurt you, Vittoria. You were safe in exile, exactly as I promised."

Vita shook her head, laughing. "And you think that was a kindness? Keeping me trapped because you couldn't bring yourself to do away with me too? You knew all along that there was no chance I was another man's child—is that the reason? You couldn't quite bring yourself to end my life, because some small part of you still recognized that it was wrong to execute your own helpless daughter? But you were fine with letting me suffer—with isolating me until I was just a shell of a person. *That* was your compassionate compromise."

If she'd been in there another decade, or two, six, seven, eight, what would have become of her? She would have forgotten more than poems.

"And even if my mother had agreed to your terms, you would have kept me away from her as a punishment, and maybe I still would have been sent away to rot in obscurity. When you decided you were done with her, you were done with me too. You already had the son you wanted; I was in the way. There was nothing I could have ever done to be a worthy heir in your eyes. You loved me once—I know you did—but that was never going to be enough in the end." His love was not stronger than his ambition, and she knew that now. When the thrill of a child in his image wore off and the promised son never arrived, he would have always found fault in what remained. "They told you to kill me, and they were right. You should have done it, because now I'm going to take your crown and your kingdom. I will strike your name from history. Your accomplishments will be forgotten, and they will remember you for only one thing: being the man who killed his wife and was usurped by her daughter. When they execute you, Father," she said, voice shaking, "I hope it's her face that you see at the end."

"Ah," Ardaric said from behind Vita. He'd been so silent, she'd almost forgotten he was there. "Why wait? You can do it now. Even better, it will be your face he sees at the end. After all, he is your monster, and our bargain promised you vengeance."

"I—you wish for *me* to kill him?"

"Why not? Who else would relish it like you will? I promised you this; he is my gift to you."

She rubbed her palms along her clothes, wiping away imagined sweat. "Doesn't he need to be killed before witnesses? So they can attest to his death and avoid pretenders?"

"Don't harm his face, and there will be no issues. His head will adorn the city gate." Ardaric took her hand, smoothing out her curled-up fist until it lay flat. He drew her dagger from its sheath, never taking his eyes off hers, and placed it in her grip. "But be quick. The light is almost gone, and there is still far more to do today."

As if in a dream, she gripped the hilt and walked to her father. Vita forced herself to recall the cries of the children caught between the walls, and the pleading wails of their mothers needing to get them to safety. She remembered her own mother, warm and soft and gentle, more a feeling now than a woman.

She'd never killed anyone up close—never killed anyone at all, at least as far as she knew, though perhaps hoping that the catapults had only harmed buildings was asking too much. Her father's calm demeanor was gone now, replaced with the pale face of terror.

Ardaric presented this as a gift, but it felt like a punishment.

"If you want a man dead, Vittoria, you must be willing to look him in the eyes as you kill him."

She was his to command, and he would force her to do this dirty act herself. Anyone else could be called upon to kill the king, but Ardaric wanted to see her agonize over her own complicity. Her wish to see her father dead was not enough—Ardaric had to make her the murderer.

He expected it to break her. Expected that, for the rest of her life, Vita would look at her hands and see blood.

And suddenly it was easy. Easy to let the anger at her father and Ardaric course through her until there was no room left for fear. Neither of them believed her capable. She would always be weak in their eyes, pliant and manipulable.

Her father tried to grab her wrist, and whether he meant only to stop Vita or to turn the dagger back on her, Ardaric stopped him. "Ah, ah, ah. Let her go. I will make your death far slower otherwise."

"You could send me away to die in obscurity. It would be a crueler punishment than death to make me watch you destroy my kingdom."

Before Ardaric could muster a response to such a pathetic effort, Vita said, "Being sent away to rot is a terrible punishment indeed, but it's not the ending you deserve."

Without another moment's hesitation, she thrust her dagger deep into his gut and twisted. He hunched over, trying to protect the wound as Vita pulled the blade out. Even Ardaric looked a little surprised as her father dropped to his knees.

"There can be no mercy, Father. Not for men like you."

Chapter Thirty-Eight

Vita wore her father's blood dried into the lines on her palms, and when she asked Ardaric to let her retire for the night, he put a hand on her shoulder, steering her back toward the great hall and promising that they would be done soon enough.

With the palace now as secure as they could make it for the time being, the hall was flooded with all of Ardaric's inner circle, half the cavalry, and just about anyone else not too injured to shove their way into the room.

"The king is dead!" Ardaric shouted as he walked in, holding Vita's hand up in victory. "Long live the king!"

The crowd cheered before dropping into dramatically low bows as he passed. When they reached the head of the room, he turned to face the audience and cried, "And tomorrow, you will see your new king crowned and married!"

He gestured the servants in, each carrying trays of celebratory food. It was meager fare—the city was nearly wiped bare, and their own stores had been low before the battle. No one would be able to go hunting until the morning, and soon, provisions would have to be made to bring food in from other parts of the island or import it from neighboring kingdoms. But still, the general and his commanders drank and laughed, even as the castle's servants, now forced to wait on a new king, cowered like skeletons in the corners.

Uncertain, she laid her hand on his wrist, hoping it would signal some kind of trust or affection that she didn't know how to otherwise feign. "Tomorrow is too soon to prepare everything. They must have spectacle, don't you think?"

"They will have a competent king again. Is that not spectacle enough for these pathetic, starving people?"

Vita tried not to frown. She had to put the wedding off as long as possible.

"Of course. But imagine a coronation feast. Perhaps a revel. We all need something to be excited for again, and the Messilians must have the chance to see you in your most majestic form. At least give us a few days. A week is all I ask. You still look a bit pale," she told him, reaching out to graze his cheek. "It wouldn't do for anyone to think—"

He smacked her hand away, and though it didn't hurt, Vita cradled it to her chest. "I am fine," he said under his breath. "Do not imply anything you do not mean to say." He glared at the room, perhaps staring at the near-empty banquet tables, the dingy decorations on the walls, and the staff. Earlier, they'd presented Ardaric with loaves of bread that were supplemented with pine needles and, in one case, wood shavings. They sat untouched on the tables, though the servants still stared at them with hungry eyes. "We will wait until we can send out hunting parties. Three days, Vittoria. That is all."

A shiver ran down her spine. This would be her final reprieve. "Thank you, Your Majesty."

The words haunted her later that night as she readied for bed. Though it was unwise, she couldn't help herself from pulling Soline under the covers beside her and curling into her warm side.

It was only that morning that she'd been loading catapults. Only that morning that Ardaric had seemed to be dying and she'd been the one giving impassioned speeches.

How easily everything could fall apart around her.

"I shouldn't stay here tonight," Soline said.

Vita wrapped her hand around Soline's wrist. "Don't go. Please. Not right now."

These rooms were unfamiliar, and though they dripped with ostentation, it was clear that they had been raided long before by desperate staff looking for anything of practical use. It was a wonder that the bed itself hadn't been the kindling in a long-dead fire.

Soline settled against her. "What happens next?"

"Tomorrow I'll release you from my service, and you can go back to doing whatever normally occupies Kasrian noblewomen. It will be better if you're far away from me when the wedding takes place."

"Vita—"

"It will be," she repeated. "Better. Safer. But we still have tonight. We still have this."

To love Soline in the quiet hours of the night would have been enough for an eternity, but it came with too many dangers. Vita could not do that to her.

Soline sighed, staring up at the ceiling for another long moment before she rolled to face Vita. Their noses grazed as Soline stared into her eyes. "We should have gone for the convent. I think about that every day. We should have just run."

Vita nodded, though she wasn't sure it was true anymore. "I think they always would have found me in the end. We'd always end up here somehow."

"If someone had come, I would have protected you. I am

good with a sword, remember?" she teased. "I would have never let them take you."

Vita bit her own lip, worrying it between her teeth. Then, unable to hold back, she kissed Soline, sweet and soft and sorrowful.

"After the wedding, you and your brothers should go back to Kasri."

"And leave you here alone?"

Vita twisted her hand in the front of Soline's nightdress, pressing their foreheads together so she didn't have to see her eyes. "I didn't understand it before, but now I do. I can't have this—I know that. But I will live through every unbearable future if it means you can get away from here and live happily."

Vita had no choice now—she had to stay. But Soline could still escape this life. Vita owed her that.

In the dark, Soline's coiled curls shone with silvery moonlight. She looked ethereal, like a goddess with the sky's constellations mapped across her freckled cheeks and shoulders.

Vita imagined her at eighty, hair white and skin paper thin. She would still be perfect. Looking at her would still feel like staring at the beginning of the world.

They would never see each other at eighty.

It was love, this feeling—grown in the cracks of her like stubborn weeds that did not care how gray the skies were. It grew without permission, disorderly and gnarled and impossible to overlook, until those cracks were filled with new life.

"There will be a way to take him down someday," Soline swore. "This isn't the end."

"Perhaps he is not meant to die after all, and I'm fighting against fate to try to rid the world of him."

Soline shook her head, adamant. "There is always a way. We just need more time."

But Vita knew that this would be their last night together. That in the morning, she would have to tell Ardaric she wished to secure a new lady-in-waiting now that she was to be queen. That whether Soline stayed three doors away or moved to the northernmost Sopian city, she would never again be as close as Vita needed her.

Her tears soaked through the shoulder of Soline's nightdress.

Vita curled her hands into fists as she marched toward Ardaric, determined to do what was necessary, but when she finally had his attention, she couldn't bring herself to dismiss Soline. Instead, she found herself saying, "Ardaric, I think I know what I wish to have as a wedding gift."

He was sharpening the blade of his axe right in the middle of the throne room as others worked around him, the display a reminder of his power. No one was allowed to tend Ardaric's weapon but him.

This time, she knew, it would be used to kill her brother, Elio. The boy who lived in parallel to her, trapped on the opposite side of the looking glass. The boy who begged their father to break the glass and have her killed.

"I have already given you a gift." He didn't look up at her as she spoke. "I allowed you to kill your father."

"Not from you, sir. From the other nobles. Surely they will bring gifts of tribute to the wedding, won't they? They must swear fealty to you."

His hands stilled, and he raised a brow as he asked, "And what would you demand of them?"

"Nothing expensive." It would be some time before anyone

was prepared to indulge again in luxury, though surely it would come. Even war could not stop that. "I know that you have granted the large estates outside of Messilio to your most loyal commanders. I only ask that they each go to their new lands and bring me three birds in good health from their woods."

"Three birds?"

"I would have new companions. They need not be crows. In fact, I would prefer any other kind. Something new. Perhaps I will entertain myself here with a menagerie of Carca's finest birds. It would keep me occupied to care for them."

Eda had perched in her new bedroom window, and in spite of everything, Zeda, Jeda, and Neda had found her again, for which she was grateful, but there might come a time when she would need to send them away too. Ardaric could never be permitted to use them against her again. Especially now that she had already been made to bury Meda.

"It will take a week at least before I can spare them to travel to their estates, survey the lands, and then return."

She ducked her head, pleased when a flush rose in her cheeks. "I hope you will forgive the musings of a silly girl, Your Majesty. Only . . . the birds would please me dearly to have. And in asking for them, you would remind your commanders that they govern these lands at your behest, and that should you demand something from them, they are duty bound to provide."

He stared at her for a moment, checking for a crack in the performance. When none came, he said, "You shall have your menagerie. And then, you will marry me without complaint. Do you understand, Vittoria? Do you see how much I am willing to give to you?"

"I do," she said hastily. "I do see it. Thank you."

He flipped the axe over with an easy grace, setting it beside his throne. There was only one in the room. Vita couldn't recall now if her mother had once had a throne of her own, or if Carcan queens were always meant to bow before their husbands the same as any other wives.

Ardaric led her over to the windows that overlooked the courtyard. The glass was brightly colored, reds and blues and greens that depicted some famous scene in Carcan history, but this close, it only distorted the world beyond the castle until it did not look real.

"Do you trust me?" Ardaric asked, not looking at her. His hair had been neatly combed that morning, hanging long and wavy around his shoulders. "After all I have done for you, do you trust that I have your best interests at heart? That we want the same things for this kingdom?"

She recalled the way he'd ranted and raved in his tent in the days leading up to his illness. It was hard to reconcile that image of him with the man before her. If she could forget Marius, she might almost convince herself that he was not all bad.

But she could never forget Marius. Could never forget how easily Ardaric turned to destruction. And though he was no longer ranting, he still had a slightly manic look about him that worried her.

"Yes," she said finally, voice unsteady, warped like the glass. "I trust that we desire the same things."

"Then I will tell you this kindly, as a wife deserves."

She drew her eyes away from the world outside, glancing up at him. "Tell me what?"

He leaned down, tucking her hair behind her ear to whisper in it. "I know that your servant tried to kill me."

Chapter Thirty-Nine

"You *what*?"

It was the only thing Vita could think to say. She reared back, trying to read in his face what he meant.

"My staff are loyal," she reassured him. "I have no idea why you would think such a thing."

"One of my aides died after the battle," Ardaric said. "Ferra, I think. He'd gone back to camp to see my things brought to the castle. When he returned, it was only an hour before he dropped dead in the middle of organizing my rooms. Poisoned. And would you not know that the only thing amiss was a glass pot of some salve or another that he'd knocked off the bedside table as he was flailing for air? Bit of a mess on the floor. But it seems he'd used it right before dying. I made one of the prisoners try it just to be sure, and I was right. The physicians have no idea what it was laced with, but there's no doubt that it's some manner of poison. Now who would have the kind of access needed to sneak something like that into my tent?"

"But—"

"But nothing. She stole from me once, and you covered for her. She was angry after the boy's death. I know she must have seen in him that upstart brother of hers. It was the serving girl."

Undoubtedly Ardaric knew Soline's name, and yet he refused to say it if only to take that last dignity from her.

"She was busy tending me, Your Majesty. Soline would never—she is *loyal*."

"Then do you know who did poison me, Vittoria? Because it was someone—someone perhaps who liked going into the woods and looking for special plants during her hunts—and that someone will pay."

Ardaric probably found the idea of Vita poisoning him ridiculous, but he allowed the threat of implicating *her* instead to hang over her head. Vita wanted to have the kind of bravery that would let her say, *It was me. I did it. I tried to poison you, and the only thing I regret is that it failed.* But she couldn't bring herself to. It wouldn't save Soline. He would likely just kill them both.

"It wasn't her. I will—I will find out who did this. We will make them pay as my father has."

Ardaric grabbed her wrist, digging his fingers into her skin and pulling her toward him until they were pressed together.

"You are too late," he whispered, letting the words settle in like venom. Never before had Vita understood the stories of forlorn lovers lining their pockets with stones to walk into the ocean and be carried off. Now it made her envious of their ease; they could escape and she could not.

"Too late?"

"Not for her death, of course. That will come later, after the wedding. There will be a public execution the next morning for all the prisoners we've taken who will not swear their allegiance. The only prisoner who will face execution prior to the wedding is your brother, and that is so we can go to our coronation with no doubts in the hearts of the people of our legitimacy. But your servant has already been taken away, and there is no chance for clemency." He squeezed her wrist again. "My word is the law, and it is final. Do not cross me, Vittoria. As you said, we have the same goals. We are not enemies. Now is not the time to make one of me."

"Then you should not condemn the innocent to die," Vita said, ripping her arm from his grasp.

"In time, you will see this as a favor. You will learn that not everyone is capable of true loyalty. That no matter how much you might like someone, they cannot all be trusted." He turned away from her, watching as the people outside the window rushed from task to task. "And if you're right, if she was not the culprit as you so obviously believe, then we can be sure at least that the real criminal will witness how Carca's new king punishes treason."

Before he could say anything else, Vita fled from the room.

For the next several hours, she tried to find the dungeons, making her way downward and inward, but no matter which path she chose, she always ran into servants and guards who would lead her back to the royal apartments.

She was sure that there must be hidden ways to access the lower levels—secret doors and passages that Ardaric's guards would not yet have discovered. But though there were parts of the castle that she could remember far better than she should, like they'd been burned into her mind and faithfully preserved, most of it had been off-limits to her as a child, places that a princess had no business being.

The worst part was, she found her own childhood bedroom without thinking, everything inside untouched and covered in a thick layer of dust. The labyrinth of the Messilian castle was one she recognized, and yet it still could not take her where she needed to go.

"Please, Isotta. I am only asking to borrow one of your dresses. That is not a punishable crime."

"It certainly is, given how you mean to use it," Isotta whispered to her furiously. "Marius is gone, and Soline will be next. We need to keep our heads down."

"Isotta!"

For three days, claiming that she needed to refamiliarize herself with her home, Vita had promenaded through the halls with an entourage of servants following behind. She hadn't complained about the gaggle's presence and allowed them to steer her away from certain guarded halls. The more of these she came across, though, the more hopeless it seemed that she'd ever find a way to Soline.

The old woman shushed her. "You know I love Soline. She is like a daughter to me. But when the general—the king, I mean . . . When he gets in these moods, there is no swaying him. You were lucky to save her from him once. The best thing we can offer Soline now is to not get ourselves killed beside her."

"If I don't find her, I'll never get to say goodbye. I know he will prevent me from seeing her until the execution."

"Vita," Isotta chided, placing weathered hands on Vita's cheeks so that their eyes met. "You know very well that you are not going down there to say goodbye. You are going down there to do something that will surely put you in danger. Once, there were four of us. If we aren't careful, none of us will survive long enough to see you crowned, and then what was any of it for? You might as well have just let him kill you on the day that you met."

"I have to do something." Vita's eyes filled with tears. Isotta had comforted her in the darkest moments of the siege—kept her fed and comfortable and done all she could to counsel Vita well. But Vita could not sit by now and let Soline die. "Please."

"I told you to be careful, didn't I? I told you that carrying on with her was risky."

"I'm sorry." What more was there to say? She was sorry, and also she wasn't. What hurt the most was knowing that her affections were a curse to people. If she did not care, Ardaric could not take them from her. She should have listened to Isotta and left Soline alone, but that could not be undone now.

Their conversation went around in circles until finally Isotta dropped her head into her hands, trying to stave off her own tears.

"I love you, Isotta. Please help me. You need not be involved beyond giving me the clothes. If I am discovered, it would be easy enough to say that I stole them."

"Fine," she sighed, her shoulders slumping. "I will bring you the dress tonight. What else?"

Vita stared at her in confusion. "Nothing else. You have promised the dress, and I have promised to ask no more of you."

Isotta let out a huff, and though it was aggrieved to no small degree, Vita could hear the fondness in it too. The love. "You cannot do this alone, and I can't stand by and watch you try. I doubt I will be forgiven my culpability no matter how little I am involved, so tell me. What else do you need?"

"Well . . . even in your dress, I might be recognized in the main halls. But surely there must be servants' passages that I'm not aware of. Do you know how I might get down to the dungeons without being seen?"

Isotta sat down at Vita's desk to draw her a crude map. Even after only a few days, Isotta could faithfully recall the castle's whole meandering interior while Vita still got lost going down any hall that wasn't burned into her childhood memory.

"Do not take this with you," Isotta warned her, refusing to hand over the paper until Vita agreed. "Study it as long as you need and then destroy it. There should be no evidence."

Chapter Forty

It took another two nights before Vita could sneak out under the cover of darkness without being seen, deciding that it would be easiest to slip by unnoticed when there were few people moving about. She kept a candle and a bit of flint in the pocket of Isotta's dress, and though once she couldn't have been trusted to light the thing, those months in the encampment had taught her several new skills.

She followed Isotta's map, relegated now to her memory, down and down into the heart of the great stone citadel, using staircases that, as a girl, she'd never even known existed.

There was only one guard standing outside the entrance to the dungeons, his blond hair bright in the wall sconce's light. Vita pressed back into a recess to watch him for a moment before she realized why his face seemed familiar.

"Halt," he said, rattling in his armor as he approached her. He drew his sword, holding it out before dropping the point to the floor with a quiet gasp.

Vita stepped out of the shadow. "Winnog."

"Princess?"

She nodded, glancing between his face and his sword with wide eyes. Quickly, he sheathed it again.

"What are you doing here?" he asked softly. "You aren't permitted access to the prisoners."

"I know, but . . ." Not wanting to reveal too much, she said, "Winnog, is my brother being held here? I have never had the chance to speak with him, and soon I never will. I came because, well . . . Truthfully, I feel that I must know—just this once, just before he dies—what kind of man he is." Though it was a lie, Vita could feel the way her eyes burned with real tears. "Can you understand that?"

He glanced back at the entrance to the dungeons, as though some other guard might appear to tell him what to do, but there was no one there. Beyond the door, she could hear the pained groans of its inhabitants.

"You cannot be here."

"Winnog—"

"If you meet with your brother, he will make it known, and then we will both be in trouble."

Having had no intention of meeting with Elio until it became a convenient cover story, Vita didn't know how to refute this. It was the groans that finally provided an answer.

"Is he well treated? Do they take care of him?"

Winnog's face twisted in sympathy as he said, "Not particularly, Princess. In fact, he would appear quite . . . altered, I imagine, from the day that he was captured."

"He's being beaten?" she asked, and he nodded. "Then when we leave, we must do what is necessary to ensure that he cannot reveal to anyone that I visited him."

Winnog stared at her for a moment in the dark, and she waited for his verdict. "You must tell no one."

"Of course," she said, letting him take the lead as he guided her to the entrance. "Thank you, Winnog. For everything."

He laughed. "Night shift down here was supposed to be grunt work."

The dungeons were nearly full, at least three or four prisoners in each cell. Some held far more, and though most inhabitants were asleep, several hands reached out toward her ankles as she scurried past. Vita was grateful that she'd covered her glimmering hair with a scarf so that no one would call out her name in recognition. Winnog kicked at the bars to keep them back.

He brought her to a solitary cell in a damp corner, far from the entrance or any other light source. It was difficult to see the boy in the dark, but Vita could just make out the sharp line of his jaw and the dark bruises marring his face.

"Ah," Elio said, his voice too quiet for the vitriol it held. The damage done to his face made it look painful to speak. "The forgotten princess returns to gloat."

"Would you like me to stay?" Winnog asked, staring at him with distrust.

Vita shook her head. "No, I will be all right. You should go back to your post so that nobody notices your absence."

"Very well. You have thirty minutes and no more; do you understand? There is a guard rotation in an hour. Once you've gone, I will deal with any loose ends."

"I understand. One day, I will repay you for this."

Winnog glanced between Elio and Vita. "Repay me by being a good queen. I have seen the hope of it in you."

She nodded, watching him disappear into the darkness again before turning to face her brother.

Now that she was here, she didn't know what to say to him. She considered squatting down to his level, but before she could, he staggered to his feet, unwilling to be below her despite the clear strain it put on him.

"What do you want?" Elio panted.

"Father is dead."

He laughed. "I know. They have told me a hundred times. They rejoice when they say it."

"And I killed him."

"They told me that too." He leaned against the bars, staring her dead in the eye. "Did you enjoy it, Vittoria? Was it everything you've dreamed of for the last decade?"

"Yes," she said, a little surprised by how easily she admitted it. "It was. I didn't think it would be, but it was."

He looked equally shocked by her candor, but his expression smoothed over again before she could give it any further thought.

"Did you really beg him to kill me all these years?" she asked.

"Of course I did. And I will curse him right to the end for never listening to me."

Vita tucked an escaped curl back into her scarf. "I never even knew about you. Did you know that? Not a name, not a face. They never mentioned you to me. Must have kept you hidden away in another wing of the castle with your own staff so that my mother didn't have to face the indignity. And even after I was sent away, I never wondered who would take my place. But you must have never *stopped* thinking about me. Never felt safe in a world where I still lived. Never let my name leave your thoughts. How I must have haunted you."

He said nothing, his glare heavy.

"And for that, I pity you. You were his pawn too. Another tool to cement his legacy—the long-awaited son. And I'm sorry for it."

"I don't want your *pity*."

She huffed out the tiniest laugh as the corners of her lips quirked up. "Don't worry. My pity isn't worth much. I cannot save you, Elio. And maybe that's a good thing, because it means I don't have to ask myself what I would do if it were an option." She leaned closer, eyes finally adjusted enough that she could see how their father's features had marked them both forever. They were two children who couldn't escape the fates he placed upon them. "I'm sorry that this is how it must end," she whispered, grabbing the front of his shirt and pulling it roughly forward until his face hit the bars. When he reeled away in shock, she forced him back, listening to the way the delicate bones of his face, already damaged, smashed into the wrought iron. "But I am not sorry to see it ending."

Fresh blood spilled from his mouth as she released him, and she wiped her hand on the dress, silently asking Isotta's forgiveness for the state she would return it in.

"Goodbye, Elio." She turned away, but in the damp darkness of the room, she couldn't help adding, "If it's of any comfort, you will die your father's beloved son."

Placing a hand on the stone wall and letting it lead her, Vita darted off before he could try to say anything else.

Winnog had given her only a half hour, and she'd wasted more of it on Elio than she would have liked. She tried not to count the remaining seconds as she ran deeper into the dungeons, knowing that each one was another that couldn't be spent with Soline.

"Sol," she whispered. Eventually she was forced to stop and light the candle in her pocket, holding it like a weapon in front of her. Voices called out, gruff and pained, but none as sweet as the one she needed to hear.

"Sol," she whispered again. The cells became fewer and fewer, and her little candle barely lit the way down. "Sol, come on."

From farther down came a wispy, nearly imperceptible "Vita?"

"Soline?" Vita waved her candle around, the flame teetering on extinguishing before she stilled her hand. The light remained, but no matter where she looked, Vita could only see a dead end. They were far enough away that she could no longer hear the murmurs of the prisoners behind her.

"Down," said the voice, cracking. "Down here."

Something moved beneath the ground, scraping the earth, and Vita saw the prison grate laid out over part of the floor.

She dropped to her knees, candle only just able to illuminate the girl trying to scale the dirt walls of her vertical prison. Without thinking, Vita thrust her hand down until her shoulder was pressed painfully against the bars. When she felt the touch of Soline's hand, Vita practically dragged her up.

"What happened?" Vita asked, heart beating in her throat. "Why are you down there?" Even her mother had been granted the luxury of a standard cell. This hole looked like it was waiting for its inhabitant to lie down and die so that the guards could cover the body with dirt and be done with it.

"You're here," Soline whispered. Her lips were painfully cracked. Had no one given her water? Vita jammed the bottom of the tapered candle into the cracks of the stone floor before running her now-free hand over Soline's cheek. It was paler than it had ever been. "You really came."

"Of course I did." Vita dug in her pocket, pulling out her flask of water. She had to uncap it with her teeth, her other hand still entwined with Soline's. If she let go, Soline would go careening down into the darkness again, unable to maintain her position perched halfway up the dirt walls. "Here, careful. I'm sorry I didn't bring more."

Soline drank it greedily. When it was empty, she whispered again, "You came."

"I would never leave you here, Soline."

Vita hadn't ever thought that anything about Soline was terribly girlish—she had often seemed so mature compared to Vita. But here, she looked like a lost child waiting to be told what to do, eyes wide and bright against the dirt on her cheeks. "I never thought they were real."

"Never thought what was real?"

"Oubliettes." One of her feet slipped, and Vita's hand tightened on Soline's as she regained her perch. "We used to tell stories of Carcan princesses getting locked away in oubliettes by the evil monsters. It's funny, don't you think? I always assumed they were as real as the monsters were. And now the Carcan princess is coming to visit me here."

"Haven't they given you food?" Vita asked, trying to peer down into the darkness, as though one of the beasts from the stories might peer back. "Or at least water?"

"What's the point? This is where they put you when they want to forget you. Where they put the people they hate the most. They only give me enough water to ensure that I don't inconvenience them by dying too quietly."

Vita blanched. How long could Soline survive being forgotten down here?

But Soline was right—what happened to her in the meantime hardly mattered to her captors as long as she was alive for the execution. The cruelty was the point.

"I'm going to get you out," Vita promised, voice shaking as she dug her nails into Soline's skin. "I swear."

"Vita—"

"I swear it."

There was a plan, still half-formed and missing a dozen pieces, but she knew that it was better than waking up on the morning after her wedding to watch Soline die. Anything was better than that.

"No. Promise me—"

"I promise," Vita repeated.

"Not that. Promise that—"

Her voice cut out as she tried not to cry, though her eyes were dry with dehydration.

"Soline," Vita whispered, leaning as close to the bars as she could get.

Soline's eyes fluttered closed. "Say it again."

"Soline." Her skin was so cold, carrying the damp chill. Usually Soline ran warmer than Vita, her own sun. "I promise I will—"

"Not that. Just my name. Say it again."

Vita chewed on her lip before acquiescing. "Soline. Soline."

"And now promise me you will keep saying it. Every day for the rest of your life, so I know you won't forget it."

"Soline," Vita chided, nose tingling with unshed tears. "I could never—would *never* forget your name. But it doesn't matter, because I'm going to rescue you."

"Just keep saying my name. That's all I'm asking for." She sounded choked, but it didn't stop her from kissing the back of Vita's hand like a prayer. "I don't want to be another person you lose. Whose name gets lost."

Vita could live whole lifetimes, could watch kingdoms rise from nothing and fall again, and never forget Soline. And in all that time, she would have nothing to give to the world, an empty, broken husk of a person—because if Soline was dead, and Marius, and Meda, too, then how much of Vita would be left behind to keep going?

"Don't say that," she ordered. Then, a soft plea: "Don't say that. I'm going to get you out. You're not dying here. Not for me—not when it was my crime."

"It's all right—"

"It's not!" Vita's lip trembled, and then the tears did come. "It's not. I won't let you die here, because if you do, they should throw my body down with yours and be done with it. They should bury me in the same unmarked grave and leave us be. But if we can't have that, then I will save you, and I will fix this. I will topple a king if that's what it takes."

"Vita," Soline said, shaking her head, "you have to let us go if you're going to survive. It's all right. But just—think of us sometimes, won't you? Me and Marius."

Before Vita could argue again, Soline steadied herself enough that she could pull her other hand off the wall. She jerked the dainty chain around her neck in one swift motion, breaking the clasp and pulling it free.

When she held it up to Vita imploringly, Vita took it without a fight.

Soline had always worn only one necklace: a gold chain with a hammered disk at the end bearing what looked like a family sigil. In the darkness, Vita could just make out the etchings. On the back, there was a simple *S*.

"You can still be free," Soline said, practically begging.

"Listen to me." Anger sharpened Vita's words. "I couldn't forget you if I tried, and I'm not going to leave you here to die for me. I can't. If you want me to remember your name, I will pay scribes to write it across time, across history, but you will be there to see it too. One day, our legacy will be carved into the very core of this kingdom, and they will remember us. But it can't happen yet. We're not *done* yet. Do you understand me? There's too much left for us to do." Then, the words catching painfully in her chest, she gave voice to the feeling that she hadn't been able to name for so long, as terrifying and foreign as it was. "I love you. I do; I love you. No conqueror on earth or any god in the heavens could ever grant me the peace that you have given me. So I'm not leaving you here. I can't, because if you die, I'll never escape these dungeons either. Not really."

"I love you too," Soline said. She clambered up the last little stretch until her face was pressed to the bars, and Vita leaned down to kiss her forehead, her eyes, anything she could reach. "Which is why I'm telling you it's all right. I love you enough to tell you to go. Take the necklace; do whatever you must with it, and escape. Pawn it; use it in a spell, whatever it takes. Just get out and don't look back."

"But it's my fault," Vita cried. "All of this."

"You didn't want to do any of it, not at first. I stole your necklaces. I kissed you. I knew how this might end."

"I should have stayed away. Isotta told me I should." Vita buried her nose in Soline's hair, weeping. "She told me I was putting you in danger."

Soline laughed. "No, Vita. I should have stayed away. It's my fault that any of this happened. I only befriended you as a means to kill Ardaric. I even broke Amara's arm to do it. I stole your jewels, and I told you about my brother just so I could manipulate your sympathies. It was the truth, but I knew you would join me if I told you. So you must see that this is my fault, not yours. I could have left you alone, but I needed your help, and all I've done is ruin your life in the process."

"You *broke* Amara's—never mind. I knew all the rest, Soline, and I chose to join you anyway. You didn't ruin my life; you gave it hope. And I still have hope now."

"You do?"

"Yes. So don't give up on me. I will save you."

Soline looked up at her, eyes shining against her dirty face. "I'm too terrified for hope. But if I know you are safe, then all will be well."

Vita smiled sadly. "I feel exactly the same."

Chapter Forty-One

"I can do this," Vita mumbled, forehead sweaty as she knelt on the ground to grind herbs. How many times had she and Soline done this exact thing and failed? But she knew the trick now. She knew how to summon something from within herself, some ancient anger that ran through the rivers and her veins and cut through the whole of the cosmos.

Fire, she thought as she worked. *Contained fire. A powder that was perpetually ready to combust.*

There was no time left to come up with a better plan. The men she'd sent to their estates for wedding gifts had returned that morning, and Ardaric wasted no time in announcing that the wedding would be the following day. Vita had only hours until she would be bound to him for life.

She put the pestle down and closed her eyes, knowing that at any moment, the concoction might burst into violent flames and melt the skin from her face. Soline's necklace, so beloved, was already lost in the spell, eaten by whatever magical force might grant Vita this reprieve.

When she finally had the courage to look at her creation, it was a brilliant poppy red, like something that a woman might apply to her lips. The powder looked remarkably different from the lilac-colored poison they'd made, but it was every bit as transformed. Vita sighed in relief.

"It worked," she said to the silence of the room. "And I will have everything that I want."

Ardaric thought that the crown was what he wanted, that being king would fill the emptiness, but it wouldn't. It wasn't a hunger that could be sated—he would need to find something new to sink his teeth into, destroying it bit by bit until all that was left were the sun-bleached bones. He could never be happy in victory.

A crown with so many strings attached couldn't make Vita happy either. But if Soline was beside her instead of Ardaric, then perhaps power might suit her after all. There were worse things in the world than thick stone walls and men with pikes standing between you and the things that wished you harm.

No convent could have protected Vita. Not forever. But she would carve out her own safety in this world, and then she would do whatever it took to keep it. And if she failed, Ardaric would ensure that she died in the attempt.

Carefully, she portioned out the powder into dozens of small canvas bags cut and sewn from her old tent. It had taken some time to scrape away all the remaining wax that had kept rain from entering, but now, though the pouches were sturdy, they were far from impermeable.

When the last of them were safely tied off and tucked away, she prayed to gods that never answered.

Vita made only one request on the morning of her wedding.

She did not complain about the elaborate gold silk dress that

Isotta forced her into, though it was a little too big and clearly made for some Carcan noblewoman who had once lived in these halls.

Perhaps she was still here, swearing allegiance to a new king. Perhaps she was already dead.

Vita didn't complain about the manacle-like bracelets or the impractical shoes either, though when she was finally allowed to look in the mirror, she painted an almost unrecognizable picture.

Noticing her displeasure, Isotta said, "The king requested this dress specifically."

"Oh?"

"I believe Helka Aventicus helped him select it."

Vita imagined the woman—taller and stronger and curvier than Vita—and it made sense now why they'd had to lace it as tightly as the fabric allowed. Helka would enjoy making Vita marry Ardaric in something from her own wardrobe.

"Is it hers? I'd assumed it was Carcan. This is a very fine dress for even Helka to own."

"No, you were correct. It's not hers," Isotta said.

"Then who did it belong to?"

Isotta grimaced but did not lie to Vita. "The queen."

Vita drew in a measured breath, wisely choosing not to ask which queen. Both answers would upset her for different reasons, but at least if she did not know, then she could pretend she carried something of her mother with her.

And still, Vita did not complain.

"Isotta," she said, taking the woman's hands, "I know there cannot be much time left, but I've gotten ready quickly, and I must make one request before we go."

"You cannot see her," Isotta said under her breath, the words sharp but not angry. She was frightened, Vita realized. Frightened of what trouble Vita might still cause herself before this was over.

It was a novelty to be cared for.

Keeping her voice only just audible, Vita said, "I know. Only . . . I need to get a message to Ivo."

"It may put Ivo in danger to visit you."

"He is already in danger," Vita reasoned. Having a second sibling killed by the general—now the king—could not bode well for him. In spite of his key role in taking both Novogna and Messilio as well as his own noble birth, Ivo remained only a captain, not ascending high enough to be granted one of the estates as some might have expected, and it was clear that Soline was the cause. "But I do not need to see him for long. Only long enough to pass along a note."

"He cannot save Soline any more than you can, Vita. Don't do anything stupid."

Vita shook her head, careful not to dislodge the hair clips pinning back her blond locks, entirely aware that there wasn't a crown for a reason. "For once, I don't think I am."

Chapter Forty-Two

Isotta could arrange only a passing moment between Vita and Ivo before the ceremony, but it was enough time to achieve what she needed. Though Vita's writing was far worse than her reading, she still managed to slip him a note with few enough ink stains that her message was legible.

She didn't remember much more of the day than that. They brought her to the castle's chapel on the eastern side, now covered wall to wall in weapons and banners bearing Ardaric's standard. At the front stood a throne and a smaller chair meant for Vita.

There was a grander cathedral in Messilio, but there could not be a public coronation there until Ardaric was certain he had the people under his fist. In some months, they would do this all again for an audience of thousands, parading through the streets to remind the Messilians of the fealty they now owed him.

She was ordered to wait at the back of the room while Ardaric was crowned. The Kasrians had brought their own priest with them, a man who rambled for at least twenty minutes about the gods' blessings in granting the pitiable Carcans a strong warrior-king who would defend them for all his days. The priest placed the elaborate Carcan crown, which Vita had seen only a few times in her life, on Ardaric's head, and he soaked up the applause and chants of the room.

Finally, Vita was beckoned forward, her existence no longer a threat to Ardaric's rule. He was king with or without her. Making Vita his wife was now an act of charity, benevolence by the victor toward the vanquished. During the ceremony, Ardaric kept a tight, punishing grip on her hands, never letting her flinch away as he pressed his vows to her forehead and cheeks in the form of kisses.

Her vows to him were different; the priest bade her to repeat promises of affection, fidelity, and fruitfulness. They were poison on her tongue but not quite merciful enough to kill her outright.

The Mother gives. The Father takes. It was the same in families too. They told this story across Carca, across the islands, across the world. *He will let me think that if I give just a bit more, I will finally be safe. But my penance for being a woman will never be paid.*

Out of the corner of her eye, she watched Ivo, trying never to let her gaze linger on him. He stood with his hands behind his back, his weapon conspicuously absent from its regular place at his hip. No one in the chapel wore one as a sign of deference to the new king.

Sensing her attention, he glanced down and back up again, the closest he could come to a nod.

Vita pursed her lips in time for Ardaric to lean in and seal their nuptials with a final kiss. And then, like that—crownless, powerless—she was married. A queen in name only.

"Come," Ardaric said, taking her hand to lead her away from the priest and his stale smell. "I promised you a splendid wedding party, and I am a man of my word."

Vita smiled up at him, tightening her grip on his hand. "Of course, Your Majesty. Lead the way."

He conveyed them down the aisle of the overfull room and into the banquet set up in the great hall. Though there had been little to eat all week, the army still working day and night to rectify the empty larders, the tables were laden with food tonight.

"How have they—"

"Hush, Vittoria," Ardaric said as he brought her to the head table and pressed on her shoulders until she sat in the smaller of the two grand chairs. "You asked for a celebration. Gifts and a feast. I have provided all that and more, so that our people may rejoice in their new king and queen."

She knew what he wanted from her as he crowded her against her chair, and she was close enough to an end to this charade, one way or another, to give it to him. "Thank you."

He grabbed her chin and kissed her, a mark of ownership. With a thumb still pressed to her bottom lip, keeping her quiet, he said, "You will be a fine queen as long as you mind your manners. Be pretty. Be silent. Wear your dresses and your jewels. We will not have another mishap like the speech you gave before the battle, do you understand?"

She nodded.

"Good. Then I will call our guests in so they may present your wedding gifts."

Soon, the empty benches at each table in the hall were filled by people drinking and gnashing their teeth around more meat than Vita had seen in weeks. As they celebrated, the esteemed commanders of Ardaric's military lined up and one at a time approached the head table. Each man would bow his head before presenting her with a cage usually carrying five or six birds. In one ugly instance, there was no cage at all, only a small wooden box with barely enough holes in the sides. That she had asked for only three from each estate did not seem to matter, but today, their pride worked in her favor.

"I have brought the finest birds from my new lands to gift to Carca's queen on her wedding day," said the tenth such man. The birds he gave her were distinctly pigeon-like, as though he intended to mock her request. Still, Vita approached the cage, letting her fingertip trace one of the creatures' heads.

"Where are your new lands, sir?"

He was bedecked in finery and proud as a peacock. The fine jewels he wore appeared to be Carcan, clashing garishly against the Kasrian craftsmanship of his garments. "Maledo, Your Grace. Twenty miles south."

Maledo.

Patubal, Ferrasaro, Lulle, and all the other names they'd listed. Vita had never visited a single one of them. She could not picture their imposing facades or beautiful woods, but she knew their positions around the city after spending months studying maps of Messilio and its surrounding seats of power in Ardaric's tent. During those lessons, Vita hadn't expected to recognize any of the names, but they'd come back to her far too easily, accompanied by hazy memories of the men in her father's entourage who each claimed ownership of one such estate or another.

She tucked the list away inside her mind.

"May you spend many happy years in Maledo," said the new queen as she returned to her seat, and the man bowed ostentatiously before retreating to his table. Another man stepped forward, and the exchange repeated.

Isotta took each new cage as it was bestowed upon her,

CRUELER MERCIES 383

placing them all in the corner of the room closest to the servants' exit, through which they would be whisked away after the gifting was complete.

When the last of the new Carcan nobles had paid tribute to Vita before rejoining their tables to laugh at her silly whims behind their tankards, Ardaric clapped his hands together.

"Now," he said excitedly, "it is time for our feast."

The others had been eating since their arrival, but the head table was conspicuously devoid of any dishes. A barrage of servants flooded the room with silver serving platters, which they placed before the new monarchs.

She imagined them lifting the covered domes to reveal heads of other messenger boys, but the food was completely average. Each tray bore a plate with a hunk of still-steaming meat and vegetables.

Ardaric tore into the meat with his hands. His fingertips must have been dulled to all pain after so many years of brutish, raucous eating.

"Here," he said, raising a chunk of the meat to her lips. "For my bride."

She could do this for Soline. She could. The night would be over soon enough.

Vita opened her mouth and let him place the food on her tongue like an offering. She chewed and swallowed slowly. "What is it?"

He grinned, taking his own bite. Vita cut into her meal with her knife, inspecting the inside. She rarely ate anything finer than chicken or liver, though this tasted a bit like the pork she'd had at one of Ardaric's first feasts in Novogna.

She swallowed another bite, watching him carefully.

"This meal is the spoils," he said. "There wasn't enough for everyone to partake, but they're all right. They have enough horsemeat to last until they pass out into their cups."

She stopped eating. "Horsemeat? I thought it was a crime to kill the horses."

"Before the battle, yes. Now we have won. Most of our stable remains untouched, but sacrificing one or two for a coronation feast is worth the expense."

The men and women around the room let out loud, grating laughs as they spoke across the tables to each other. "Whose horse?"

"Don't be sad, darling. You won't need Vipsania anymore. Now that you are safe in the castle, there will be no cause for you to leave."

Guests chewed and licked their fingers and tore through flesh again and again, never minding what exactly they were eating.

"Vipsania?" she asked, lips numb. Vipsania, who stood beside her when they buried Meda. Vipsania, who had been the one who provided that small taste of freedom in the early days of the siege.

Ardaric's eyes were wide and still too bright. She wondered if the feverish temperatures he'd suffered during his brush with death hadn't addled his mind more than they'd realized. "Yes, but just for the others. I would never make *you* eat that. I know you cared for her. It would be cruel."

His goading hung in the air—he wanted her to ask. If they were not eating her horse, what were they eating? What spoils did they share?

Vita didn't have to ask to know the answer already. It was obvious: they were eating the only thing he could give to her that was more deranged and horrific than her horse.

She made herself saw off another hunk, and she smiled when she forced it down her throat. He'd taken Soline, made Vita wear a dress that in all likelihood belonged to her father's mistress, and fed her horse to his guests. Ardaric wanted to hurt her, and all she could do was refuse to be hurt.

"And who is this, then?" she asked, cutting another piece. She would not cower. "My father or my brother?"

Ardaric barked out a laugh, surprise flashing in his eyes. "Mine is your brother. Yours is your father. Perhaps we might switch halfway through. What's mine is yours, after all."

She kept eating, wishing she could wash it down with the wine in her goblet but careful to leave it untouched. "I'm suddenly ravenous, husband," she lied. She dropped her fork and began eating with her fingers, letting the gravy stain the corners of her mouth.

Ardaric raised his brows. "Ravenous? In that case, we should end the party now and proceed straight to the marital bed. And then tomorrow, perhaps you will enjoy the festivities of an execution more than you anticipated."

Vita finished her whole plate and then asked for more, giving no attention to the mention of Soline's fate. The liveliness of the room never wavered, but she noticed the way people watched her eat, waiting to see her gag or weep or vomit everything up.

She wouldn't give them the satisfaction no matter how heavily the meal sat in her stomach.

"More wine for my husband," she called to one of the servants. "In fact, another round for everyone!"

People cheered, and over the next hour, they indulged in drink after drink. Even the servants were making merry behind a wall where they thought they could not be seen, wanting to celebrate after months of hardship. There were only a few sober people in the room: Ivo, his most trusted confidants, and Vita herself.

"I must relieve myself," she said, using Ardaric's shoulder to lever herself up as though she were also drunk. She let out a loud peal of laughter. "I'll be back."

Ardaric said nothing, clapping along to a balladeer's song.

She exited, stumbling and giggling behind her hand before taking a turn down a dark hall where no sconces were lit.

"Is everything prepared?" Vita asked as soon as she was able to slump against the heavy wooden door behind her.

The room was largely empty. It had once been her mother's secretary's chamber, if she recalled correctly. Everything of use in it had long ago been stripped away, the walls bare and the floor collecting debris. In the corner, though, were cages and cages of gifted birds waiting by a window. Dozens of beady eyes watched her.

"I need the final list to pass along if you have it," Isotta said. "The riders want to know where they'll be going. Some know specific areas better than others and think they would be best served on familiar grounds."

Vita recited the memorized list of the estates, starting with Patubal. Mentally, she plotted their locations like a wheel around Messilio. Lulle to the north. Maledo to the southeast. Those who had been in the hunting parties in the earliest days of the siege might know the territories well indeed.

Isotta repeated the list back to herself once before nodding. "Then we are ready. How long will they need to fly?"

"The closest might arrive in a quarter hour or so. The slowest may need a full hour or more. They will be faster than the horses, certainly."

They planned the order for how they would release the birds, trying to remember which cages belonged to which estate.

From an old cabinet with a broken lock tucked away in the

corner, Isotta gingerly drew out the pouches Vita had prepared. Vita approached the cages, and with reverent gentleness, she tied a bag to each bird's right leg. She tried to stop her palms from sweating, aware that one wrong move could destroy the entire room.

"Thank you," she whispered, running her fingertips along their heads. Some ducked away, but some leaned into her like cats. "And I'm so sorry."

It broke her heart to send them off like this—defenseless and wanting nothing more than to fly toward the familiarity of home—but they were her only weapon.

For Marius, Vipsania, Meda, and all those whom she couldn't save.

For Soline, whom she could.

"You know when to release them?" she asked, turning her focus to Isotta.

"Yes. Are you sure this will work?"

Vita laughed wetly. "Not at all."

"In that case, let's pray for a miracle."

Chapter Forty-Three

Vita slipped back to the feast, dodging the blindingly drunk dancers who had overtaken the hall. They stumbled and skipped through several traditional Kasrian dances that only half the participants seemed coordinated enough to follow. Ardaric repeatedly took his crown off and held it up for the room to marvel at before putting it back on his brow imperiously. He was too ruddy-cheeked from the alcohol to pull off the look, but most of the room was worse off and didn't notice.

Vita took her seat again at his side, pretending as though she'd never left it. After several minutes, he gestured so widely that he almost elbowed her in the nose. "Vittoria!" he cried, genuinely delighted to see her.

Maybe plying their husbands with copious alcohol was how all weary wives survived marriage.

Vita allowed herself to be dragged onto the dance floor. Ardaric ranted about the music and the wine and how he longed to initiate her into the world of matrimony properly while his hands brushed over her skirts. The dancer beside her stepped on her feet three separate times, and when he stumbled into Vita at the end of the song, Ardaric was a split second away from hitting him.

When the dance ended, he handed her off to Sorrel Aventicus with a flourish, happy to trade partners for a song. Sorrel said next to nothing for the entire duration of the dance.

Vita tried to drag him into conversation through gossip she'd picked up at the edges of the room. She slurred her words, talking far faster than she normally did, but he responded in disinterested grunts until enough time had passed that he could hand her off again.

Eventually, she was passed to Aart Svaldalur, whose leg had been injured in the battle but had seemingly healed well enough for him to attend the festivities, though not so well that he could dance. They stood off to one side to watch instead.

"Don't mind Aventicus," he said, though Vita hardly needed his permission.

"He doesn't seem very pleased tonight. Is he not happy to be right hand to the king?"

Svaldalur frowned, the wrinkles on his cheeks cutting deeper. "He will be tomorrow. But he's smarting over his new lands."

"Lulle? But it is the most beautiful of the estates." Only days before, he'd been bragging about Lulle's decadent architecture and resplendent collection of art and furniture. Though neither man would admit it outright, it had some amenities that even outshone the Messilian castle, a detail Ardaric undoubtedly knew. Messilio had sustained a lot more damage than a place like Lulle.

"Oh, it's lovely, but it's right under the king's thumb, barely six miles away."

"But he is the second most important man in the kingdom now. Surely he will have to stay close if he means to keep Ardaric's favor."

"He will. But there will be no escape either. The king can

monitor all that he does if he is so close. The estates farther afield will have more authority over their own lands."

There were plenty more estates far from Messilio's epicenter that might still be distributed if Ardaric wanted to make enemies of all the original Carcan nobles, but Vita knew now that Sorrel would be granted none of them. Or if he was, it would be one at the farthest edges of the island, where he would never deign to go.

Friends and enemies alike must be kept close.

"Ah," Vita said, nodding. "I see why he is so upset."

"He will get over it soon."

Vita glanced out the warped glass of the window they stood beside. It was such a small dot in the distance, but she felt nearly convinced that there was a spark of light in the darkness.

"I'm sure he will."

She excused herself from Svaldalur's company, and he gave her a small bow.

It would all be different tomorrow. This was the only promise she could afford to make to herself.

Too nervous not to keep moving, she approached some of the guards watching the doorways. They, like the servants, had clearly snuck in a drink or two, but she grabbed a pitcher of wine on her way to them.

"Gentlemen!" she said, nearly shouting. "You are our guests tonight. Please, have a drink!"

Vita began doling them out before they could decline, and it took very little prodding on her part to encourage them. When the cups began to empty, she refilled them.

"We only crown a king once," she reminded them, slurring her words.

By the time the first riders arrived, everyone was pleasantly foxed, and the enjoyment was so pervasive that the messengers looked embarrassed to intrude, their urgent pace slowing to a dead halt.

"My lord," one of them said, leaning near Ardaric's ear.

"Majesty," Ardaric corrected, letting out a belch as he did so.

"Yes, sorry." The boy shook his head. "Your Majesty. There is . . . an issue. In Lulle."

"Lulle? Aventicus! What did you do?"

With his back to Ardaric, Sorrel rolled his eyes before turning to inquire as to what exactly he'd done. Helka, now belligerently drunk, made to jump in on her husband's behalf, but before she could, the messenger quietly said, "It's caught fire, Your Majesty."

Though the room was far louder than his voice, the word *fire* rippled through the crowd. The jaunty music cut off as the players questioned if they should continue.

"Fire?" Sorrel asked, face paling.

"Must be some upstart Carcans," Ardaric said, patting Vita dangerously low on her back as a reminder of who among them was kin to the perpetrators. Vita bit the inside of her cheek to stop from scowling. "You should ride for Lulle immediately, Aventicus. See what can be done to mitigate the damage."

Sorrel nodded, already herding his wife and their retinue toward the doors.

"Your Majesty," said a woman as she stepped forward from the throng of onlookers. She was one of the captains who had been in the strategy tent before the final battle, an ally of Ivo's. "Will you allow my company to join them for protection? If there are rogue arsonists out there, we will need to be on our guard."

"Of course," Ardaric said, waving a hand and already turning away to get more wine. The music started again without any fanfare as the Aventicus party left for Lulle.

It was only twenty minutes later, when a second group of harried messengers arrived, that anyone considered something was truly amiss.

"Sacarpa is on fire" was shortly followed by "My lords, Quarta is burning."

Then Ferrasaro, Maledo, Galona, and Patubal. Before anyone could do more than run around in a drunken panic, there were a dozen recently bequeathed castles alight. Those who had risked everything in following Ardaric to Carca saw their winnings burning to the ground while they feasted. Flagons of wine were forgotten as they prepared to make harried journeys back to preserve what they could.

"You will need aid," Ivo said, voice booming through the din, though he did not yell. "Protection in the dark and hands to fill buckets if we are to stop the flames. I will rouse as many as I can in the barracks to follow along to each estate."

"See—see that you do," Ardaric said, hiccuping. Though clearly concerned by the turn the night was taking, he was now so drunk that he tilted heavily to the left even while sitting. He could not have ridden out to fight off dissidents even if he'd wanted to.

Ivo arranged the parties, putting Kellen in charge of one of the missions and his allies at the head of several others. They took only those that they could trust. The stables were emptied to accommodate the late-night rides. Vita stood at the window, pushing it open and leaning out to watch the troops riding off. She wanted to cry out when she saw Berimund among one of the contingents, so grateful to know that he'd survived, but she did not want to bring attention to either him or herself. Instead, she called down a farewell to those departing, punctuating it with a hearty, *There can be no hope!* which she thought fitting enough. Berimund glanced up toward her window, and from atop his horse, he dropped his head and shoulders in a low bow.

Soon, the great hall was nearly desolate, the tables littered with half-empty tankards and stray flecks of meat.

Ardaric listed over, all his strings finally cut. Only the guards on the door were left, the rest of his protection detail sent out to watch the main entrances of the castle. With half the infantry patrolling the streets of Messilio and much of the remainder sent out days before to secure the roads all throughout Carca, they needed those guards elsewhere, making sure a riot wasn't coming for the castle next.

"Would you help the king back to his rooms?" Vita asked one of the remaining men. "I expect the celebration has exhausted him."

The guard was hardly faring better than Ardaric, though he gave an animated nod and shuffled toward his charge, ready to lug him up a staircase or two before giving him over to his bed for the night. He didn't notice when Vita plucked the key ring from his side and slid it into the pocket of her skirt.

Winnog did, though, still standing at attention by the door. But when she met his eyes, he only nodded before helping to lead the king away.

Chapter Forty-Four

Footsteps came from around a corner, and Vita dove down the wrong path, walking several paces and taking another turn before she heard the servant veer off in a different direction.

"Shit," she murmured, the word a prayer. Though she had studied Isotta's map so thoroughly that she could see its imprint behind her eyelids, few of the sconces were lit—either because the castle was so empty or else because lighting a fire seemed now to tempt fate. The more anxious Vita grew, the harder it was to recall the turns. She retraced her steps, finding herself back in a hallway that looked like all the others.

Surely it was the right one, though. If it was, she could make a left, travel down a long, curved hall, and then the next right should bring her to a staircase.

Vita held her breath long enough that it became difficult to run, but she found the staircase exactly where it ought to be.

She ran down the winding spiral, fighting not to lose her balance. The stairs descended several flights, and though the only windows were thin arrow slits, she could see a great blaze in the distance every time she circled.

The stairs spilled out at the entrance to the dungeons, and though she was sure the prisoners' only crimes were refusing to serve Ardaric, she did not have time to free anyone as she ran past the crowded cells. Not sparing a glance for the one that had once held her brother, now empty, she bolted down the long passage, heading for the oubliette where Soline waited.

Falling to her knees before it, she reached down through the bars and pawed at the darkness.

"Soline? Soline, I'm here."

There was nothing in the depths to see until the whites of two eyes appeared. "Vita?" called the voice. It was hoarse with the memory of broken sobs. "You're here?"

"Yes," she said, one hand still reaching down while the other tried unsuccessfully to shuffle keys around the key ring, testing which would fit the rusted lock.

"To say goodbye?"

Vita's hands stopped. "No. Never that. I'm here to free you." She closed her eyes as she heard Soline's jagged breathing. Vita took a second to collect herself before injecting false cheer into her voice. "I told you I would. It has been a complicated mess, I'll have you know. Everyone's in on it. Truly a nightmare to organize. Now, can you climb up again? I have to get you out."

"I'm so tired, Vita."

"I know. After this is over, I will let you sleep in the finest bed in the castle for as long as you like," Vita promised, hoping it was a vow she could keep. "You will not have to rise for anything if you do not wish it. But right now, I need you to try climbing."

Had Soline slept at all in this horrible place? Or had the waking world and her nightmares melded together so seamlessly that now she could not be sure this was real?

Soline gave her no answer, but her hands scraped at the walls, slipping and sliding without finding purchase.

"Just a little farther," Vita said. She had found the correct key but could not use it until Soline was closer. Vita needed the grate beneath her if she was going to take Soline's hand and help her up the last few feet.

Finally their hands met, and Vita struggled to hold on until they could settle Soline into a stable position at the top of the hole. Vita unlocked the grate with shaking fingers and dragged Soline out onto the cold flagstone.

"I can barely feel my hands," Soline said, staring at them in bewilderment. They were scraped raw and bloody, but the skin beneath was a shocking grayish white. Vita took them in her own hands and placed them on her neck. It was the same trick she'd often used to warm her own hands during the many cold winters spent in her tower. Then, she kissed Soline's forehead and let herself linger there.

"Do you want me to take you somewhere safe? We can find an empty room and bar the door."

"Where will you go?"

"I have to finish what I started. Ardaric must die tonight."

"Surely you don't mean to go alone? You'll take someone with you? Ivo would help."

Vita knew how much it cost Soline to offer up her brother's aid like that, aware that to be caught in collusion with her would mean his death. Unfortunately, he was firmly entangled elsewhere in her plan.

"He is already off helping to kill Ardaric's men."

Soline reeled back. "He's *what*?"

Vita explained it all then, in clipped half sentences and trailing thoughts. How she'd managed to make a flammable powder from the necklace Soline gave her. How she'd known— or hoped, really, given that it could not safely be tested— that water would have a similar effect on it as it had on their original fire, igniting the powder and making it grow to deadly proportions.

How she had used the same sleep tonic that Isotta had given her while she was sick to dose the bottles of wine. Ardaric's cup was given special attention so that he could barely walk by the end of the party, though nearly everyone was affected, given their liberal drinking. How she and Ivo and all his trusted compatriots had carefully abstained all night.

How she had asked for birds from each commander—birds whose only aim when released from an unknown tower would be to fly home, even if they carried the combustible powder with them, ready to set alight anything they touched as a fine morning dew coated the estates. Even that little trace of water would be enough for such a volatile substance.

If the story of Carca's capture needed a villain, it would not look to Ardaric. To Nicolo. It would look to Vita the Merciless, whose birds rained fire from the sky, and she would oblige.

"And now you will kill him?" Soline's hands shook, but Vita did not release them.

"Yes. For everything he did to you, and for everything he did to me."

Soline nodded, drawing away to stand and fix the torn hem of her skirt. She looked like a colt on unsteady legs, but she kept her chin tipped up. "Then I will come with you."

"You don't have to. The castle is not as well guarded as it normally is, but that does not mean there won't be any danger."

"We have come this far together, Vita. I started all of this. I'm not going to hide away in a broom closet while you finish it."

"Soline," she breathed, permitting herself another touch. "You're trembling."

"Then put a sword in my hands and they will be still."

Chapter Forty-Five

Vita had taken every possible precaution she could think of to destabilize the castle and empty it of its guards, but even she was impressed by how easily she and Soline evaded notice ascending from the dungeon.

The hall leading to Ardaric's chambers included recesses for six guards to stand watch at all times, but tonight, there was only one man present, slumped against the door itself, eyes half-closed. He was the guard that Vita had tasked with bringing Ardaric here. She wished that it was Winnog at the door instead, but he must have been ordered away after Ardaric was safely in bed. The remaining guard was still taking sips from his hip flask, like his drunkenness had reached a point of no return.

"Princess," he slurred, eyes squinting to see her in the darkness. Vita did not bother to correct him on her title.

"I am here to attend to my husband on our wedding night." Though the clips in her hair were askew and she was covered in a sheen of sweat from hauling Soline out of her prison, Vita was still a bride. This was what a newly wedded woman did: get escorted to her husband's bed to fulfill the marriage contract.

"King's asleep," he said, short and gruff.

"It's tradition. I must go in."

"Not much to look at in there."

"If the marriage isn't consummated, who do you think the king will blame?"

The guard shrugged but did not move. Vita let out an annoyed huff, ready to continue arguing, but she was cut off by Soline stepping forward and punching him in the throat. It wasn't a particularly hard hit—Soline was far too weak for that—but he started back all the same, stumbling over his own feet before collapsing to the ground. A swift kick knocked him out cold.

"There, that's better."

"What if somebody sees him?" Vita whispered, staring at the limp body in frustration.

Soline glanced to the right and left, seeing long stretches of empty hallway in both directions. "Who is going to come looking? We passed at least five guards and servants sleeping only inches from their own vomit between here and the dungeons. Anyone will assume he was a too-rowdy guard who failed in his duty to stay awake." She toed at the flask on the ground by his hand, a foul-smelling liquid leaking from it onto the floor.

"Should we at least move him?"

Soline groaned. "Fine. But only around the corner. We can't drag him far."

The guard was summarily dumped in an alcove farther away from the king's door. Soline made to grab his sword, but Vita stilled her hand.

"That's too conspicuous. Take his dagger if he is wearing one, but no more. And keep it sheathed until you have no other option. You aren't strong enough to fight Ardaric like this."

Soline scowled but acquiesced, pinching the smaller weapon at the guard's side. It was short enough to fit into her pocket. Then, the girls approached the room together, hand in hand.

It was locked, but it only took trying two of the keys on her stolen key ring before the lock clicked and the door creaked open beneath her touch.

Vita drew in a ragged, painful breath. He was there, half-undressed and sprawled in the mussed sheets. There was a massive canopy above him, boxing him in like a gift. Like a head on a tray presented joyously.

It seemed all too easy. His snoring was the only sound in the room, cutting through the stifling silence that made Vita's heartbeat ring loudly in her ears.

Vita had once been a girl made of spider's silk, easy enough to brush away or leave to languish in forgotten corners. For so long, she'd seen hope the same way, too delicate to survive a gust of foul wind.

But hope was not like that at all. It was the gravy still staining the corners of her mouth, the blood that would soon sit slick and sticky on her palms. It was an ancient rage that slumbered fitfully until it could be unleashed. Vita's rage, her mother's rage, the rage of the women who died in the space between enemy walls, begging for escape. It was the rage of peasants and queens, all suffering the same small cruelties again and again. It overflowed until she was prepared to drown in it, and Vita knew that she would never again dam this anger—this hope—to please another.

She approached the bed, motioning for Soline to go around behind Ardaric. His long brown hair spilled across his forehead, and she pushed it back, tucking it behind his ear.

When she imagined a moment like this, she thought it would feel out of control. A maelstrom within her. But the fear, the anger, the hate—they were as cold and cutting as they'd always been, only now they had somewhere to land.

She touched his lips, dragging her fingertips over them. Soline motioned for her to get on with it, but Vita ignored her.

His eyes fluttered open, a bleary film covering them. "Vittoria," he mumbled. "My bride."

"It's our wedding night," she teased. "Do you mean to forget me?"

"Of course not. Come here." He took her hand, pulling her onto the bed. Vita followed, climbing onto the mattress without resistance.

Ardaric pushed onto his elbow, staring up at her. With his free hand, he traced her leg, drawing back her skirts as he went. Though she wore braies beneath her dress, the length of her leg was bare to his touch. She shivered.

"Do you remember when you told me that it is for men to win wars?" She leaned farther over him, touching his chin and tipping his head up to lock eyes.

"Yes. And I have. Carca is ours now."

"You told me I could be like Queen Magda someday." Vita leaned down to brush her lips against his. "But I suppose even under your tutelage, no one would ever expect that little Vittoria was capable of winning a war."

"You weren't destined to fight. Not like I am."

"Ah." Vita laughed, unable to contain the burst of pleasure. His hand settled high on her thigh. She crawled forward, nearly in his lap now. "There was a moment, just briefly, where I thought it was all over. So much hard work, so much planning, all for nothing."

"During the battle? You should have more faith in me." He moved to kiss her again, but she drew back.

Vita tilted her head to take his measure, hand playing with the hem of her skirt. "No, not then." She let the words linger on his lips in puffs of warm air. "No, you see, you almost chose the wrong leg."

Then, before he could ask any questions, she drew her dagger from the sheath strapped to her untouched thigh and thrust it toward his neck.

He toppled backward, the alcohol and sleeping tonic unsteadying him. Ardaric tried to parry the dagger with his bare hands, but Vita drew a clean line across his collarbone before he pushed her away. Blood spilled from the wound, and he rushed to stanch it, the slickness coating his fingers. He bucked against Vita, trying to shove her to the floor. With shaking arms, Soline grabbed his shoulder and held it down, pressing the tips of her fingers into his wound and using all her weight, knees on the bed, to keep him from moving. Ardaric's hands came up to push her off, and Vita had only a moment before he would overpower Soline.

The dagger was silent when it entered Ardaric's throat. Warm, wet blood spurted upward and out across the white bedcovering. Vita's skirt was soon drenched, but she didn't let up. Instead, feeling vindictive, she wiggled the dagger around in the wound. Marius had taught her where to aim to kill quickly, but she was only a silly girl playing with a weapon after all, so no one could expect her efforts to be too clean.

"This is for Marius," she snarled. "And Anselm, and Meda, and my fucking horse." He gasped as the blade shifted again, hitting something that cut off his keening cries. "But mostly, this is for every person in this kingdom that you would have let suffer. For Soline." She jerked the dagger again. "And for me."

Sorrel, Ardaric mouthed, either a threat or a prayer, but Vita laughed.

"He can't avenge you. He's probably already dead. You didn't think those fires were an accident, did you? They were your wedding gift to me."

He released a gurgling sound, eyes shiny. His body slackened, no longer pathetically fighting off Soline.

Vita's mouth quirked up at the corner. She'd thought killing would be harder than this—and perhaps it would be, if it were any other person at the end of her knife. But he'd taught her how to look a man in the eye as she ended his life only days before in the garden with her father, and now it was no trouble to turn that hatred back on Ardaric. Vita leaned down, kissed him once more on the forehead, and whispered, "Thank you for delivering me my kingdom."

Chapter Forty-Six

The first of Ivo's groups arrived back at the central courtyard just as sunlight started pouring in through the stained glass, and more followed swiftly behind. They laughed and jostled each other's shoulders while a few unlucky men ferried the dead nobles inside. Vita recognized many of the still, waxen faces of the deceased, Helka and Sorrel among them. Their bodies were laid out on the cobblestones side by side, waiting to be brought in. Neither would have expected that the troops sent out for protection would turn and attack them in the darkness. The nobles had been drunk and sluggish, while the soldiers hadn't touched alcohol all night, ready for the order to strike.

Ivo's efforts to sway the army against their general had worked after all. Things had been in flux ever since Ardaric's erratic behavior, but it was her speech, he said, that was the deciding factor for many. Vita drew in a deep breath of relief. Up until the last moment, she hadn't been certain anyone had the stomach for more war. She'd worried that maybe Ardaric's surprise appearance and victory on the battlefield had been enough to bring the dissenters back under his thumb.

She turned away from the window as the soldiers began entering the keep.

Sounds of excitement echoed up through the halls. Kellen and Ivo were the first to arrive at the throne room. Their whole party went silent as the doors opened.

Vita still wore her golden wedding dress, a massive bloodstain covering the fine silk all down her front. Flecks of it dotted her cheeks as well, dried brown like new freckles.

Atop her disheveled hair was Ardaric's crown. It was the crown of her ancestors, jewel-encrusted and imposing.

At her side stood Soline, a hand on Vita's shoulder, which Vita held in her own. A tether. The Merciless Queen would never forget the reason for the events of this night, and she would swear before every witness present that she would do it again if she must. Eda perched like a sentinel on the other shoulder.

And at her feet, cheek smushed into the ground by her slipper, was Ardaric's head, eyes still open.

No one knew what to say as they approached her, though several soldiers went down with haste to their knees.

Vita knew what to say, though. She knew what the whole of her life now looked like, meeting petitioners and assembling councils and passing laws. She knew that she could fix this wretched, broken place that left wives killed and daughters abandoned. This world that sent out children as pawns and watched them perish when the gambit failed. She knew that Ardaric had spent so much time arguing about the failure of reforms, but if she did not make them, then no one ever would. She would burn down the whole of Messilio if it meant building something better in its ashes.

"Ivo, as head of my armies, you will assemble my first council to discuss the rebuilding of Messilio. Choose wisely, as I will not suffer traitors." She stood, turning away and brooking no argument. Instead, she kissed Soline in front of the whole room, knowing that for at least this moment, nobody could stop her.

"And ring the bells," she said, facing the audience again with her chin held high. The crown sat heavily on her brow. "The people must know what has happened here. Nicolo is dead. Ardaric is dead. Long live the king."

Acknowledgments

Writing a novel is easily the most soul-baring thing I have ever done—so much so that most of my friends and family didn't know that I even *liked* writing until there was already a Publishers Marketplace announcement posted. Nonetheless, there are many people who have, knowingly or otherwise, helped bring this book to life.

First, to Zoranne Host, there is no thank-you big enough for the opportunity you have given me. Going through the process of publication with you at my side has been the greatest joy, and I only wish that I could have you with me for every book hereafter. You are a radiant light, and you are going to do amazing things for so many authors. My sincerest thanks as well to the wonderful members of the Fantasy & Frens community who have made the publication of this novel possible.

Meghan Harvey and Matt Kaye, thank you for creating an entirely new publishing path that will uplift so many talented writers. Your willingness to champion Vita's story has changed my life.

Kristin Duran, Katherine Richards, and the rest of the Girl Friday team, thank you for making the publishing process feel endlessly smooth even when I'm certain it was anything but!

Janice Lee, I am immensely grateful for your help in shaping this story into exactly what I always hoped it would be. It is hard to believe that one of my favorite scenes would never have existed without your editorial guidance. Thank you to Jane Steele for your meticulous copyedit and for catching my many egregious misuses of the subjunctive mood and to Michael Schuler for the proofread.

My thanks to CJ Alberts at Bindery and Brittani Hilles at Lavender PR for all that you have done to make the launch of this book a success. Charlotte Strick, thank you for your amazing eye for design and evident love for Vita's story, as well as a million font changes along the way. Camille Murgue, you have created the Vita of my dreams. No matter how many times over I see the cover, I will always be in awe of your talent.

Thank you to Laci Felker and Cassie Follman, who saw some of the truly rough drafts of the initial chapters and worked their magic to make Vita's introduction into the world far stronger.

To my amazing history and English teachers from grade school up through uni: thank you for instilling in me a love of storytelling. I imagine many of you will never read this book, and yet it could not have existed without the profound impact that each of you had on me.

It would be remiss of me not to mention the inspirations behind the book: Elizabeth I and Anne Boleyn, Ivan VI, Julius Caesar and Vercingetorix, Olga of Kyiv, and, of course, Artemisia Gentileschi's Judith. Your stories have inspired me, or haunted me, or kept me awake wondering what it would be like to walk in your shoes.

Thank you to my mom, my siblings, and my niece and nephews for always being home. My thanks as well to my high school and university friends—especially Meaghan, Charlotte, and Kailey—who had absolutely no idea that I was writing a book but immediately jumped on board when it was revealed.

Finally and perhaps most importantly, thank you to Poppy Grunova, Fe Lea, and Tere Nandez. I am unimaginably lucky that watching a bad TV show brought me the three most supportive friends, and luckier still that our different time zones mean that there is always someone awake when I spam the group chat with increasingly bizarre writing questions. Each time I got lost in the metaphorical forest of this story, the three of you pulled out flashlights, took my hand, and led me exactly where I needed to go. I would not be the writer I am today without your friendship. Thank you for believing in me when I could not.

Thank You

This book would not have been possible without the support from the Fantasy & Frens community, with a special thank-you to the Dragon Fren members:

Fowzi Abdulle
Ian Beck
Michelle Robbins
Calista Wielgos
Michelle Campbell
Braeden Weir
Lindsay Chung
Janine Chambers
Brett Foster
Haylee Slocum
Jessica McFarland
Mtreiber
Caralee Stover
Liam Crowley
Courtney Wyant
Natasha Renee

Shyla Northup
Stevie N. Slawson
Ava Gaughen
SHatiAuthor
David B. Kranenburg
Whitney Massey
Faze
adlitam
Fairiedancr
T Throneberry
Alina Dennis
Cristina Rowe
Sammie Gillam
Lillie McAdams
midnight91princess
GabbyVegaa

Christian Bellman
Becca Langewicz
Lilacfairy16
Burns
RCTechTech
SamRush
Jill Smith
V.J. Hugaux
SGP
JackieM88
Amanda Berroyer
jbrando
LexC
KattReads

About the Author

MAREN CHASE is a writer and frequent museum wanderer. She studied history at Regent's University London, where she led tours through monastic cloisters and across plague pits on the weekends. Since returning home to Pittsburgh, Pennsylvania, she has worked in the contemporary art world, and in her spare time, she devours stories about vengeful women, forbidden romance, and the inherent angst of immortality. For more information, visit marenchasewrites.com.

Fantasy & Frens is an imprint of Bindery, a book publisher powered by community.

We're inspired by the way book tastemakers have reinvigorated the publishing industry. With strong taste and direct connections with readers, book tastemakers have illuminated self-published, backlisted, and overlooked authors, rocketing many to bestseller lists and the big screen.

This book was chosen by Zoranne Host in close collaboration with the Fantasy & Frens community on Bindery. By inviting tastemakers and their reading communities to participate in publishing, Bindery creates opportunities for deserving authors to reach readers who will love them.

Visit Fantasy & Frens for a thriving
bookish community and bonus content:

fantasyandfrens.binderybooks.com

ZORANNE HOST is a book reviewer from Cleveland, Ohio, who shares her love for fantasy with over 150,000 followers across TikTok, Instagram, and YouTube. Zoranne has a highly engaged audience and is the founder of the online fantasy book club Fantasy & Frens, one of the largest groups on Fable with over 17,500 members.

TIKTOK.COM/@ZORANNE_

INSTAGRAM.COM/ZORANNE_

YOUTUBE.COM/ZORANNE_